'A truly monstrous rom[...]
grotesque, kinky and [...]
Step[...]
Julia Armfield, author [...]

'Messy lesbians fight a horrifying monster in a small town.
Sophisticated and petrifying, it genre splices so well that it's not a
splice any more. I've never read anything like it!'
Tamsyn Muir, author of the Locked Tomb series

'Beautiful, greedy and terrifying, this book makes an intimate home
for itself right alongside your bones.'
Freya Marske, author of The Last Binding series

'*Feast While You Can* is a singingly clever and gnarly tale of hunger
and possession. Lesbian pulp meets literary horror – the sexiest
book you'll read this year!'
Yael van der Wouden, author of *The Safekeep*

'A fresh, queer spin on possession horror with a sharp focus on
deeply complex small-town dynamics.'
Kirkus Reviews

'*Feast While You Can* has the delicious compulsion of a thriller and
all the lush prose and tenderness of a love story. I devoured it
and it will devour you.'
Sarvat Hasin, author of *The Giant Dark*

'Monstrous, feral, and unspeakably hot. The sentences are delicious,
the butch swagger more so, and the merciless tension building
left me gloriously wrecked. I'm obsessed.'
Jane Flett, author of *Freakslaw*

'Seriously hot, deeply unnerving, this is a powerhouse of queer
horror. While Angelina is a brilliantly brattish protagonist, it's
unforgettable Jagvi who joins the ranks of Byronic heroes.'
Victoria Gosling, author of *Bliss and Blunder*

Also by
Mikaella Clements & Onjuli Datta

The View Was Exhausting

FEAST WHILE YOU CAN

**Mikaella Clements
& Onjuli Datta**

SIMON &
SCHUSTER

London · New York · Sydney · Toronto · New Delhi

First published in Great Britain by Simon & Schuster UK Ltd, 2024

Copyright © Mikaella Clements and Onjuli Datta, 2024

The right of Mikaella Clements and Onjuli Datta to be identified as authors of this work has been asserted in accordance with the Copyright, Designs and Patents Act, 1988.

1 3 5 7 9 10 8 6 4 2

Simon & Schuster UK Ltd
1st Floor
222 Gray's Inn Road
London WC1X 8HB

Simon & Schuster: Celebrating 100 Years of Publishing in 2024

Simon & Schuster Australia,
Sydney

Simon & Schuster India,
New Delhi

www.simonandschuster.co.uk
www.simonandschuster.com.au
www.simonandschuster.co.in

A CIP catalogue record for this book is available from the British Library

Paperback ISBN: 978-1-3985-4211-2
eBook ISBN: 978-1-3985-4212-9
Audio ISBN: 978-1-3985-4213-6

This book is a work of fiction. Names, characters, places and incidents are either a product of the author's imagination or are used fictitiously. Any resemblance to actual people living or dead, events or locales is entirely coincidental.

Cover design © Caitlin Sacks
Cover photo by Stocksy
Print book interior design by Taylor Navis

Printed and Bound in the UK using 100% Renewable Electricity at CPI Group (UK) Ltd

FEAST WHILE YOU CAN

I

Look for Angelina right in the middle, grinning and dissatisfied. Part of her wondering where her derelict older brother is, and what the guilty note in his voice meant when he told her he'd be late. Part of her longing to be back in Cadenze's main square, where thirty minutes ago the last tourist bus of the summer had trundled in, bearing Angelina's last chance to get laid for the year. And part of her cheerful right here at this family party, drinking wine from a mug because they'd long since run out of glasses, hazily conscious of disco music on the stereo and the sharp tang of woodsmoke in the air.

Her uncle Franco's farm was not impressive in grandeur or beauty, but it was abundantly rugged, strewn with chicken wire and fig trees, and it smelled like home. It fit all the Siccos, just about: the older generation playing cards, aunts and uncles trading gossip, the cousins on parade with their pretty wives all dolled up for the occasion in lipstick and flowery dresses, the children yowling through the crowd and rolling in the vegetable garden smeared in mud and overripe tomatoes, the farmyard cats ganging up on Angelina's dog. Their long shadows stretched out in the late summer dusk and the mountains crowded around them. In the center stood Angelina, in her own flowery dress and lipstick, her hair running riot and her mouth running more riot. To her right, her uncle Sam pinching her cheek. To her left, somebody's shy girlfriend wondering where Angelina's brother was. Before her, the ominous sight of her mother moving through the crowd, looking for

1

her. Nothing behind her because everyone was always grabbing her elbow, turning her toward them, begging for her attention.

It wasn't that Angelina didn't want to be here; she wanted to be everywhere. It annoyed her to miss anything in Cadenze, the tiny ugly town that she privately believed belonged to her. She didn't want to be only a queen among her family, celebrated and beloved, glittering at the heart of the night. She wanted omniscience. She wanted to be a god stretching out the fingers of her influence everywhere, all-seeing eyes peering into every cranny. At least she had envoys. And here came Gemma now.

Gemma was not a Sicco, but she was a born-and-bred Cadenze local with no outstanding family feuds, welcomed by Angelina's clan as a favored albeit second-class citizen. She slyly elbowed Angelina's mother out of the way— good woman—and launched herself at Angelina, kiss on each cheek, strong smell of neroli, pink lipstick cracked at the corners of her mouth.

"Well?" Angelina demanded.

"Oh my godddd, I'm not as good at spotting lesbians as you," Gemma moaned. "Okay, let me think. There were two women with leather jackets. Three with short hair, but two of them were at *least* fifty. I dunno if that matters to you or not." She leered at Angelina affectionately. "I think I saw one girl with a nose piercing? Or maybe it was her septum? Or?"

Shaky intel at best, but it wasn't really Gemma's fault. She made a valiant effort, scouting crowds for Angelina's potential flings. Gemma simply did not have the discerning eye that Angelina required, and even when looking for leather jackets, short hair, facial jewelry, pins and badges, T-shirts flashing Ani DiFranco or Sleater-Kinney, loose jeans riding low and the like, she could not see beyond them. She could not spot an anxious spine nor a loping swagger; she would not catch a woman's gaze and wait to see if that gaze was pleased to be caught. But she tried her best, and she'd more than earned the brimming cup of wine that Angelina handed her.

"Nice work," Angelina said.

"There's something else, too," Gemma said, cheeks pink with excitement. "It's really good."

"Oh, yeah?"

"It's *really* good," Gemma said, which meant she had a secret. Gemma with a secret was unbearable. She'd spend the next hour lingering joyfully on its juiciness, assuring Angelina that she would not *believe* what Gemma was about to tell her, before sharing some insight that inevitably fizzled upon its revelation. Gemma had divorced her husband young, and Angelina suspected that Gemma considered the divorce worth the heartache for the secret she possessed before the news leaked. It had been a brutal breakup that left her an outcast among their generation's set of Cadenze married women. Misfortune begets misfortune, after all, and nobody wanted Gemma's marital affliction to contaminate their own. Angelina was the only one among their peers who had no fear of Gemma's bad luck with men rubbing off on her. As friends they had plenty in common: both twenty-five, unmarried, and defiantly happy that way, still loyal to their beloved shithole hometown, two fallen angels busy building an ugly paradise.

"Nini," Angelina's mother, Caro, said, finding her way through at last. Caro looked stressed, fine lines deepening around her mouth. Threads of silver glinted in her long blond hair, which she always wore down, tumbling girlishly over her shoulders. "Your grandmother wants to say hello."

"Where is the old witch?" Angelina asked, and then, spotting her a few paces behind: "Nonna!"

She stooped to give her shriveled grandmother a kiss, ignoring Caro's troubled sigh. Nonna always seemed on the verge of winking at her, eyes bright with secret affection, like they were two friends caught by accident on opposite enemy lines. Caro avoided her mother when she could, complaining of childhood mistreatment ("Nothing I did was good enough, I could never please them! You can't imagine what it's like to grow up with five brothers and not one is on your side!"), but the three women were usually dragged together for a photo at every family event.

As a rule, the Sicco family bore boys. In terms of blood relatives, Angelina had five great-uncles (four deceased), five uncles (one deceased), nineteen male cousins (two deceased), and a brother, Patrick. There was one exception in every generation. Angelina and her mother and her grandmother formed the lineage of Sicco women, a cluster of anomalies with a reputation for wildness. Sicco women made up their own minds and flouted convention, and when they married, which was not often, they did not take their husbands' names. Angelina's grandmother had been a partisan in the war, seducing Nazis and harboring fugitives. Her great-grandmother had been known for a protective streak and extremely good night vision; she had lived nocturnally, patrolling Cadenze's farms, sometimes felling a wolf with a well-aimed stone to his forehead. Angelina's mother had run away from Cadenze at seventeen, only to return pregnant, penniless, and heartbroken (more stupid than wild, her uncle Sam said, but that was Caro all over). Patrick's father was a married man from San Michele who wanted nothing to do with them, and Caro spent nearly two years raising Pat alone in stricken obsession, writing letters that came back unopened, sequestering herself in a crumbling house, and (as Nonna told it) screaming down all attempts at help or advice, until she met Angelina's father: an itinerant worker who nobody knew much about, except for the fact that, judging by Angelina, he was not white. He disappeared before anyone even knew that Caro was pregnant. Contrary to Patrick's father, Caro was not lovesick over him, did not rue raising her next born alone. She was fond of telling Angelina, "You're all mine, baby." But Angelina's skin said differently.

Long before Angelina had committed any real deviance, the Sicco family decided Angelina's foreign appearance and mysterious father were proof enough of her own wild nature. Then she'd surprised them again when she was twenty-one, by coming out.

"Hair's getting so long," Angelina's nonna remarked. "You look like a Spanish dancer."

Angelina gave a lackluster clap of her hands above her head, and her nonna giggled. Despite Caro's persistent suspicion that Nonna was trying to steal Angelina's loyalty, the old woman was essentially harmless, even if she did have a collection of vintage rifles mounted to the wall above her bed. She clutched Angelina's wrist with a wrinkled claw. "Going to stay the night, baby?"

"Nini has her own house, Mama," Caro said.

Nonna shot her daughter an acidic look. "She knows she's welcome here."

"I'll see how drunk I get," Angelina said, appeasing them both.

"It's a good party," Gemma chimed in, doing her best to defuse the tension. "Your auntie's doing tarot readings, did you see?"

"I already got mine," Angelina said. "Knight of Pentacles. Same as always."

Caro laughed. "Well, Jethro brought a girl who reads palms."

Gemma nudged Angelina's ribs. "Literally everyone's trying to tell your future."

"You're looking at it," Angelina said cheerfully. The party sprawled before them. Dusk now but light everywhere, the streaking sunset in fiery orange cream across the mountain-cut horizon, the candlelight flickering against her family's gathered faces, the firepit spitting sparks, the porch lights swaying in their heady cloud of moths and mosquitoes.

"I've got a little something-something to add," Gemma said, beaming. "Just a pinch of seasoning for the next few days, a morsel of news, if you will—"

"San Rocco save us," Angelina's nonna said. "The Valenti girl has a secret."

Gemma looked abashed. Caro said, "Nini, where is your brother?"

"On his way." Angelina had no idea whether this was true, but she moved instinctively to obscure Patrick from their mother's appraisal, smiling wide when Caro turned a narrow-eyed look on her.

"When you see him, tell him I need to discuss something with him."

Angelina doubted this. What Caro actually needed was to put her arm through her tall son's and trot him around the yard to demonstrate to her brothers that she had a handsome and devoted young man at her beck and call. Angelina would protect Patrick from this indignity, if she could, but she still wished he would materialize. His absence tripped her up. There were plenty of people to talk to and a big pot of rabbit stew in the kitchen beside a stack of buttered white bread. There was her idiot dog, coming up to butt her mournful mongrel head against Angelina's leg. Angelina didn't need her big brother, but it was strange not to see him among the men, catching her eye as he howled along to the chorus of whatever seventies ballad their uncles had put on.

Gemma pulled her aside. "So you're not gonna even try and guess?"

"What if I accidentally get it right," Angelina said, "and ruin your whole night?"

"There's *no way* you'll get it."

Angelina laughed, squinting out over the crowd. For one final moment, the Sicco family and the rich finale of a Cadenze summer evening belonged to her, her control and confidence uninterrupted. Then her brother appeared, long hair freshly washed and tied back, faded jeans and a Morbid Angel tour shirt, climbing up the hilly path to join them, and Angelina guessed Gemma's secret. She knew it exactly, from the relaxed set of Patrick's shoulders and his smile that revealed both anxiety and relief. He held himself like he knew exactly who he was, and who he was worried him a little. And he only looked like that around one person.

That person arrived behind him a split second later, cresting the hill to stand at Patrick's side. Behind her shoulders, all the light in the evening stilled and then began to sink.

II

"Aw shoot, she blew my news," Gemma said. "I didn't think Patrick would bring her straight here. I saw her get off the bus just now, and she had a big fuckin' bag and everything. It looks like she's staying a while. Did *you* know Jagvi was coming to town?"

"Kind of," Angelina said.

For a long time, Angelina had thought that Jagvi looked the way she did to deliberately fuck with Angelina, to be so obviously, openly handsome that Angelina would let her guard down. She watched Jagvi approach with the cool eyes of a prizefighter sizing up her opponent. Jagvi was shorter than Angelina, the ideal height to sink a fist into Angelina's stomach. She had short, sleek black hair in jagged tendrils down her neck, practically a mullet, the latest in a series of dykey haircuts she'd paraded in front of Angelina over the years. Dark skin, high cheekbones, and a mouth that seemed to hold a neat hook of scorn in its corner. And those hands, hanging open at her sides, square fingers beckoning.

A quiet ripple of murmurs rolled through the party as people noticed her. Like most of Cadenze, Angelina's family did not know what to do with Jagvi. They didn't trust her still face or the wolfish grin she regularly wore, that shocking flash of her teeth. She surveyed the world from atop a high wall; or at least, she surveyed Cadenze that way. Heavy barricades kept her features smooth, her eyes half-lidded, her speech considered and condescending. She was like a pit of snakes concealed by a trapdoor, her smooth countenance a heavy wooden surface belying the venom hidden beneath. Every so often one of the vipers lunged up and sank its fangs into Angelina before Jagvi snapped it back, unmoved.

Patrick had been expecting Jagvi for weeks, and in his lengthy expectation, Angelina had found safety. It would be just like Jagvi to leave Patrick hanging. It would be just like her to say, *I'll be there soon*, and then make him wait months, even years. In the decade since Jagvi and Patrick broke up and Jagvi left Cadenze, she had visited only a handful of times. Once to spend three nights ostensibly with her dad but actually on Patrick and Angelina's couch, lounging around in her basketball shorts and baiting Angelina, so that everywhere she turned she found Jagvi's faux polite face and another pointed question. One Christmas holiday that Angelina never allowed herself to think about. Another trip eight months later, when Jagvi and Patrick fought so badly—Patrick would never say over what—that Angelina had dared to hope their friendship was done for good. But a year after that, Jagvi had been back again, driving past Angelina drinking on the roof of Gemma's house, making inscrutable eye contact.

She'd been here six months ago, too, but Angelina had not begrudged her that trip.

Now the guilt in Patrick's voice earlier made sense. He'd attempted to smuggle Jagvi in as though she could join the party unnoticed, glancing toward Angelina, half warning and half appeal.

He probably expected a scene. He knew all about Angelina's antipathy. No matter how she tried, Angelina had never been able to convince Patrick that it was his ex who caused trouble, that Jagvi was the chaos element in Angelina's equilibrium, that maybe Angelina couldn't keep her temper, but Jagvi couldn't leave well enough alone, making a beeline for Angelina at every opportunity. Tonight was no exception.

"Hi, Angel," Jagvi said.

"Don't call me that," Angelina said automatically. Jagvi was the only person who used that nickname. The first time, Angelina had been thirteen and drunk, sneaking back into the house. *Big night, Angel?* Jagvi had said, raising her eyebrows, and Angelina had been so intimidated and awed by her brother's fifteen-year-old girlfriend that she hadn't dared correct her. By the time she'd gathered the courage to protest, Jagvi was unswayable and Patrick thought it was sweet. *It's nice you guys have a thing*, Patrick insisted. These days Jagvi called her Angel not with the indulgence of an upperclassman, but like a taunt, like she was savoring each uncomfortable syllable.

Jagvi grinned at her. Pointy canines. "How've you been?"

"I'm always the same. How about you?"

"You guys are so polite to each other," Gemma said. "It freaks me out. You want some wine, Jagvi?"

Jagvi shook her head.

"Well, I need more," Gemma said. "Back soon. Welcome home, I guess."

Angelina watched displeasure track across Jagvi's face, like it offended Jagvi's sensibilities to be reminded that she was from here, and not just a reluctant visitor. "Don't worry," Angelina reassured her. "You won't be here long."

"Are you telling me not to worry or yourself?"

"You and I have always been very simpatico like that," Angelina said. Jagvi laughed. That old teenage thrill ran down Angelina's back; she was used to ignoring it by now. She didn't want to impress Jagvi anymore, but sometimes her body forgot. "Did you come straight from work?"

Jagvi nodded. Angelina's gaze flicked down, checking out Jagvi's loose jeans, the battered leather jacket. Jagvi looked amused. "I changed first."

Angelina flushed. "I guess the uniform would have been a bit bloody for the bus."

"Too early for Halloween," Jagvi agreed, with a straight face that gave no sense of how gory her day had been. Patrick's accounts of Jagvi's work as a paramedic swung between dragging crumpled bodies from wreckage and fixing old ladies cups of tea.

"How's the city?" Angelina asked.

"Do you care?"

"No."

"It's really good, Angel," Jagvi said. "Endless excitement."

"Listen." Angelina cleared her throat, discomfort prickling through every limb, but it had to be said: "I'm sorry about your dad."

Jagvi looked interested, rocking forward on her toes toward Angelina. "Are you?"

"I know it must be…" Angelina hesitated; like most people in town, she had disliked Jagvi's drunk of a father, though not nearly as much as Jagvi had hated him. Angelina had not gone to Riccardo's funeral, back in the spring. Patrick had. He'd come home tired and sad and gone to bed without saying much. "Complicated."

Jagvi nodded.

"You don't wanna talk about it," Angelina guessed.

"I don't wanna talk about it," Jagvi agreed. "Tell me something else. How's work? Are you seeing anyone?"

"Uh, no," Angelina said, and only after she'd answered did she wonder whether it was a strange thing for Jagvi to have asked.

Jagvi looked pleased, either by the confirmation that she'd done right to leave Cadenze and its utter dearth of queer prospects, or because she liked watching Angelina stumble. Angelina wasn't sure when she and Jagvi had ended up alone in the middle of the yard. A neat force field of two or three feet had formed around them, another of Jagvi's defenses. Angelina knew it was different in the city, had seen the way girls crowded close to Jagvi when she was in her element. But in Cadenze, Jagvi was the half-caste daughter of a grumpy old bastard, and people kept their distance.

The Sicco family tolerated Jagvi's presence for Patrick's sake, and without much grace. Angelina had once overheard her nonna praying to San Rocco that Patrick would finally give up on Jagvi. "He will do anything that girl asks," she'd said, confiding in Cadenze's patron saint like he was another old lady gathered around her kitchen table to play scopa. "It's not healthy." Jagvi's hold over Patrick was a well-trodden family problem, somewhere on the scale of severity between Uncle Sam's drinking and Caro's melodrama.

Gemma returned with a bottle of red and Angelina's cousin Jethro. Together they looked like the prototypical Cadenze couple: Gemma's straggly waist-length blond hair and heart-shaped face ("I'm a three in the city," she once told Angelina, "but that makes me a Cadenze eight") and bulky Jethro's big shoulders and small black eyes.

"Come on," Jethro said. "Cave time. Oh, hi, Jagvi. Welcome back." He made significant eye contact with Angelina over Jagvi's shoulder.

"Thanks," Jagvi said.

"Cave time!" Gemma pushed the wine into Angelina's hands. "Pat's here now, let's go!"

"You guys still go down there?" Jagvi asked.

"Sure we do," Gemma said. "Who doesn't love a big ugly haunted cave? It's the coolest hangout in Cadenze."

Angelina leveled a glare at her, and Gemma added, "Sorry, Nini."

Her shallow penitence made Jagvi grin. Jagvi had told Angelina a few years ago that she shouldn't take every criticism of Cadenze as a personal insult. It was at the summer festival, late afternoon, and Angelina had been too drunk for a good comeback. Not so drunk that she'd forgotten how it felt, wavering angrily in her bikini top and combat boots while Jagvi stood there looking smug and licking an ice cream cone, strawberry ripple dripping over her knuckles. When their eyes met now, Angelina knew Jagvi was remembering it, too.

"Still not over that?" Jagvi asked.

"Nope," Angelina said. "And you still don't belong here."

"Yeah," Jagvi agreed. She turned smiling as Angelina's brother joined them. "But I like to try my luck. Keep you on your toes. Hey, Pat. You coming to the cave?"

Patrick punched Angelina's shoulder in welcome as he joined them, but his gaze was set on Jagvi.

"If you are," he said, which was the whole problem.

III

It was a lovely cave. Pitted walls of rock soared up to the high ceiling, and generations of Sicco graffiti scarred the lower stones. Higher up, out of reach, were paintings by artists unknown, of ancient eyes layered with smoke from centuries of campfires. The occasional glimpse of a sword, the line of a richly embroidered robe.

The cave lay under Franco's corner of the mountains, just before the land tapered into a ravine. It was an unofficial haunt for the younger generations, their own den where they could moan about their elders and take whatever there was to be taken and drink the rest. One time Angelina and Jethro had spent a whole night out there, sharing stolen oxy and shaking with cold in the cave mouth with the stars wheeling before them. Another night Patrick drank too much and fell asleep while everyone else was still talking, then sleepwalked over to their campfire and pissed into it.

At the back of the cave lay a neat line of stones, barely calf high, placed more as a sign than any genuine barrier. Beyond them stretched the pit. It yawned down, deeper than anyone could tell. Little children were kept away, and adults stopped going once their eyesight began to fade. Sicco teenagers sometimes sat on the edge with their hearts catching in their throats. If they dangled their legs into the pit, there was an acknowledged touch, a curious stroke along the arch of the foot, and then a nudge like a knuckle pressing up against the sole, turning them back.

The air stayed fresh in the cave despite its small mouth, and even a little light seemed to fill it with warmth and honey. The Siccos were proud of it and so kept it to themselves, as they did with all their favorite things.

"My pa said he hid out here for a week," one of the cousins insisted. "Said he barricaded the entry with rocks and left a little nook for his rifle's muzzle."

"How'd he eat, then, dummy?" Angelina said.

Several of the cousins gave her stubborn looks: Sicco family legends were not to be questioned. Despite a fair amount of petty theft and violence, it had been generations since the cops took much interest in the Siccos, so stories like their great-great-great-grandfather's standoff in the cave over a crate of stolen morphine had taken on mythic dimensions. Nowadays there wasn't even a police department in Cadenze. The boys in blue were outsourced from Myrna, showing up occasionally to bust meth houses or search for runaways. Like everyone in her town, Angelina distrusted them and steered clear of all federal uniforms. Even the fortnightly garbage collectors made her hackles rise.

"He'd left supplies up here," tried Cousin Eugene, a teenager with yellow hair and a glass eye. "Just in case."

"I heard he took some of the morphine," another suggested. "Kept his appetite down."

"And his shooting straight," Patrick said, exchanging a grimace with Angelina. The two of them had been raised with Caro's disdain for her forefathers' exploits. The once-in-a-generation daughters were the significant members of the Sicco clan, Caro had explained, dropping a conciliatory kiss on Patrick's head. The men were just there to support their lone and courageous women. *Thanks, Ma*, Patrick had said, his face tight like he knew it was true and felt all its weight. Angelina was fifteen then, and she and Patrick had been living on their own for two years.

"You two only like the really gruesome stories," Jethro complained.

"Nothing too gruesome!" Angelina said. "But Beloved Great-Whatever-Paw-Paw just seems tame when you think about the Myrna kid killer. Or the thing in the pit."

"That's not about our pit," Patrick said comfortably. "No matter how much you want it to be."

13

"It could be our pit!"

"The thing in the pit is on the other side of town," another cousin said. "Under the Pepper Grinder."

"I heard it was back Maudoro way, not even in Cadenze."

"Wait," one of the girlfriends said, frowning. "What's the thing in the pit?"

Whoops of delight through the cave, and a mild argument sprang up as to who should tell the story. Patrick won, eager to take the stage, perhaps because of Jagvi's presence.

Patrick always looked best when he was performing. He dabbled as a front man for fledgling local rock bands, and he liked to lose himself in the set, his long, dark hair released from its customary ponytail and swarming around him while he snarled into a microphone. At home he was quieter, more thoughtful. He could be a stickler for rules and followed a constant duty to behave well, as if some absent authority were always hovering over his shoulder. He hated to be late for work and couldn't leave a parking ticket unpaid for more than a day, his mouth thinning as he worried over some new favor their mother had asked of him.

But he changed when there was a crowd before him. Shoulders squared, expressive hands. His jaw sloped slightly toward the left, and paired with his deep-set eyes, it gave him a devil-may-care attitude that looked excellent on a band poster or amid the boys at happy hour or now, in the yellow lantern light of the cave, telling the story of the thing in the pit. He leaned forward with his beer held high.

"Okay, so," he said, "once there was and once there wasn't a monster that lived in the mountains. This monster wasn't like the wolves, who ate flesh, or the bats, who drank blood. This monster came down into town once in a while to eat a whole life."

A chorus of protest: already he wasn't telling it right, he'd already missed—

"It's my version!" Patrick maintained. "You can have your turn telling it later. So. The monster hounded the town. Fathers woke up with no sons where an heir used to be, just an empty bed and a wardrobe full of clothes with no memories of the person who wore them. Men appeared at their weddings only to find their girls didn't exist, even though the church was filled with flowers and the priest was waiting to be paid. That's the thing about this monster. It's not hungry for your death, it's hungry for your life."

"No, no," Eugene said, shaking his head. "See, this is why your version doesn't make sense. It doesn't eat your life. It eats your future."

"Same difference," Patrick said.

"Actually, it's not," said another cousin, Matthew, a community college teacher about a decade older than the rest of them, clearly only here for the weed. He took a lordly toke from the joint circling the crowd. "Your version ends with death, and death is fast. It's just another moment in your life. The last moment, but still a moment, and often a short one. The legend says that's not enough sustenance for the thing in the pit. It wants the future that could have been yours, and it eats every morsel."

"Fu*tures*," Eugene corrected. "Because you could do all kinds of things, you know, like maybe you marry this girl or maybe that one, and that changes your life. And maybe you become a priest or maybe you become a farmer, and that changes your life, too. And the thing from the pit eats all of those lives, all that potential, and that's how it gets full enough to sleep for as long as it does. And in the meantime, you're not dead and gone to heaven or the grave, you're being *consumed*, forever, it licks every trace of you out of the world, until no one even remembers your name."

"Eugene's getting way too excited about this," Jethro said.

"Yeah," Angelina said, starting to giggle with him, "tell us more about being *consumed*—"

"You guys are ruining the story with all this technical bullshit," Patrick complained. "You wanna hear what happened or not?"

General laughter and agreement that yes, they did.

"One day, the monster's walking down the road when it sees a girl with a tasty-looking life. Or future, whatever, it can tell she's young and pretty and it wants to eat her."

"Eat every *possible* version of her," Eugene cut in, "every kid she might have, every song she might sing—"

"Every guy she might fuck," someone interrupted. Even Patrick laughed this time.

15

"Yeah, exactly. It wants to take all of that away until she's just a shell without a past, or a future. Worse than being a corpse. But then her husband steps in."

Angelina added, "And he's like, *What was that about her fucking other guys?*"

"Thanks, Nini," Patrick said. "No, the husband steps in and says the monster can eat him instead. He can't bear to live in a world where his wife never existed. It's a noble sacrifice. The monster agrees, probably the man's life is even richer food than his wife's. So it's about to sit down to eat, when the wife says, 'Wait, you shouldn't eat him on the side of the road, you don't want people gawking at you or interrupting. I know a cave further down the hill, why don't we go there together and then you can eat.' And the monster agrees."

"Classic mistake," Jethro muttered to Angelina, who snickered into her palm.

"And when they get to the cave, the monster's already gnashing its teeth"— Patrick bared his canines—"when the wife says, 'Oh, but it's so cold here at the mouth of the cave, why don't we go further back, where it will be warm.'"

"Women *always* have to be warm," somebody grumbled, and the others shushed him.

"So they go to the back of the cave. And the monster's really ready to eat now, it's starving. But they've delayed for so long that the sun is setting, and it's so low that the light is coming into the cave. So the wife says, 'I can see that the light is bothering you, why don't you move back a little further?'" He widened his eyes in mock-feminine innocence. "And the monster takes one more step back and falls straight down into the pit." He clapped his hands, loud enough that the sound bounced around the cave's steep walls. One of the girlfriends yelped.

The rest of the party cheered, in part for Patrick's storytelling and in part for their own pit, the star of the show.

Angelina said, "In Caro's version, the wife pushes the monster in herself."

"That's the feminist version," Jethro said. He wagged his finger at Angelina. "Don't you get too carried away with that kind of talk, young lady."

Angelina laughed. "Too late. I've been indoctrinated."

Jethro made the sign of the cross. "Then may God have mercy on your soul."

"But did it die, when she pushed it in?" Eugene's little girlfriend asked. She twisted to stare behind her. "Or is it still down there in the pit?"

Eugene hugged her close. "It might not even have been this pit. There's plenty of holes in the caves around here. The biggest one was in a cave that fell in years ago, during the Second World War. I heard there was a whole family hiding inside when it collapsed."

"That could have been the inspiration for the whole story," Matthew said. Behind his back, Jethro caught Angelina's eye and mimed shooting himself. "I always thought the way the thing eats futures is like a war, isn't it? You have all these grand plans for your life and your family and your country, and then the war arrives and takes it all."

"The story's older than the war," Gemma objected. "My great-great-grandpa used to tell it to my grandpa. Gramps said that when he got to the bit about the pit, he'd open his mouth and smack his gums at Gramps and say that when you got old, the monster pulled out all your teeth and found somewhere deep inside you to hide."

"Ewwwww," Angelina said, delighted.

"So it's still not the Sicco pit," Jagvi said.

"Our pit looks the type, though, doesn't it," Patrick said, nudging her.

Quiet as the family turned to look back at the line of stones, the dark chasm gaping beyond.

"Ughhhhh," Eugene's girlfriend said. "I hate ghost stories. We need a protector." She snuggled in closer against Eugene.

"Men don't work," Matthew said, voice solemn. "Didn't you hear? It eats men's futures up." He considered. "There's legends about animals resisting it."

"Oh my god, where's Your Dog?" Jethro asked Angelina, and the cousins cracked up.

"My Dog would be fucking useless," Angelina said. "If she met a monster, she'd roll over for it to scratch her belly."

"Where is she?" Jethro asked.

"I left her up at the house," Angelina said. "Haunted or not, she'd run straight into the pit. Forget about the monster eating lives, I can't let it eat my damn dog."

"San Rocco wouldn't let it," Jethro said. "Nonna told me once that the stupider a dog is, the more San Rocco protects it. Idiots go straight to heaven."

"No wonder he's Cadenze's patron," Patrick said. It was a mean joke, made for Jagvi's benefit. Angelina gave him a derisive look, and he stuck his chin out, stubborn.

"My mama used to say that the thing in the pit was San Rocco's dog," Eugene put in. "And that he'd send it to chase children home if they stayed out too late."

"*My* mama used to say that the thing in the pit was the saint who lived in Cadenze before San Rocco claimed it," Jethro said. "And all its love and care for the town had twisted to hate because we don't remember it."

A few of the cousins turned inquiring looks on Angelina and Patrick. Jethro and Eugene's mamas, though respected Cadenze matrons, were not Sicco blood; only Angelina's mama could make the final, definitive call. Angelina shrugged. "There's a million versions of it."

"They all mean the same thing in the end," Jagvi put in. Angelina startled, surprised that Jagvi cared enough to have an opinion. "This town swallows up options."

The mood in the cave soured. Angelina's cousins considered the outsider with distrust. Jagvi didn't seem to notice, leaning back on her palms, eyes on Angelina like it was still just the two of them. But Patrick laughed.

"You've always hated the thing in the pit. You prefer the Bloody Doctor," he added, referring to the myth of a Cadenze physician who had gone crazy and run into the hills, preying on unsuspecting hikers to practice his rusty surgery skills. Patrick's hand folded around Jagvi's head like a big cap, tousling her hair. "Something you can punch."

A bottle of wine reached Angelina, and she took a swig, considering her brother. If you threw something into the pit at the back of their cave, you could wait forever and never hear it land. Patrick had a similar pit inside himself, and it was where he kept his love for Jagvi. No matter how many times she messed up, Patrick never stopped forgiving her. The wine hit Angelina's throat harshly. "The thing in the pit too frightening for you, Jag?"

Jagvi answered her directly, untroubled. "It frightened me a lot when I was a kid, yeah. When I was six, one of the other kids in my class told me that Cadenze was haunted by the thing in the pit and once it had eaten your soul, you just walked around like a zombie, all eaten up. And even if I thought people were normal, they'd actually be gone. He said maybe it had eaten my dad."

"Kids are so creepy," Patrick said.

"The pit is creepy," Jagvi said. "Kids get it."

"Maybe you just need to get to know it," Angelina said, standing and taking another swig from the bottle before she handed it on. "Now that you're on your big welcome home tour."

"I'm not sure a Sicco family party counts as a tour," Jagvi said, but she watched Angelina closely. As Angelina wandered over toward the pit, she thought she even saw Jagvi tense.

"No? Well, let's invite someone else," she said, and cupped her hands around her mouth, stooping to the deep black of the pit. For a moment the depth was dizzying, and then Angelina got her balance. She called down into the drop, her voice bouncing. "Yoo-hoo! Jag's home! Wanna come say hello?"

"You're gonna kill yourself leaning over that," Jagvi said.

Angelina kicked one of the rocks gathered at the pit, knocking it over the edge. Her thirteen cousins and their respective girlfriends fell silent, listening to it clatter and fall, until the sound faded beyond their reach. No one spoke.

Then Angelina turned and shrugged. "Guess it's not one of your fans."

Her cousins laughed, and Patrick shook his head, rolling his eyes. Jagvi slouched against his shoulder, exuding the indulgent air of someone allowing a child to act out at a party. It was the same condescending energy that Angelina had loathed her entire adult life, and it should have thrown her into the usual mix of embarrassment and annoyance. Instead she felt pleased.

Good joke, said the pit.

Thanks, thought Angelina.

IV

Only on the way home did Angelina stop feeling pleased about her Good Joke and begin to wonder if she was frightened. She got a ride from her cousin Marc. Patrick and Jagvi had disappeared, Gemma was hooking up messily with Angelina's second cousin Tom, the uncles shouted back and forth about politics, and her mother looked despondent in the kitchen. Angelina had work tomorrow, and the night wasn't good enough to be worth a hangover.

The voice she alone had heard echoed in the rumble of the engine. Marc's headlights cut across the landscape, sloping farmland and a distant bevy of stars and the peaked crowns of laurel trees lining the road. In the bustle of the party, she had been able to push the voice aside. It was nothing, she told herself, just a trick of her imagination, an extension of her own exuberant interior monologue. Barely even a real thought. But as they cut through the night in Marc's old hatchback, it kept coming back to her. *Good Joke.* According to who?

"How long is Patrick's ex gonna be here?" Marc asked, and Angelina shrugged. Marc lit a cigarette and exhaled thoughtfully out the window. "She's a lesbian, right?"

"That's right," Angelina said.

"Whew." Marc offered her the cigarette. The drunken drag didn't have its usual flavor; almost sweet in comparison to the dirty adrenaline flooding her mouth. "I'm glad you don't feel the need to look like a man just 'cause you don't like them, Nini."

"I'd love to see a man manage to look like her," Angelina said. Marc didn't seem to know what to do with this, so he laughed. Angelina felt only faint pity that Marc couldn't see the way Jagvi moved, the lean line of her body and the points of her tits, the nape of her neck when she bent her face, and her hair feathered around that jawline. Sometimes Jagvi was manly, and often she was handsome, but there wasn't a man alive who looked like her. If Jagvi were in the car right now, Angelina wondered if her own heart would be beating steadier, if her breathing would be surer. Or if she would just be trading one form of danger for another.

Angelina loved Cadenze, and she knew Cadenze loved her, too. But she wasn't used to Cadenze answering back.

At home she climbed straight into bed, hoping she could fall right asleep and forget whatever had spoken in her head when she kicked the rock. She was drunk, probably; she was unsettled from Jagvi's return, definitely. She needed to sleep it off. She fell exhausted onto the mattress, as though she'd been wrangling with her own disbelief in a wrestling match, and slept, and woke. Her bedroom was very dark and her body was covered in chill sweat. My Dog lay on her feet, snoring and weighing her down. She couldn't tell how long she'd been asleep. Something in the air had changed, a thin metallic note that she felt in her nose and her teeth. Her heart pounded, and she could smell the fear rising off her, from her armpits and wine-rotted breath.

Worse, her bladder was full and uncomfortable, which meant she had to get up.

She spent what felt like an hour thinking, *This is stupid, just go piss*, in the hope that finally she would look out her window and see the first touch of light in the sky. But the night stayed vivid black and cool, and My Dog snored on, and Angelina lay there thinking in rapid succession of every horror film that had ever frightened her, every angry man who had ever tried to pull his weight on her, every urban legend and Cadenze myth. She thought about stories she'd rolled her eyes at, headless murderers and vengeful surgeons.

She thought about Patrick leaping out to frighten her when they were kids. She thought about Caro's most dire cautionary tale, lying awake in a foreign apartment, listening to a man trying to break through her flimsy door. She thought, *Hey, whatever you do, don't think about*—and immediately remembered a new night terror. She thought about her own failures, her missteps and cruelties, both accidental and not. She thought about Jagvi admitting she was afraid of the pit. Her limbs, heavy and inexorable, sank deep into the bed, and her head was light with fear as though it would swell and float to the ceiling, her body dragging her in different directions.

My Dog yawned and rolled over. *I am actually going to wet the bed as an adult*, Angelina thought, and used the fresh wave of embarrassment to pull herself up.

Flinching away from the cheap floorboards, as though at any moment one would turn into a hand curling around her ankle. Shuddering back from the breeze on her sticky neck, as though it would reveal itself to be a mouth grazing across her skin. Grabbing her doorframe at the unexpected rumble behind her, like a beast preparing to charge, before she realized it was My Dog snoring.

By the time she made it to the bathroom, she was almost laughing at her own fright. She wondered if it was the ghost stories in the cave that had done it, or her drunken thought that she'd heard something speak back. Her annoyance in the car with Marc, his mild-mannered bigotry conjuring up the feeling of some greater danger, like something loping behind them on the road.

She had one last test to pass. To wash her hands and make eye contact with herself in the mirror and hope there was nothing behind her. Angelina remembered her own childhood promise to herself: as long as you think obsessively about the worst thing that could happen—your dad coming back and taking you away, Patrick dying—it makes it so unlikely that it won't ever happen. So picture the worst thing, again and again.

She stood up, flushed the toilet, and washed her hands. She lifted her head to look in the bathroom mirror. Behind her, the thing from the pit looked back.

V

Angelina opened her mouth to scream. The thing behind her pinched her lips shut, a brutal and effective move that felt as though it had yanked her jaw off her face and squeezed its fist closed.

Staring at the thing and not being allowed to cry out was awful; Angelina turned away. This was permitted even as its hard grip kept her mouth shut. Shock rang through her. For the first time, she understood the concept of a swoon, as though her consciousness, her sense of sanity, might shake its head and make for the exit. *That's enough for me, folks.* She staggered to the floor, landing hard on her knees, and the thing staggered with her. A tugging sensation on the back of her neck felt like the thing was trying to yank her up. She kicked out behind her and struck something, but the showerhead made a metallic clang as it fell, and all she'd hit was the glass shower wall.

Already the specifics of what she'd seen in the mirror were shattering into a handful of panicked impulses, to kill it, to run, to cry for her brother or her dog. She had lost her bearings. The thing pulled her hair, her head rising a dizzying few inches off the ground and then thudding hard on the tiles.

Stand.

The same voice she'd heard at the edge of the pit, speaking inside her own head. It was not speaking out loud; she couldn't *hear* it. The words just appeared in her brain, kicking aside her panic to make room for themselves. But it was here physically, too, at her back. Present and yanking her up by her head, her knees burning against the ground as the rest of her body rose another inch in its grip.

Stand Or I'll Have To Drag You.

Angelina shook her head so viciously that the thing lost control of her mouth, and she spat a mouthful of saliva and blood onto the tiles and screamed, "PAT!"

Don't.

It clamped her mouth shut again. This time the pressure felt thinner and sharper, its fingers like needles slicing through her lips to sew them together. While she scrabbled at her face, touching nothing but her own skin, the thing began to haul her into the hallway. One knee caught on the threshold bar, raised from years of damp showers. It had her head, dragging her along by her hair, but she flailed her body about, slapping at the wall and leaving scratches in the yellow wallpaper, digging her bare feet down and trying to grip the edge of each floorboard with her toes. She could feel that it wasn't strong enough to carry her, so she fought hard to wrestle free. When they reached the top of the stairs, she lunged forward and wrapped her arms around the banister. It tugged once, twice, and couldn't dislodge her.

In the tussle it lost her mouth, and again she yelled for Patrick. Her chest thumped down into the floor and she thought it had punched her in the back but the pressure remained, anvil-heavy on her torso, holding her there on the ground. It clutched her mouth shut again, and in the silence they both waited, tears pooling at the corner of Angelina's eyes—*Be home, Patrick, be home*—but after a few seconds, it released her mouth on a pitiful gasp.

He's Not Here. Scream As You Like.

"Get out of my head!"

Its touch was cold like wet rock, soft like the sandstone her ancestors had used to build their homes, chalky fingertips tucking her damp hair behind her ears, petting at her sore scalp as if it were sorry. Stale air tickled her nostrils, musty, a buried smell that had not known daylight for years. She was still crying as it peeled her hands from the banister and dragged her by her wrists into her bedroom. My Dog, asleep at the foot of the bed, didn't even stir when the door creaked open, only grumbled in her sleep as the thing from the pit pulled the sheets back and dropped Angelina onto her mattress.

It Could Just Be A Nightmare, Baby. We'll Feel Better Once We've Had Some Sleep.

It locked itself around her in a stubborn embrace. She couldn't tell what was an arm or hand or some other type of limb altogether. And there was something else, too. Now that the thing had her where it wanted, it was doing something to her mind. Once, when she'd needed her wisdom teeth out, she'd been put under, made to breathe in gas that shut her brain off to pain and noise and light. What the thing from the pit was doing to her seemed like that; a slow-blooming, unnatural peace. *Stay awake*, she thought. *Stay awake!*

She tried to remember what she'd seen in the mirror, but she could only picture her own terrified face staring back at her, whites of her eyes bulging. Did the thing have eyes? Did it have teeth or hands? Did it climb up from its hole rock by rock, dragging itself from ledge to ledge, or did it drift up like a feather on the breeze? That sinking, silent dark swept up through her mind. She stood on the edge of the pit again, making fun of Jagvi, toeing a rock over the edge. The black mouth opened to greet her. The dog on the bed sighed in its sleep.

VI

"Be a nightmare," Angelina said, swarming up to the surface of consciousness. Daylight nudged at her eyelids, which were screwed tight. Covers tangled around her like she'd been thrashing in her sleep, so she woke overheated and sweating, already garbling around her dry tongue, "Please be a nightmare, please don't be real, please be gone, ah, fuck, c'mon!" She fisted her hands in the sheet, frustrated by her own cowardice, stomach knotted with tension. Too scared to open her own eyes. A new low. She hiccuped a laughing, breathless gasp. "Okay, I'm gonna, I can open my eyes, it's not real, please don't be real anymore." It took another parcel of seconds to get her courage, and then she opened her eyes. The bedroom was empty, and Angelina was alone.

"Ooof," Angelina said. Her whole body relaxed, like some reverse waking, muscles that had been tight with fear melting against the sheets. Her mouth pooled with the saliva it had lost in anxiety. Everything was okay and Angelina was in control again. She put her hand in her underwear and jerked off, more on instinct than anything else, the tension and release in her body demanding it. She thought about nothing and came almost immediately, slick and throbbing like she'd been on edge for hours. Downstairs the front door banged open.

"Is Angel still here?" Jagvi asked, voice carrying through thin walls, and Patrick answered, "Yeah, I don't think her shift starts for a while." He thumped his fist on the wood paneling that lined the staircase, making her bedroom wall shake. "Nini? You up?"

Angelina sat up in bed and rubbed her forehead. The nightmare should be fading now. She couldn't remember what she had seen in the mirror, what had been so awful, but she could still feel the bathroom tiles under her knees and the sense of something catching her by her hair and dragging her to bed. Her jaw felt stiff and overworked like she'd been grinding her teeth in her sleep. Her scalp ached; she rubbed it, and checked her legs for bruises, but the only marks there were days old and probably from lugging kegs around at work.

She looked around the empty room again. After a moment, she flopped over the edge of her mattress and checked under her bed. Nothing there either.

"Nini!" Patrick called again. "You want coffee or not?"

"Coming!" Angelina yelled back, and climbed out of bed. She opened her wardrobe and rifled through coat hangers, running her fingers over its plywood back. More nothing. So it had been a nightmare.

Downstairs, Patrick was already in his work clothes, blue coveralls with his hair tied back and fresh stubble, slicing a baguette into thick chunks. Jagvi sat on the kitchen table, knees pointed at opposing walls. She didn't seem hungover, but there were dark shadows under her eyes to match her outfit, all black again except for a large silver belt buckle. Jagvi's mouth quirked as she took in Angelina's paisley shirt, swirls of red and pink hanging open over the white tank top she'd bought in a five-pack at the hypermarket, a tiny satin bow resting at the dip of her cleavage.

"Morning," Jagvi said. Angelina narrowed her eyes, unprepared to deal with Jagvi so early.

"Nutella?" Patrick asked, looking over his shoulder. "You can put the coffee on."

"Oh, fuck youuuu," Angelina moaned, digging out the stovetop pot. "You led me astray, I thought you'd already made it—"

Patrick made an obscene gesture at her. "I'm not your servant."

"Will you at least toast the—"

"I am, Christ. Your Dog's more help than you." Patrick tossed the brown paper bread bag to My Dog. "Hold, girl."

My Dog caught the bag between her teeth and gave a muffled bark, soft brown ears pointing up in delight. Angelina surveyed her fondly as she tried to wrench their ancient coffeepot open; the top was stuck again.

Angelina had found My Dog tied up and abandoned by the side of the highway, a young hip-high mutt with a feathery tail and her head bowed to the ground. Her ribs protruded through mangy brown fur, and Uncle Franco said it would be kinder to let her die, and if she did survive, she'd surely be feral. But Angelina took her home anyway, and after a few good meals, My Dog revealed herself to be a loving, slobbering fool. She followed Angelina with devotion, happiest when running at her heels with no clue where she was headed. She guarded stray footballs with her life even when she couldn't fit her long, narrow jaw around them, and she frequently ran into walls. Because she was kind of a dumb dog, Angelina had only been able to think of dumb names for her. But it felt cruel to draw a mark of shame on the dog's forehead. *I dub thee Numbnuts.*

At first Angelina and Patrick had both called her The Dog, and then as allegiances formed, she became Your Dog (Patrick's preferred usage) or My Dog (Angelina's). People in town caught on and paused in the street to say, *Hello, Your Dog!* and *Isn't Your Dog a good girl?*

Now My Dog stood happily in their kitchen with the bread bag held between her teeth, doe eyes fixed on Angelina as if the coffeepot she was wrestling with might have beef jerky hidden inside.

"Neat trick," Jagvi said.

"She just thinks he's given her a present," Angelina said. "Look, she won't give it back now, she thinks it's hers. Drop it, girl."

The universe loved to prove Angelina wrong in front of Jagvi, so My Dog immediately opened her mouth and let the slimy paper fall to the floor.

"She did that to fuck with me," Angelina said. The coffeepot still wouldn't give; she thunked it sadly against the countertop.

"I forgot about this," Jagvi said. Voice low and frayed like she hadn't woken up all the way. "The Sicco morning show. A privilege to see it again. Give me that, Angel."

"What?"

"Yeah, it's such an exclusive," Patrick said. Jagvi took the coffeepot from Angelina, unscrewed it with one hard twist of her wrist, and handed it back. "We're short on cast, though. Wasn't Ricky coming over this morning?" Ricky was Franco's youngest, a good-for-nothing who grew weed at the far edge of the property, and the only son who enjoyed their uncle's unconditional adoration.

"He changed his mind last night." Angelina busied herself putting the coffee on. She couldn't look at Jagvi, sitting at ease on the table, wide palms braced on the wood.

"Probably knew he'd be hungover today," Patrick said. "Hey, what the fuck did you do in the bathroom last night? It looked like a bat got in."

Angelina jerked guiltily. "I tripped. I was mostly asleep. Whatever." She hadn't checked the bathroom this morning: Had she been sleepwalking? Had any of it been real? A needle of fear slid through her. No—it was a nightmare, and one she didn't want to admit to in front of Jagvi, so instead she said, "I think Ricky just didn't want to risk running into Jagvi."

"Ouch," Jagvi said, but she didn't sound very hurt. The insults of Cadenze could not penetrate. Patrick did not possess such defenses, and he shot Angelina an aggravated look.

"Don't be a dick."

"It's fine," Jagvi said, still smiling. "Good to know people's attitudes haven't changed."

"It's more about your attitude than his," Angelina said, still unsettled by this much Jagvi this early in the morning. "He probably didn't want to start his day being treated like an idiot hick."

Jagvi's face smoothed back into distant neutrality. "You didn't seem that drunk last night, Angel. To be so hungover now."

"I'm just good at holding it."

Jagvi's evident disbelief was unfortunately a fair reaction. As a teenager Angelina had been a lightweight of the most humiliating degree. She often had to seek Pat out at parties, asking him tearfully to help her find a lost shoe or hold her hair while she vomited. Jagvi had helped, hunting down Angelina's lime-green sandal or fetching a bottle of water while Patrick patted Angelina's back as she keeled over the toilet. The only saving grace was that Angelina had a good recovery time and could normally pull herself up again within fifteen minutes, rinse her mouth out, and kiss Pat on the cheek for his trouble. Awkward nod at Jagvi as she passed. Shot of tequila to drown out the incident. Repeat.

"I've had a few years to build up a tolerance," Angelina reminded Jagvi.

"Good work," Jagvi said.

"Thank you," Angelina said, putting both hands in her hair to adjust her ponytail. Jagvi's belt buckle flashed at her.

Patrick cleared his throat and began comparing their timetables. Saturdays were a double shift for Angelina. First eight hours at the call center reading government survey questions from a laminated script, and then she'd drive to Old Timers Bar and work until close. Patrick worked the day shift at his garage, and on Saturday evenings he normally rode into Myrna with a band of Cadenze bachelors, to drink lager in a rock bar and crow over a pool table and flirt with the bartender, a chick with a Mohawk and shaved-off eyebrows who worshiped the Clash. Patrick's taste in women tended toward oddballs: girls who had green hair, who kept ferrets as pets, who took GHB or had been abandoned as children or stretched out their earlobes with black plugs. Marc and some of the other Siccos gave him shit for it, said he had a fetish for freak pussy, but Angelina thought it distinguished him from other men.

Deep down Patrick was as conservative as the others, wanted a wife and a household and bright-eyed kids to call him Papa. But he'd had a fascination with nonconformity since he was a kid, and a sympathy for female outcasts that he'd never been able to shake.

Case in point: Tonight he wasn't going out at all. Instead he would head back up Big Joe after work, to help Jagvi with clearing the crap out of her dead dad's house.

Jagvi's plan was to stop by the hardware store for supplies, then burn most of his belongings in the front yard before ferrying the rest to the dump in

Patrick's truck. Angelina wondered if she was imagining the twinkle in Jagvi's eye when she talked about destroying all of her father's things. Jagvi probably wished she could raze the whole building to the ground, erase any proof that she or her forebearers had ever called these mountains home.

"Are you driving to work, Nini?" Patrick asked. "You'll be late if you walk."

Angelina drained the last of her coffee. "I guess so."

"You can give Jag a lift, then, she needs to get into town."

It was skillfully done, a classic Patrick maneuver, just blatant enough to feel like an order but subtle enough that it was petty for Angelina to refuse. She glanced at Jagvi, who seemed uncomfortable but shrugged. If Jagvi wasn't going to protest, Angelina definitely wouldn't.

Angelina tied up My Dog in the backyard to keep her from following them out to the cars, kneeling to stroke her head and accept the sloppy good-bye kisses. The scratch of land out back really belonged to the mountain, just a tumble of rock, a few shrubs gone lopsided from the wind, and their one tall chestnut tree. Angelina wondered if it was just the remainder of her nightmare that made her feel so uneasy standing under the mountain's shadow. Something stirred on the back of her neck, and when she turned, she wasn't sure whom to expect, Jagvi or the thing from her dream. But there was no one.

VII

The bulk of Cadenze rested in a valley at the intersection of three mountains: Big Joe in the west, Little Joe in the north, and Regular Joe in the southeast, which most people called the Pepper Grinder due to the black ash littering its peak. On an atlas it looked like the three Joes were an offshoot of the mountain range that split the country, but anyone who had seen them up close would assume these peaks stood alone, the result of an entirely separate geological phenomenon. Caro liked to say that if their province were a face and the southern mountains its proud mustache, then the three Joes were flecks of old food in its teeth.

Angelina and Patrick's house sat off the road that snaked across Big Joe's flank, about halfway to the summit, and Jagvi's father's house lay a half mile above them. If she squinted across the valley at Little Joe, Angelina could just about see Caro's shack, the green-yellow blur of weeds that surrounded it and the sunlight reflecting off its corrugated iron roof.

Round the bend and down the hill, and the valley unfolded below them, revealing Cadenze in all her gray glory. In the fifties the Christian Democrats had sent envoys into the far-out reaches of the country to track damage left by the war. Not much fighting had ever happened in Cadenze, but officials streamed into the valley anyway, sticking their noses into everyone's business. They attempted a land survey of the region's honeycomb network of caves, but canceled it when two men disappeared. During the investigation into the deaths, every townsperson gave the same answer: What else did those men expect, rooting around in caves that didn't belong to them? What did they think they'd find down there other than trouble?

The officials' report labeled Cadenze a nexus of poverty and deprivation, and announced their plans for a new age of running water, electricity, and concrete. People living in huts up and down the Pepper Grinder were first encouraged, then forced to move into new concrete tower blocks. A concrete industrial park granted generous leases to the same officials who had appropriated government funds to build it. The lurching concrete shopping center became home to the hypermarket that would eventually drive half of Cadenze's store owners out of business, as well as the slot machine arcades where Cadenze's spinsters traded gossip and performed fortune-bringing rituals verging on the heretical.

The only part of Cadenze not gutted was the old town, which held some potential for tourism. Even now there remained a clear divide between the old medieval Cadenze, with its cobblestoned streets and weatherworn war memorials, and the new reformed Cadenze. Nobody ever put the new side on a postcard. The regulars at Old Timers said what the CDP had done was sacrilege, that they'd forced fake tits on a natural, sagging beauty. But Angelina couldn't find fault with the tower blocks and concrete. She liked how severe and unphotogenic the new side of Cadenze was, resisting the temptation to blend in with the rugged glamour of the mountains, uninterested in pleasing anybody or anything. Some of the best nights of her life had been spent in the asphalt parking lot of the hypermarket, where they could blast the car stereo as loud as they wanted and her cousins performed feats of physical fitness while she sat drinking with their girlfriends on the roof of somebody's minivan. On quiet weekends she and Gemma went to play the slots, drink aperitifs in the neon light of the arcade, and politely decline the advances of Paul, the eighty-year-old who ran the all-night bar.

But Jagvi had grown used to finer things. Angelina imagined her holding grim eye contact with Cadenze from her view in the passenger seat, counting the seconds until she could escape to civilization. She flicked Jagvi a dismissive glance, and found that actually, Jagvi was looking straight at her.

Angelina startled. Amusement rippled across Jagvi's face, and Angelina hurried to preempt anything she might say by asking, "How long are you here for?"

"A week," Jagvi said. "Less if I can help it."

"It's not that bad. Lots of things have changed since you lived here."

"I heard," Jagvi said. She leaned back against the passenger window, body angled toward Angelina. "You've been busy, huh? Pat says you're like the unofficial tourist ambassador."

That was an overstatement; probably Patrick had been making fun of her. He tended to deride her town improvement activities, or treat them as some kind of adorable pet project. Angelina didn't mind. They weren't for him.

Angelina had realized a long time ago that if she wanted to live comfortably in her hometown, she was going to have to work for it. She loved so much about Cadenze: her brother, her cousins and uncles and mother, the old ladies who kept treats in their tracksuit pockets in case they ran into My Dog, the stories the Old Timers regulars told about the war, the fascists and the partisans, tales so distant from Angelina's happy existence they might as well have been folklore. August nights with Gemma on the plastic chairs outside of Old Timers, watching tourist families line up to take pictures by the town fountain. Even the fountain itself, Cadenze's one instance of creative expression, a stone hand turned palm up to the sky.

But there were certain things the town couldn't offer her, unless she created the circumstances for them to appear. Such as cool parties. Such as cultural events. Such as girls.

"I just do some events for Old Timers," she told Jagvi.

"And the film festival," Jagvi said.

"That was a one-off."

It was a one-off because it had been unsuccessful—Cadenze's city council was skittish about licensing, and so she'd had to limit her selection. The only people who showed up were Cadenze locals who seemed bemused by her choices of cult horror and obscure modern dramas, their only connecting feature that they each involved some kind of dykey subtext. Most audiences could, at least, be relied upon to cheer heartily at the sight of a bare tit.

The women's poker night had been similarly unpopular, mostly attracting wives from the surrounding farms who told stories about things they had seen in the woods and offered tips on how to discipline your husband but provided nothing to Angelina in terms of hookup options. Her most ingenious tactic had been the campaign to offer summer tourists a free drink at Old Timers. She kept a stack of the flyers behind the bar so she could hand them out at will.

Cadenze was not a highly ranked vacation spot, but it was secluded and cheap on a city salary, which meant it attracted groups of college students wanting to spend a weekend drinking wine and hiking the Pepper Grinder, and single women longing to get away from it all. Angelina made sure they had a good time—fixing them drinks, reciting the best bits of town lore, giving them a number to call if they were looking for weed. And occasionally one girl dropped away from the pack to sit up at the bar and ask Angelina to do a shot with her, or the lone woman from the city acquiesced when Angelina suggested a game of whose hand is bigger, raising her palm to press it flat against Angelina's. Angelina had fucked in three separate rooms of the motel, in old town apartments with gold fixtures and mountain views, in tents pitched up and down Little Joe, in the backs of vans flanked by ugly cement. She brought women back to her own house only if she was sure they could handle My Dog barking outside the door and Patrick's awkward morning-after small talk.

"And people are okay with this stuff?" Jagvi asked. "They just let you do whatever you want?"

"I mean," Angelina said. "It's not like I'm hosting orgies."

Jagvi laughed. "I guess they haven't run you out of town yet."

A few years ago Angelina might have argued with her, but she'd become reluctantly aware that her experience did not align with Jagvi's. The allowances made for Angelina were not made for everyone; as Angelina's foreign parentage had been brushed off, so had her sexuality, just another quirk of this generation's Sicco girl. Angelina's proclivities were amusing, novel, even titillating at times, as long as she stayed polite and discreet. People did not look at her the same way they looked at Jagvi, who'd made a damn fool out of Patrick, turned herself into a dirty joke overnight, and still flaunted herself around town every time she came back. Compared to that, Angelina was harmless.

"I heard Myrna had a pride march last year," Jagvi said.

"It was crap," Angelina said, making another turn.

"Yeah?"

"Just a handful of men waving flags. And a bunch of students showed up as a joke. I mean, obviously it was crap. It's Myrna."

"Obviously," Jagvi said, although the town rivalry clearly didn't mean much to her anymore. "You don't go to Lyonette, then?"

Lyonette was the gay bar in Myrna, the only bar of its type in the county.

"Rarely. Only when I'm desperate," Angelina said, intending to imply that she was rarely desperate. Jagvi snorted instead, as if Angelina had said something funny. "When did you go to Lyonette, anyway?"

"When I was eighteen," Jagvi said, and glanced at Angelina, and stopped smiling.

Angelina reached the rough cobblestones of the old town and switched into second gear, the car resisting with a groan, her mood souring. Her voice came out leaden. "Right."

"It was after everything, Angel."

"Okay. Doesn't matter, anyway."

"Well," Jagvi said, and she sounded almost gentle. Angelina watched Jagvi's hand lift before she let it drop back against her knee. "Don't lie."

"I'm not," Angelina said, though obviously she was, but she didn't like Jagvi to write her off as childish, unable to shift old grudges even when Patrick himself had moved on. "Did you like Lyonette?"

"Not really. I think I was a little freaked out."

Angelina scoffed.

"You don't have to believe me," Jagvi said mildly. "But I didn't really get the hang of the whole gay thing until I went to the city. I was either terrified or oblivious or—I don't know, acting on instinct."

Recognition stirred in Angelina's chest. *Instinct* was the right word. Her desires felt obvious and natural and feral, as though all the straight people in her life were tamed and housebroken creatures and Angelina alone prowled through her town, wild and hunting. She did not like to identify with Jagvi. She did not like to find anything clear and understandable about Jagvi, and know that Jagvi was understanding her right back.

"You're always going on about that. Like it's impossible to realize that you're gay in Cadenze." She pulled into a parking spot in front of the hardware store and turned to Jagvi. "What do you think, heterosexuality's in the water or something?"

Jagvi nodded. "Maybe the air, yeah."

"Such bullshit," Angelina said. "It's not Cadenze's fault you didn't realize it about yourself. You either know you're gay or not, okay? Like me."

Jagvi laughed. She popped open her door. "That's not why you knew."

"Oh, it isn't? Enlighten me."

"You knew because you had me," Jagvi said, and patted the roof of the car. Angelina gaped at her. "Thanks for the ride," she added, and strolled off across the square.

Angelina banged the steering wheel and cursed. Who did Jagvi think she was? How dare she? And what did she mean, anyway?

Did she mean that Angelina had been thirteen and fixated on Jagvi, on some hidden dykeiness that, when Angelina thought back, wasn't entirely hidden? As a teenager Jagvi had sat with her legs spread, one square palm rubbing at the back of her neck. She'd given Angelina the same head-jerking *what's up* nod Angelina knew from truckers passing Cadenze on the highway. She'd never paid Angelina much attention, but now and then something would attract her gaze, like the time Angelina got home having gashed her arm open climbing a fence to find Patrick gone and Jagvi on the sofa with her homework. Jagvi snorted and said, "What did you do, you little idiot?" and took Angelina into the bathroom to apply iodine and wrap it in Patrick's tennis ankle bandage. Her grip sure on Angelina's wrist, turning her this way and that, the kindness so unexpected and the pain so sharp that fifteen-year-old Angelina had teared up. Did Jagvi mean that some tiny, urgent bell in Angelina's body had been jangling every time Jagvi walked into the room, even when Angelina couldn't recognize the sound? Or did she mean—did she mean—

VIII

Angelina and Jagvi had known each other since Angelina was twelve and Jagvi was fourteen.

Jagvi's family on her dad's side had owned the house on Big Joe for generations, but her parents only returned to Cadenze to live in it when she was four years old. From the start Meera and Riccardo Marino resisted the pull of the town, and never came downhill to say hello to the Siccos. In retaliation, Caro never sent Patrick and Angelina up to play, and it took years for the two families to interact at all.

When Jagvi turned five, her parents enrolled her in the private girls' prep beyond the valley. Her parents didn't think a little mixed-race girl would do well among the white farm kids at Cadenze's ratty elementary school. Angelina managed okay, but Angelina had Caro. Her mother worked as a teacher's assistant in the infant school, clutching children to her in viselike cuddles, joining them in their tears over scabbed knees and stolen lunches, slipping candy to her favorites. Everyone knew her, and knew Angelina as her kin; local, respected, and safe. Jagvi had her mother, Meera, whose skin was a dark brown that most kids had only seen on TV before and who had a strange maiden name that no one could pronounce. Riccardo was Cadenze born and bred, but no one liked his family.

It wasn't until Jagvi turned fourteen that her father decided the private school fees were too much and his daughter too ungrateful. He sent her to the state secondary school in Myrna that all the kids in the district attended.

It was a forty-minute trip each way from Cadenze; on the first morning, Patrick saw Jagvi on the bus and realized that he'd spent the past few years deliberately avoiding her. Everyone Pat knew disdained the Marinos, and he hadn't wanted to taint himself by association. That day on the bus he was struck by a shame so profound that he almost turned around and got off again. Instead, he took the seat across the aisle from her. He held out his hand to shake, and just like that they started talking.

"About what?" Angelina would probe.

"Music and stuff."

After a while, Jagvi started picking him up on her way downhill to the bus in the mornings. Sometimes Caro wanted Pat to stay home for the day, and it was Angelina's job to run outside and tell Jagvi her big brother was sick. Jagvi always accepted this news with a hard little nod.

Usually, it was actually Caro who was sick. Patrick made their mother up a bed on the couch and the two of them fussed around her, fetching her food and water and listening to her symptoms with wide, sympathetic eyes. Patrick, whose conception had been Caro's undoing, had a particular duty of care. Tending to it would make him a good man.

Once Caro had a fever and needed Pat to stay home and look after her three days in a row. On the fourth day when Patrick came outside, Jagvi was so pleased to see him that she cheered and pumped her fist. Patrick embraced her, kicked away a piece of gravel, and asked, "Do you want to be my girlfriend?" Jagvi said yes.

In some tangled part of Angelina's mind, she could draw a line from Jagvi's appearance in their house to Caro's departure. It had gotten crowded, or maybe Caro just thought, with the old-world logic she pretended to scorn, that if Pat was old enough to be in love, he was old enough to run a household. The balance had shifted. Patrick no longer gave Caro his full attention, and Angelina was a woman of her own. She'd learned to deploy that irreverent Sicco humor, cackling relatives crowded around at every party, this newest Sicco girl living up to the legacy in ways that Caro herself never had. The kids at school hung on Caro's sleeves all day and then she came home to her two little adults, still expecting her to baby them, cook their food, wash their clothes, divine their every need. It was all too much.

She told thirteen-year-old Angelina and fifteen-year-old Patrick that while she loved them, she also needed her own space now and then. She'd scoped out an abandoned cottage on Little Joe, and planned to spend one night a week there, or maybe two, as her sanity required. On the nights she was away, Patrick and Angelina ate cereal for dinner and stayed up in front of the TV. Sometimes Jagvi came over with a battered VHS tape, an old horror movie or one of the Bollywood films she and Patrick were fascinated by, to watch with her feet in Patrick's lap.

Those were tense days, long stretches of lonesome quiet punctuated by painful confrontation. Patrick and Caro had bitter spats in the kitchen over who'd finished the milk and a standoff over an unpaid phone bill that lasted a week. Angelina did her best to mediate, but Patrick usually told her to keep out of it, which was easier said than done. Hiding up in her room only did so much, especially when Caro was apt to storm upstairs and find her, like the time she slammed Angelina's door open and started gathering a random assortment of Angelina's T-shirts and underwear.

"You'll have to come with me today," Caro said, in a voice intended to carry downstairs. "Your brother demands some relief from the burden of your company."

Patrick had chased her up, and Angelina turned to him in the doorway. "Fuck you," she said, stung. "That's what you've been complaining about?"

"No!" Patrick said. "Ma, come on. I didn't mean it like that."

"He feels like a full-time babysitter," Caro told Angelina, her voice somehow managing to convey both immense pity and deep satisfaction. Angelina knew she wasn't misreporting—one look at Patrick's miserable expression was proof enough. Caro always told the truth. *Wouldn't you rather I'd be honest with you, babies?*

Angelina stayed with Caro for only one night. The shack had one single bed, and as Caro repeatedly said, it wasn't ready for visitors. The plywood door rattled in the wind. Angelina lay curled in a kidney shape at Caro's back and didn't sleep at all.

Back at home the next day, she resolved not to be a burden, not to drive Patrick away the way she had Caro. If Patrick and Jagvi weren't around, Angelina sat on her bed staring out across Cadenze. She picked out every house she could see from her window, and when their lights came on and smoke billowed from their chimneys, it made her feel surrounded by people, even though her own house was empty. She slept in strange places because it didn't seem to matter; on the couch, at the kitchen table, in Caro's empty room. Once Patrick found her curled up in the backyard, an old blanket of Caro's tangled around her legs and morning dew coating her bare skin. Jagvi stood in the doorway with her arms crossed and an angry dip in her brow, though she said nothing.

One night Angelina realized it had been four days since she'd seen Caro at all. Caro's shack didn't have a phone line connected yet, and even if they'd had a car, Angelina couldn't drive. Patrick and Jagvi had already gone quiet in his room, and Angelina had been doing her best not to annoy them. Instead she unearthed a flashlight and shone it across the valley, switching it on-off-on-off, in a pattern that she imagined spelled out M-A-M-A. Eventually she was rewarded with a return flash, the lights in Caro's windows flipping on and off in a similar pattern, so Angelina could pretend that it spelled out N-I-N-I.

Caro came back the next night, but her next spell away lasted ten days. She said she knew they were having plenty of fun on their own: What teenager doesn't dream of a whole house all to themselves? She would continue to pay rent and she'd drop by now and then with groceries, at least until Pat found a job. Angelina stood in the doorway waving goodbye to her ("Like I'm going off to war!" Caro said, laughing as she drove away) until Patrick yelled for her to come watch TV with him. She sat stiffly on the couch and her throat hurt and her eyes burned. Patrick reached out and grabbed her hand without looking away from the screen, even though they were too old for that.

They'd been living alone for weeks when Uncle Franco came to check up on them. He took in the kitchen full of empty soup cans and molding pizza crusts, the stacks of unopened mail littering the hallway, the pits of dirty laundry that constituted their bedrooms, while Patrick and Angelina sat in the midst with guilty, shifting eyes, waiting for him to start yelling.

Instead, he left, and returned an hour later with two daughters-in-law, who got started on the laundry, a secondhand truck for Patrick, and a wad of cash along with a stern lecture about spending it on food and gas *only*.

After that they were rarely left alone for more than a few days. Franco intermittently fought with Caro but couldn't convince her to move back. Angelina was glad; a gruesome thought, really, to imagine her mother trapped back at home with them, like a wild fox baited into a cage. It was easier to let Caro's retreat become another family oddity, the whim of another Sicco woman who couldn't be controlled.

Angelina got used to coming home from school and finding one of her cousins fixing a broken shelf, or an aunt batch-cooking pasta sauce or pinning laundry on the line. Sometimes a gift would be waiting on the table: a stack of videocassettes, a tomato plant, a gallon of gasoline. Patrick used the truck to drive them over for a hot dinner at Franco's three or four times a week, crowded around the table with a cluster of uncles and aunts and cousins. Caro was conspicuously absent, complaining that after years of neglect, the family's new efforts to help were deliberate insults, meant to shame her. She refused to be punished for the crime of being a normal woman with normal flaws. In her stead, Angelina took pride of place beside her nonna.

She was technically taking Caro's seat; if her mother ever showed up, she reasoned, she would gladly give it up.

Angelina liked it best when the adults told stories about the war, the man from Cadenze who shot a Nazi for assaulting his daughter, the people who hid in the caves to evade deportation. More often the talk was of government corruption and elites who thought they were so much better because they lived in the city, where nobody's your friend and nobody gives a fuck, where you don't know your neighbor's name but you still have to hear him take a shit every morning. Thank God they *weren't* in the city, Angelina's nonna said, thank God Caro hadn't run off after Patrick's father like she'd wanted to, thank God Angelina's dad hadn't whisked them away to some distant bazaar. Thank God they were home where they belonged and where family bonds still held strong, where weak links could be superseded and where the ground beneath them was rich with ancestors glad to kiss their feet.

At school Angelina's friends told her how lucky she was not to live with her parents, and gamely she agreed. Patrick touted his freedom to his classmates and offered Caro's old bedroom up as a practice space for anyone who wanted to start a band, heralding an era of screeching guitars, offbeat drum solos, and a parade of grungy guys with nicknames like Mutt and Dingus who taught Angelina how to roll joints one-handed and asked what the deal was with Pat's stuck-up girlfriend.

Occasionally, Angelina longed for more: for Caro to miss them enough to move home, or—her most alarming desire—for her own father to appear. For some reason she always pictured him limping in on foot, as if he'd been walking thousands of miles to reach her. Maybe it was easier to picture his staggering silhouette than his face. She tried to subtract Caro's features from her body and make sense of what was left. Minus the straight nose, the green-gray eyes, the narrow shoulders, and full pocket of belly. Her forehead was wider than most kids', her brow more protruding and her eyebrows thicker; she had more hair in general, actually, thick heavy waves of it, coppery brown in the summer and almost black in the winter but always frizzing up beyond her control. She thought she could see her father most in the rounded set of her chin. But that didn't make a full face. She had nightmares of a stranger with no eyes and a toothless mouth banging on the windows, coming to take his daughter away.

Her father must be responsible for her height, at least. The women in her family skewed small, birdlike, but by fourteen Angelina was already on a level with Patrick. At family dinners Angelina stretched her legs out, threw her arm around the back of her nonna's chair, preferring to act like her boy cousins than scrunch herself up into a little girl. Probably she could have tried harder to fit in, but it was easier to show off instead. She played the difference as an advantage. Hair more luscious, legs longer and leaner, tits bigger, and sweetly freckled skin with a permanent tan even in the winter months when the rest of her family went anemic pale. She stood out, but she was a Sicco girl, and standing out was the point.

Patrick, already well on his way to manhood, grew his hair down to his shoulders and spent six months sporting a wispy black goatee. He took over more of the household tasks, and asked Angelina to stop calling Franco about burst pipes or broken toasters. He said he could handle them himself. Angelina didn't see the issue with accepting family help, assuming that one day she would help another Sicco in turn, but with every new day Patrick found it more shameful to depend on others.

Increasingly, the only person Patrick would lean on was Jagvi. Jagvi could bring him a paper bag of painkillers when he was sick, Jagvi could quiz him before his tests, Jagvi could hole up in his room with him on bad days, blasting hardcore and pretending not to hear when Angelina knocked on the door. Jagvi bought him a Raw Power T-shirt on his seventeenth birthday, and he wore it so often that holes formed in the armpits and the hem unraveled, which they both agreed only added to the look.

In her father's absence, Angelina wondered if Patrick saw himself as something of a father by proxy. Sometimes he yelled at her in a vaguely paternal manner for hitching a drunken ride home with strangers or skipping school to lie in the sun reading magazines, but it was hard to take him seriously when she knew he was also skipping school and smoking questionable substances with their cousins and getting into fights in the hypermarket parking lot. Sometimes, too, he yelled at her for blaring her beloved Eurotrash or other trivial offenses that meant she got to holler back at him, and so Angelina always felt qualified to ignore his instructions. Authority hovered somewhere between them, uneasy and prone to switching sides. Angelina was just as likely to take control, make demands, give instructions: joining her nonna in pressuring him to finish his vegetables, or making him phone the school and say she was sick. "I have period pain," she announced, which Patrick accepted as an excuse about three times a month until Jagvi sold Angelina out.

If Jagvi was pleased about Caro's absence and the privileges it allowed her and Pat, she kept it to herself. She didn't spend much time with the wider Sicco family. Patrick said that there was some ugly history between her dad and Uncle Franco, planning permissions denied by Riccardo's council office, rumors that Franco had stolen a youthful girlfriend from under Riccardo's nose. Behind Patrick's back Franco said that the Marinos were conceited, and that Jagvi was no exception.

Back then Jagvi wore her hair in a long braid, and dressed in linen shirts and workman's pants and combat boots like she wanted early admission to the Communist Party. In the chaos of the school hallway, Jagvi's silent composure seemed like an indictment on the whole scene. Most kids thought Jagvi was a snobby foreigner and said that her ma wore garish clothes like she was proud of them even though they basically looked like pajamas, and her dad was a drunk who would scream at you if he saw you cycling on the wrong side of the street. Jagvi kept her mouth shut and her chin high. Patrick had grown up with Angelina for a sister and was well enough acquainted with provincial racism not to be surprised. Patrick told Angelina that if anyone said shit like that to her, she should rise above it, exactly like Jagvi did. Angelina got her fair share of racist comments, but she always sidestepped them with a laugh, and she worried that Jagvi would catch her one day, joking around with the worst of them, and write Angelina off for good.

Once it almost happened: Patrick played a show opening for a more established band from Myrna, thrashing around on his guitar with Jethro offbeat on a borrowed drum set, and Jagvi and Angelina both came to watch. While they waited for him to finish packing up his gear, a bartender brought them a round of shots, smirking as he rapped two glasses filled with blue liquor before them.

"Hey, ladies. Didn't know we were serving dark meat tonight."

Jagvi looked down, her mouth a hard and fixed line.

"Too bad you could never afford it," Angelina said sweetly.

"Fuck you," he said, but he was laughing despite himself, shaking his head. "Everyone's right about you, you're a handful."

"Better luck next time," Angelina said, winking so he wouldn't take it too hard. When she turned back, Jagvi was watching her intently, half frowning and half admiring in a way that made Angelina self-conscious.

"Doesn't that bother you?" Jagvi asked.

"That's just everyday shit," Angelina said. "It's harmless, Nonna says."

"Is it?" Jagvi asked.

It felt like a rebuke, and Angelina shrugged, a little crestfallen. "I think it's not worth being angry all the time."

Jagvi didn't say anything, dark eyes glittering in the low light.

"You don't agree."

"No," Jagvi said. She picked up her shot. "To your health."

"And yours," Angelina said, and they both drank, slamming the glasses on the sticky tabletop. She'd wondered, after that, if Jagvi would talk to her more, if maybe it was something they could bond over. She'd wanted to know more about Jagvi's anger; she couldn't imagine living like that, hidden inside a cold high tower of fury. Wasn't it better to joke and coax your peers into accepting you?

But it was clear that Jagvi had more pressing concerns. By the time she and Patrick were seventeen, she only wanted to talk about the future: timelines, options, career plans. She was blunt about her desire to leave Cadenze, working as a cashier but never spending any money. At the table with Angelina, over a meal of oven pizza and bagged salad, she and Patrick talked about the most insane things: buying a car and driving until they hit the coast; applying for scholarships so they could afford their own place in Rome, or Paris, or New York; traveling to India together to meet Jagvi's extended family. Jagvi didn't have the same starry-eyed naivete that Angelina's friends had when they talked about becoming movie stars or fighter pilots. She was pure determination. Once she fell asleep on their couch, and Angelina noticed that she slept with her fists clenched tight.

Angelina cornered Patrick alone. "Is that really what you want? To leave?"

He looked uncomfortable. "It might be cool to see more of the world. Play music, maybe."

"You suck at guitar. Yesterday you tried to play standing up and dropped it."

His jaw jutted out. "I could get better."

"Nobody's gonna pay you to get better."

"I'd work as well."

"Doing what?"

"I don't know. I'll wait tables or clean cars."

"Jagvi said you'll have *better* opportunities if you leave."

"Well, Jag wants to go to university."

"That's what she wants. It's not what you want. You'd just be her sidekick. You wouldn't have any friends."

Patrick stood up. "Just because you can't imagine a life outside Cadenze doesn't mean that none of us can." He glanced away, then seemed to find his resolve. "I'm in love with her. If she goes, I will, too."

Angelina watched him leave, panic swarming through her. The next time they saw Caro, Angelina raised the point again, hoping that Caro's own experiences would compel her to intervene. Caro's foray into the outside world was her favorite tragic tale. Just like Patrick, she had craved something more, without a clear idea of what *more* was. Failing to meet the impossible standards of her family, branded a disappointment because she didn't kill a wolf or fight in a war, she ran away looking for the recognition that Cadenze had denied her. Instead she'd found destitution, humiliation, people who laughed in her face and ditched her in nightclubs, and a fickle romance that cost her her future.

Angelina thought Caro would be horrified at Patrick's plans. She had even hoped her mother might throw a tantrum, sob and wail that he couldn't leave her side. Instead, Caro lifted her head slowly from the fried shrimp she'd been peeling.

"If that's what you want, darling," she said to Patrick. "I'll be just fine here on my own. And I'm sure Nini will, too. She's almost sixteen, after all."

Despair tugged at Angelina's chest.

Patrick told Angelina that in a few years she could come and join them. The offer disgusted her. She didn't want to follow them across the country like a lost dog, to lie on their couch in some crummy apartment, watch them get married, have kids, the two of them shooting off to a separate Pat-and-Jag planet while Angelina hung on to their wings by her fingertips, a shadow from their past they couldn't quite shake off. No thank you. Angelina was beginning to fully appreciate the benefits that came from being the Sicco girl, and she wasn't about to give that up for her brother's girlfriend's pipe dreams.

More than once at a party, some thick-necked guy had eyed her and told her to go back where she came from, only to be interrupted by a similarly thick-necked friend who warned him she was the Sicco girl. Her cousins hosted grown-up parties with live music and free booze, the sort of parties her rabble of school friends couldn't hope to get into without Angelina's help. The girls always came over to her place to get ready because they could pre-game without adult supervision. She had reached the level of coolness that a sixteen-year-old confuses with invulnerability.

Patrick never came to those parties anymore, so he couldn't see how high Angelina had risen. He stayed home studying, or working late shifts, whatever was necessary to keep up with Jagvi's ambitions. That meant he wasn't there the night he should have been. It was left to Angelina to report everything that happened, to kick all his scrappy dreams to the floor. It was so unfair. Even now, with the benefit of nine years' cooling off, Angelina still thought it was so drastically unfair that the reason Pat wasn't there that final, shitty night was because Jagvi didn't want him to be.

At a party in Lavra, a town about an hour from Cadenze, somebody handed Angelina a joint that made her dizzy. She could still remember the heady nausea of bad weed, the room spinning away from her and the five shots she'd already downed churning in her belly. She stumbled upstairs on her own, hoping for an unoccupied bathroom. Instead she took the wrong door, into a bedroom.

Inside Jagvi was on the bed with a girl. For a long moment all Angelina could see was the other girl's face, blond hair spilling back over the mattress, her cheeks flushed and her eyes shiny and her mouth swollen and pink. Her back arched up toward Jagvi, her shirt tangled around her armpits, both hands clutching onto Jagvi's arms, her pretty voice pleading. And Jagvi, in her sports bra and those workman's pants Angelina knew so well, caging the other girl with her body, her fingers inside the other girl's underwear, the unmistakable jerk of her knuckles, a heady fuck with the other girl squirming and begging for more and spreading her legs. Almost worse than all of it was the expression on Jagvi's face, hot and devoted, so taut with desire it was nearly angry, and the way that expression warped into shock and shame when she turned her head and saw Angelina.

IX

Nine years later, Angelina spent her Saturday double shift in a bad mood. She got to Old Timers still fuming at Jagvi's assertion that she had triggered Angelina's sexual identity; the implication that the very worst thing Jagvi ever did, the thing that hurt Angelina's brother maybe even more than their mother moving out, had been some kind of come-to-Jesus moment for Angelina. As if heavenly hosts hallelujahed and angelic light enveloped the sordid scene on the bed, showing Angelina what she wanted.

And now she was tired, too, and unsettled. Not enough sleep last night, so the bad dream about that thing in the mirror stuck around like a hangover, and her anger at Jagvi jangled her already-tight nerves. Her brain bounced back and forth from the dream to Jagvi, feeding off its own unhappy energy. She couldn't stop remembering the sensation of being seized by the back of her neck and hauled roughly to the ground.

A bad, no-good weekend, Angelina decided, slamming down barstools. A terrible twenty-four hours. Let Jagvi back into Cadenze, and nightmares and humiliation were sure to follow.

It didn't help to have Jagvi's dead father lying in state on Angelina's bar, his picture in a cheap frame beside a candle. Cadenze mourned all its deaths like this, although the only picture anyone had of Riccardo was the one from his municipal ID card. Patrons gave his photo a perfunctory nod as they came up for their house wine and schnapps. Sooner or later there would be a new picture to replace him—one of Cadenze's ailing pensioners, or a kid who'd taken too much or driven too wildly—to which people could bow solemnly and blow kisses. After the landslide on the Pepper Grinder eight years back, they had fourteen frames lined up on the bar for weeks.

Riccardo had never been a kind man. After Jagvi and her mama left town, he took on a more gnarled demeanor, a failed tyrant huddled in his empty hall. He retired from his job at the county office and stopped coming outside except to buy canned food in bulk like he was stocking up for doomsday. The town had some sympathy for him—the wife leaving was one thing, but that daughter abandoning him, too, was a heavy blow. Who knew how much better Riccardo's life might have been if he'd just picked out a nice local wife? Well, that's what comes from mixing.

Angelina always laughed at this sort of talk. *Yes, fellas, mixing was definitely the problem, and not the fact that Riccardo's a bitter old asshole.*

Oh, but they didn't mean Angelina! She could always count on someone taking her hand at this point and telling her not to worry, Sicco blood was too strong, Angelina was Cadenze born and bred. By then Angelina was used to the whole town speculating about her parentage. Old men were forever telling her authoritatively that her father must have been Black, or an Arab, or maybe from the Philippines; a teacher had once patted Angelina's six-year-old cheek and said kindly there was every chance he was just Greek, as though Angelina's genes were a threat that needed defusing.

She was relieved when Old Timers began to fill up. The bar was more sociable than the call center, more distraction from Angelina's own mind. Francesca-Martine, the owner, pored over an accounts book with a bottle of wine. Her husband usually appeared at Old Timers half an hour before the football kickoff to fondle his wife for luck and bring a hot meal for the night crew, then go home to yell at the TV. "Sometimes I think if his team was winning, he'd switch sides," Francesca-Martine said. "Usually men just need something to be angry about." His tobacco-stained stubble reminded Angelina of her uncles, and she wished him a full season of heavy losses and sound sleep.

As co-owners, he and Francesca-Martine did not mind Angelina using their bar as a pickup spot for wayward tourists. They permitted the free drink flyers, let her stage whatever subtextually queer events she wanted in their back room, and had even given consent for Angelina to offer Old Timers as a venue to any riot grrrl or punk band she liked, should any of them deign to reply to her letters. Francesca-Martine and her husband were not, in short, immune to the Sicco girl's charm.

Tonight, Angelina was especially grateful for their leniency. She had come to work an hour early, after driving the car she shared with her mother to Caro's place, reasoning that walking to and from work was better than being tricked into ferrying Jagvi around. She had avoided a trip home between shifts, unprepared to face that messed-up bathroom again, the scratches her fingers had left in the wallpaper, the bathroom mirror winking at her. She kept running it over in her head, trying to make sense of it as she handed out foaming glasses of beer. She'd been sleepwalking, or half-asleep and easily spooked by a shadow in the mirror—"Sorry!" she said, overpouring a glass of red and licking the excess off her fingers—or she'd been drunk and clumsy in the bathroom and then gone back to bed and dreamed up an explanation. Her home and head felt newly unfamiliar. She stood wiping a rag over the same clean stretch of counter for too long, until Gemma startled her back into her surroundings, dumping a handful of dirty glasses on the bar.

Gemma's green eyeshadow was smudged up to her eyebrows, headphones hooked around her neck with her Walkman still playing. Angelina could just hear the buzz of another recorded self-help guru chanting affirmations.

"Am I supposed to empty the dishwasher by myself?"

"I'm getting to it," Angelina said. The bell above the door rang and she jumped. But it was only another band of regulars, nodding absently at Riccardo's picture as they passed.

Gemma followed her gaze. "You expecting someone?"

"Who would I be expecting?" Angelina asked, rattled by Gemma's close attention.

Gemma shrugged, unstacking tumblers. "Someone said they saw Jagvi getting out of your car this morning."

"Pat made me drive her into town."

"And?"

"And that's it."

"What was she like? Did she do anything weird?"

Angelina shoved a dish towel into one of the wineglasses and gave it a lackluster polish. "Just implied that she triggered my entire sexuality."

"Ha!" Gemma said. "So arrogant." She stacked a few tumblers onto the back shelf and glanced over her shoulder at Angelina. "Did she?"

"No," Angelina said. "It's the dumbest thing I've ever heard. You went to school with Jagvi, by that logic you'd be gay, too."

"Ugh, don't tease," Gemma said, with a self-pitying grimace. Admittedly due in part to Angelina's boasting and bravado, Gemma had a very idealistic view of what it meant to be queer. Whenever she complained about men, which was often, she was prone to throwing in a casual *you don't know how lucky you are*, and it didn't always register when Angelina responded with an incredulous *at least you're getting laid, dude*.

Tonight, Gemma put her hands on Angelina's shoulders in a dreamlike caress. "Just think how nice my life would be. We'd probably be married."

"Don't be gross."

"Don't be homophobic!" Gemma grasped Angelina's ponytail and gave it a playful tug.

Angelina whirled and tossed the remnants of melted ice from a rum and Coke over her shoulder at Gemma's face. Gemma screeched and cursed, swiping at her damp face with a rag.

"Sorry." Angelina's heart was pounding. The hand in her hair, the body against her back. For a moment she'd been back in that dark bathroom fighting off something too awful to see. It was only a nightmare. It had told her so itself.

"What is wrong with you tonight?" Gemma demanded.

"Sorry," Angelina repeated. "I had a bad dream last night, it's put me in a mood."

Gemma's expression softened. "Were you smoking Ricky's hash? Because last time he gave me some, I thought I saw a gnome in my parents' kitchen and started screaming but it turned out just to be my gramps."

"No, it wasn't like that. I think I was sleepwalking and I saw a ghost or something." She rubbed her knuckle against her nose, feeling almost self-conscious about it. "I trashed the bathroom trying to escape."

Francesca-Martine looked over, curious. "Why didn't your brother come and wake you up?"

"He wasn't there."

"Pat," Gemma said, exasperated, as if it were Patrick's job to stay home and tend to his adult sister's night terrors. "What did it look like?"

"I can't remember. But I think I saw it, in the mirror. It was standing behind me."

"Oh, don't creep me out," Gemma said, backing away. "If you talk about it too much, I won't be able to sleep."

"Maybe it'll come for you next," Francesca-Martine said, chuckling when Gemma crossed herself.

"No really, stop. I bet it was all those scary stories last night. What do you expect if you sit around in caves talking about demons?"

Francesca-Martine shook her head. "Not Franco's cave? You Siccos, honestly. Franco ought to have that thing boarded up before one of his boys falls in."

"Angelina was playing around on the edge," Gemma said, and Francesca-Martine tutted disapprovingly.

"Anybody who falls into a hole is dumb enough to deserve it," Angelina said, words of wisdom she'd learned from her nonna. "You're probably right, I just creeped myself out. I thought I was awake, but I guess I was dreaming."

"Ugh, really, let's stop talking about it," Gemma said. "This is the type of conversation I can only have in the daylight."

Angelina turned to the window. "It's after sunset already?"

The days had been getting shorter since August, but only now did it strike her that summer was really over. The last tourist bus had come and gone and a new season had begun. Outside the streets were already quiet and the fountain switched off. The stone sculpture of the giant hand rose from the still pool of water, its palm facing up to the sky and its thick fingers silhouetted by streetlights. The cobblestones beneath the fig trees were littered with fallen fruit. Autumn already. Jagvi talking riddles, nightmares lingering, and wind stirring the dead leaves.

Angelina ought to take a cue from her town and pull the shutters down. No more hanging around in caves, no more one-on-ones with Jagvi, and most of all no more thinking about the thing from the pit, because then she'd just invite it in. That was what she'd done last night, thought and thought and thought about it, until it finally appeared.

Her friends were already filing into the bar to distract her, Jethro and Ricky and the girls from the call center in their tight jeans and heels. She would work hard tonight and then go home and pass out without thinking of anything, and in the morning she would clean up the mess in the bathroom and steer clear of Jagvi, and life would be calm and safe again. Gemma had the right idea. Angelina wouldn't talk about her nightmare, wouldn't think about it. Otherwise, she only had herself to blame.

The phone rang. Gemma spoke rapidly into the headset, then hurried back to Angelina.

"Marc's coming here with all the warehouse guys. The first ones already left."

"We'll need extra vodka," Francesca-Martine said.

"I'm not going in the cellar," Gemma said. "Nini's freaked me out."

"You need to grow some balls," Angelina told her. "I'll go."

"You need to grow some self-preservation instincts," Gemma retorted. The sound of men's cheerful singing filtered in through the window. "Better get some rum, too."

Angelina had always thought she looked after herself pretty well; she and Pat both had long years of practice. Even in her nightmare, she'd put up a good fight. But there she was, thinking about it again. She just needed to fetch a few bottles, and then the men would be here to distract her. They stored all the extra bottles beneath the bar, down ten wooden steps with a trapdoor that people occasionally tripped over. The cellar was a cold and cluttered room full of shadows. Once, Angelina had hidden down there and jumped out at Gemma, who had literally pissed herself.

If that thing's real, it will be down here, Angelina thought as she hit the first step. She cursed herself for breaking her own resolve again. But some things in this world couldn't be conjured by thoughts or speech alone; some things existed whether Angelina Sicco thought about them or not. She could feel her heartbeat like a pulsing fist of tension in her chest. She descended the wooden steps into the gloom. The air was heavy and warm, like something down there had been cooking.

X

The cellar had never been well organized. Crates of bottled beer stood in unsteady towers. Angelina was always afraid they would topple over and crush her, so she kept them stacked close to the wall, but tonight several of the towers had moved. Someone had dragged them forward into a triangle formation, leaving a hidden space behind them.

Worse than the uncharacteristic warmth was the smell. Stale like deep earth, like air trapped under rock for too many years and left to seethe in a lightless pit. The smell of monstrous fingers stroking her face in a nightmare. Angelina's breath came quick and loud, and she couldn't get it under control.

"This is something I dreamed up," she said to the dark cellar. "It's only because we were talking about it upstairs."

The singing men chanted for shots at the bar. Their stomping feet shook the ceiling.

She hauled five bottles of rum and five of vodka out of their boxes and lined them up by the stairs ready to carry. She started sweating in the heavy air, but nothing happened while she worked. Nothing spoke and nothing tried to touch her.

Why do I even assume it's gonna do that, she wondered.

Because I Can Speak. Because I Have Hands.

Sheer terror pulsed through her; it *hurt*, her limbs flaring with heat and chest seizing with panic. Angelina howled, and the thing behind her snatched her voice out of the air before it could get far. Her scream hunched up in her throat. She almost choked on the saliva her mouth was suddenly full of. It was so much stronger than the night before, silencing her without even touching her.

"You okay down there?" Gemma called from the top of the stairs.

Tell Her You're Fine, the thing behind her said. Don't Be Such A Baby.

Its voice had weight, a pressure like heavy hands on her shoulders, and she scrambled to obey.

"Fine! Sorry. It's dusty down here."

You're Suuuuuuch A Good Liar, the thing said admiringly. You Should Flex That Muscle More Often.

Angelina whipped around, but all she could see behind her were the liquor shelves, dirty light on dirty wood. Her hands hung limp at her sides. Something touched her forehead, very gently, reaching around from behind her. A cool brush against her skin, like Caro checking to see if she had a temperature, but it wasn't quite hands, it wasn't quite fingers.

Okay, So I Lied A Little, Too, the thing said. It Wasn't A Nightmare.

I'm going to be eaten by a town legend in my own fucking bar, Angelina thought. Hot tears pricked at her eyes, and she couldn't catch a full breath. She panted, tongue too thick for her mouth. Her organs rioted, lungs full and stomach heaving and guts squirming like earthworms. She hoped her cousins were wrong and that it would be quick.

So Dramatic. I Just Wanna Get To Know You. I'm Interested In Your Appeal. You Can Go Upstairs, Would That Make You Feel Better?

Please, Angelina thought fervently, *please, please, please—*

Don't Beg. It's Unbecoming. Up You Go.

Something heavy knocked at the soft hollows behind her knees and shoved her into motion. Angelina scrambled up the steps, almost falling in her haste to get out of there. She emerged into the warm chaos of Old Timers gasping, sweating, hands empty of the bottles she'd gone down to get. Gemma glanced over, measuring out a round of tequila slammers. "You okay, Nini?"

Angelina poured herself a shot of vodka and took it in one, hands trembling around the slim glass. She gasped, took another. Gemma laughed at her.

"Save some for the rest of us."

"I can't go down there," Angelina said, gesturing at the cellar. "I can't get the, the stuff we need, I'm sorry—"

"The liquor?" Gemma blinked at her. "Babe, you literally just carried it up. Wait, are you already drunk?"

Angelina turned. The bottles of rum and vodka stood neatly on the shelf behind her. Had she carried them up? Her arms were aching. Did Gemma think she was losing it? Would telling her there was a monster in the cellar make Angelina seem more or less crazy?

Better Not Risk It, the thing said cheerfully, leaning over her shoulder, vast and invisible. You Can Say Thank You For Helping You Out.

"Thank you for helping me out," Angelina said. Hands numb, vodka sinking in.

You Are Welcome, said the thing.

Saturday night at Old Timers, normally one of Angelina's favorite times and places, started to spin. The music rang in her ears, the colors were vivid and blurry, the night reformulated before her eyes like some hideous carnival. And while she worked in a humming, appreciative crowd, the thing rummaged through her head. Flickering images paired with the sensation of moist hands digging deep into her cranium, hands that wouldn't stay solid and kept *dripping*, like wax or sweat sliding down folds of gray matter, making her stomach drop and heave. The glass of whisky she clutched steadied her a little, made her able to bear what it was doing to her, and bear it, the thing said, she must. It had meant what it said about getting to know her, and this, it told her, was easier than boring old questions and answers.

"You won't mind if I get wasted, then," she said. The bar was heaving at this time of night, and nobody noticed her speaking behind her glass. "I'm not sure if I can handle this sober."

Ripple of appreciative laughter, but no response: the thing was busy sorting through Angelina's life. Daddy issues, not interesting. Mama issues, slightly more interesting! Do You Think The Lack Of A Present And Supportive Mother Turned You Into A Lesbian?

"No," Angelina said, pouring out fresh pints for the boys. She tossed back the last of her whisky; it made her tongue looser, her sentences smoother. "Shouldn't an ancient uncanny beast be a little more creative in its homophobia?"

Who Are You Calling Ancient? I've Only Been Around Since The War.

It was the first solid piece of information she'd heard. "The fascists threw you in that pit?"

Fascists? No, the thing said idly, The Other Ones, With The Spears. Shut Up And Drink. You're Attracting Attention.

But Angelina wasn't. No one looked over her shoulder, where she felt the thing looming over her; no one asked whom she was speaking to. Maybe Angelina wasn't talking at all. Maybe Angelina was hallucinating their indifference. There seemed so many different ways she might be going crazy. She wanted Patrick badly.

That Makes Sense. Rely On Him A Lot, Don't You?

"I do not," Angelina said, but the thing flicked through her head with speed, pulling up its evidence: Angelina calling drunk from a party in Lavra, needing Patrick to come pick her up at three in the morning; Angelina, aged sixteen, spending the first Christmas without Caro, rugged up on the couch with Patrick, reading his palm, demanding he take her out with his friends that evening; Patrick helping Angelina get the gig bartending at Old Timers; Patrick speeding to Myrna's hospital with a shard of glass embedded in the arch of Angelina's foot; Patrick teaching her to drive over long, patient hours in his truck. Angelina's face was hot. "He's my brother. Who else would do those things?"

Looks Like You Never Bothered To Find Out.

What the fuck was this thing, her mother? "I look after him, too."

True enough. The thing didn't seem particularly interested in Patrick's deprivations, but it skimmed desultorily through to track them. Yes, Angelina was a bright counter to Patrick's melancholy, pulled him out of the house on the days or weeks when he succumbed to that male Sicco moodiness. Yes, she was minutely better at housekeeping, and she'd taken over the washing and grocery shopping despite her resentment that he saw no problem with sliding any apparently feminine chore into her hands. Yes, the thing could see now that Angelina kept Patrick secure in the Sicco clan; that where she was valued and special, Patrick could have slipped out of view, just another boy, and a fatherless one at that. Angelina had pushed him forward, made sure that everyone knew her big brother was no one to be challenged or underestimated. Not even Caro was permitted to insult Patrick without reason; Angelina didn't keep out of their fights anymore. Dull deeds for a dull life, the thing supposed, but fair enough. Angelina looked after her brother, with a tougher love than Patrick turned on her.

Oh Hey, What's This?

"Fuck off," Angelina said. "That's private."

More Private Than Anything Else? Interesting. In Angelina's memory, Jagvi moved against the girl on the bed in vivid color. Fascinating! What A Betrayal. Angelina had been very good to tell Patrick, to keep him from being cuckolded, to rescue what was left of his dignity.

"Leave it alone," Angelina said.

Jagvi's mouth, wet and gleaming like her knuckles. The arch of Jagvi's back as she hunched over the nameless girl, like an animal tearing at its prey. Where had she learned to kiss like that? Surely she hadn't kissed Angelina's brother like that.

"Fuck *off*," Angelina said.

The other girl's tits spilling into Jagvi's groping hand. Jagvi's fingers pinching at a pink nipple. The rough, competent way Jagvi handled her. The thing's slimy interest smeared over the scene. Had it really been the first time?

"I don't know," Angelina moaned. "It doesn't matter. Don't keep looking, it's so embarrassing."

Embarrassing for Angelina, really? Surely it was only embarrassing for Jagvi. Unless...how long had Angelina stood there watching? It was a vivid little clip, playing over and over, memorized and known by heart. How could the thing resist knowing it, too? Mouth, nipple, teeth, hand, hips. Jagvi shoving her cunt down against the girl's leg, grinding at her.

Oh, Don't You Like That Word? Not In Connection With Jagvi?

But that was what Jagvi had been doing, after all, even through her heavy workman's jeans (And Really, Did They Never Tip You Off, Nini?): pressing the hot tight core of herself against the girl's leg, searching for friction, dragging denim against her clit.

Shall We Play It Again?

Mouth, nipple, teeth, hand, hips, cunt, kiss. When Jagvi broke away and saw Angelina, a strand of saliva linked her mouth to the girl's on the bed. It hung there for a moment, then snapped. Angelina stood in the doorway cold and sweating.

You Don't Like This Part? The shame and desire on Jagvi's face and the way she jerked away from the girl and tried to scramble after Angelina, crying, *Angel, Angel*, her voice breaking with fear and desperation, only Angelina was already shoving her way through the party, back to the car, back to Cadenze, back to tell her brother what Jagvi had done. How, about two weeks later, Jagvi at their door with her mama waiting in the car outside, she was leaving town for good and she wanted to say goodbye to Patrick, and Angelina was the good tough little sister saying, *No. You can't see him. You've done enough already.* You Don't Care To Linger On That? Shall We Rewind?

Jagvi and the girl on the bed. Mouth. Where did she learn to kiss like that?

Angelina poured another drink, and the thing laughed oleaginously, a greasy wave cresting. Oil dripped through her head.

All Right. Let's Move On.

Angelina drank steadily. She drank through the fights breaking out and the pop songs about surfing at the beach and running from the law; she drank enough to hold Marc while he cried about his ex and then led a rousing performance of "Now Our Men Are Home from War." As the bar emptied out, Angelina knew that she was running out of time. Her mind reeled with alcohol and cruelty, and she couldn't think how to fight it off. She hoped she was drunk enough that it wouldn't hurt too bad, whenever the thing finally grew bored and moved on to its true purpose. She hoped the liquor would muffle her terror as the thing tore into her abdomen like it had torn through her brain.

Gemma, on her way to a party in Myrna with some of the boys, wanted Angelina to join them. She grasped Angelina's hands and pleaded for her company while Angelina sweated and the thing behind her crooned in admiration, She Loves You, Baby, She Really Does! It felt too much, overwhelming, to have both of them clutching at her, the thing from her nightmare and Gemma's laughing, demanding grip. Angelina wrestled herself free and stood over the ice bucket. Gemma followed her. She tucked a strand of Angelina's damp hair behind her ear.

"Are you okay?"

Angelina swallowed and shook her head. "My nightmare—" She gestured behind her to where the thing's voice came from, the empty space over her shoulder where it resided. "It's back in my head."

"Oh my god, stooooop it," Gemma said, giggling. "You've already freaked me out, okay, you got me!"

"Gem," Angelina said, "Gem, really, please, stay here—"

Gemma took her by the shoulders and spun Angelina around in a neat circle, her sneakers catching on the tacky floor behind the bar. "Okay, we've done a full three-sixty check," she said, in the sweet sympathetic voice she used on drunk men who needed to go home. "No ghosts or demons or anything behind you."

"It's invisible," Angelina tried, "it's hiding—"

"You *tease* when you're drunk," Gemma declared, already whirling and tossing her hair over one shoulder, one of the guys drawing her close with an arm around her waist. "I'll see you soon, okay? No more nightmares, Nini!"

Don't Take It Personally, the thing said. These People Really Care About You. I've Watched Them All Night And They Love You So Much. You Comfort And You Entertain, You Pour Poison Down Their Throats, You Make Them Feel So Interesting. They're Just Having A Different Night Than You.

Yes, Angelina could see it, Gemma swept up in the energy and fun of an Old Timers night, easy to brush off Angelina's dour drunkenness at the bar. She tried again. "Gemma?"

"Everything's okay," Gemma called, blowing kisses. Marc caught her hand and held it up, and she spun a tottering turn in her heels as he escorted her toward the door. "You're just a little trashed, baby. Call me in the morning!"

The door closed. They'd left so abruptly it felt deliberate, a hidden presence rushing them out. Now it hovered behind her, pleased.

Angelina stood in the empty bar. She heard the rev of Marc's motorbike and watched the red taillights swinging around a corner. Sometimes Patrick stopped by at closing time on his way from the rock bar to steal a free beer and hear the night's gossip before they walked home together. But tonight he would be with Jagvi. No one was coming to save her. She raised her eyes to her reflection in the dark window. She looked dizzy and pale, her long hair frizzing out, her T-shirt stained at the pits. There was nothing behind her. Still she spoke aloud.

"Okay. I'm ready. You can do it now, whatever the point was of all this."

No. It's Your Turn. Be Good.

"I don't want to be chased," Angelina said. Her voice wobbled.

Then You Be The Chaser, the thing behind her said. We've All Got Things We Need To Do. If It Makes You Feel Better, You Can Run.

XI

Angelina ran up the mountain for home, sodden with drink and fear. The night felt large, enveloping, and she did not trust the thing not to follow. But the mountain stayed quiet, just the granite peak of Big Joe leering over her, and then she was part of the peak, climbing higher, and there was a circle of light that was her home. Angelina put on another burst of speed and landed panting in the porch light.

Jagvi looked up at her in surprise. She sat alone on the front steps: no, not alone, My Dog lolled at her feet, Jagvi's hands in My Dog's fur. Her face was a strange blend of startled affection, like she was still mostly focused on smiling at the dog, and her hair was limp, flat around her face. She must have been sweating, working hard today, her T-shirt sleeves rolled up even in the cool of evening. There was an open tub of cherries by her side and a small pile of pits sucked clean. She looked so competent and secure that despite everything, Angelina wanted to swoon at her feet. A knight-errant here to guard Angelina against the dark.

"Why are you back so early?" Jagvi asked, and then: "Did you run all the way up here?"

Angelina rubbed her mouth, still panting, woozy with whisky. "It's not early. Where's Pat?"

"I think he passed out inside. We got my dad's liquor cabinet open, and he drank most of it in celebration. Here." She passed Angelina a bottle of water, and Angelina lunged for it, mouth cotton dry and gasping. She sank onto the steps and downed it, choking on the last swallow in her eagerness. Jagvi reached out, gave her three hard slaps on the back as she coughed. "Easy. Pat said you probably wouldn't be back until four in the morning."

"What time is it?" Angelina demanded, still breathing heavily but calming now, the dizziness of the run and the alcohol receding. Jagvi checked her watch.

"Just midnight. You okay, Angel?"

"What?" Angelina shook her head: that was absurdly early, for a Saturday night at Old Timers. "It can't be."

"Really, are you okay?" Jagvi said, and leaned forward, frowning. She caught Angelina's chin between her fingers and tilted her face toward Jagvi, examining her like there was some answer to be found. Their eyes met and they both startled backward.

"Uh," Angelina said, trying to think. "I guess everyone left early. Shit. I'm kinda drunk."

"I'll get you some more water," Jagvi said, and took the bottle back inside.

The minute Jagvi was gone, Angelina dropped to the ground and checked under the porch for anything that might be hiding beneath it. She hadn't managed to catch sight of the thing today, but she kept looking for its unknown form all the same. My Dog came with her, sniffing the night air with baffled enthusiasm, the dark markings over her eyes like furry eyebrows drawn together in concern. Angelina stood up again and scanned the front yard. Not even the leaves in the trees were moving.

She sank back onto the porch steps, rubbing her forehead while My Dog licked the sweat from her shins. She was too fucking drunk, though the cool air and water were doing a cruel job of sobering her up, leaving the echoes in her mind nowhere to retreat. That oily sensation had gone, and now she felt dried-out, sticky, much too awake. My Dog whined gently, pressing in closer to Angelina, and Angelina put her head against the dog's flank.

"Here," Jagvi said, pressing the bottle back into Angelina's hand.

"The night got away from me," Angelina said.

"Drink some more water."

"I don't understand what's happening."

"You're drunk, Angel," Jagvi said gently. She touched Angelina's hair so swiftly that Angelina wondered if she'd imagined it. "Have some more water."

Angelina peered up at Jagvi. "Why aren't *you* drunk?"

"I don't drink much anymore. Health-care thing."

"Oh, you're too smart to get wasted? I'm glad I'm dumb."

"You're not dumb," Jagvi said, but not in a conciliatory way, more annoyed, like it bothered her to have to correct Angelina. "A couple of years ago I was drunk and sleeping it off and then my neighbor came and banged on my door 'cause her kid was having this crazy allergic reaction and couldn't breathe. I had to use the cricothyrotomy needle and I was terrified I was going to fuck it up and kill him quicker."

"A crico-what?"

"Cricothyrotomy needle." Jagvi made an alarming jabbing motion. "You use it to puncture someone's throat to get them oxygen."

"Christ," Angelina said. She could almost picture it, Jagvi hazy and hovering above a kid, making her incision. "But you weren't on duty?"

"No, but I had my kit and there wasn't time. He would've died if we waited for the actual ambulance." She sat on the step, too, arms folded across her chest and frowning like it was a problem she was still trying to work out. "Anyway, since then I don't really like to be out of control. Feels like every situation is a potential emergency."

"Did the kid make it?"

Jagvi nodded. She took another cherry from the bag, dragging the flesh from the stalk with her teeth. "Yeah, he was okay."

"Well. I promise not to have a medical crisis if you want a beer now."

"You can't promise that," Jagvi said. She sounded tired. "I should get going."

Angelina straightened up. She didn't want Jagvi to go. Alone time with Jagvi was another thing she'd sworn to avoid, but if it was a choice between that or sitting by herself, waiting for the thing to catch up with her, then better the devil she knew.

"Don't leave on my account," she said, and tried to smile. "Are you scared to be on your own with me?"

"I meant to go earlier," Jagvi said. "Pat's been asleep for hours." Then she blanched, like she hadn't meant to say that.

Angelina raised her eyebrows. "Waiting up for me, Jag?"

Jagvi looked away, embarrassed. "Fuck off, Angel," she said, and something clicked for Angelina; Jagvi rarely expressed any anger, and Angelina could count the times Jagvi had been mad at her on one hand. For Jagvi to snap meant that she already had to be in a truly foul mood. And Angelina liked to see Jagvi in a bad mood. It gave her a glimpse below the trapdoor, a chance to watch the snakes writhe.

"What's going on?" she said. "Bad day?"

Jagvi gave her a swift, disbelieving look, then laughed, a rough sound. "Leave it alone."

Angelina took a swig from the water bottle. "Spill it. I'm still in bartender mode."

"I don't need you to bartend me," Jagvi said. "I hate this place, that's all. I can't believe I have to go back up there tonight."

"Your dad's place? Just crash on the couch," Angelina offered. That would be good, to have Pat and Jagvi in the house all night. If she yelled, they would both come running.

But Jagvi shook her head. It was not an option, according to implacable Jagvi logic that she would never bother explaining to Angelina. "Doesn't matter where, really. It's this whole town. It's like a pit of quicksand."

"Ooh, that's a new one. Guess you've had some time to work on your Cadenze metaphors."

"You asked," Jagvi said, and added another cherry pit to the pile.

"I did," Angelina agreed. She didn't mind, anyway. She felt sorry for Jagvi, that Jagvi couldn't love her hometown like Angelina did, and that her hometown didn't love Jagvi back. "I guess you've been back more than usual this year."

"Funeral and fix the house. Two super-fun errands. Thanks, Dad."

Angelina cocked her head to the side. "You don't really seem like you're grieving."

Jagvi laughed again, this time in a startled burst. "Man, how drunk are you?"

"Pretty drunk," Angelina said. "And I don't wanna sleep yet, so we have to keep talking." She took a cherry for herself, scanned over the yard and the road again. Nothing moved. "*Are* you grieving?"

Jagvi stared out, too, but her gaze strayed uphill, where the roof of her dad's house was usually just visible over the tree line. Too dark to see it at this time of night.

"How do you want me to grieve, Angel? What would anyone like me to do? Even Ma doesn't know. If you have some ideas, I'd actually genuinely appreciate it." She folded her hands tightly together in her lap. "One of my friends said when someone dies you only remember the good stuff, but I didn't like him when he was alive and I fucking hate him now. He had nearly thirty years to be someone I would miss, and he spent the whole time telling me I was the one who needed to try harder. Now I can't even try anymore."

"You're so upset," Angelina realized. Jagvi looked away, face shadowed. "You never talk to me like this."

"That's not true," Jagvi said, her voice plain and direct in a way that reminded Angelina of the conversation they'd had years ago in San Michele or, worse, the Christmas holiday she did her best never to think about, and so she hurried on.

"You know what I mean. You're always working on your mysterious allure."

Jagvi's shoulders relaxed, like she was more comfortable being sniped at. "Oh, Angel. I'm an open book. Ask me anything."

"Anything," Angelina repeated. "Okay." A good question for Jagvi would be, *What the fuck do you think is happening to me? What did I call up from the pit, and what is it going to do next?* But probably Jagvi would answer the same as Gemma, only worse: *You're drunk. You're messing with me. Go to bed.* Angelina watched Jagvi peel the plastic label off the water bottle and hand it to My Dog, murmuring, "Hold." The pink gray of My Dog's mouth closed around her fingers. All night the thing from the pit had rifled through Angelina's memories. "Tell me about the girl you kissed. The one I saw you with, when we were kids."

Jagvi blinked. "You're still thinking about that?"

"You're the one who brought it up. That was what you meant this morning, wasn't it?"

"I shouldn't have said that to you."

"But you did."

"It was a long time ago."

"I remember it pretty well. Don't you?"

"I remember it," Jagvi said, but she looked at Angelina like she was remembering something else, her expression distracted and out of focus.

Angelina said, "I can tell you about my first kiss, if that makes it easier."

"Yes," Jagvi said immediately, snapping back to attention.

"I was kidding," Angelina said, flustered.

Jagvi blew a breath out of the corner of her mouth, an annoyed scrunch in her forehead. "I already know it was Demonic Dani, anyway," she muttered. "What do you want to know?"

"How did it start?"

"That's your question?"

"It was the first time you kissed a girl, right?"

"Yes."

A little thrill jolted down Angelina's spine. She had never been sure. "So how did it start?"

Jagvi took another cherry from the tub but didn't eat it, pressing the fruit between her fingers. "You know when you just go to touch a girl casually but once your hand is on her it doesn't feel casual at all? I cupped the back of her neck and she shivered."

"Her neck?"

"Yeah."

Angelina pulled her hair out the way. "Show me how."

Jagvi gave her a delighted look, coaxed out of her bad mood despite herself. "No, I'm not gonna show you how."

Angelina rolled her eyes. "So you touched her neck. What next?"

"I don't remember."

"Yes, you do," Angelina said, leaning forward, and Jagvi tilted her chin up, considering Angelina just long enough to make Angelina want to walk it back. Jagvi had that dangerous expression she got sometimes, the face that made Angelina feel as though she were inching along a tightrope, doing her best to balance above an outcrop of empty, hungry space.

Before Angelina could say anything, Jagvi nodded. "I think I just liked it when she shivered, and I wanted her to do it again, so I squeezed harder and she made this noise."

"Uh," Angelina said.

"Yeah," Jagvi said, satisfied, "kind of like that, and then she leaned forward and put her hand on my knee—we were on the couch, I think, and I knew she was going to kiss me, and it felt like all these little hooks in my brain that had been pointing in different directions and getting all tangled up in each other suddenly all turned toward her and zoomed in and I knew exactly what I wanted."

"So you kissed her."

"No, I bit her. Pretty hard."

"Where?"

"Her lip."

Angelina touched her bottom lip, thumbing the edge of it. Jagvi, leaning forward and watching intently, said, "More in the middle. Yeah, there."

"Ouch," Angelina said, pressing down. "But she liked it."

"I think so. She wanted to go upstairs, anyway." My Dog got up to scrabble at the front door. Jagvi's gaze followed her, and the sight of the Sicco front door made her bow her head, that promise of danger fading from her face, leaving only weariness behind. "You know the rest of the story."

Flash of the bed. Mouth, nipple, teeth, hand—

"Yeah, I do. Asshole," Angelina commented, but lightly. She felt almost completely sober now, and tired, like she'd run a marathon. She didn't want to go inside the house. The thing had not chased her home, but it also hadn't promised not to come find her. It could already be upstairs waiting in her bed. It had told her to be good, but it hadn't told her how.

"You know I'm sorry, Angel."

Angelina raised her head. "For what?" Jagvi was glum, her sharp features gone soft with a teenager's dismay. "Oh, for kissing that girl? Jagvi. It's not like— You didn't cheat on *me*."

"I worry sometimes that I really fucked him up. Like I'm the reason he never—"

"You sound like Caro," Angelina said. Jagvi flinched. "Relax. I don't think he ever would have left Cadenze for long. We're Siccos. We stay put. He likes his job and his friends, and he's with his family, he belongs here. He's even got a new band, did he tell you?"

"Yeah," Jagvi said. She stared out at the valley. The craggy tip of Little Joe was a black cutout against the stars. "The Crushing Defeats. Any good?"

"He's done worse." Pat had never really committed to the guitar, but what he lacked in technical skill he made up for in stage presence, stalking around in his ripped jeans like a self-ordained rock god. The last time she'd got him a slot at Old Timers, he made out with a girl in the front row halfway through the set to raucous applause. Angelina was at the back with Gemma, both hollering, "MANWHORE, MANWHORE," until Pat came up for air long enough to blow them a kiss.

Angelina loved to see Pat perform, especially in the back room of Old Timers, where she could control the lights and turn his mic all the way up. It was a constant relief that he wasn't playing alone in some city bar where nobody gave a shit who he was. She got a selfish thrill from watching Patrick unleashed onstage, all his raging, spiteful expressions and his uneven singing, voice slinging from a growl up to a wail. It was like a cage opened, and the real, reckless Patrick came striding out. It made Angelina acutely proud. Only those who knew her brother well enough would understand what a rare metamorphosis had taken place. Within Cadenze's borders there was nothing dull about Patrick or the way she loved him.

"I don't know if you're right," Jagvi said. "If this place is right for him."

Angelina bristled. "That's just because you hate it."

"No," Jagvi said. "It's because we're pretty similar, me and him. I know what it's like to want to belong here, and know that you don't."

Jagvi wasn't totally wrong, but she was outdated, still stuck on teenage Patrick in his battered Raw Power T-shirt, scowling at their uncles after another conversation turned sour. Patrick was an adult now, free to chase freak pussy, scream his heart out onstage, get into debates at Old Timers on the eve of every general election, and still be a Sicco and live with Angelina and belong, just as Angelina herself belonged.

The way Jagvi acted, you were dealt a card when you were born and that was that. Belong or don't. It didn't surprise Angelina to hear Jagvi say something so unequivocal. What surprised her was the disconsolate, tender note in Jagvi's voice, like Angelina had hit a bruise.

"When did you ever want to belong here?" Angelina demanded, and Jagvi stood, shaking her head.

"It's my hometown, too, Angel," she said, fists balled at her sides again. All that endless determination, pointing somewhere Angelina had never been able to see. "There are things I want from it. I'm gonna go."

"I know it is," Angelina said, stuttering. "I just didn't think— Are you sure you don't want to stay here tonight?"

Jagvi's shoulders hunched higher, and she turned her head, hiding her face. "Yeah. Go get some sleep."

Angelina held on to My Dog's collar and watched Jagvi leave. The soft fur against her fingers, the bitter taste of adrenaline back in her mouth. For the third time that night, she wanted Patrick around badly. When Jagvi was just outside of the yellow circle of porch light, nothing more than a shadow, Angelina called, "Jag!"

The shadow turned.

"Be careful out there, all right?"

The shadow nodded and flexed a bicep. "I'm all good."

Angelina threw a cherry pit at her, but she was too slow. The night swallowed Jagvi up. Angelina swept up the pile of pits and hurried My Dog inside.

No monster waiting in the hallway. Instead she found Patrick asleep on the couch. He'd taken his hair out of its ponytail, fanned around him like a grungy halo.

"Pat?"

He frowned and threw his hand over his eyes. "No. Sleeping."

"But I'm lonely."

"So call your friends."

He buried his face against the couch cushions. Angelina sat on the floor beside his head, while My Dog trotted in a circle and curled up at her side. Three sets of lungs breathed in and out, and Angelina strained to hear the other familiar night sounds, cars passing through the valley below or night owls calling to one another or the screams of the junkyard foxes. There was only quiet, and the prospect of the monster.

Angelina felt as alone as she had the night Caro moved out. She curled her arms around her knees and realized she was still holding Jagvi's damp cherry pits. She wished she could ask Jagvi what to do about the monster. She wished Jagvi had spent the night. If that thing showed up in the bathroom mirror again, there was no way Jagvi would sleep through her screaming.

She raised one of the pits to her mouth and swallowed it whole, letting it scrape down her throat. Patrick reached out in his sleep to ruffle her hair. Angelina fed herself the pits one by one, sucking down the sweet round stones until all of them were gone.

XII

The year she turned seventeen had been good for Angelina. There was a pleasant sense of aftermath in Jagvi's absence, like the days after a coup, cleaning up and sorting through. Tending to Pat, drinking wine with her nonna, reading pulp novels under her desk at school. The story of Jagvi's betrayal had made Angelina even more popular. She'd spied out an injustice—and what a lurid, titillating injustice—and rectified it. Jagvi didn't even stay in town long enough to sit for her exams.

There was no question of Patrick going with her, or going anywhere at all. He seemed determined to curl up and die. He stopped going to school and spent his days locked in his room with the stereo on full blast. If Angelina made dinner, he shuffled out for a plate and ate without speaking. At Angelina's request, Jethro took him out to drink his sorrows, only to return him at four in the morning with a black eye, a fat lip, and an old sock held to his bloody nose.

Angelina sat on the toilet while Patrick cleaned himself up. He was still drunk, and he kept dropping the antiseptic wipes. Angelina wanted to help him, but he batted her away and told her to leave him alone.

"I just want to know what happened," Angelina insisted.

"Nothing happened." Patrick hissed as he dabbed around his purple eye. "Just some guys talking shit."

"Which guys?"

Patrick scowled. "No one you know." He ran his tongue over his teeth, checking if any had come loose, and muttered, "Homophobes."

Angelina hugged her knees and curled her toes around the edge of the toilet lid. She pictured Patrick snarling nose to nose with a bully. She wondered what the guy had said, whether his mockery had been focused on Jagvi or Patrick himself. Even some of Angelina's friends looked at Patrick differently now, no longer the idolized older brother but a humiliated shell. If Angelina had been Patrick, she would have been delighted to fight someone over it, to prove her manhood before a cheering crowd.

"Did you at least get a good punch in?" Angelina asked.

"Nope. Spat some blood on his shirt, though."

The end of Angelina's teenhood was a balancing act of supporting Patrick without crowding him. She felt pity, but she couldn't let him feel pitiable. Angelina had no parental power over Patrick and none of Jagvi's spellbinding thrall, but she had methods of her own. She grouched so tirelessly about having to take the bus that Patrick started driving them both to school again. She enlisted her cousins to have his back in any future fights. At home she told him she'd drank all his booze with her friends, and sat in her room with his whisky stashed beneath her bed, smiling satisfied to herself while Patrick yelled and thrashed about below. Whenever he sank too deep into sadness, Angelina put on her most sympathetic face and offered to call Caro over to cheer him up. It usually shocked him out of his mood. Angelina would stand poised with her hand on the phone. "You're *sure* I shouldn't call her? She wants to help!"

And Patrick stumbled out of his room, pulling on a clean T-shirt, cursing, "You're such a little shit, Nini, I swear."

"Haven't you heard? Some wounds only a mother's love can heal!"

"Fuck off," Patrick grumbled. He grabbed his keys. "Come on, let's go for a pizza."

They drove their take-out boxes to a lookout halfway up the Pepper Grinder, and Patrick said that Caro seemed to find it even harder to move on than he did. She had asked him which was worse: the pain a teenager feels in their first heartbreak, or the pain a mother feels seeing her children get hurt?

"Christ," Angelina said.

"She told me she's been asking San Rocco for help."

"How's *he* gonna help?"

Patrick wiped his palms on his jeans. "I dunno. Turn Jag straight again, probably."

It took Angelina too long to laugh. When she did it was stilted. Her face felt hot, and she knew that Patrick could tell she was uncomfortable, although he had misinterpreted why.

"Sorry. Bad joke."

"Whatever," Angelina said. "I'll tell Caro to start praying for a porn star's car to break down outside our house instead."

Patrick clasped his hands together and turned his face up to the cloud-mottled sky. "You hear that, San Rocco?"

It took a long time for the squirming in Angelina's stomach to die down. She was lucky that Patrick was so preoccupied with Jagvi and his own misery that he hadn't noticed how much his own sister was hiding from him. Her priority that year was her brother, but even Patrick couldn't fill all her hours, and in the in-betweens she had found a new way to pass the time.

Somebody had palmed her a magazine article that taught you how to make yourself come, and she managed it on the first try, and on every night after that. She jerked her hips up to greet her own touch and collapsed in on herself. She hooked a pillow between her legs, pretending it was a denim-clad thigh. She forced herself to take it slow, picture the shy entreaties, the husky invitation to come up to her room. And then in a lightning burst of images seconds before orgasm: a girl, another girl, a *woman*, holding her down, fucking her, teaching her to fuck, wet on Angelina's thighs.

Her friends decided that Angelina was "too good" for boys their age, and she skated by on plausible deniability. There was just one gay kid at her school; he wasn't out but people could tell, and he took a lot of shit, WARNING: AIDS scrawled in Sharpie on his locker and the occasional beating to keep him in check. But lesbians were more of a punch line than a threat. Months later, people still laughed about Jagvi, boys waggling their tongue between their fingers while girls squealed, "*Gross!*" Angelina had yet to meet anyone who needed to know her secret.

Eventually she would turn her bedroom fantasies into reality. She watched her friends couple up and felt that twinge again, longing for something beyond her reach. Sometimes she wondered how Jagvi had managed to find a girl out here. It felt wrong to be jealous of the person who had broken her brother's heart, but she wanted a dash of Jagvi's luck. Up until Patrick approached her one day in late summer, she hadn't been able to think of a solution.

"I need to tell you something," he said. "Mostly so you can't call me a dick for lying."

Angelina had been sprawled on a towel in the backyard with a transistor radio at her hip, midway through a Madonna-fueled daydream. She raised her sunglasses to look at him. "What did you do?"

"Nothing!" He sat down beside her. "I've been talking to Jagvi a little."

She wanted to slap him. All that hard work, that endless well of patience and sympathy that she'd cultivated for him, gone swirling down the drain. She had dedicated herself to his recovery, and the whole time he'd been sneaking back to the source for another hit.

"Why would you do that?"

"She sent me a letter a few months ago. She's really sorry, Nini. I've called her a couple times, and I'm thinking about going to visit her. She's at the university in San Michele." San Michele was the capital of their province, a blotch of a city hugging the coast, about half a day's journey from Cadenze.

"Pat. No. That's a terrible idea."

He shrugged and looked away. "I wasn't asking your permission."

"You've only just gotten over her!"

"Why can't we stay friends?"

"What if it's awful? What if you see how happy she is without you?" Angelina sat up. "What if she has a *girlfriend*?"

"She might. She's been dating, I think." He sounded deliberately casual, and already Angelina could tell that he'd made up his mind to be okay with

Jagvi's new life. He'd smile politely as Jagvi made out with some girl or flirted with their waitress. But Patrick had no idea what it was like to see Jagvi kiss another girl. Angelina knew how intense it was, how obscene. Whatever he was imagining, the reality was a thousand times more extreme.

Most of Angelina was disappointed in Patrick and furious with Jagvi, both of them unable to leave well enough alone. But the hidden part of Angelina, the hungry part, had pricked its ears. It had been starved for so long, and its belly was rumbling. Jagvi was *dating*. The verb implied continuous activity: multiple nights, multiple options, the dreamy multitude of willing gay girls that a city might harbor.

Cities held their negative reputation in the family lore, but Angelina wasn't a frantic runaway like Caro had been. She could sneak out like a knight on a quest, chaperone Patrick, fend off Jagvi, and gather whatever trophies she came across on the way.

"What if I come with you?" she said. "Then if it's shitty, you won't be on your own."

"Great idea!" Patrick said. "Turn up with my baby sister holding my hand. Cool look."

"But you don't care what Jagvi thinks," Angelina reminded him. "You're over her."

"I still want this to go well."

"I'll be nice, Pat. I'll have your back. Don't I always?"

Patrick frowned. Finally he stood up, shrugged, and said, "I'll think about it." He raised a warning finger. "This isn't a yes."

Angelina watched him walk away. "It's not a no," she said, and put her sunglasses back on.

They had to take three separate trains to get to San Michele. On each new connection the upholstery got fancier and the inspectors got meaner. Patrick's bag was searched twice and their tickets were checked over and over, often by the same person.

Angelina hadn't realized how easy it was to spot them as Cadenze kids.

Her unstyled hair, her rough accent, the ripped hem of her denim miniskirt and the fraying sleeves of Patrick's flannel. It seemed like once they slipped out from Big Joe's shadow, everyone they encountered wanted to send them back. Tension crept into her shoulders well before they saw the high-rise buildings on the horizon.

Patrick drummed impatiently against the seat, and Angelina picked at a thread in her skirt and made her plans. Apparently Jagvi had offered to take them both to a student party, where Angelina hoped she'd find ample targets for her desires. She would keep an eye on Patrick, politely grit her teeth with Jagvi, and slip away as soon as she knew he could handle it. She wasn't in the habit of prayer, but she made a silent request as their train pulled into San Michele's airy central station: *Lord, please deliver unto me a babe to kiss and rut against. San Rocco, if your hand reaches this far, do a solid for your girl.*

The city disorientated Angelina immediately. The station was full of more people than she'd ever seen at one time, and all of them were strangers. But Patrick didn't seem lost: he craned his head over the crowd, and then he took off, bounding toward the one familiar face. Angelina had expected Patrick to be diffident or uneasy around Jagvi. Instead he shoved his way through the throngs of people and hauled Jagvi easily into the large frame of his body, already laughing and talking. It was Jagvi's knuckles, clenched in the back of Patrick's shirt, that went pale with strain.

Angelina followed more slowly. Jagvi's physical presence was a shock after a year of absence, a faded photograph come back to life. She leaned into Patrick, her face desperate and relieved, but Patrick held her close, and by the time they separated, Jagvi was grinning. Patrick never saw that she'd been worried at all.

"Took you long enough," she said.

"It's a long way."

"I remember," Jagvi said. "I thought you were bringing your sister?"

She looked around the station, unconcerned by the crowd, gaze lingering where she liked. Her eyes flicked up and down Angelina, lazy and assessing, before she turned away.

Then her head jerked back, embarrassment dawning on her face.

"Hi," Angelina said.

"What the fuck?" Jagvi said. "You got so tall." And then, stuttering a little, "Hey, Angel." They shook hands gingerly.

Over Jagvi's shoulder Patrick made a placating face that meant Angelina must be nice, and Angelina realized that she herself was the wild card here. The last time she'd seen Jagvi, she screamed at her to stay away. Angelina was so used to the two of them ignoring her that she wasn't sure what to do with all this nervous attention.

"You can relax," Angelina said. "I'm not gonna bite you."

"Don't let her freak you out," Patrick agreed. "I'm starving, is there gonna be food at this party?"

"We can stop for dinner on the way," Jagvi said, and led them out of the station and along the rain-slicked streets. The walk made them awkward again. Patrick and Jagvi used to hold hands, or he'd sling a comfortable arm around her, and now their elbows bumped and they had to lean in to hear what the other said over the roar of the boulevard. Pat didn't move fast enough for the city traffic, and cars honked at their little group as they dawdled over the street. Jagvi kept throwing accusatory glances back at Angelina, like their discomfort would have been okay if Angelina hadn't been there to witness it.

Angelina slouched along behind them. She was in no mood for indulgence: people kept knocking into her or splashing her with their umbrellas. The plan of reaching out into that faceless crowd and snagging a girl seemed ludicrous. Her mood turned jagged, catching on the corners of every ugly street.

In the diner Jagvi wound her way to their corner booth, holding a tray of beers and greasy burgers with fries. Angelina dunked three fries in her beer before she shoved them in her mouth, a Cadenze custom. Jagvi watched Angelina lick the foam off her fingers, lips parted with disgust.

"You look different," Patrick told Jagvi.

"Not really," Jagvi said, voice guilty. She was wearing a black T-shirt and jeans, her hair in its usual braid, but Angelina knew what Patrick meant. There was something open about the set of her shoulders, and Angelina had watched her chatting to the waitress; friendlier here, without the hunted, guarded look she'd always worn in Cadenze. She had her first ambulance ride along next week, she told them.

"You're still set on staying in Cadenze?" she asked Patrick. Angelina rankled at the question and the disappointment it implied, but Patrick nodded as if they'd already discussed it.

"For now," he said. "I got that mechanic apprenticeship, at the garage on the other side of Big Joe."

Jagvi reacted with over-the-top delight, clashing her glass against his in a clumsy toast. Angelina almost felt sorry for her. It must be hard to know how to act around Patrick, to feel the fragility of his forgiveness. If Jagvi still wanted Patrick to leave Cadenze, she couldn't risk voicing it. The version of Patrick who might have left was a version who'd been in love with her, and that was impossible now.

"How did graduation go?" Jagvi asked.

"It was fun," Patrick said. "Nini made Ma cry."

Jagvi blinked at her. "You did?"

"Not on purpose," Angelina said.

But Patrick was already telling the story. When Patrick announced his apprenticeship to the family, Caro took the news badly. "Of course I'm happy for you," Caro had said. "I just can't help thinking about everything you've lost."

"He's done very well," Nonna had said. It had been her idea to hold a graduation party for Patrick, and before the other guests arrived, she had taken Angelina aside for a private toast in the kitchen. "To a job well done," she'd said. When Angelina protested that all she'd done was bring balloons, Nonna shook her head. Now she turned to Caro, who had spent the party draining a bottle of white wine and muttering about how she'd been much too busy with a lice outbreak at the school to help with party planning. "You should be proud of your children."

"Obviously I'm proud of him," Caro snapped. "But he was going to travel, or be a great musician—if Jagvi hadn't ruined everything—"

"Ma," Patrick tried, but Caro shook her head.

"Don't pretend you aren't still hurting. I can see it in your face."

"If his face is upsetting you, you don't have to look at him," Angelina quipped. She'd meant it as a joke, but in the stunned silence that followed, she realized how Caro would interpret her. She watched Caro's face fall, those deep breaths that meant she was mounting to a sob.

The story made Jagvi crack up. Angelina wasn't used to seeing her laugh like that.

"Good for you," Jagvi said. "And your nonna. I guess you're the only two who can stand up to her."

"What does that mean?"

Jagvi shrugged. "The whole Sicco women thing."

"I'm pretty sure talking back to a Sicco woman counts as heresy," Patrick agreed.

Angelina rolled her eyes. "Wouldn't that be convenient."

"C'mon, Nini, you know it's true. Ma's always going on about it."

"Of course she is," Angelina said. "She's insecure about how the family feels about her, it's all she's got. The Sicco girl is a fun little myth. Toss the ladies a bone. Meanwhile Franco still runs everything."

"Only since Nonna got tired," Patrick argued. "I thought you liked Franco, anyway."

"I do," Angelina said. She wished they weren't having this conversation in front of Jagvi. "All I'm saying is that being a Sicco girl is just a story. You have to know how to use it."

"Is that right," Jagvi said.

"No," Patrick answered. "It might be a story if you're the star. From the outside, it feels pretty real."

Angelina set her jaw. Usually she liked to take Patrick's side in family disputes, but this time it was Angelina who was outnumbered. "Maybe it's just the first time you've ever felt left out," she told him. "Everything else in Cadenze is open to you, even if it's not to me."

"Oh, don't play the girl card," Patrick said, and Angelina saw Jagvi make a face. It made her feel worse. She didn't want to argue about sexism with Patrick, and she didn't want to talk about what it was like to be visibly foreign among the Siccos, and she definitely didn't want to do either of those things in Jagvi's earshot. She didn't need an ally. Maybe what she needed was to go home. Her pulse spiked at the thought, the gut-rising nausea of wanting to turn and run.

Jagvi looked between them and spoke in a conciliatory tone that didn't suit her. "Small-town politics are a minefield."

"Exactly," Patrick said, as Angelina said, "Oh, shut up."

"It's not an insult, Angel," Jagvi said. "You'll see when you leave."

"But I'm not ever gonna leave," Angelina said, and felt a little better for having made her position clear, and for the way Jagvi looked troubled, like she had only just discovered that maybe the whole world wouldn't come running to her like Patrick did.

The party was on the highest floor of a grimy apartment building. Inside were tall windows pushed fully open, scarves draped over the light fixtures, and girls. Girls spilled out through the warren of rooms, girls stood around smoking, girls with knowing smiles and buzz cuts and tattoos. There were hardly any men, and everyone seemed to know Jagvi so well. She introduced Patrick and Angelina to a wave of people with sophisticated names that Angelina immediately forgot. One of them, with a severe blond bob, grinned at Angelina and said, "Hi! How old are you?"

"Seventeen," Jagvi said, and stepped in front of Angelina.

Two girls were wrapped around each other in a corner. Angelina looked away, and then worried that looking away was homophobic, and then worried that staring was too obvious. She panicked: Could everyone tell? But when she turned back to Jagvi, Jagvi was watching her with a condescending expression, and the blond girl hooted with laughter.

"Look at the baby! She doesn't know what to do with herself!"

"Leave her alone," Patrick and Jagvi said at the same time, worse than no defense at all.

A few people looked at Patrick curiously, their eyes flicking between Patrick and Jagvi like they couldn't understand the connection. Jagvi introduced him as "a friend from home." Patrick shook hands gamely with every offered palm. There had been a flash of confusion on his face when Jagvi called him friend, as if he'd forgotten for a moment that they weren't together anymore. He recovered fast, and pretty soon he found the one other man at the party, a somber goth who liked the band on his T-shirt. Angelina wondered if Patrick would be daunted by his black nail polish and eyeliner; this arch boy was nothing like Mutt or Dingus, Patrick's metalhead friends. But Patrick seemed more fascinated than repelled.

Angelina took her beer through a series of rooms, trying to float as easily as she did at parties in Myrna. But she had never been an outsider like this. The accents were sharp and polished. The outfits were stylish, nearly everyone in black like Jagvi, and Angelina's treasured cable-knit sweater felt juvenile. Groups of chattering women paused to look at her. Angelina didn't know what they could see.

What had they thought of Jagvi when she showed up here? Could they tell she was gay right away, or had she made it clear to them somehow—should Angelina make it clear? But what would they do if they knew? Or worse, what if they didn't believe her? What if they told her kindly that she'd been mistaken, that jerking off doesn't count, that she wasn't from here and couldn't be anything like they were? And what were they like? Angelina had hoped she might find girls like her, but none of these women felt familiar.

She was draining her third beer when the blond girl found her. She'd brought a friend, with hair dyed violent pink. The blond said, "Hey, it's the baby!"

Pink Hair waved at her. "Hi, baby! You need a drink?"

Angelina accepted the new beer mutely.

"We didn't frighten you, did we?" Blond said.

"No," Angelina said. "I know Jagvi, don't I?"

They both laughed. "You're right, baby." Blond gestured to Pink. "You hear that? She knows Jagvi. We're small fry."

"We're honestly so excited to meet you," Pink confided, her pointy face alight with interest. "You can tell us all about baby Jagvi! Do you know Jagvi's mama too? We all call her Auntie, she's so nice to us."

Angelina tried to reconcile this with the sour-faced, unhappy woman she had known.

"Tell us about Cadenze," Blond demanded, pronouncing it wrong. "Jagvi makes it sound like hell on earth."

"She actually almost never talks about it," Pink countered. "It's like this *trauma* that she's carrying around with her. Her whole *body* changes when it comes up." This last with a significant tone: someone who knew Jagvi's body. Angelina's face crawled with heat.

"You can tell us," Blond said. They both leaned in, poised for Angelina to tearfully admit that she and Patrick slept in a barn with three cows for warmth. Angelina was full of contempt for everyone and everything, especially herself.

"It's my home," Angelina said. "We have three mountains and I live on the biggest one—Jagvi did, too. In the winter it snows and every spring when the snow melts it sends last season's dust through the town. There's a fountain in the center of town in the shape of an open hand and you can sit in the palm and get drunk and feel like something's holding you over the water."

Neither Blond nor Pink looked very impressed. "So you're thinking about studying here?"

Angelina shook her head. "I'll probably just get a job back home."

Her interrogators exchanged looks. "Is there an art scene? Good music?"

"No."

"Is it beautiful? The mountains?"

"No. It's ugly."

"But you like it?"

"I love it," Angelina said.

"*Why?*" Blond pushed. "What's so good about it?"

She sounded genuinely frustrated. For the first time all evening, Angelina felt good. "Nothing," she said, and took another swig. "It's not for you."

"Fuck," Pink said. She laughed, but her face was hard, unhappy. "They make the bigots young there, huh?"

"I'm glad Jag got away," Blond said, and caught her friend's elbow. "Come on."

Angelina reminded herself that these people did not matter and she would never see them again. Her eyes prickled, hot in her skull. She knew that she should find Patrick, but she couldn't stomach it.

She found a quieter room instead, with a big couch only occupied at one end by three girls who ignored her. A mirror ball spun woozily from the ceiling, and the light coming in through the open window had a lilac hue, a TV playing in the apartment across the damp alleyway. The booze and travel were catching up to her. She felt sick and tired, and she leaned with her forehead against her palm, wilting in the dimness.

"Angel?"

Angelina looked up. Jagvi frowned and turned to the girl she was with, intimidatingly glamorous with dark lipstick and a diving cleavage. Jagvi touched her elbow. "I'll find you later."

"You don't have to sit with me," Angelina said, when Jagvi did.

"I know," Jagvi said, and tilted her head to the side, more curious than anything else. "Seems like you don't really need babysitting anymore."

"Did you expect us both to be exactly the same?"

"I wasn't even sure you'd show up," Jagvi said, toying with the label on her beer bottle, voice fluid; she was a little drunk, too, Angelina realized. "It's actually really nice that you're both here. Sometimes I feel like I've landed from another planet, or that I made home—made Cadenze up."

"Ha, yeah, it's all too real," Angelina said, and maybe it was because the other girls had been so cruel about it or because she felt so homesick, but she kept talking. "This year they tried to start a monthly town meeting, did you hear? It fell apart because people kept starting fights and they were worried there was gonna be a big new feud. Oh, and Alfred Marchesi told everyone that working as a security guard at the hypermarket is enough experience to become our first official sheriff."

Jagvi groaned. "I hated that guy so much. He used to follow me and Ma around when we went grocery shopping. Once he actually told me that he was keeping an eye on me."

Angelina nodded. "He does the same thing to me. Jethro and I worked out that I could lead him down the hair-care aisle while Jethro was stuffing steaks down his pants."

Jagvi yelped with laughter. "I never thought of that."

"Gotta stay alert," Angelina said, tapping her temple.

"It was interesting what you said, about being the Sicco girl," Jagvi said. "Don't look at me like that, I'm not attacking you. I never thought about it being so much pressure."

"Pressure?"

"Doesn't it feel like pressure?" Jagvi shrugged, uncomfortable. "My parents always made it clear I had to get good grades, get a good job, get out of Cadenze. I'm glad I did, but I remember feeling sick for years, like if I didn't, I'd be letting everyone down."

Angelina hesitated, then turned, both of them sitting sideways on the couch and leaning toward each other. "That sucks. I think my family's just annoying. If I ever impress them, they'll be like, *Well, of course, she's the Sicco girl*. No matter what, I'm part of the story."

Jagvi had never paid this much attention to her, amused and wondering at the same time. She batted a moth away from Angelina's shoulder. "So you're gonna break the mold?"

"I'm gonna run my town," Angelina said.

"What!" Jagvi started laughing again, but there was a note there that kept Angelina from rising to the fight, like Jagvi was impressed despite herself. "Don't you want to set your sights a little higher?"

Angelina scoffed. "They *are* high."

"I'm just saying, you could do cool things here. Or in other cities—"

"You don't get it," Angelina said. "You've never understood it."

"You don't know what it was like for me," Jagvi said quietly. "I know you have a hard time, Angel. Pat can't see it, but I can. I know what it's like to be an outsider in that town. If you want to fight to make them accept you, more power to you, but you're starting way ahead of me. You have your whole family behind you, and your skin's light enough they can pretend you're almost the same as them. I was the little brown freak, and even dating *Patrick Sicco* didn't make me fit in. And now…no one in Cadenze knows what to do with a dyke."

She shook her head, spreading her hands. Her fingers were blunt, fingernails clipped, a capable crook to her knuckles. Angelina had the sudden, wild thought that she'd come to the city looking for girls like her and here she was on a couch with one, and recoiled on instinct.

Jagvi's mouth twisted down. "Sorry to bring it up." Unhappiness glittered in her dark eyes.

"I didn't—"

"It's fine." Jagvi sank back on the couch, not facing Angelina anymore, and took a pull from her beer. "It's just where you're from."

"You're so fucking condescending," Angelina said. "You and all these bitches here. You think you know everything. You think you invented gay people."

"Angel…"

"For the record," Angelina bit out, "at least I actually know I'm gay. When you were my age, you still wanted to marry my *brother*."

Jagvi swung around. She stared at Angelina, her face gone hazy and confused—or maybe that was Angelina, flushed from the alcohol and the confession and this series of small rooms that had given her nothing that she wanted. She stumbled to her feet, ready to find her brother and demand they go home, except she couldn't leave on that declaration, because this city had proven to her that she was a coward, and she hated it, and she never wanted to return.

She paused, trembling, and then she said, "Don't tell Patrick."

"No, Angel," Jagvi said. Still staring, lips still parted in shock. "I won't."

XIII

In Cadenze, Angelina woke up on the living room floor with Patrick's hand still in her hair from the night before. Her mouth felt fuzzy from drink, a faint taste of cherries. Why had she slept here?

In case the monster followed her home. The night came back to her in a rush: the thing from the pit skulking in the cellar at Old Timers, the way it flipped through her memories like a photo album, its mocking voice, the scene it had replayed over and over. Running home, *Be Good*, and Jagvi.

Patrick's hand combed through her hair until his fingers stalled on a knot and he paused to untangle it. It made Angelina's scalp prickle—she wriggled, but Patrick wouldn't release her. "Cut it out," she said. "Are you as hungover as I am?"

I Doubt It.

She whipped around. An empty couch, just an indentation where Patrick had been. She ran to Patrick's bedroom, throwing herself through the doorway to find his bed empty and no sign of him anywhere, just his overflowing ashtray and his neat shelves of vinyl, the record player taking up too much space in the corner. Her scalp crawled where the thing had touched her.

"Where is he?" Angelina demanded.

Who Cares?

She sprinted outside. The front yard was empty except for My Dog, who cantered over with her big dopey eyes full of hope for a walk. Patrick's truck was gone, and down in the valley the bells rang to remind everyone it was Sunday.

Angelina's breath flooded out of her in sweet relief. Right. Sunday morning Patrick always went to Caro's place to make repairs and either drown in praise or hear a litany of complaints, depending on how their mother was feeling.

She Keeps Him Well Trained.

"Don't talk about Patrick," Angelina said, and all of her hair leapt straight up into the air, like she'd flattened her hands against the static electricity conductor at Myrna's pathetic attempt of a science museum. It made her laugh despite herself, smoothing her hands over her curls until they dropped. "Quit it."

I'm Getting Stronger, the thing crooned. Can You Feel It?

"Yeah," Angelina admitted. The hand in her hair had felt as solid as Patrick's; even its voice seemed louder. Angelina had never thought of her skull as a penetrable barrier, but the thing's words nestled inside her head, and there was nothing she could do to stop them.

The knowledge that Patrick was safe at Caro's calmed her spike of panic. It had not come back to kill her in the night. This morning made it three times that the thing from the pit had found Angelina and not hurt her. Angelina couldn't help herself: she was starting to warm up to it. Its attention felt like Cadenze itself, a dangerous affection that Angelina loved to try to win. Talking to it reminded Angelina of joking with her cousins about being gay, aware that she was leaning into stereotypes she shouldn't encourage but too cocky and pleased with herself for making them laugh to stop. She had that old pleasure of performing, the feeling that if she was trapped in the thing's grip, well, it was eating out of the palm of her hand.

Told You We'd Be Friends.

"I could do without you," Angelina said. "What do you want?"

I Like Spending Time With You.

"I'm flattered," Angelina said. "All right, well. I gotta take My Dog for a walk. Should I take you for a walk, too, nameless demonic entity?"

There was a warm thud behind her, like an approving hand clapping her square in the middle of her back. Angelina and her dog and her monster set up the mountain.

"Why do you talk like that?" Angelina asked.

Like What?

"Like What," Angelina intoned. My Dog ran ahead, oblivious to the eldritch presence that trotted behind Angelina. Before Angelina was Cadenze's endless blue sky, ready to fold itself around some new horror. "It's not how I thought the thing from the pit would talk. But I guess I didn't imagine it talking at all. Just, you know." She raised her hands into rabid, hungry claws. "Nom nom nom!"

Silence behind her.

"Aw, did I offend you?" Angelina had a vague thought that she should not be enjoying herself so much, but the day was bright and warm, an easy early Sunday of climbing up Big Joe with her dog and feeling as though everything in Cadenze belonged to her, even the monsters. "Was it 'cause I've stopped taking you seriously? Was it 'cause I called you a thing?" She considered. "Actually, are you even the thing from the pit? I just assumed. It felt like you followed me home. Are you the one from the stories?"

From Some Stories.

"Are you a saint? Or a saint's dog?" Angelina laughed. "Pat was mad enough when I brought home an ordinary mutt."

You Have No Idea What I Am.

"But you *are* the thing from the pit?" Angelina pressed, and felt something give behind her, a rush of condescension that did nothing to disguise the fact that Angelina had won, that Angelina could nag even a supernatural being into giving her answers.

Yes, it said.

"So my family's right," Angelina mused. "It is our pit."

You're So Proud Of That Family.

"Yeah," Angelina said. "But I don't understand what you want. Do you want to eat me?"

Would That Be A Good Meal? the thing asked, and it sounded curious. Like it was genuinely inquiring. Angelina shuddered.

"I don't know. If you're going to eat me, why not eat me already? The only thing I can think is that you're, like... fattening me up. My life, or soul, or whatever it is you eat."

You Are Scrawny, the thing agreed. Not Much Of A Meal.

"Well, take your time," Angelina said. "I've decided what to do with you."

I Am The One Who Does Things To You, Baby.

"For now," Angelina agreed. They paused to watch My Dog, rustling birds out of the undergrowth and snapping her jaws as they flew away like she was admonishing them. *Aw, c'mon, stay a while! I just wanna get to know ya!* "But I'm gonna run the risk of being crazy. I'm going to tell someone about you."

Another wave of curiosity lapped over her. Who?

"I've got options," Angelina said airily, strolling up the mountain with her hands clasped behind the small of her back. She wore the thing from the pit draped over her shoulder like the latest hot accessory, stylishly paired with her bike shorts and the big Fila T-shirt she'd stolen from Patrick. "You're right, I am proud of my family. But I could tell Gemma you're real, she'd do a séance and chase you off. Francesca-Martine's husband is drinking buddies with the mayor. I'm telling you, your time is up."

You Could Tell Jagvi.

Angelina laughed, startled. "What?"

You Like To Tell Her Things.

"Fuck off," Angelina said reflexively, and then: "No."

I Think She Would Be A Good Choice.

"Oh, well, I'll definitely prioritize your opinion. No, I'm not gonna tell Jagvi. I'm not even gonna tell my uncle Sam, though he'd fucking love it, I'm pretty sure a demon is the only thing he hasn't shot at."

Angelina shielded her eyes against the glare and squinted: there was a waver in the air, and for a moment Angelina thought it was some veil opening, a doorway. Then she caught the thin smell of smoke and realized it was a heat shimmer, a fire lit by the other inhabitant of Angelina's lonely mountain. She shook her head.

"I'm not gonna tell Jagvi," she repeated. "I'm gonna tell my brother."

The thing shoved her in the back. A solid, heavy force that sent her stumbling forward, almost tripping. She yelped, catching herself, and swung around to see nothing.

"What the fuck!"

Another shove caught her shoulder, and this time she fell hard, landing on her knee, blood beading up, vibrant red against brown. Angelina panted, heart pounding, and waited for the thing to descend. It didn't. The quiet was almost worse than the violence, the feeling that she'd misjudged, that she'd lost sight of the stakes up here, alone.

But she wasn't alone. Angelina wiped her forearm over her eyes and squinted toward the heat shimmer. She could just see a small, slight figure moving beyond it, and she hauled herself up to her feet and set off at a fast clip toward Jagvi's father's house.

The thing sped up behind her, little pinches at the backs of her legs with My Dog yelping joyfully at her side. Down the twisting path, close enough now to see the surprise on her face, Jagvi looked up and caught sight of Angelina hurtling toward her, and came running, so that Angelina bounced into her and Jagvi caught her shoulders.

"What?" Jagvi demanded. "What!"

The thing behind Angelina paused. Angelina croaked, "Can you, can you see something? Behind me, is there—"

"No?" Jagvi tilted her head, her hands sliding down Angelina's arms to steady her, fingertips pressing into Angelina's bare elbow. She was looking right where it should be with no comprehension on her face. Definitely not the right person to tell; Jagvi with her medical training and her city allegiance, shrugging off Cadenze's small-town shame and superstitions. And especially not now that the thing had essentially dared her to tell Jagvi. Angelina wasn't stupid enough to run where it led.

All the same, as if the thing behind her was embarrassed, its presence retreated. There was no pressure on her back, no voice in her head. That anxious prickle of observation on the nape of her neck faded away. And now Angelina was embarrassed, too, even as Jagvi said, "Did someone hurt you? Are you okay?"

She scanned Angelina up and down. Angelina stood under Jagvi's restless hands and waited for the thing's mocking voice to ring through her head, for its invisible limbs to shove at her or drag her away, for it to sew her mouth shut and bring her to her knees. There was nothing.

Scaredy cat, Angelina thought scornfully, hoping it could hear. *That's still three times. You're all talk.*

"Angel," Jagvi said, frowning up at Angelina, worry making her eyes bright.

Angelina shook her head. Jagvi's fingers tightened around her arm, her sharp, attentive face trained on Angelina. Terror felt close, so close Angelina could reach out and stroke it. Instead she gave Jagvi her best liar's smile.

"Hiya," she said. "I thought I'd come see how bored you were."

XIV

"You scared the hell out of me," Jagvi said, entirely unscared, as she came out of the house with a red bag and a glass of water. She handed the second to Angelina and went through the first for sterile wipes and bandages, turning her attention to the scrape down Angelina's leg even as Angelina made a half-hearted attempt at protesting. "Why'd you come running up here like that? Some farmer freak you out?"

"Something like that," Angelina said. "It's nothing."

Jagvi looked unconvinced, even when Angelina offered her most confident smile. But Angelina felt sure. She kept thinking about the moment Jagvi had caught her, and the way the thing had stuttered in its chase. It was interesting, playing it over in her head. Last night there'd been no sign of it on the porch when Jagvi was there, and here, too, the only inhuman presence was her panting dog. Crowds didn't bother the thing from the pit—at Old Timers it had gone unnoticed—but like many of Cadenze's native sons, it seemed to shy away from Jagvi. Angelina allowed herself to feel comforted, sitting under the shambolic eaves of the house Jagvi had grown up in, with Jagvi tweezing gravel out of her knee.

It was not a comforting house. Smaller even than Patrick and Angelina's own tiny property, the house sat squat in the middle of the dirt-streaked lawn, patchy and yellow at this time of year. Grime streaked the walls, and paint peeled in thick strips down to the ground. Beetles and earwigs scuttled in dank corners. Filth smeared the windows so thickly that Angelina couldn't see through to the curtains drawn shut behind them.

The patch of airborne heat belonged to Jagvi; she'd been tossing paperwork in a small fire burning out front, huge boxes beside it stacked high with years of junk mail and bills. Now she frowned over Angelina's injuries, a smudged streak of ash on her cheek and tawny hair striped down her legs. Angelina's brain tripped over Jagvi's black sports bra, the easy dip of her tits underneath, and hurried onto the pale yellow shorts she wore.

The shorts made Angelina pause. They weren't Jagvi's standard style, and featured a small, familiar logo.

"Jagvi," Angelina said, "are you wearing…"

Jagvi glanced up from Angelina's knee. "Uh, yeah."

Angelina cracked up laughing, partially relieved to find she still could. Every moment in Jagvi's presence eased away the feeling of the thing, the sense of being hounded.

"The Caracals? Really? They haven't ever even won a tournament!"

Jagvi looked offended. "That's not why you support a team."

"Oh yeah?" Angelina reached out and touched the angry cat logo, with its spiky black-tipped ears. Cadenze's basketball team was one of only two local teams that had ever qualified for the minor leagues; the football team was below average, but the Caracals were famously terrible. The working theory went that they were only allowed to compete to create a reliable bottom rung of the ladder. "Since when are you into basketball?"

"I used to go to games a lot when I was a teenager."

"With Pat?" Angelina demanded, because she had no memory of this.

"No, he hates basketball." Angelina flinched as the scrape flared with pain and Jagvi smoothed her hand down Angelina's shin. "You're doing well," she murmured. "I got you." That practiced bedside manner, Angelina thought, and hoped Jagvi hadn't noticed the goose bumps prickling on her skin. Jagvi continued, "I went on my own, mostly. And now I see the Caracals when they come to San Michele. What?"

"Nothing," Angelina said, wrenching her gaze away.

"All right, then." Jagvi's expression was closed and amused, the same secretive streak as ever. Maybe she'd share the joke if Angelina asked, but Angelina wasn't going to ask. "You going to tell me what happened just now?"

"It's fine, I overreacted. You can flip the paramedic switch off."

"That's not really how it works," Jagvi said. "Not even after you quit, apparently." She tapped Angelina's leg, and Angelina straightened it, letting Jagvi wrap the bandage around the scrape. Tight enough to feel like a hand gripping her.

"You're gonna quit?"

"Everyone quits eventually. You quit or you teach or you die young. That's the basic career trajectory."

"So what are you going to do?"

Jagvi shrugged. "I'm going back to school when I can afford it. Maybe next year, or the year after. I'll get my MD."

Angelina scoffed. "That famously unexhausting career choice?"

"At least you get to sit down now and then."

"If you're burnt out, why don't you just stop? Give up on it already."

Jagvi smiled at her. "I don't do that."

"You gave up on Cadenze," Angelina said.

"I guess, kind of." She touched the logo on her shorts, then dusted her hands off, taking a seat next to Angelina. She left a careful gap of space between them. "I've never been able to stop anything once I started. Even if it was hopeless. Even if it wasn't any good for me."

That hook of a smile in the corner of her mouth. Angelina swallowed and managed, "Your breakups must be hell."

Jagvi laughed, short and wry. "You already knew that."

Sitting side by side on the steps, Angelina could feel the heat coming off Jagvi's body. "That's not what I was talking about."

"No? What did you want to talk about, when you came running up here?" Jagvi's voice was still light, unassuming, but Angelina was growing hotter. "You always seem to have a list of questions. You had plenty of questions last night."

"Jag," Angelina said, and then corrected herself. "Jagvi."

"Yes, Angel."

Angelina was on the verge of something dangerous, and she didn't know what it was. Jagvi could always find new ways to throw her off balance. She could try telling the truth about what was happening. It seemed ludicrous that Jagvi would believe her, but Angelina could almost imagine what it would be like to have Jagvi on her side. She would love to expose the monster to Jagvi's sure, determined gaze. She would even let Jagvi be condescending about it. *Of course there's a way to stop it, Angel. Just do as I say.* But conversations with Jagvi never went the way Angelina expected.

"You talk to me so much easier when you're drunk." Jagvi leaned back on her elbows, tipping her chin up to the sky. "I don't know whether I should be hurt or pleased."

But she sounded pleased. Angelina shot her a dark look. "It's because I know better than to talk to you when I'm sober."

"Is that what it is?"

Angelina couldn't look Jagvi in the eyes. She stared at her scuffed sneakers in the dirt, instead, and Jagvi's knee with the white scar that twisted up on one side from when she and Pat had tried to jump a fence at the Myrna music festival. Then her gaze wandered along the silky line of Jagvi's shorts and into Jagvi's lap. Angelina blinked. The shorts were baggy and fell loose, but they had ridden up, and now Angelina could see, subtle but unmistakable, a line at the V of Jagvi's hips. Not a line: A curve. A bulge.

"Uh," she said. "Hey, are you wearing something in your shorts?"

Jagvi hooted with laughter. "Okay, I guess sober you're still pretty easy."

"Shit," Angelina said, and covered her face. "Sorry. Shit. I was just—surprised. I just noticed it, I wasn't looking on purpose." A thought occurred to her, somehow both thrilling and awful, and she blurted out, "Do you have a girl here?"

Jagvi laughed even more. Back on one elbow, unembarrassed, looking up at Angelina with genuine delight, like she'd stumbled upon some strange and fascinating species. "Hidden in my dad's shitty house while Angelina Sicco comes running up my drive? No, I don't have a girl here."

"Then why would you—what are you—"

"It's a packer," Jagvi said. "It's not for sex. Not really. I can't fuck with it, anyway. I didn't think you'd notice it."

Angelina frowned, too curious to bother being polite. "Is it...why wear it, then?"

"It feels good," Jagvi said, her voice almost sleepy, a deep and lazy burr catching in the back of her throat. "I felt good this morning and I wanted to keep feeling good."

"Right," Angelina said, and looked again. Grain of yellow silk, rise like a gentle hill. She wondered what the packer looked like underneath, whether it was skin colored or like a dildo with their bright, ludicrous hues. The dip of her eyes hadn't been subtle, but when she turned back to Jagvi's face, Jagvi was attentive and smiling, like she had enjoyed watching Angelina look. Like she had enjoyed Angelina's questions, like she wasn't offended or guarded about this, at least not with Angelina.

"Hey, Jag," she said, "can I see it?"

"Nope," Jagvi said.

It wasn't a rebuke but an opening, a first move that Angelina knew she should not meet. "Can I touch it?"

"Why would I let you do that?"

"Because I've had a hard morning?" Angelina offered. "Because you want to calm me down with your paramedic expertise?"

"I didn't realize you had such an instinct for health care," Jagvi said, grinning.

Angelina couldn't believe that it was daylight. She'd spent her whole Sunday morning flirting with danger, and now the sharp, visceral fear of the thing from the pit gave way to a different type of risk. Better the devil she knew. Her breathing had picked up, but Jagvi was polite enough not to mention it.

"C'mon, you said yourself it wasn't a sex thing." Just intellectual research: the great depths of dykery that she had yet to explore. Angelina drew in a breath. "Please?"

"Okay," Jagvi said.

It was softer than she'd expected, elasticity under the silk like it was real flesh, tissue giving under her fingers, and Angelina's palm went tentative as a result. She'd thought at first she'd just poke it, but she cupped Jagvi instinctively, rubbing her hand along the soft line. Her palm formed a gentle hollow, and it fit so well. She could feel the line and thread of the shorts' seam, and slid her hand along the packer in one sure movement, thumb gliding over where she thought the head might be. She wanted to know what Jagvi's face was doing, but she couldn't look away from the inviting sprawl of Jagvi's lap and Angelina's own hand, Angelina's own daring.

"I'm not gonna, uh," Angelina said as her fingers curled around the packer, trying to map out its edges, wondering if she could lift it, jerk it off, maybe. She'd never interacted with a dick before. One of the women she'd slept with had a strap, but she was drunk and struggled getting into the harness, and when Angelina laughed, she stormed out of the room. "I don't wanna—do anything, this is just, uh, a fact-finding mission."

"Sure," Jagvi said. "Investigate away."

"Don't be weird, Jag," Angelina said, and she did look up, watching Jagvi's gaze trail down to her mouth, her tits, back up again. "Don't act like this is a big deal, just be normal about it, okay? Don't make it a weird thing. Can you feel it?" She squeezed.

"Yeah," Jagvi said, and her hand dropped to Angelina's wrist, gripping it in the circle of her fingers. For a split second Angelina had thought Jagvi would close her hand over Angelina's, grind Angelina's hand down harder against Jagvi's dick, turn the touch from a curiosity into something real. Angelina squeezed again, and Jagvi squeezed her back.

"Fuck," Angelina mumbled.

"Don't be weird, Angel," Jagvi said, singsong, making fun of her. "Don't quit. There's nothing else good to do in this shithole."

Angelina scowled on instinct. "There's plenty. Why don't you come hang out at Old Timers?"

"Not this time."

"Oh, you'd rather lure unsuspecting locals up here instead?"

"You're the one who came running to find me."

"Ah," Angelina said. Fingers curled around Jagvi's dick, eyes fixed on Jagvi's face. This was going too far, she knew, beyond sparring, almost beyond flirtation. The morning's leftover adrenaline made her heart flutter, skin oversensitive in the breeze. She wanted to say something bold enough to snap the tension. The first time her voice came out in a low rasp. She cleared her throat and tried again. "I can't believe you're so bored here you're even considering fucking me."

"Angel," Jagvi said, and her voice was still light and playful, but she wasn't smiling anymore. "I've wanted to fuck you for years."

A thin line of heat radiated down Angelina's spine. In another second she would lean over to Jagvi's mouth, so instead she melted, shoulders crumbling, stooping to press her forehead against Jagvi's knee and breathe. After a moment she felt Jagvi's hand on the back of her neck, fingers pushing through her hair to press against the top of Angelina's spine. All of Angelina's breath came out of her in a rush.

"I gotta go," she mumbled against Jagvi's thigh.

"Yeah," Jagvi said, and this time she did sound serious.

Angelina stumbled to her feet. She forced herself not to look back as she returned the way she'd come, whistling for My Dog and keeping her face resolutely toward the road. She was still breathing hard, dizzy and overwhelmed. She could not fuck Jagvi. She absolutely could not fuck Jagvi. It would be the very worst thing she ever did to Patrick. She could not fuck his ex-girlfriend and the former love of his life, even if the love of his life had just made it clear for the first time that was an option. She stepped blindly out onto the road and toward home.

That's Enough, the thing said. Its voice stung in her head, lanced with fury. My Turn.

It seized her by the back of her neck, and Angelina was gone, she was out of her head, she was done.

XV

Okay, So There's Two Kittens. Stop Squirming.

The thing carried her body up the mountain. Every time Angelina tried to reach into her fingers, her limbs, jerk a knee or twist her head, it cut off the impulse before her muscles could respond. Her mouth closed tight over the scream she wanted to let loose, her face turned smiling up to the blue sky. My Dog trotted beside her, panting and happy. Two nights ago, the thing from the pit had barely been able to drag Angelina along the bathroom floor, and now it slipped itself inside her and moved her as it liked.

You Want To Hear The Story Or Not?

Angelina wanted to throw her body to the ground, wanted her brother, wanted to be hit by a car, wanted to run back down Jagvi's drive.

Can't Do Any Of That. So There's Two Kittens! Or Dolls, Or Dogs, Whatever You Like. You're A Dog Person, Huh?

The thing reached Angelina's hand toward My Dog, and Angelina felt her throat vibrate as though she were moaning, though no noise made it out to the open air. *Please don't hurt my dog.*

Let's Stick With Kittens. Two Little Kittens, And One Of Them Is Yours. She's Got A Pointy Snout And Big Green Eyes And She's Black All Over With Two Tiny Bald Spots On Either Side Of Her Forehead. And The Other Kitten Looks Exactly Like Your Kitten. You Can Only Tell Them Apart When You Play With Them, Because The Other Kitten Plays Too Rough.

The thing veered Angelina off the tarmac road and onto scrappy green. Up here was no one's property. Her legs walked confidently over the scrubby ground. The thing had been here before. It knew its surroundings.

The One Other Way You Can Tell The Kittens Apart, the thing continued, Is The Not-Yours Kitten Has Such An Appetite. If You Take Too Slow A Bite Of Toast, It's Hanging Off The Other Corner. If You Leave Out A Pot Of Jam, It Drowns Itself In Strawberries And Sugar. It Eats Anything. You've Seen It Eating Flies.

The thing forced Angelina's gaze down to My Dog. Pocketed gray stone against the dying green grass at the end of summer and Angelina's dog sniffing out rabbit holes. Angelina thought about pushing My Dog to the ground and kneeling on her soft throat. She thought about catching My Dog's silky ears between her fingers and stroking her furry cheeks and catching her adorable furry little face between her hands and snapping it hard to the side. She thought about using her teeth to tear through the pinkish skin of My Dog's belly, fumbling through My Dog's insides to find the reddest, juiciest parts to eat, sinking into the coil of intestines face-first and gorging herself on guts and only wanting more, more, more. The more she thought about these things, the more the part of Angelina that wanted to protect her dumb dog faded, like she was a stranger slipping out of view over the horizon, even as she tried to call them back, grabbing their shirtsleeves. But that stranger had no authority here.

Not Hungry? the thing behind Angelina said. Okay. Your Kitten Feels Bad For This New Hungry Kitten And She Tries To Help. She Points Out Mouseholes. She Even Takes The Other Kitten Down To The River And Then They Sit There With Their Identical Fishing Rods.

A blow to Angelina's head slammed her to the ground. The pain was strong enough that she could feel it even in the corner of her mind the thing had shoved her into. She reeled and gagged on the ground. The thing made her swallow her vomit, a clump of something hard in her esophagus, which spasmed wildly, before it sank back into her stomach and left her throat stripped raw and stinging.

It Doesn't Have To Be This Bad, it told her. Remember That Next Time, Okay? I Don't *Need* To Hurt You.

Now Where Was I. Oh Yes, The Kittens Fishing.

They Also Have A Picnic Basket. It's Soooo Cute.

Angelina could feel her consciousness blinking on and off. That swoon from the first night, the darkness descending on her head. Did it even need her brain? What was it doing with her legs? It hauled her to her feet, but she couldn't take in what she was seeing, where she was going, only the thing's voice in her head, knocking aside thoughts of fear or escape.

Your Kitten Begins To Realize That When You Have An Appetite Like The Other Kitten's, Food Always Tastes So Good. It Tastes More Real. If You're Hungry Enough You Can Eat Past The Flesh And Get Every Possible Part Of Its Life. Not Just The Fish In Your Paws But The Fish That Could Have Escaped, Too, The Fish That Would Have Gone On Swimming And Seen Other Streams And Had Little Fishy Adventures, Every Fish It Ever Could Have Been. For Every Fish The Other Kitten Eats, It's Actually Eating A Thousand Possible Fishes. No Wonder The Other Kitten Is So Strong.

The ground was arid brown like the surface of another planet. Angelina and her friends never came this high; there was never any point. Nothing up here but snake holes and hidden ravines and a view of the fields beyond their valley, brown and yellow squares of territory. Not even the mountain climbers chose Big Joe, preferring the muddy forests of the Pepper Grinder or the wildflower charm of Little Joe. It might take them weeks to find her body up here.

The thing jumped her off a boulder and landed her wrong. Her ankle felt mushy, and a signal that she knew was pain came creeping up her spine. Every step she took felt more mangled, a clumsy puppeteer jerking at the marionette strings, but she could not stop climbing. My Dog struggled to keep up.

Sometimes You Accidentally Pet The Other Kitten, Because It's So Hard To Tell Them Apart. And Sometimes You Think It's The Other Kitten And Actually It's Your Kitten, Maybe Feeling Hungrier Than Normal. But You

Like To Think Your Kitten Is More Sophisticated. Do You Think You're Sophisticated, Little Nini? Do You Know What That Word Means?

Insults didn't sink in, not when Angelina did not belong to herself. Pain did not sink in either. She knew her ankle hurt badly, but her brain could not make the knowledge anything real. It was like reading about pain in a book. She knew she was afraid, but the thing would not let her scream.

They reached the gray cliff of rock that made up the highest peak of Big Joe. It rose like a barrier, smooth from the wind and rain, impossible to climb even when the thing made Angelina run and leap at it. No matter. It walked her to a mound of white stones, flatter than the rest and arranged deliberately into layers. It sat her against the ancient wall.

I Wore You Out, it said. This Is Where I Used To Sleep.

The air was cold and thin this high up. Angelina needed to take a deeper breath, but the thing wouldn't let her. It had taken over her lungs and kept her breathing at a slow, comfortable pace, her eyes tracing the shapes of clouds in the sky.

It Was Nice Up Here Once. Now It's Just The Past.

My Dog sniffed the wall, searching for traces of the ancient hands who had built it or maybe just for the lizards in its cracks. The thing put Angelina's hand on the animal's back, stroked up the knobs of her spine one by one. Angelina made a long, high-pitched sound. Her belly felt tight. Her body was revolting, desperate, pleading for one big breath, one deep lungful of air.

Whoops, the thing said. Come On, Then.

It wrenched her upright. The slope of Big Joe rolled down below her and it took a moment to notice that she was running. Sprinting down the mountain, too fast, leaping over boulders and landing hard on her sprained ankle and she fell, of course, more than once. Sometimes it caught her, but sometimes it let her hit the ground and tumble over, rolling ragged over the thistles before it dragged her back up and set her running again. My Dog galloped behind her, yipping in mingled delight and distress, and the speed made tears stream from Angelina's eyes.

Ready For The End Of Your Story? You Don't Trust The Hungry Kitten. Sometimes You Worry It Will Bully Your Kitten. It's Stronger And Smarter.

Angelina's leg bled steadily and somewhere her face hurt, too, wet and warm dripping onto her upper lip. The thing dabbed at it with her tongue, then swung her body over an old wire fence. The hillside streaked past in a blue-brown blur.

You Decide To Protect Your Kitten. You Keep It Close. You Feel Like A Good Responsible Kitten Owner, And You're Still Feeling Good The Night You Wake Up And Your Kitten Is Lying Next To Your Cheek And Purring And The Other Kitten Has Chewed Clean Through Your Intestines.

She fell, and this time it didn't pick her up. Angelina lay on her back staring up. This was where it would finally kill her. Chew up her intestines just like it said. She saw herself lying with her guts spilled out, still smiling dopily up at the sky.

Wrong Again.

A new, rough grip on her arm, shaking her back and forth. Angelina moved like a rag doll, and the thing laughed and made her smile. Whose face was that before her? The jaw that sloped left, the mouth caught in a grimace. Patrick shouted at her, but the words took such a long time to filter through that by the time she deciphered them, he wasn't even speaking to her anymore. Her gaze drifted, uninterested, around her surroundings. The hard wood of the porch, the peeling painted door before her eyes. Her own front door. Crawling home to die like a dog.

"Hang on," Patrick said. "Nini, please hang on, just wait a fucking minute, Nini, I called and she's close." And then he whirled and threw his hands up in the air like a signal. "Here! We're here! I found her like this—"

A new voice, breathless and strong, racing toward her. "Did you call an ambulance?"

"They take too long to get out here," Patrick said, voice cracking. "Jag, you gotta do something—Nini, Nini—"

"Get out the way," Jagvi said, and landed on her knees by Angelina, and then her hands were on Angelina and Angelina came howling back to life.

The thing from the pit shrieked, too, furious, shoved aside and out of Angelina. Angelina rocketed upright, gasping and gagging, spitting up thick wads of phlegm. Patrick and Jagvi crowded around her, but it was Jagvi's hands on her shoulder and her back that felt like a brand, and the thing peeled away from Jagvi's hot palms.

Jagvi grabbed Angelina's wrist to check her pulse, other hand swiping up to Angelina's clammy forehead. Angelina grabbed her, hauled her in, hand fisted in Jagvi's hair, trembling in her arms.

"Don't let go of me," she garbled out, "don't stop touching me, that's what gets it out. I worked it out, that's what chased it off before, too, and it's so mad—"

"Angel," Jagvi said, easing Angelina's fingers out of her hair, which Angelina didn't mind, because it meant she could hold Jagvi's hand instead, her shaking sweaty palm in Jagvi's steady grip. "What did you take?"

Angelina laughed, cracked and hoarse, fully crazy now and ready to admit it. Jagvi knelt at her side, arms around Angelina, and Angelina's brother bent terrified before them. Angelina leaned forward, grabbing Patrick by his shirtfront.

"It's the thing from the pit," she said, panting and still shuddering back into her brain. "Pat, I swear. It's the thing from the pit, it's found me. It's gonna eat me."

XVI

Four drops of olive oil made the sign of the cross in a clay bowl of water. Angelina wondered what bread her uncle Franco had in his kitchen and whether she'd be allowed to mop up the leftover oil once the ritual was over. She'd felt too weak to eat yesterday, and this morning Caro had arrived on their doorstep in full nursing mode, meaning she wept at Angelina's bedside for two hours, delivering orders to Patrick between sobs. *Raise her leg. Fetch another pillow. Put those flowers in a vase, they'll die. Call your uncle. Tell your sister you love her. Tell me again how you found her.*

Angelina had succumbed to Caro's frantic attention. As if they were extensions of herself, with injuries that she felt in her own flesh, Caro was always overcome by her children's pain. While Angelina lay bruised and bandaged, Caro asked Patrick repeatedly to check her own pulse and temperature, to confirm that this was real and not a nightmare. A small, spoiled part of Angelina reveled in her mother's care. Neither Caro's mood nor her attention would last, and it did no harm to enjoy them.

When Patrick escaped downstairs, Caro climbed into bed with Angelina and cradled her eagerly, pulling Angelina tight against her chest. It was nice to hear Caro's steady heartbeat, though it hurt Angelina's ear after a while; she'd nicked it at some point on the mountain, just a shallow cut but enough that Jagvi had washed it with antiseptic twice. Jagvi had also washed and plastered the fresh gashes on Angelina's knee, iced and bandaged her sprained ankle, fed her some painkillers, and done a concussion test before she allowed Angelina to hobble upstairs to bed. Whenever Angelina tried to bat her away or protest that she was fine, Jagvi fixed her with that black-eyed, incredulous stare until she submitted.

Late last night Jagvi found the homemade cream that Francesca-Martine had gifted Angelina on her birthday, labeled WITCHES' BREW, and dabbed it onto Angelina's bruises.

"Thought you don't believe in magic," Angelina said, half-asleep. Patrick had promised to sleep on her floor tonight, and Jagvi took the couch. Neither of them were willing to leave Angelina alone for longer than five minutes: Patrick because he wanted to tackle the thing from the pit to the ground and kill it, Jagvi because she kept waiting for Angelina to take more of the drugs she was convinced Angelina was hiding. My Dog wagged her tail mournfully, banished to the armchair so as not to disturb Angelina's sore ankle. They'd placated her with a lamb bone.

Jagvi used her thumb to rub the Witches' Brew into the purple rose blooming below Angelina's wrist. "It's just arnica."

At first Jagvi had dismissed Angelina's announcement that she was haunted as traumatized babbling, but when Angelina didn't take it back, Jagvi appealed to Patrick. In the hours since the thing retreated she'd given him multiple theories on what had happened to Angelina: snakebite, heat-stroke, psychosis, overdose.

"She was completely out of it and then back to normal the second you touched her," Patrick said. "What drug wears off that fast?"

"I don't *know* what kind of drug," Jagvi said, turning to Angelina. "That's the point, that's why you have to tell the truth."

"She is telling the truth," Patrick said. "What's the use of lying? What would she have to hide?"

Angelina watched with interest. She didn't often see them argue. Patrick was more defiant than she would have expected, and calmer than when he fought with Angelina. He never snapped. Instead he was implacable, considering each of Jagvi's theories before he offered logical reasons to dismiss them: no snakes on Big Joe, the temperature mild, Angelina's mental health sound, and her taste in narcotics limited to weed and the odd line of coke on a Friday night. Jagvi's brow scrunched tight like it physically pained her to disagree with him.

The more Angelina denied taking drugs, the more worked up Jagvi seemed to get, like she was angry at Angelina for not being a secret addict. There was no critical damage to Angelina's body or mind—she would limp for a week or so, but her head had been returned intact. In Angelina's opinion, the main thing to be upset about was the existence of a monster with the will and ability to hurt her. But Jagvi didn't believe in that, so why be so upset?

In the morning as Caro clutched her close, Angelina could hear Jagvi downstairs, arguing with Patrick in their low, brotherly tone. She wanted to take Angelina to a doctor or a psychologist or even the police. What if she'd been attacked?

"Police," Patrick echoed, unimpressed. "No. She's okay now. Ma's with her."

"Pat, come on. She needs proper help."

"I know. We'll get it," Patrick said.

Help didn't come from a doctor or a cop, but from Nonna, sitting at the head of the table in a bobbled cardigan, holding Angelina's hand and dropping oil from Angelina's pinky finger into the bowl of water. The golden drops quivered on the surface of the water but did not sink. Angelina's grandmother murmured under her breath. Now and then she raised her hands to the ceiling and asked San Rocco to guide the way.

Gathered around the table, the Siccos bore witness to the spell. Patrick had been calling around all morning and now here they all were, Franco and his wife and three of the other uncles and all their grown-up sons, Jethro and Ricky and Matthew and Eugene and Marc, an assortment of girlfriends and wives, a baby asleep in Uncle Robert's lap. By the time Angelina, Patrick, Caro, and Jagvi drove up to Franco's property in Patrick's truck, the house had been full and Angelina had been received into a series of crushing hugs and tender greetings. Franco slipped her a mug of whisky, and now she took furtive sips and enjoyed their concern. Nothing like her family in conference mode, gathered together to solve or save. Teenage pregnancies, town feuds, the bullfrog plague twelve summers back that turned harvest season into a slimy bloodbath.

Angelina was relieved that nobody had called in a priest. They were not a very religious family, but in a situation like this, God threatened to raise his head, hoping to score some loose change. Luckily the church didn't intrude much into Cadenze. It was San Rocco's territory, and most locals were surprised at any reminder that technically, San Rocco answered to a higher power. Once a week a roving priest showed up to conduct Sunday Mass and hasten to his car before the bells finished ringing. A shrine to the Virgin Mary hung above the door of Franco's barn, a plaster bust and an electric candle with a dead bulb. When they were kids, her cousin Marc had balanced an army man action figure onto the tips of the Virgin's praying fingers, and it took the adults six months to notice.

For the third time, Angelina dipped her finger into the plate of oil and scattered droplets into the bowl. She'd watched her uncle Carl's wife, Sara, do the same thing after her miscarriage. For the third time the cross held, and despite its holy silhouette, Angelina didn't see God reflected in the water, only the grimy cracked base of Franco's bowl.

Angelina's nonna peered over Angelina's shoulder, too, then waved her hand dismissively. The group relaxed, Angelina settling back into her chair with her sore foot in her mother's lap. Caro squeezed Angelina's big toe. "Did it work?"

Nonna raised her empty hands, lips pursed. "There's no sign of evil here."

"You see?" Uncle Carl said, pinching his wife's cheek. "It's not the evil eye."

Sara looked skeptical. "Maybe you should do it again." Both Caro and Nonna shot Sara sharp looks, and she added hastily, "If the other women agree, I mean. Wouldn't it make sense? It targets pride, it goes after those who draw attention to themselves, and..."

"You can admit you're jealous of me," Angelina said. Almost everyone laughed. "Look, the eye is one thing, but I'm not talking about bad luck or sickness, am I?" Caro gave her a nod of encouragement. "It's the thing from the pit."

"But how can you be sure?" Sara asked.

"It told me so."

Out the window pale clouds gathered over the farm. The vineyard stretched in rows over the curve of the hill, and Angelina could see the chicken coops, the heap of ash from the bonfire, and the grassy pasture where Matthew's kids were playing.

This was Angelina's people's land, but it was her monster's land, too. Those caves had formed long before any Sicco set foot here. It lived here, it slept here, it might be sleeping now. Angelina hadn't heard or felt it since yesterday afternoon when it left her outside the house, gasping in Jagvi's arms.

Jagvi leaned against the windowsill with her arms folded, watching the family talk. She had refused a seat at the table, an insult that the Siccos had not missed. Whenever Angelina caught her eye, Jagvi stared at her intently, like she was urging Angelina to give her something: a confession, a cry for help. But Angelina was already telling Jagvi the truth. She looked back, wide-eyed and sincere. *Anything else you want, Jag?*

Franco said, "We didn't find anything down there." He'd taken a party of men down to the caves this morning to check for disturbance around the pit. "Just one stone displaced. Jethro says it's the one you kicked down at the party."

Angelina had forgotten doing that. Maybe that was how she'd woken it up. It seemed unfair that such a simple act could wreak such havoc. She'd been looking for attention, but not of this kind.

"Does anyone know anything else about that pit?" Patrick asked. He glanced at Jagvi and added, with careful emphasis, "Anything factual? Like a historical record?"

The older generation whooped with laughter. Even Caro had a watery smile on her face. Angelina did not want to betray Patrick by smiling, but she didn't interrupt as the elders of her family asked one another: Historical records? A list of names and places in a dusty old book? The only people who wrote those types of things were invaders, and the only reason they did it was to categorize what they wanted to steal or destroy. Did Patrick mean the records of the reformers who tore Cadenze down, or the fascists who used it as a prison, or the landowners who swindled their ancestors out of what was rightfully theirs? Did Patrick think any of those people gave two shits about a pit in a cave?

"Further back than that, though," Angelina said. "It said something to me about men with spears."

"You could have got that from the paintings in the cave," Jagvi said. "There's a soldier somewhere up there, isn't there?"

"Right, thanks, Jag," Patrick said. "Any history about who drew those?"

That wasn't what Jagvi meant. She meant that Angelina had seen the paintings and they had worked their way into her subconscious somehow. Angelina blew out a breath, considering the tight line of Jagvi's shoulders, the hard set to her mouth. On the drive to Franco's, Angelina had watched Jagvi's concern mutate into anger, and with every minute Jagvi's temper rose. Angelina could track it, and she knew Patrick could, too, from the increasing number of placatory looks he directed at Jagvi. Her old and familiar fury against Cadenze and the inner workings of a place that seemed to exist in opposition to everything she believed.

Angelina's uncle Robert listed possible artists for the cave drawings while the baby on his lap batted at his fingers. "Monks. Shepherds. Romans. Angels."

"Oh." Angelina remembered. "I think it took me to something Roman. Up on Big Joe."

"The Romans didn't build much out here," her nonna said.

"Maybe it was an outcast group," Jethro suggested, smirking. "The Romans must have had losers, too. Where else would they come?"

"Actually," Matthew said. Angelina, Patrick, and the rest of the cousins exchanged mild looks of derision. Matthew's *actually*s tended to be dull and patronizing, like Matthew himself. "There are peasant ruins all across these hills. Just because it 'looked Roman' doesn't mean it was."

"Well, it looked old as shit," Angelina said. "Maybe next time the thing from the pit will drag you up there and you can date it for us." Caro tittered. "It said it used to sleep up there. I got the feeling that someone, like, kicked it in the pit. Banished it."

"There you go, then," said Sam, the youngest of the uncles, that generation's problem child with a cauliflower ear and a habit of hitting on the younger men's girlfriends. "That's what you do when something like this comes along, just tell it to fuck off." He leaned across the table toward Angelina, and she leaned forward in kind, propping her chin on her palm. "Do you know about the time I saw the devil?"

"We've heard this a hundred times, Samuel," Caro said disdainfully.

"Twenty-nine years ago," Sam began.

"Angelina isn't like you," Caro bit out. "She isn't a useless drunk!"

"Carolina," Nonna snapped.

"Ma, she isn't. You know she isn't. You *all* know my daughter is special. We are all special, the Sicco women, we are *special*," Caro said, her voice high and strained, like she half expected one of her brothers to laugh her down, "and that is why the thing wants her. Everyone knows the stories. The monster in the pit wants the best and brightest, the most beautiful and promising life, and *that* is my daughter."

"Ma," Angelina said, grateful and embarrassed at once. She had learned from Nonna's example that it was poor taste for a Sicco woman to describe herself as special. "Anyone who has to explain how important they are," she'd told nine-year-old Angelina, "probably isn't so important." The same year, they'd returned from a family dinner and Caro had thrown herself to the floor, howling with miserable rage. "They have *never* respected me," she'd sobbed. "They think I am *trash*, all because my only purpose was to be a new, better mother, to break away from their traditional *bullshit*!" Angelina had crouched helplessly beside Caro while eleven-year-old Patrick plucked at her shirt and assured that she wasn't trash, she was perfect.

But now Nonna only looked thoughtful. "It's true that Nini stands out from her cousins," she said. "In more ways than one." The family sat nodding in agreement. Jagvi's mouth twitched like she wanted to laugh or sneer.

"Nevertheless," Sam said doggedly. "Twenty-nine years ago—"

"God help us," Caro muttered.

Twenty-nine years ago, Sam was walking home one day along the highway when he saw a beast with black wings and a spiky tail and red glowing eyes. It stopped him in his tracks and demanded that he swear allegiance to the devil and join its demonic horde.

"And"—Sam turned around the table, waiting for the boys to join in chorus—"I told him to go fuck himself! Did you try that, Nini?"

"I did actually try that," Angelina said. "Sorta. But the thing from the pit didn't ask me to do anything. It said it wanted to eat my guts."

Patrick flinched. "Christ," Jethro said, and several of her uncles made the sign of the cross. Her nonna reached across to hold Angelina's hand. Angelina squeezed back and then let go, aware of Caro's presence. But Caro had folded her hands across her face in a gesture of horror. Their reactions unsettled Angelina, as if she were already lying dead on the table, guts eaten, in front of them. On the windowsill, Jagvi made no sound and did not look away from Angelina's face.

"I don't get it," a girl piped up. Eugene's latest girlfriend, the easily frightened one from Franco's party, whose name Angelina couldn't remember. "Since when does this thing eat your guts? It eats a life, that's what he said in the cave." She pointed at Patrick. "Or like the others said, it eats your future. And everyone else forgets you ever existed."

"God help us," Caro repeated, and this time her voice cracked. "I don't know if I can do this, Nini. I don't."

She put her head on the table, her shoulders shaking like she was crying again. Angelina didn't know how she had the energy left. She rubbed her mother's bony shoulders and said, "Ma, please, it's gonna be okay." Angelina found herself wishing, for a moment, that the thing was here and poised to attack. No more wondering about motives, no wading down in the mud of family folklore and Cadenze history.

"Maybe you should lie down, Caro," Franco suggested. "Take a nap in Ricky's room."

"It was just a story, Ma," Patrick said. "I was telling ghost stories."

"What did it actually say to you, Nini?" Jethro asked. "Just like, *Ra ra, I'm gonna eat your guts*? Because the thing is, like, if it's going to do that, why not do it already?"

115

"Um." Angelina considered her mother folded over the table, not wanting to make it worse.

"She can take it," Sam said.

Patrick added, "Ma, leave if you need to, okay?"

The heap of Caro on the table said, "Uhhhuuuuh."

"It said something about fattening me up," Angelina said. "Or I said that, and it agreed? I can't remember. And it said that I'd been feeding it really well." She dug her fingers into her palms. "Like it was already eating me."

"Maybe it eats pain," Franco said. "It hurt you."

"Maybe," Angelina said. She tried to remember. "It said something about fish. Eating a fish and tasting every fish it could have ever been, or tasting all these different possible fish until it was full. Something like that."

"Isn't that just a Bible story?" Jagvi said. When the Siccos turned to her, she shrugged. "Sorry, but isn't it? A thousand fishes in one? It sounds like what you guys were talking about in the cave, too, all the potential lives. Has that been on your mind?"

"Girl, you need to be quieter," Franco said, and the others joined him in a family chorus of disapproval.

"Fuckin' chill out, guys," Angelina said, and Patrick snapped, "Hey, none of that, okay?"

"Sitting here judging us," Nonna said icily.

"Come on, Nonna, you've got resting bitch face, too," Angelina said, and Patrick said, "Jagvi stays, okay, she's the one who got rid of it—"

"I'd rather go," Jagvi said, unmoved except for the distaste she couldn't hide.

"Jag, please," Patrick said, and stood up, joining her at the window. Their shoulders pressed together, defiant in the face of Sicco disapproval. The image didn't do much for Jagvi's rehabilitation. It was just a reminder for a group who knew Jagvi best as a traitor, caught with her hands on another girl. Angelina wanted to tell Patrick that there were better ways to integrate Jagvi than setting himself and her as a pair relentlessly apart, but he wouldn't appreciate it, he wouldn't understand, he hadn't had to work to make Cadenze love him. He thought it was romantic to be an outcast. He turned his obstinate face to his family.

"Nini says Jagvi scared it away," Patrick said.

Angelina nodded. "Three times." After Old Timers, at Jagvi's dad's place, on the porch with Angelina fully out of her mind. Angelina had put it together; it wasn't that the thing kept showing up and not hurting her. It was that Jagvi kept stopping it.

"There's nothing in the stories about that," Angelina's nonna said.

"So that means I'm not just copying what I heard," Angelina said. "Doesn't it, Jagvi? There's nowhere I could've got that from except from feeling it."

Jagvi looked helpless, her mouth softening out of that hard line. "Angel…"

Caro lifted her head. "I just remembered— Ma, what about Maria?"

Maria, Angelina's great-great-great-grandmother, had been the exception of her generation, and one of the few Siccos to be driven out of town under a cloud of scandal. When Angelina was a kid, Patrick had told her that really Maria was tossed in a well by her angry family members and left to die at the bottom of the deep hole, and she still held a grudge against Sicco descendants and came crawling out of her well to kill their children. It had given Angelina nightmares for months.

Nonna, frowning at Caro, said, "That's women's business."

"It's about the cave."

"It's irrelevant. That's just about weakness."

"Come on, we all know," Marc said. "She threw her baby into the pit, didn't she?"

Angelina blinked, turning to Patrick. "I didn't know that. Did you?"

Patrick shook his head. Nonna said, "It's the worst kind of weakness. A woman abandoning her children." She was still looking at Caro with stern satisfaction.

"Wild definition of abandonment," Jethro commented.

"Maybe she didn't want it to happen that way," Caro said. "Maybe if her family had been kinder to her—"

"Hey," Angelina said, her hand on Caro's back. She could feel old familial patterns rising around them, leading them off track.

"I thought the stories are all about free will. How you have to sacrifice yourself. So maybe Maria was trying to cheat the sacrifice or something.

Isn't that a big part?" Jethro asked. Angelina shot him a grateful look, and he nodded at her.

"I think maybe the Catholics are responsible for that little embellishment," Matthew said.

"Shut up, Matthew," said his brother Eugene.

"If Maria was trying to beat the thing, that means Angelina's not the first Sicco who's been attacked," Sam said. "Maybe it took the form of the devil to get me."

General eye rolls around the table, but Marc piped up, "Dad told me once that Uncle Louis was attacked by the thing from the pit."

Jethro grimaced. "Isn't that kind of messed up? Uncle Lou had brain damage."

"He wasn't born with it," Nonna said. "He hit his head."

"Yeah, *in the cave*," Marc said. "He went out there whole and came back half-gone. And he died young."

Angelina leaned toward Jagvi. "Is a fall enough to do that to someone? Give them brain damage?"

"Depends on a million factors," Jagvi said. "Yes, sometimes. You know what's not gonna do that to someone? A make-believe demon."

"Does she *really* need to be here?" Marc asked.

"She's important, we told you," Angelina said.

Patrick nodded. "She touched Angelina and it was gone, just like that."

Quiet for a moment, Marc annoyed and sinking back into his chair, Caro pious and sniffling, the shuffle of the uncles' feet. Then Sam said to Nonna, "Tell them what you told me."

"Oh, it's..." Nonna gave Angelina a glance that was almost apologetic. "Something my husband used to say. The thing from the pit doesn't come alone. It always has a friend—a dark companion."

Jagvi laughed, a harsh, strangled bark.

"Uh," Patrick said. "Wasn't Nonno, um, a huge fucking racist?"

"Yeah," Jethro said, "that seems kind of convenient..."

"Not that type of dark," Nonna said. "An evildoer, someone who helps it, infiltrates the family and tricks you into trusting it."

Jagvi slipped off the windowsill, saluted, and walked out of the kitchen, which exploded into disorder. Sam pounded his fist on the table, Franco asked loudly if this was an admission of guilt, Marc and Eugene got the giggles, and Patrick cursed over the top of them: they were a bunch of assholes, Jagvi had saved Angelina, none of them fucking deserved her, and then he stormed out, too.

"You know a dark companion could also be me," Angelina said lightly into the new quiet. "If we're going by skin tone."

"Nini," Nonna said, and patted her hand.

"That girl overreacts a lot," Franco said.

"You remember who her dad was, right?" Angelina said, and that made the rest of the Siccos laugh: yes, that old bastard, no wonder a temper ran in Jagvi's veins. Angelina reminded them of the time Riccardo had spat in Franco's face during a council meeting; well, Jagvi's manners were definitely better than her dad's, even polite when they accused her of being the devil's favorite lil fella. She kept talking and they kept laughing.

Sometimes Patrick looked down on Angelina, told her that he'd never seen anyone run their mouth like her, and Angelina had never been able to explain that it was work, hard and cautious labor disguised by frivolity. She could unpick the threads of tension with enough sly nudges and jokes at everyone's expense, including her own, to stitch herself into the tapestry of the town. She knew how to make herself familiar, known, beloved. She could stitch Jagvi in, too, if she were given the opportunity. But Jagvi had never wanted that from her. Until recently, Angelina had thought Jagvi didn't want anything from her at all.

Angelina waited until the tension had seeped out of the room, and then she picked up her crutches and excused herself.

Outside Jagvi and Patrick sat huddled by the bonfire ashes, talking closely with their heads bent together. They looked up when Angelina hobbled over on Franco's old, oversized crutches.

"Guys, they're just being dumb," she said. "Of course the folklore is dodgy, it's a fuckin' million years old. There's no need to storm out. It's just Cadenze, Jagvi."

"I know it's Cadenze," Jagvi said. "I grew up here, too, Angel."

"No," Angelina began, then stopped. She didn't want to sound like her uncles or any of the other people, including Angelina herself, who'd told Jagvi she didn't belong here. Jagvi had grown up on Big Joe, she knew the way these people's minds worked, she had history here. She had her own connections, roots, desires. She'd wanted to fuck Angelina for years. Angelina's face went hot and she said, "I didn't mean it like that."

"Okay," Jagvi said, and then, relenting: "I know, Angel. It's all right."

"Should we go back in?" Angelina asked.

"We've got all we're gonna get," Patrick said. "They're all too freaked out to come up with anything but blame. Not the next Sicco matriarch in trouble..."

"Give it a rest," Angelina said, eyes narrowed. "At least they believe me. They'll stay close. They'll be on alert."

"That's good, but..." Patrick shook his head. "I dunno, Nini. When I found you, it was like you were—completely gone. I couldn't do anything. I don't know what they'd be able to do. The only one who helped—"

"Pat," Jagvi said.

"If you could just stick around," Patrick said.

"I'm supposed to be leaving on Wednesday."

Angelina squeezed the handles of her crutches. She hadn't noticed the days passing so quickly.

"Just give us an extra week or two."

"Don't do this to me," Jagvi said, her voice tight, almost panicked, like she could see the walls closing in on her. Like Angelina and her brother had come up with the perfect trick to drag Jagvi back into Cadenze and all its evils and archaisms. "You know you shouldn't do this."

"You'll be fine," Patrick said.

"Pat, come on, please—"

"For me," Patrick said.

Jagvi paced away, moving in such fluent fury that Angelina thought for a moment she would run and never be seen again. But she stopped a few feet from them, then turned around, miserable and defeated, a hot look of venom directed at Angelina.

"One more week," she said.

Angelina would have taken it. But Patrick had full access to the twisting years of demands and gifts, promises and betrayals, the stained and hoary ropes binding him and Jagvi to one another, and he shrugged his shoulders.

"We'll see," Patrick said. After a moment, Jagvi nodded.

XVII

Angelina's new guard dog paced around their yard. She made two laps of the house while Angelina sat out on the deck with her ankle stretched before her, tracking Jagvi going past, disappearing out of view and then back again, her hands in her pockets and her jaw clenched. Angelina watched and painted her fingernails tangerine. After a while Patrick came out to lean against the railing.

"See?" Angelina said. "You spent all those years bitching at me to be nice, and it turns out she hates me, too."

"She doesn't like feeling trapped," Patrick said. "Jag, come have a beer."

Jagvi shook her head, already on the next loop.

There was something almost stern about Patrick's face, fond and empathetic but unforgiving, like he'd made his decision and Jagvi had to pay the cost. Jagvi and Angelina had agreed to every order Patrick made as they drove home: Angelina would take a week off from her job at the call center; she had to keep working at Old Timers, couldn't afford to lose every shift, so Jagvi and Patrick would keep her company at the bar. Patrick would work every other day, and they'd make it through the financial hit. Jagvi only spoke once, offering money ("Fuck off," Angelina and Patrick said as one). To every other plan she only nodded. Patrick seemed unfazed by Jagvi's obvious unhappiness. He'd asked her for something and she'd agreed. That was all.

"Okay," Patrick called. "Well, come inside when you want. *Baywatch* is on."

Dusk came creeping over the face of Big Joe. My Dog whined in her sleep, and Angelina watched Jagvi's long shadow blend into the rest of the shadows that crawled out. Cold gripped the air and shrill birdcalls echoed from somewhere higher up. Angelina shivered and reached out tentatively, groping into the empty air behind her, trying to feel any kind of presence. But there was only Jagvi, wearing a path around their house.

"You hungry?" Angelina asked, and Jagvi stopped, turning toward her. "Nonna gave us some dumplings."

"I want to apologize," Jagvi said.

"Uh." Angelina scratched her head. "Okay?"

"I shouldn't have— I let it go too far." Angelina couldn't track Jagvi's expression, the shadows hiding her face and her eyes black and burning. "At my dad's house. When I said—"

"Jesus. You're sorry for *that*? What about telling me I'm a lying drug addict?"

"I was wondering if I upset you. If it was too much. And if you did something and then felt like you couldn't tell Patrick why—"

"How weak do you think I am?" Angelina snapped. "You tell me you want to fuck me, and I go off and overdose? I'm sorry you don't believe me, but I could do without all the patronizing. I'm hot, Jagvi. Lots of girls want to fuck me. I haven't gone crazy yet."

Jagvi blew out a breath, half laugh and half fury. "I don't think you're weak."

"But you think I'm lying."

"Angel, patients lie all the fucking time, and it would be a lot easier if you were, but, no, I don't think you're lying, I think something really bad is happening and your whole family is just going to believe that it's *magic*, and stop you from getting help when you need it!"

Angelina hauled herself to her feet, clutching her crutches. She wasn't interested in debating the thing's existence anymore. "Why do you flirt with me?" she demanded. "If you hate me this much?"

"I don't hate you," Jagvi said, a rough edge to her voice that Angelina didn't trust.

Angelina made an impatient gesture. "If you hate my town and my family, and you still say this shit to me, you still get me all..." She stopped, shook her head.

"I can't help it," Jagvi said.

Angelina laughed, scornful and miserable. "Right. I forgot you're the lady-killer of San Michele. Spot a pretty skirt and can't help chasing it, huh?"

Jagvi said nothing, hands open at her sides. She stood still at last, back straight and nothing on her face that Angelina could read.

"Patrick was the one who asked you to stay," Angelina said. "I'm with you, Jag. I wish you were long gone, too."

She went inside, threw a shoe at Patrick to express her displeasure, and hobbled up the stairs.

At midnight Angelina shuffled back downstairs, bored and sleepless and wondering if they had any wine, then paused in the stairwell at the sound of voices. Jagvi's was a deep drawl. "That time your uncle Sam fell over drunk and managed to pants you on the way down. Uh, when Big Tits Bianca dumped you in the middle of your birthday party—"

"Fuck youuu," Patrick said, laughing, something soft and worn-out in his voice. Angelina crept down another few steps. She could see their silhouettes in the dim lamplight of the living room, Patrick stretched out on the couch with his head in Jagvi's lap, Jagvi's legs slung up on the coffee table, one hand carding through Patrick's hair. "You remember all the great disasters of my life, I'm so glad."

"Yeah, from every angle," Jagvi said. Her thumb stroked over his eyebrow. "I'm just saying, you've been through a lot. Your sister being in trouble is a minor issue. You can take care of her."

"If she lets me," Patrick said.

"She seems freaked."

"She is *now*," Patrick said. "Give her a couple of days and she's going to get stir-crazy or confident that she can take down a demon from hell—shut up,

I'm not arguing with you about it again—or she'll decide the demon's her best friend, and keep insisting everything's perfect right until it eats her."

"Well," Jagvi said, a rough scrape to her voice. "That's Angel."

"Yeah," Patrick said, and Angelina slipped back upstairs.

Patrick worked the next day. Angelina woke up with a knot in her stomach at the idea of being alone with Jagvi, but she needn't have worried—the house stayed busy all day. Caro came by before she started work to drop off their shared car ("In case you need it, my darling," as though they just needed some extra horsepower to outrun the thing). After Caro left, Franco's wife, Lucille, arrived with a fresh hamper of food and her tarot cards: "So, you haven't changed too much," she said, turning over the Knight of Pentacles.

Then it was Francesca-Martine, who'd heard of Angelina's mysterious illness through the Cadenze grapevine and dropped by with a jar of caramelized garlic and a candle she used to remove Angelina's earwax under Jagvi's silent supervision. She reminded Angelina about the Halloween festival they'd been planning, a night of music and street lanterns that Angelina had masterminded to lure tourists during the quiet season, planning to dress as a lurid damsel from an Argento movie and winking at every girl she saw until one winked back. But now Angelina was caught up in her own horror story, and so far it was much less glamorous.

"You know you can hang out with us," Angelina said when Francesca-Martine left. She had a guilty flash of her eavesdropping from last night, Jagvi consoling Patrick; she should try to be kinder in gratitude. "Patrick didn't hire you as a bodyguard."

"I'll pass."

Angelina whistled, long and marveling, any kind impulses fleeing. "When did you turn into such a dick?"

"Guess it's in my genes."

"Right," Angelina agreed, and then, distracted: "Wait, did you say *genes* or *jeans*? Like with a *g* or a *j*—"

Jagvi barked out a laugh, bright-eyed across the kitchen. She stood up, shaking her head. "I'm gonna raid Pat's records. Call me if you get possessed."

Out front Jethro pulled up honking his horn, with a rabbit-foot for Angelina and a punching bag for Patrick. Angelina helped him drag it around the house to the backyard and their one scraggly tree. They were arguing about the best way to put it up when Patrick got home and whooped joyfully for Jagvi. Together Patrick and Jagvi suspended it from the sturdiest branch.

"Thought it'd help to be prepared," Jethro said, taking a gulp of the beer that had circulated as reward for a good day's work.

"I dunno," Angelina said doubtfully. "It doesn't really feel like the kind of thing you can punch."

"We don't know what we can do to it," Patrick said. "You've been on your own so far, Nini. It's gonna be different now. Hold the bag, Jethro." He took a couple of jabs, but Jethro refused to put down the beer and ended up spilling a decent amount over himself. Jagvi swapped in, bracing herself against the bag while Patrick let out a karate cry and chopped high and low. Angelina felt a weary sort of embarrassment. She pulled Jethro to sit on the back steps with her, eating the food their aunt had left and throwing rocks for My Dog to chase.

"No sign of it today, Nini?" Jethro asked.

Angelina shook her head. In the shadow of the mountain, Patrick and Jagvi took turns hitting the punching bag, until Patrick slipped and caught Jagvi's hip instead, and Jagvi tackled him to the ground. They shoved at each other on the prickly grass, My Dog running in anxious circles around them, Patrick laughing uncontrollably as Jagvi got him into a headlock. All that laughter and energy felt like a beacon, flaming high, but the oncoming night was as quiet as the one before and the one before that. *Where the fuck are you*, Angelina wondered, and heard no response.

Her uncle Sam called the next day to tell Angelina more about the dark companion. "Your nonna says it could be the spirit of an unbaptized baby. So you can tell your brother not to be so offended, huh? It might not even be his friend's fault."

Angelina yawned. "Oh, no? What else did Nonna say?"

Her uncle reminded her of the story they all knew, where the wife tricks the monster into falling into the pit before it can eat her husband. In some versions she wasn't a savior at all, but more like a lackey who attended to the monster's needs. "She's a witch who made a deal with the devil," Sam said, "until she gets too greedy and decides she wants the husband's future for herself."

Angelina scoffed. "So it's about wives who want to kill their husbands? Super original."

Sam explained that it could also be a little monk out running mischief, pinching at Jagvi's ankles to make her turn in the right direction, hanging on to her coattails. But Jagvi didn't even wear a coat, Angelina thought, while Sam talked on in her ear. Every now and then Jagvi threw on that leather jacket, but mostly she flaunted her arms and her shoulders and the ripple of the long vein that ran down her forearm and into her hand without distraction. Nobody wanted Angelina and her brother to kick Jagvi out, her uncle continued. They just needed to be careful. Why was the thing backing off when Jagvi touched Angelina, anyway? Her role in this was not clear.

Angelina listened idly, perched on the kitchen table and twirling the phone cord around her finger. On the floor before her, uninterested in Angelina's conversation, Patrick and Jagvi had started reinstalling the sagging kitchen counters. Jagvi had said this morning that if she was going to be hanging around here, she might as well be useful. Patrick stayed home today per their agreement, ostensibly to keep an eye on Angelina, but neither of them paid much attention to her. Patrick's fear melted away with every second that he and Jagvi spent together, their shoulders pressed close, a force he didn't believe any power could get through. Angelina wanted to tell him that his confidence was strong for a pairing that had been so flimsy in the past.

"Now listen," her uncle said. "We're taking care of your mother. Franco was over there today, she's very upset, of course, but he's looking after her. We don't want you two to worry about her."

"Oh," Angelina said. She wondered if Caro had used up all her stamina for weeping at the family conference, or if she was still going strong. Hopefully the uncles were keeping her hydrated. "Okay, I won't."

At four, the three of them walked down to Old Timers for Angelina's shift. The end-of-summer light made Angelina feel as though she were limping straight down from the sky, hazy blue around her shoulders and the ugly concrete plain of Cadenze rolling itself before her. Traffic hummed in the distance, Jagvi and Patrick talked quietly to one another, and the whole world felt agonizingly normal. Angelina shrank with every step. The crisis had faded and instead she felt embarrassed and young. Patrick missing work, Jagvi tied to their company, and nothing to prove any of it was necessary except Angelina's word and a twisted ankle and handful of fading bruises that—as Jagvi insisted—could be explained in so many other ways.

Angelina did not think she had gone crazy. But where was it? She did not think she had imagined it. But where was it! Its absence felt half as frightening as its presence, both the fear of it leaping out, and the anxiety that it would never come back, and eventually everyone would decide she *was* crazy. She did not doubt her experience, but how long before everyone else did? What if this was her legacy? What if her family was wrong and she wasn't the golden shining girl of her generation? Perhaps Angelina was fated not to be one of the Sicco women who had adventures or starred in scandals, not one of the beloved legends of her family history and not even a disappointment like Caro, but another vagrant or baby killer or warning, another monster at the bottom of a well.

"Coming, Nini?" Patrick asked, looking over his shoulder. Angelina frowned, and refused to hurry, hands deep in her pockets, goose bumps prickling on her arms, lilac T-shirt and blue jeans, hobbling over the road.

"Baby," Gemma said, wrapping her arms around Angelina and squeezing tight. She presented Angelina with a little bundle of mayweed tied with a pink ribbon Angelina recognized as one of Gemma's favorite hair accessories. "Is everything okay? Francesca-Martine is being gloomy as shit."

"Fine," Angelina said. "I just banged my ankle up on the mountain, but it's fine, I'm not even using crutches anymore."

Gemma tutted over the scrape on her arm and the bruise on her elbow and didn't press for information, turning instead to exclaim over Jagvi's presence. "I haven't seen you here in *ages!*"

"Yeah," Jagvi said absently. She was looking at the framed photo of her father on the bar. Angelina wanted to direct Patrick's attention toward her, but he was embracing Gemma, kissing both her cheeks while she flexed her usual mix of flirtation and maternal scolding. Jagvi put her hands in her pockets and didn't take her eyes off her father's black-and-white scowl.

"You can turn it over," Angelina said. "Or shall I put it away?"

"It's fine," Jagvi said. "But thanks, Angel." Angelina's face went hot.

Jagvi didn't look away from the photo until Gemma turned back to her, dusting her hands. "Seriously, when was the last time you came to Old Timers?"

Jagvi's gaze jerked from her dad straight to Angelina, guilty and struck.

"Four years ago, I guess," Patrick said, a little wry. "Christmas. No wait, New Year's. That was a messy night."

"It was Jagvi's fault," Angelina said, on instinct.

Jagvi nodded. Patrick said, "Not really."

Angelina busied herself limping back and forth to unpack the dishwasher. She wished Gemma hadn't brought attention to Jagvi's presence. When she returned to the group, Patrick was laughing over that ill-fated Christmas vacation, when Jagvi had returned to Cadenze to spend the holiday with her father.

"…picked Jag up at the bus stop and she was all rugged up like a fucking yeti…"

"Oh, that winter was awful," Gemma agreed. "Me and my ex ate dinner in bed 'cause the house got so icy."

Patrick nodded. "But Nini was working, so I took Jag into Old Timers, and we were getting out of our coats and hats and shit, and it turned out Jagvi had shaved her entire fucking head. Scared the life out of me."

Jagvi smiled, rubbing her palm over her jaw. Angelina didn't know what to do with her hands. She could see it clear as a picture, the moment four years ago when Jagvi had pulled her beanie off and revealed that buzz cut, hair short as a boy's, bristly and close around her skull. She'd looked tough and somehow taller, all the delicacy drained from her features in favor of a challenging severity. *Try me.* The sheer arrogance of the haircut had made Angelina hot with fury. Like a test, giving herself the dykiest haircut in the world days before she descended on Angelina, waiting for Angelina to give herself away.

Angelina still hadn't come out, back then. After the party in San Michele, she'd kept the secret to herself. The only person in Cadenze who knew that Angelina was gay was Angelina. Until Jagvi came into her bar.

"Was that the first time you cut your hair, Jagvi?" Gemma asked earnestly. "Was it a lesbian thing?"

Patrick looked annoyed. "It was for work. Some guy grabbed you by your braid at a scene, right, Jag?"

"That's right," Jagvi said, gaze flashing at Angelina and back. Jagvi had told Angelina the real reason, later that week, running her hand over its soft grain while Angelina did her best to pretend she didn't want to touch it, too. *I wanted to upset my dad*, she'd told Angelina. Old Timers had been almost empty. Angelina had said, *Mission accomplished.*

Patrick did not know about that confession. He had not been there. He didn't know that Jagvi and Angelina spent one long evening alone in Old Timers together, and he didn't know about the shots they'd downed or the secrets Angelina had confessed across the bar. He didn't know that Jagvi had rested her chin in her palm and listened like there was nowhere else she'd rather be. Or that Angelina had pulled off her baggy sweatshirt and clipped her hair up just for the thrill of Jagvi's eyes on her bare skin. Most of the time Angelina pretended she didn't know, either, but it was more difficult with Jagvi here and back in her bar, the secret cupped between them.

"Help me set up the outside tables, Gemma," Angelina said.

Gemma followed her out into the sunset, the town square bright with gold, the fountain's hand clawing against a pink-streaked sky. Angelina fussed about lighting candles and mosquito coils while Gemma did the heavy lifting, ushering Angelina out of the way when she tried to help.

"Look after that ankle of yours," Gemma said. "Hey, Nini. You okay?"

Angelina looked back over her shoulder at Jagvi's silhouette through the bar. She was so incongruous in Old Timers, like Angelina had opened the door and invited one of the mountain wolves to come in and take a seat. Angelina didn't trust any of her own instincts. Jagvi was laughing at something Patrick had said and stretched, pushing her hands up toward the ceiling. Angelina stared at the slope of her bicep and imagined being a fairy or pixie, small enough to flutter up onto Jagvi's arm and wrap herself around it, squeeze the muscle hard between her legs.

"Jagvi said she wanted to fuck me," Angelina said.

"Jesus!" Gemma dropped the table she was moving, eyebrows gratifyingly high. "When?"

"Few days ago." Angelina grinned at Gemma, pleased to be saying the words aloud to someone whose presence didn't turn her silly. "We haven't, obviously."

"Small blessings," Gemma said, shaking her head. "She shouldn't do that."

"Fuck me or say it?"

"Either, really. But *definitely* not the first one—"

"I wouldn't let her!"

"Oh, good," Gemma said. "That would be a really bad idea. Phew, she really plays with fire, doesn't she?"

"*Yes*," Angelina said, relieved. "She fucking does."

"Are you okay about it?"

"Sure. I can handle Jagvi."

"I know you can," Gemma said, and touched Angelina's arm. "Are you also okay about...everything else?"

The first stars pricked out, visible just beyond the vivid chaos of the sunset. Angelina said, "My family is taking care of it."

"I don't know what's going on and I don't wanna," Gemma said, laughing. "God protect whatever the Siccos turn their minds against."

Days of quiet. Gemma's bundle of mayweed wilted and died in the vase after Angelina forgot to water it, and she lost Jethro's rabbit-foot somewhere in her bedroom. Still no retribution arrived. Patrick worked, called in sick, worked, then asked Angelina if she thought it would be okay if he went back to full-time. "I'm not far if you need me," he said. Angelina studied his face, trying to ferret out doubt or disbelief. She saw only his plain practicality and the fact of their gas bill. Guilt stirred in her chest. Her ankle felt better; the bruises were fading. Some nights she thumbed the cut on her ear and tensed for the shallow spark of pain. It had been real.

"Yeah, go," Angelina said. She told him she'd check in with her boss at the call center, too, and pick up the next free shift. They were coming up to Jagvi's one-week deadline, though neither of them mentioned it. *We'll see*, Patrick had said. But what was he seeing?

Jagvi slept on the couch and lived out of her backpack. Angelina overheard her on the phone apologizing to her boss, explaining that she'd been unavoidably delayed in Cadenze for another week, maybe two. She seemed distant, existing as though she occupied a separate yet near universe, her atoms brushing past Angelina's without managing to make contact.

Angelina knew that Jagvi felt claustrophobic here. She left all the doors open so that the sharp fall breeze found every corner of the house and My Dog galloped from end to end with glee. On a hot afternoon she came outside and found Angelina in her daisy dukes and bikini top. She turned down Angelina's offer of a beer in favor of sticking her head under the cold outdoor tap, shaking off a wave of water that arced across the backyard and slapped Angelina in the face.

"Not really the return you imagined, huh," Patrick said one evening, out on the back porch with red wine and moths fluttering around their heads.

Jagvi shrugged.

"Since when did you imagine a return?" Angelina asked, irritated. "I thought the whole point was to get out of Cadenze and never look back."

Jagvi stretched out her legs, wineglass untouched by her side. "Everyone imagines what it would be like to come back sometimes."

"I remember angry little Jag," Patrick said, tipsy enough that Jagvi's seventeen-year-old ghost made him happy. "She wanted to show up like some kind of conquering hero. Prove everyone wrong about her and claim her prizes."

"What prizes were you gonna find here?" Angelina asked. She was genuinely curious, but the question landed wrong with Jagvi, who rolled up to her feet.

"Yeah," Jagvi said bitterly. "What fucking prizes, Pat." She disappeared back into the open mouth of the house, rapping her knuckles against Angelina's head in farewell.

All through the days, Angelina practiced her prairie wife smile, accepted visitors, accepted gifts, accepted favors, like a hungry black hole had set up shop on Big Joe. She was not the golden girl but something that took and took. Her family's care began to feel shameful, like she was tricking them. The thing had dragged her across the bathroom floor, it had stalked her into Old Timers, it had taken full possession of her body and carried her up the mountain and hurt her. Leaving her entirely alone now was the worst cruelty of all. Allow her monster to abandon her, and how long before her family followed suit?

"No one thinks you're lying," Jethro said, and her uncle Sam said, "These things are tricky, Nini, and we're hunting now, so you gotta be patient, you gotta wait for your prey," and Caro called and said that she was barely sleeping, she was so worried for Angelina. They spoke for a few minutes, and when Angelina hung up, she found Jagvi leaning in the doorway watching her.

"Everything okay with your ma?"

"She'll be okay. I shouldn't have gotten her involved. It was childish."

"Was it?"

"It would probably have been kinder to tell her when it was all over."

Angelina worried at her thumbnail. "But she doesn't like being kept in the dark either."

"Difficult," Jagvi commented.

Angelina twitched under her steady regard. "It's fine. Did you need the phone? Want to call your city friends and tell them the redneck drama is getting you down?"

Jagvi managed a smile. "That one's not your best."

Angelina ran her hands through her hair, unable even to retreat to the old comfort of being furious at Jagvi. Here Jagvi was, doing her a favor, and Angelina was just another Sicco sniping at her. She mumbled something to this effect, tense and waiting for Jagvi to seize on another opportunity to talk Angelina into going to see a doctor.

Instead Jagvi said, "I kind of like that you think I don't belong here."

"What?"

Jagvi shrugged. "Everyone else thinks I don't belong because I'm brown. You just think I don't deserve this place. That makes more sense to me. Like maybe I'm too shitty a person for this shitty town."

"That's not why you don't belong," Angelina said, staring. "It's 'cause you think you're too good for Cadenze."

"Is that what I think?"

"Yes," Angelina said. Jagvi was smiling at her, like they were just joking around, no self-pity or fishing for affirmation involved, and that made it worse, because Angelina thought Jagvi might be telling the truth. "Why are you a shitty person?"

"Why not," Jagvi said lightly.

"You're annoying, not shitty," Angelina said. "Maybe I misinterpret what a snob you are. It's your whole strong-silent-type thing backfiring on you."

Jagvi laughed. "That's bullshit. Every time I start talking to you, I can't shut up. You know that."

Angelina stumbled. "Just because you've found a new tactic for freaking me out this visit..."

Jagvi shook her head. "What about that Christmas?"

"Jag—"

"It's been weird," Jagvi said, "being back in Old Timers."

Angelina nodded, helpless.

"I keep thinking about that night."

"Me too," Angelina said.

"You look good there," Jagvi said. Embarrassment and regret flashed across her expression. She turned away. Angelina stared at her, starving. "I'm gonna…I'll be outside, okay, Angel? I know I can't leave, and you and Patrick think I'm some kind of magic…I just need some space."

"Yeah," Angelina said. Her throat hurt.

When Jagvi left, Angelina sat down at the kitchen table and wondered if she was going to cry. She didn't think she'd ever felt so small, so selfish, so desperate. Even the acute pain and terror of the thing shrank in the face of this long week, leaving her needy and contained. She rested her cheek on the wall, grainy plaster against her cheek. She was lonelier than she'd been in a long time, and she wanted to re-enter her life, which she loved, and she wanted to prove that she'd been right to ask for help, and she wanted the monster back so that she hadn't made it up.

A wet nose snuffled at her ankle. Angelina dropped her hand to stroke My Dog's furry head. But My Dog wasn't there.

Hi, Baby, the thing behind her said. I Missed You, Too.

XVIII

Angelina bolted out of her seat, and nothing stopped her. She knew not to bother looking behind her, but she did anyway and jumped at a shadow looming outside the window. It was only the punching bag hanging from the tree. The rock face beyond was painted red by the setting sun. There was no monster to be seen, but Angelina knew what she'd heard.

"Don't hurt me," she said.

Of Course Not, Baby. I Didn't Hurt You Last Time.

Angelina snorted in disbelief. "Okay, sure."

You Fell.

"You made me fall." She took a step toward the hallway, and when it didn't stop her, she took another. She didn't want to anger it with a sudden move. "Where've you been?"

Sleeping.

"You sleep a lot, huh?"

Everything Needs Rest. That's How We Get Stronger. Look.

It lifted her clean into the air. She yelped, reaching for something to tether her down, but her hands were not her own and stayed glued to her sides. She hung suspended about a foot above the kitchen threshold. Tennis shoes dangling. She told herself to keep calm. Jagvi was close, she was just outside, and with one touch, it would be gone again. And if Jagvi saw her hanging from thin air like this!

You Like It, Too? I'm So Pleased. It lowered her slowly, careful not to put her weight back on her sore ankle too fast. Angelina wondered if it felt bad for hurting her. She took another few steps down the hallway in the guise of testing her body again, confirming that it would still let her move. She could hear My Dog yapping to Jagvi in the front yard.

"I've been resting, too," she said. "Resting and thinking." Another few steps. The floorboards creaked beneath her, and she started talking to drown them out and keep that amused attention on her voice. "Everyone's trying to figure out exactly what you want. There's stories about you eating my life, or my future, but nothing actually makes sense. Are you listening?"

Yes.

"Okay, good. So I've been thinking, maybe you hang around aboveground attached to me and, like, feel the sunlight on your face or, or on my face, whatever, and slowly make me look crazy to everyone I love, and that's how you steal my future. You take it over. You get to have everything I have."

What Do You Have?

Questions were good. She wanted to keep it talking until she reached the door. "My whole life! My body, my friends, my town. My family."

Your Family Doesn't Know How To Help You Now.

"Yeah, you're right." She had the door unlatched. "None of us know what to do. But I figured one thing out." She shoved the door fully open with her shoulder. The setting sun was blinding. Angelina squinted into the red light and shouted Jagvi's name and braced for the thing to whisk her away, shut her up, maybe lift her off the ground and throw her back, or slam the door and lock it so that Jagvi had to break it down to get to her. But nothing happened.

Jagvi was on the grass with My Dog and a hose. She'd been washing mud off My Dog's fur. Water pooled around her boots. "Yeah?"

Angelina stood on the deck. "It's here."

The sunlight reflecting on the windows must have been in her eyes, because Jagvi used one hand to shield them, frowning at Angelina.

"The thing from the pit, I mean. It's here." Angelina paused. Even My

Dog was quiet, peering at her through wet locks of fur. Both Jagvi and the dog looked unimpressed. "Come on," Angelina muttered under her breath. "What's the problem? Got stage fright?"

Gamely, the thing behind her gave her a push. She stumbled forward and landed on one knee, her hands stinging against the wooden boards of the deck, and finally Jagvi dropped the hose and came over to her. "Angel, maybe you need to lie down."

"Didn't you see that?" Angelina demanded.

"I saw you trip." Jagvi wiped her hands on her jeans, leaving wet prints on the denim. "Are you feeling dizzy?" She reached out.

"Don't touch me!"

Jagvi stood back, her hands held up.

Oh? I Thought This Was Your Whole Plan?

"I don't want to get rid of it yet," Angelina said. She pulled herself upright again and came down the steps. "It's finally back, Jag. If you get rid of it, then we're just back where we started."

You Missed Me *So* Much, the thing crowed. You've Been *Pining* For Me.

Jagvi crossed her arms, jamming her hands under her armpits. She'd been wearing the same black T-shirt for a few days now, and it was stained with dust and dirt. "Angel, I'm sorry we fought, but you don't have to do this."

"I'm not *doing* anything," Angelina said. "You don't have to believe me. Just stay close in case it, um, pounces, okay? Please." She wished she had Patrick's knack for making Jagvi do things. She couldn't mimic his careful words or the way he seemed to find the rope of obligation hidden between them and pull it tight. All Angelina could do was fix pleading eyes on Jagvi and hope that the thing behind her didn't interfere. But it was quiet, too, curious, like it wanted to see how this new development turned out, Angelina almost panting in her eagerness, leaning toward Jagvi, who stood still and tense, her elbows jutting out sharp as knives.

Eventually she nodded.

"Okay," Angelina said. "Thank you. So, um." She didn't like the way Jagvi was watching her, expectant, like she'd asked Jagvi to come watch her do a trick and was now failing to perform.

Oh, Come On, the thing said. It took hold of Angelina's legs, and suddenly she was walking across the gravel.

You Finally Got Her Attention, And Then You're Gonna Freeze Up?

It marched her over to My Dog and clicked Angelina's fingers for her, ordering My Dog inside with a sharp jerk of her head. My Dog wasn't usually well trained enough for something like that to work, but she seemed to sense some new authority. She dropped the stick she'd been chewing on and trotted into the house.

Jagvi watched My Dog, who sat acquiescent in the hallway with her eyes fixed on Angelina. The three of them formed a triangle of eyes, Jagvi's on the dog's on Angelina's, which were guided or permitted by the thing to study Jagvi's face for any sign of what she was thinking.

Wherever I Take You, She's Going To Follow?

Angelina's mouth was loose with the permission to speak. "Yes. Jagvi comes."

Then Let's Go.

XIX

Angelina and her monster and her bodyguard walked down her mountain toward her town. Once it had got them moving, the thing gave back her body and let her set the pace. The last flies of the year buzzed around their heads, and the air was pink and cool. Angelina's footsteps were so light she almost wasn't walking. There was no shoving or forcing this time, no horror stories about killer kittens. The quiet made Angelina jittery, but she followed the easy pace the thing set. She had wrested back some control. One wrong move and Jagvi would touch her and wipe it out.

They were already halfway down Big Joe, the lights of Cadenze flickering on to welcome them. Her beautiful crumbling town that she'd shaped so well. She'd made it fun, made it safe, she could subdue its racists and its homophobes, and she could subdue its monsters, too.

Your Theory Has Some Merit, it told her.

"Which one?"

Eating Up Your Whole Life. There Are Parts Of This I Enjoy.

Angelina nodded. "That's why you got so mad last time, too, right? Because I cut you off."

Jagvi glanced over her shoulder at Angelina, her face sour and uneasy. Farther up the mountain, Angelina had offered to tell Jagvi what the thing said, but Jagvi had responded with a curt *no thanks*. She hadn't spoken since, as if saying another word would encourage Angelina to include her in the conversation.

The thing from the pit didn't seem bothered by Jagvi. Angelina kept expecting it to try to get away, maybe seize Angelina's body again and have her make a break for it across the scratchy fields. Instead it ignored Angelina's question and said, It's Good That She Follows.

Angelina frowned. "Why?"

I Wonder How Long Before She's Had Enough.

"She won't when she sees what you can do," Angelina pointed out. Jagvi's head twitched at the word *she*, but she did not look around or ask what they were discussing. If the thing would only lift Angelina up again…

There Are Rational Explanations For Most Things.

There was no rational explanation for levitation, but as she studied the back of Jagvi's downturned head, she wondered if Jagvi would come up with one, anyway. She was sure the thing in the pit could prove itself to Jagvi if it wanted to, but she guessed that it didn't want Jagvi to believe in it, because it didn't want her to keep protecting Angelina.

Jagvi glanced back again and noticed Angelina watching her. "What?"

"Nothing. Sorry."

"Finished talking to yourself about me?"

"I can't control what it asks me about."

"Of course you can't," Jagvi said scornfully.

She's Going To Abandon You. Angelina worried her bottom lip with her teeth. She's Going To Leave You Alone With Me. Jagvi was waiting for a response, but when Angelina didn't say anything else, her face softened and she said, "Sorry. I'm in a bad mood."

No shit, Angelina thought, but she heard herself say, "Why?"

It wasn't her. That wasn't her question. It was in her mouth, using her to speak to Jagvi. And Jagvi didn't notice; she matched her pace to Angelina's and walked by her side, responding to the question she thought Angelina had asked. Angelina tried to recover her mouth, to gurgle or cry out, but her muscles were locked and numb, beyond her reach.

"I had a fight with Pat this morning. I hate fighting with him. I said something cruel."

"Oh," the thing said. It made Angelina sound disappointed. "Who Cares?"

Jagvi slanted her a glance, unconcerned, used to Angelina's disdain. "You fight with him often enough that it's normal. But I don't, and I hate it."

"Whatever You Said, I'm Sure He Deserved To Hear It." *It's not me*, Angelina thought, *it's not me. Look at me.* But Jagvi stared into the distance.

"I said he wants this thing from the pit to be real. I told him he wants you to be in danger because then he can force me to stay."

"You're Probably Right."

"No. He wouldn't lie to me. Why are you putting on that voice?"

"Is It Creeping You Out?" the thing asked, and nodded Angelina's head casually in the direction of the town square, guiding Jagvi through the streets as they talked. Angelina couldn't make it stop. And Jagvi just thought Angelina was fucking around.

"I just know that Pat thinks I'm not coming back again, now that Dad's gone. He thinks I won't come just to see him."

No, Angelina thought. I need to talk to her. Let me talk to her.

"Is That True?" the thing made her say.

Jagvi shook her head, dip of a frown between her eyebrows. "Pat's my oldest friend. He's the first person who ever really took my side. I'm not just gonna disappear from his life." She shrugged, and Angelina tried hard to trip herself up, fall against Jagvi and shake the thing away, but it kept a good grip on her ankles and her tread did not falter. "In some ways Cadenze is more appealing without my dad here. Makes this place seem less oppressive, somehow. You remember what he was like."

I Don't, the thing said to Angelina, I Don't Remember, Show Me, and before she could even parse what it meant, it was rifling through her head again, the way it had that first night in Old Timers. That horrible thick liquid, dripping, clawing, taking everything. She didn't have many firsthand memories of Riccardo, but there were things that Patrick had told her, angry and ranting after Jagvi had gone home for the evening, and now the thing scanned through them. How Riccardo demanded that Jagvi visit him in Cadenze but he didn't even give Jagvi a proper bed, he didn't pick her up from the station or wait up to greet her. He expected her to make up for years of lost caretaking whenever she was back, cook and clean and shop for him, behave like the daughter she had always failed to be.

Boring, Boring, Boring, said the thing, shoving through Angelina's brain and flicking Patrick's outrage aside, and then: Ah. Here. That Christmas four years ago, when Angelina was twenty-one. It was Riccardo who had driven Jagvi out of her house and into Old Timers. The thing from the pit wanted to see all of it, the bell ringing above the door, the snow falling outside, "Week-end à Rome" on the radio, Angelina looking up from her book and meeting Jagvi's hunted eyes. The way they'd stared at each other.

"My dad locked the liquor cabinet," Jagvi had said. "Can I just get one drink?"

"I mean," Angelina had said. "It's a bar."

Not now! Angelina thought, *I don't want to remember this now!* But the thing oozed forward, seeping deeper into her head, and she could do nothing to beat it back.

What's So Bad About This, Huh? Seems Like You Had A Nice Time Together. Look How Young You Both Were. It's Cute!

Woozy memory, coming in and out of focus. Angelina twenty-one, Jagvi twenty-three. They had seen each other only once or twice in the four years since the party in the city. Nobody else in Cadenze knew the truth about Angelina, and in the intervening years, her secret had soured. She had never planned to be in the closet. It was as though she'd just been living her life, enjoying her private desires, and someone else had knocked up the walls around her. She didn't know how to open the door and exit.

It hurt to look back. Those awful years of evading Patrick's questions, letting Caro believe she was just a late bloomer, offending her cousins when she refused to let them set her up. And then along came Jagvi, who already knew everything, who was impossible to resist. When Jagvi asked, "How's life?" Angelina said, "Well. There's this girl."

"There's this *girl*," Jagvi had responded. Twenty-three. Hair buzzed down to nothing and her arms not as bulky back then, hollows beneath her eyes. And that was how they ended up talking about Daniela Vitanelli, whose name Jagvi didn't recognize until Angelina sighed and confessed, "Demonic Dani.

She was in your year in high school." Jagvi hooted with delight: Demonic Dani had been a high school legend, with a wonky self-administered penta-gram tattoo on her left breast and a homemade altar to the Great Mother Goddess in her locker.

Angelina had been hooking up with her for a few months by then. Dani's whole room smelled of patchouli and stale cigarettes in a way that felt both stomach turning and semi-sexy to Angelina, so that every revolted breath was laced with desire, every orgasm with a roll of nausea. She was the closest Angelina had ever had to a girlfriend, and no one else in Angelina's life even knew that she existed.

Jagvi laughed at Angelina's concern that she wasn't falling in love. She said, "Shit, Angel, you don't have to like a girl to want to fuck her." She told Ange-lina about bad dates that she'd been on, and when Angelina asked if the buzz cut was the hot new lesbian look in San Michele, she said, "No, there's plenty of femmes like you." She turned a coaster over and wrote down a list of things Angelina should try to acquire: a sexy book, a radio show that might broad-cast this far, a dyke magazine that printed classifieds for free. "You could tell lesbians if they come all the way out to Old Timers you'll give them a free drink," Jagvi said. "See if you find someone you like better than Dani."

At midnight Patrick called and said he'd drive down to pick Angelina up. She did not mention Jagvi's presence, but after she put the phone down, she said, "He can give you a lift, too, if you like."

Jagvi looked up and Angelina hung there, in the moment of their eyes meeting.

"That's okay. I was thinking about leaving now, anyway."

"It's snowing pretty hard out there."

"My coat's thick," Jagvi said, and Angelina had known then that they were making a quiet agreement, that neither of them was going to tell Patrick about this evening, and she felt sick and dizzy. Which should have been a familiar combination, but it was nothing like Dani's room at all, nothing like anything she'd known, not least for how shy and happy she felt. She gave Jagvi a shot of whisky for the road. The way they were looking at each other could have been a handshake, for what a covenant it felt like.

And the next night was New Year's.

Angelina's rapid heartbeat must have alerted the thing, because it skid-ded forward through her memories of that night, the party at Old Timers, the bar jammed full with people, Patrick onstage with a borrowed guitar, Angelina pouring out shots and Jagvi's arm resting on the bar, brown palm outstretched, sheen of sweat in the hollow of her throat, the thing's grease pouring over it—

"That's private!" Angelina said. "Stop it!"

We're Getting To The Good Part!

In its haste to consume her memories, the thing had let her tongue slip free, and she stood shivering in the middle of the town square, working her jaw, trying to dislodge it from her brain.

"Stop what?" Jagvi raised an awkward hand. "Should I touch you?"

I Missed This Last Time, the thing said, delighted.

"Leave it alone!" Angelina hissed. And now the memory was here, all around her: that icy New Year's Eve, Angelina stepping out into the snow just before the midnight countdown, Jagvi leaning against the wall on her own, staring up at Big Joe in the dark...

"Angel!"

The thing seized Angelina's mouth back and dragged it into a nasty smile. "All Right," it made her say. "If You're So Desperate."

Jagvi faltered, then narrowed her eyes. "Don't mess me around," she said, and cupped Angelina's cheek.

This time the thing put up a fight. It did not want to leave, and it snarled at Angelina and used both her hands to shove Jagvi, but Jagvi stepped closer, putting her arm around Angelina's shoulders and drawing her into her side. The thing snarled, She Still Doesn't Believe You, Angel! She Thinks You're Crazy! but Jagvi's palms were sweet hot fire, and they burned its presence away, sodden smoke spitting into the wind.

XX

Jagvi held on to her long after the thing in the pit had gone. They made a strange sight, huddled together in the town square. Angelina rested her head on Jagvi's shoulder, and Jagvi stroked the pale skin behind Angelina's ear with her thumb. It was dark and there was no one else around.

"I need to sit down," Angelina said finally. Her head felt scratched through by long claws, and her knees trembled from residual fear or exhaustion.

"Okay." They both looked toward Old Timers, the only business on the square with its lights still on. Angelina was uneasy on her feet, muscles sore and head pounding. She could just see Francesca-Martine through the grimy window, her eyes fixed on the TV, and as she watched, even Francesca-Martine stood and yawned and made her way toward the back office. The town felt abandoned, like Jagvi and Angelina were the last living beings left.

"Let's just sit in the hand." Angelina gestured to the fountain in the middle of the square. Its wide palm beckoned.

"Really?" Jagvi looked skeptical.

"Didn't you and Pat ever come sit in the hand?"

"No," Jagvi said. "I think it only got cool after our time."

"God forbid you ever be uncool," Angelina said, and Jagvi managed to laugh.

"Then lead the way, hepcat." She let go of Angelina. Angelina tensed, but nothing happened, no voice or anger or retribution.

146

Angelina stepped from the rim to her favored spot in the center of the palm, climbing over the still, scummy water to lean back on the middle finger. Jagvi hauled herself up onto the thumb, one knee pulled to her chest and the other foot dangling over the water. After a moment she put her hand on Angelina's outstretched leg, wrapping around her bare shin, and gave Angelina a defiant look like she thought Angelina was going to mock her for it.

Relief rushed through Angelina. "It wasn't me, Jag. You could see it wasn't me."

"Yeah," Jagvi said, but she shook her head. "No. I don't know. That was fucking scary, Angel."

"Do you believe me yet?"

Jagvi stared down into the mulchy fountain water, scattered leaves littering its surface. "I don't know."

The cold stone was turning Angelina's ass numb. The fountain had been in the square for Angelina's whole life, built with rock from the surrounding hillsides. She put her hands on the chiseled groove of the pointer finger. She flexed her fingers and legs, rolled her head on her neck, a checklist of the muscles that were back under her sole control. *Mine, mine, mine.* "Can you talk to me for a minute?"

Jagvi turned back to Angelina with a hunted look.

"It doesn't have to be about the thing," Angelina said. "I can't just sit here in silence, and I'm not ready to walk home."

"Okay." Jagvi rubbed her upper arm with her free hand. "What do you want me to talk about?"

Angelina tried to recall the thread of what Jagvi was saying before, the conversation the thing from the pit had stolen from her. "Tell me what you meant when you said Cadenze is more appealing without your dad. I thought he was the only reason you ever came back."

"Not the only reason." Jagvi swallowed. "I mean, Pat's here. I miss the mountains. The skies are bigger. Different flowers. And it smells different out here. San Michele is so gross in the summer, the whole city reeks of sewage. You're lucky you came in the rainy season. Not that it made much of a difference to you, I guess."

"Not really," Angelina said. Jagvi smiled at her, some notch of tension in her shoulders easing. "What else?"

"I don't know. My dad thought he had me all figured out, and it's fun to pretend I might prove him wrong. It'd be a good way to say *fuck you*. Keep his place and make it my dyke summer house. Bring my friends out here to see where I grew up—I have nicer friends now, Angel."

"I'll believe it when I see it," Angelina said.

"Yeah, well, maybe you will. Or I could bring my own kids out here someday."

"You want kids?"

"Yeah, if I can. Don't you?"

"I don't know," Angelina said. "I don't think about it much."

She fidgeted in her seat, her body so relieved to escape the thing that it wouldn't settle, jiggling her knee, twisting a strand of her hair between two fingers. She could still hear the thing in her head, words it had dropped that sat like sediment at the bottom of a wineglass. It seemed absurd to talk about life ahead of this moment, to imagine future endeavors beyond her monster. She wondered what it felt like to be Jagvi and to see the future like a series of options. So many potential Jagvis, doctors and mothers and scholars. But there were no possible Angelinas, only this one who really existed.

"My dad told me I'm responsible for the death of his family line," Jagvi said. "It was one of the last things he said to me, actually. A great phone call."

"Your dad said a lot of fucked-up shit."

"He was just an angry old man. He had a lot of disappointments."

"He told you you were defective."

Jagvi tilted her head. "You remember that?"

"I remember it because it was such a fucked-up thing to say." It had been while they were alone outside Old Timers, waiting for the New Year's countdown. Jagvi confessing her dad's words like they were her own sins. "You told me he blamed your ma, for raising you wrong."

Jagvi nodded slowly. She skated her thumb through the hairs on Angelina's calf. "You said you thought she'd raised me right." She slanted her eyes at Angelina. "You're always so different from how I remember you."

Angelina couldn't meet her gaze. "I'm always the same."

"No," Jagvi said. "You're the only thing in this town I can't predict."

The thing was gone; it did not speak, it did not touch her, it did not have control. It couldn't rifle through her head, it couldn't call up memories for her to relive, but she felt that New Year's all around her now. The two of them standing in the snow, and the music streaming out of the bar, Angelina's people singing "Fuck the Bastard Year" as ice turned the town silver around them. The fog of their breath mingling and Jagvi staring at Angelina like she'd done something astonishing. Angelina had tilted her chin down, and Jagvi's gaze had dropped to her mouth. Angelina had made a noise, objection or invitation. For the span of a second, she thought something was about to happen. She could almost taste Jagvi's breath. But then Jagvi had said, "Fuck, no," and startled back.

Here was where the thing from the pit would have crowed, bent its face to Angelina's memory to inhale greedily. It liked these moments where Angelina's humiliation met her desire; it liked to laugh at how many years Angelina had spent on guard for Jagvi to shoot through town again, a disastrous comet that spun everything off its axis. But Angelina still felt most miserable about what happened next. Jagvi had pulled back from her and demanded, "When are you going to tell Pat?"

"What?" Angelina had said, still reeling.

"He asked me if I thought it was weird you hadn't had a boyfriend yet," Jagvi had said. "Why are you lying to him? Do you think he's going to react badly? That's unfair—"

"I'm not interested in what *you* think is unfair to Patrick," Angelina snapped. "Why is this any of your business? I don't need a lesbian mentor, and if I did, I would pick someone who actually has their shit together. You came out in the messiest fucking way—"

"I was a kid," Jagvi said, "and you're nearly twenty-two—"

"You can't tell him! It's not up to you."

"That's not what I was saying—"

"Yes it was! You're always trying to keep hold of him, you always keep yourself so fucking invested in his life—"

"He's my friend!" Jagvi yelled. "And actually, Angel, I'd be careful what you're accusing me of. Only one of us has ever outed someone!"

"Who else needs to be outed?" Patrick had said, in a strange, strained voice, coming up from behind them. For a moment, the three of them just stood there. The memory was as clear as a photograph. Angelina's face burning and eyes prickling, Jagvi shocked and defeated, Patrick's anger dawning in slow motion.

Now, cupped in the hand of the fountain, Jagvi said, "Patrick never talked to me about that night."

Angelina blinked, discomforted by how easily Jagvi's thoughts had followed hers. "No? I don't think you missed a lot. We didn't speak to each other for a few months."

It had been a long, miserable winter. Angelina cried herself to sleep, and Patrick went about looking shell-shocked, and they avoided each other at home. Eventually it became clear to Angelina that she had cut Patrick to the quick by excluding him in the same way she had their wider family, by treating him as another potential problem rather than an aide, and Patrick thawed, mumbled that of course it was up to her to tell people as she liked. She did tell people: first Caro, who spent one evening in despair before deciding that she'd known all along; then a handful of cousins, whose responses veered between titillation and skepticism; then Franco, who smoked a cigarette in silence before he clapped Angelina on the shoulder and laughed and said, "Okay, girl." She even invited Dani for dinner with Patrick, an incredibly stilted evening that cemented her decision to break things off. Springtime was awful and shy. But Patrick and Angelina shuffled back toward each other. And it was out, *it* being Angelina or the secret or the revulsion. Some mornings that year she woke up and had to put her head to her knees and pant, feeling something clean swarming through her body.

"I know it was bad." Jagvi looked away. "I'm really sorry."

"You're—what?" Angelina laughed, surprised. "How is *that* one your fault?"

"If we hadn't been out there, that night—"

"He had to find out one way or another," Angelina said. "You didn't know he'd followed us out."

"But I was so angry," Jagvi said. "I think part of me was glad. I was even glad you and Pat were fighting."

"Why?"

It took Jagvi a moment to reply. "I wanted it to be your fault. All the secrets and that weird—whatever it was between us. I liked that you hadn't come out to Pat, I liked having a reason to keep secrets from him, and I felt shitty about it."

Angelina blinked. "So you had some emotions one time?"

"Angel."

"If this is part of you being too shitty a person for this town, I've got some bad news for you," Angelina said. "Those are pretty mild emotions as they go. Sometimes I fantasize about dismembering one of my cousins."

Jagvi's mouth twitched. "Matthew?"

"Obviously. Anyway, it could have been worse. I'd rather Pat caught you accidentally outing me than us—" She stopped.

"Making out?" Jagvi suggested.

Her mouth still had that warm crook of amusement. Angelina needed to look away from it. She had the same feeling she'd had up at Jagvi's house, trading one form of danger for another, as if the thing from the pit kept inadvertently hurtling her headfirst toward Jagvi. She said, "Why didn't you kiss me that night?"

"I thought it would be dangerous."

"But you wanted to."

"Yeah," Jagvi said.

The streetlights flickering on painted Jagvi's face in tawny stripes: her sharp jaw, the soft line of her mouth. Angelina said, "You still want to."

"Yeah. I told you that already."

"Even though you think I'm crazy."

Jagvi shook her head. "I think you're sick. I want to help you."

"Do you have a thing for damsels in distress?"

"No," Jagvi said. "I have a thing for you."

It felt like the slow change of dawn, the night drifting away and the daylight unfolding, and now Angelina could acknowledge what she had begun to know some time ago. Her voice shook. "Are you going to apologize for saying this later, too?"

"No. I've given up trying."

"That was you *trying*?" Angelina said, and they both laughed, weak in the dark. Angelina shifted her weight. The stone had gone warm beneath her.

Jagvi said, "I have to leave eventually."

Angelina nodded. "I know."

"I want to help you and Pat, but you know I can't stay here forever."

"I never expected that," Angelina said. "I'm more realistic than my brother." Jagvi attempted a smile. Angelina's throat was tight. "Jag, it doesn't matter. Even if you did stay..."

Jagvi nodded. "I know."

Angelina said it, anyway. "We couldn't do it to Patrick."

Jagvi kept nodding, very fast, not looking at Angelina, her mouth pressed into a flat line. "I know," she repeated.

"So it's a deal," Angelina said, and laughed, harsh and mirthless.

"Deal," Jagvi said, and put her hand out. There was something so chivalric and stern about it that it made Angelina's stomach dip. She took Jagvi's hand all the same, calluses against her fingers, and they shook.

It felt like a betrayal already. The worst secret Angelina had ever kept from her brother. There was an awful knot in her throat. Vibrations in her chest made her wonder if she was going to weep, right here in front of Jagvi, but she was wrong. It was the fountain.

The pointer finger of the hand moved with a groan, stone grinding against stone. It was as fast as a human muscle but bent like no human joint could, twisting to clamp its thick knuckle around Angelina's waist. It coiled tighter, squeezing her in its grip.

"What the *fuck*," Jagvi said, and lunged forward. She caught Angelina's face between her hands, the warm touch that had banished the thing last time, but it wasn't in Angelina, it was in the stone, the finger around Angelina's waist squeezing so tight that Angelina's stomach tipped and lurched. Jagvi's hands slid firmly down her face, onto her neck, under her sweatshirt to squeeze her shoulder, and achieved nothing. "Why won't it stop!"

"It's not in me, it's—"

There was another screech as the ring finger curled around her, the joints cracking as it folded back over itself at just the right angle to wrap around Angelina's neck.

Jagvi swore in a steady stream now, local curses and some of the lowland dialect that Angelina didn't know as Jagvi grappled with the stone, wrapping her arms around the finger on Angelina's throat and trying to drag it back. The ring finger was less steady than the one on her waist, but it gained strength by the second, clamping against her windpipe, making her gag. Angelina broke her fingernails on the stone as she struggled, kicking her feet and bruising her heels against the palm. In her head was the image of the cars at the wrecking yard near Patrick's garage and the scraps of twisted metal that had gone through the crusher. In her head was the fact that she'd been wrong. The thing wasn't here to hang around her shoulders and talk to her friends, it was going to squeeze all her life out of her like a fist around a rotten orange. The hand was going to pulverize her, and Jagvi gave up wrestling with it and touched her anywhere she could, Angelina's face and her hands and her bare shins and knees, but nothing was working anymore.

Angelina gurgled. Already her vision was blurring and her eyes watered, something warm streaming out of her nose that could have been snot or blood, and then Jagvi caught her by the chin and kissed her.

The world was dark pain and Jagvi's hot mouth on Angelina's and her teeth against Angelina's lip, kissing hard enough to bruise. The little air that Angelina had left rushed into Jagvi's mouth and was swallowed, and Jagvi's tongue was in her mouth, begging for more. The greediest, messiest, most demanding kiss Angelina had ever received, and then the thumb of the fountain reared over them and flicked Jagvi, knocking her off balance so she tumbled into the water.

Angelina heard Jagvi cry out, and a splash. Then another grinding screech that she thought must be the fist closing around her, bracing herself for the final pulpy squeeze, her eyeballs gooey and her throat imploding. Instead the hand opened.

Every finger released, moving languidly back to its original position. It uncurled like a flower and left Angelina gasping for breath in its palm. Jagvi swore in the dark water below, and Angelina lay deposited on her back, her feet dangling off the edge, held up like an offering.

XXI

"I believe you," Jagvi said, stumbling and wading through the fountain's fetid water to grab Angelina, panting in the stone hand. "I believe you, I believe you, fuck. Fuck!"

Angelina kept heaving, trying to suck in a full breath. Her thoughts ran messily across different train tracks. Her throat hurt, her mouth buzzed, and the thing from the pit had finally tried to kill her. She shook her head, ears ringing.

The only sound she could hear clearly was Jagvi, climbing up onto the palm and repeating, "I believe you. I believe you," like they were the only words left to her.

Angelina coughed and gagged, hacking up a mouthful of phlegm. She wiped her streaming nose. Jagvi touched her neck, her chin, turning her gently from side to side and inspecting the tender bruises on her throat, but Angelina didn't want that kind of touch. She knew the kind of touch that saved her. She lurched forward and tucked her face against Jagvi's neck, and Jagvi wrapped her arms around Angelina and held her tight.

"I'm so sorry," Jagvi said, bewildered. "I believe you. It's real."

"Okay," Angelina croaked, her voice shredded. "That's good."

Jagvi laughed. It sounded watery. "Angel." Her T-shirt left damp patches on Angelina, cool against her burning skin.

"I wanna go home," Angelina said.

"Yeah," Jagvi said, and slipped out of Angelina's hands. She never quite let go, her palm cool against Angelina's forearm, her knuckles tapping Angelina's knee. Off the fountain she opened her arms, and Angelina stared at her, disbelieving for a moment, and then crawled straight into them. She hooked her elbows around Jagvi's shoulders, legs up around Jagvi's waist. Jagvi adjusted her weight and hoisted her up, and then she climbed out of the grimy water and started up the hill toward home, Angelina shivering in her sturdy hold.

"It's gone?" Jagvi asked as they climbed. Her shirt clung damp and hot between their two bodies. "It's definitely gone?"

"Yeah," Angelina said. "Ah, fuck. Jag, my teeth won't stop chattering—"

"Adrenaline," Jagvi told her. "You're okay, Angel, I've got you. And you're sure it's gone?"

"It's not speaking, it's not touching me—maybe you beat it," Angelina said, snorting and laughing, with a hitch that meant she was worryingly close to tears. It felt like fairy-tale logic: a kiss to banish a monster. Was that what had saved her? She clung tighter. Angelina wasn't light, but Jagvi carried her with a quick step through Cadenze's empty town square and up toward home.

"I can't believe it," Jagvi said, and laughed, harsh and cracked down the middle. "This fucking town." Angelina's fingers knotted in Jagvi's wet hair; if she lifted her face, she could rest her cheek against Jagvi's, feel Jagvi's warm breath as she spoke. "I'm so fucking sorry, I know you're not a liar and I know this town is crazy, didn't get education or progress or fucking electricity until half a century after everyone else, I bet the Inquisition never bothered coming through either—"

She was panting, taking tottering steps as they went up the hill. "You can't carry me all the way up," Angelina rasped. "Put me down. I'm okay, it's just the shock."

"I'm not gonna let go of you," Jagvi said. "Why does that *work*?"

Angelina flushed. "You can hold my hand."

"Hm," Jagvi said, and then she set Angelina down on one of the short stone walls that bordered the outskirts of town and turned, presenting Angelina with her back. Angelina hesitated. She looked down at Jagvi's dark head, the ends of her hair curling as they dried, the sharp point at the apex of her spine. Something cracked inside her, deep and sweet where even the thing couldn't reach. She climbed onto Jagvi's back.

Jagvi walked steadier now, arms looped around Angelina's knees, Angelina's wrists knocking against Jagvi's collarbone, her thighs squeezed around Jagvi's hips, with the first blinks of stars above them. Angelina tried to work out what time it was and whether Patrick would be home yet. The sun set earlier and earlier.

"How do you know it's gone?" Jagvi demanded. "How do you know when it's here? What does it feel like? Does it really talk to you?"

Angelina felt a little better, and laughed. "Yeah. Now you believe me, you're gonna scientifically categorize it?"

"I'm gonna kill it," Jagvi said.

The determination in her voice made Angelina's throat close up again. She clung to the pillar of Jagvi's back. Her lips still stung from Jagvi's kiss. When she could speak, she said, "I hope Patrick's home."

"We'll tell him," Jagvi said. "Don't worry, I'll explain, I *saw* it—"

"Yeah, Jag, but I hope he's already home when we get there. Because we just made a deal."

Her breath came sharp and fast. Her wrists hung at Jagvi's chest, and she could feel Jagvi's pulse pick up. "Angel."

"I'm just saying." Angelina couldn't stop trembling. She squeezed her knees around Jagvi's hips and had to bite back the noise that wanted to climb out of her throat. "It'll be easier to stick to the deal if he's already there. So I hope he's home."

Jagvi twisted her head, trying to look Angelina in the face. Her fingers dug into Angelina's thighs. "Me, too."

Angelina nodded. She laid her cheek against Jagvi's hair, felt the bunch of Jagvi's muscles under her as Jagvi took steady strides up the mountain. "I really, really hope he's home, Jag, 'cause—the deal sucks."

"I know, Angel," Jagvi said. "I hope so, too."

The air hung cool and fresh around them. Angelina wanted Patrick's truck to come rumbling past them. She wanted the pain in her neck and her chest not to be something spurring her on. She wanted Jagvi to tire or stumble, wanted to slow down, wanted to meet a barricade or beast in the road.

They climbed up the mountain untroubled. At Angelina's house there were only the tire tracks Patrick had left as he drove away this morning. Jagvi set Angelina gently on the ground. Her fingers curled around the back of Angelina's neck.

XXII

The house had the settled air of vacancy. Angelina called her brother's name anyway, her voice bouncing off the walls, making the dust stir in its place. My Dog came to greet them in the hallway, inspecting Jagvi's soaked boots when she kicked them off before carrying one of them away in her teeth, her wagging tail the only movement in the house. Jagvi's fingers were so light under the curtain of Angelina's hair they might not have been there, hidden from view. Plausible deniability. Angelina could feel every minute shift of a callus.

"What if the thing's here?" Jagvi asked. "What if it beat us back?"

Angelina shook her head. She didn't think that the thing from the pit could hide in emptiness; it occupied it. There was no presence here. Angelina felt sure of it. Her new theory had taken root, unreliable yet persistent. Maybe it really had worked. Maybe the fairy-tale logic was right, and Jagvi's kiss had broken the spell. It could have killed her in the fountain, and it didn't. She caught the edge of her lip between her teeth. It felt tender, just touched.

Jagvi's eyes were on her, insistently waiting for an answer, her body rigid like she wanted Angelina's permission to stand at ease. Angelina coughed, her throat seizing with the movement. "I think it'll be gone for a while again now. It told me that it gets tired. And it must be harder to possess stone than me, right?"

"Maybe," Jagvi said. "So if I stop touching you, it won't get you?"

"Not right now," Angelina said. Jagvi hesitated, then let her hand drop

159

back to her side. Angelina shrugged her shoulders, entirely herself. She smiled a little foolishly. She didn't know where to look. "Just me."

Jagvi's gaze dragged over her, inch by inch, then jerked back up to her face. "Seems like it."

Angelina swallowed. She stood teetering on the edge of something, the cliff top above the waiting, starving space. The snakes writhing beneath their trapdoor. If Angelina wobbled even a little, she'd be falling. "Maybe I'll check if Patrick's upstairs."

There was a flash of Jagvi's old condescension. "Okay, Angel."

Angelina started up the stairs. The back of her neck prickled.

Behind her, Jagvi said, "Angel."

Angelina turned. Jagvi stood on the step below her, her shoulders relaxed. She caught Angelina's T-shirt in her hand and drew her down, slow enough to allow Angelina's heart to accelerate. Angelina let out a shivering breath and waited for Jagvi to stop, just another moment in a series of moments they'd ignore for the rest of their lives, and Jagvi tilted her head to the side.

She looked so serious, so careful. Her eyes were so dark Angelina couldn't see the pupils. She pulled Angelina down to her and hesitated another second there. Cautious before she made a move that couldn't be walked back, especially not with Angelina breathless before her, giving up all thought and decision, forcing Jagvi to make the bad call for both of them. Jagvi kissed her anyway.

Angelina's lips parted; her knees went weak. Already stooping into the kiss, she wanted to fold completely, drape herself against Jagvi and let Jagvi decide what to do with her, but the fist in her T-shirt tightened, holding her upright. Jagvi nudged her up the stairs. The hot slide of Jagvi's tongue, the nip of her teeth.

"Jag," Angelina mumbled, all her adrenaline leaping eagerly for something better than fear: relief, and the heat coiling through her. "Jagvi. I'm really glad you believe me."

"Fuck," Jagvi said, and kissed her harder, like Angelina had something of hers and she wanted it back.

* * *

In Angelina's bedroom, Jagvi said, "Take your shirt off."

Angelina stumbled over a laugh. "C'mon, man."

Jagvi raised her eyebrows impatiently. It felt like a warning.

Angelina's laughter died in her throat. She stood beside her bed. After a moment, Angelina pulled her sweatshirt off and over her head, let it drop on the floor. Jagvi made an impatient gesture, and Angelina yanked her T-shirt off, too, stood there flushing and unsure in her bra and bike shorts. Her body felt stripped raw, and she knew what had happened at the fountain amounted to a near-death experience, but she wasn't dead. She was with Jagvi, who had kissed her and saved her and carried her home, and now they stood alone in her room, and right now she would do anything that Jagvi asked.

Jagvi looked fascinated, hot-eyed, like Angelina was something she'd never seen before. "Shorts, too," she said.

"Jesus," Angelina managed, and shoved the bike shorts down, hopping out from the tangle around her ankles, trying not to think about it too much. Goose bumps kept sweeping across her skin.

"Cute," Jagvi said, lips parted as she took in Angelina's plain black cotton underwear, and the curve of her belly, her eyes catching on a purple stripe of bruises already forming along Angelina's abdomen, where the fountain had gripped her. Angelina stood trembling under Jagvi's inspection. When Jagvi's gaze fell to Angelina's hips, Angelina put an unsteady hand on the waistband of her underwear, touching the fabric like a question.

"I'll take care of that," Jagvi said.

Angelina nodded dumbly. Jagvi was close now, close enough to touch.

"You're sure it's gone?"

Angelina nodded. Jagvi's heat rolled off her, the smell of clean sweat and dirty water. Angelina's mouth filled with saliva.

"Okay," Jagvi said, and caught Angelina's hips in her palms, making Angelina gasp at the solidity of her hold. Her fingers curled over Angelina's hip bones, skimmed under the hem of her underwear. Heat pulsed in Angelina's stomach and her pussy ached, clenching nothing. "It couldn't get in you now, huh?"

"No."

"Why?"

"Because," Angelina said, her voice a low scrape. "You're touching me."

Jagvi nodded. She ran one big palm up over Angelina's hip, her stomach. Her fingertips brushed the bruises already forming. Beneath her easy calm, her eyes were dark and furious. The muscles in Angelina's stomach jumped to meet the calluses on Jagvi's fingers. "You can lose the bra."

Angelina reached up behind herself and unhooked her bra, let it fall to the ground. Jagvi's mouth opened.

"Uh," Jagvi said, and then Angelina's nipple was between her teeth, and Angelina was crying out, arching forward. Jagvi's palm folded flat over Angelina's pussy, a hard press holding her through her underwear.

"*Hurts*," Angelina said, and Jagvi made a helpless sound and bit harder. When she tongued over Angelina's nipple, the soft touch was almost worse than the pain.

"You're soaked through," Jagvi ground out, like she hadn't been ready for it, and Angelina couldn't stand it anymore, couldn't be good. She wrapped her arms around Jagvi and dragged her down, toppling them both back onto the bed. Somewhere in the fall they started kissing, and then Angelina lay flat under Jagvi's weight, clutching Jagvi's shoulders while Jagvi kissed her bruising and brainless.

It felt like a wave, like some big animal pressing her into the long grass, like giving her body up again. Jagvi was still mostly dressed, rough denim against Angelina's legs, belt buckle knocking against her poor bruised stomach, and Angelina couldn't stop wriggling beneath her, arching her hips up, trying for something, anything. She knew this was shameless, knew it was a bad idea. But she had spent most of the night with a monster who wanted her dead, and so Angelina gave in to the luxury of having very little left to lose.

"I won't let it touch you," Jagvi said, "don't want it anywhere, not your leg—" Her hand wrapped around Angelina's inner thigh, pulling it up, stretching the skin so that Angelina felt like she was already being opened for Jagvi, crying out. "Or your ear"—teeth scraping against Angelina's earlobe, making her laugh and yelp. "And definitely, definitely not in your head, that's, Angel, I don't want it there, not ever—"

"You're the only thing in my head," Angelina said. "Please, Jag, please, please touch me—"

"I am touching you," Jagvi said, satisfied. She evaded Angelina's anxious grip, kneeling between Angelina's ankles and flipping her over, her hand knotted in Angelina's hair. Jagvi was sure of herself and relentless, pulling Angelina neatly up onto her knees, knocking Angelina's thighs apart, reaching around to cup Angelina's tits, squeezing them together. Angelina grabbed fistfuls of the sheet, and Jagvi drifted easily down, mouth against Angelina's spine, then biting her hip, then sliding her underwear down.

"Jag," Angelina said, the only word left to her. She could feel Jagvi's smile against her hip, and then Jagvi's fingers slid hot inside her, knuckle-deep, curling up and out and in again.

Angelina made feral, incoherent sounds against the pillow as Jagvi fucked her, those square fingers lighting Angelina up. And then her thumb slid over Angelina's clit and Angelina yowled and arched, flinging her head back against Jagvi's shoulder, Jagvi crouched over her now and holding her steady. It felt like Jagvi was everywhere.

"You're sweet," Jagvi said, with a vicious twist of her fingers that forced out a ragged moan. "Someone should have fucked you properly before now."

"No," Angelina managed, "no, no, no, only you, please," and Jagvi made a rough noise and turned Angelina back over, settling between her thighs, fingers deep inside and thumb sliding sure and rhythmic over her clit, and tongue licking into Angelina's mouth. Angelina's whole body seized with an animal instinct to get closer, yanking off Jagvi's shirt so they both ended up tangled up in the collar because Jagvi wouldn't stop kissing her, frantically pulling at Jagvi's belt buckle and getting it open just before Jagvi made Angelina come, spasming and surprised, clenching hard around Jagvi.

Jagvi's voice was anxious and uneven as she ground down against Angelina's thigh, *uh-uh-uh*, Angelina's hands sliding over her, shocked and thrilled by each new inch of skin. "Kiss," Angelina demanded, "kiss," but instead of complying, Jagvi grinned at her and shifted down the bed.

Angelina said something garbled that ended in a strangled squeak as Jagvi licked over her, a few hungry swipes of her tongue, and then her mouth fixed over Angelina's clit. Angelina couldn't hold it together, her panting loud and harsh in the small room. When Jagvi's fingers beckoned inside her, Angelina came again, begging and jerking against Jagvi's mouth, sweating and shivering at once, breath catching in ragged hiccups until Jagvi took pity on her and let her have a break. She sat up and Angelina crawled into her lap, clinging to her shoulders, pressing her face to Jagvi's throat.

Jagvi laughed low and warm in her ear. "You're so sensitive."

"You're fucking unstoppable," Angelina said, slurring a little. "I didn't even get to see your tits, you're so rude." She twisted in Jagvi's lap, clumsily pushing Jagvi's sports bra up, dark nipples and pointy breasts that made Angelina groan, lowering her mouth to taste, and then the truck rumbled into the drive and My Dog started barking her welcome.

Angelina froze.

"Fuck!" Jagvi said, and yanked her bra back down, scrambling for their discarded clothes. "Shit, okay, here"—and she tried to help Angelina back into her underwear and put her own T-shirt on at the same time.

"I can't," Angelina said. Her mouth was stinging, she felt sticky all over; she couldn't imagine what she looked like. "I can't see him right now."

Jagvi cursed, then said, "Stay here." Her face drew tight with misery. "Shit. Stay here. I'll tell him—"

Panic lurched in Angelina's chest. Guilt hovered above her, heavy and ready to descend, but there were more urgent matters at hand. "No! Don't tell him, are you fucking crazy—"

"About the *fountain*," Jagvi said. "I'll say you're resting. I won't mention the—the kiss. Angel. Angel, you have to call me if it comes back, if you sense it, even the slightest thing," and she leaned down to Angelina's mouth, kissing her messily, hungrily, making Angelina's chest tighter. Wet on her thighs, misery in her heart, Angelina was all full up of Jagvi, and she tried to push her away but couldn't coax her fingers to let go.

"It's gone," Angelina said, trying to be reassuring. "You chased it off. It's tired. It won't come back that fast."

The front door opened. "Jag?" Patrick called from downstairs. "Nini? You guys here?"

Jagvi jumped up, buckling her belt. She swiped her hand through her hair and went to the window, cracking it open; Angelina went hot all over again, wondering what it smelled like in here. Sex. Her. Jagvi drew in a breath of fresh air and turned around. It was strange, watching the wall go up, the way she lifted her chin and looked in control again.

"We can't do this again," Jagvi said.

Angelina nodded. "I know."

"We can't ever do it again." Jagvi leaned over the bed, fingers on Angelina's jaw, tilting her up to her mouth, a deep and hungry kiss. "You're so good. Angel. You're perfect. Fuck. We can't ever do it again."

"I know," Angelina said, and shoved Jagvi away, and listened to her jog down the stairs.

The conversation after that was hushed. Angelina could only pick out Patrick's tense, worried tone, Jagvi's voice soothing in response.

Angelina curled up under her blanket. She felt wrung out and well used, her neck sore, her mouth swollen, her sides aching, her cunt hot and tight. She could feel a bite mark throbbing on her chest. Her room was all shadows, the hulking old furniture leaning closer, the moonlight cast across Angelina's ancient poster of Gabrysia Milanowski with her glittering belly button piercing. It became harder and harder to keep her eyes open.

But Angelina did feel safer. Jagvi believed her. Jagvi had held her down and touched her so the thing couldn't get near. There was no way the thing could take her when Jagvi had staked such a definitive claim. Angelina drifted into sleep thinking about Jagvi's mouth on her, Jagvi's fingers inside her, Jagvi's wide palms skating over every inch of her skin. The thing from the pit could have been a dream, crouched beside her, lapping hungrily at everything Jagvi had done, everything Angelina still wanted her to do.

XXIII

Patrick drove Angelina to work the next morning. Outside the call center he said, "So I'll come pick you up this evening and we'll go to Franco's. You're not frightened, are you?"

Angelina shook her head. "It took a whole week to come back after last time. And we need the money."

"Yeah," Patrick said, grimacing. "Just don't second-guess yourself, okay? If you notice anything, call us."

He leaned forward to adjust the scarf Angelina had wrapped around her throat to cover the bruises from the fountain's stony grip. His hands smelled of tobacco and touched her with tentative care. The bruises were worse this morning, red and purple down to her collar, and she had to eat breakfast in tiny bites to avoid the pain in her throat.

Angelina frowned. "Are *you* frightened?"

"No," Patrick said immediately, and then made a face at her. "No. It was just weird to see Jagvi so freaked out this morning."

Angelina's tongue felt too big for her mouth. This morning she'd come downstairs and announced she was going to work, enough was enough, and Jagvi's head popped up over the back of the sofa. "It *just* tried to kill you," she had said, already wound tight with anxiety despite being bleary-eyed and barely awake. While Patrick and Angelina debated the pros and cons of returning to the call center, Jagvi paced back and forth in the kitchen and laughed harshly when Angelina posited her theory again, that Jagvi had

166

scared it off. Her shoulders coiled tight, her eyes dark. When she looked at Angelina, it was with a sort of bewildered fury.

"I guess it's only just sinking in for her," Angelina said carefully. Jagvi had touched her only once, a hard grip around the wrist when Patrick left the room. *Please don't go*, she'd said, and Angelina had replied, *You want me to stay here with you instead?* and Jagvi flinched away from her. "Now that she finally believes us."

"Yeah," Patrick said, but he was still frowning. "Well. Okay. Have a good day. Jag's gonna be at her dad's place later, remember—"

Angelina patted her pocket. "I have the number." Jagvi had scrawled it on a scrap of paper, leaning over their kitchen counter, while Angelina forced herself to look away from the line of Jagvi's back, the way her fingers curved around the pen. Those fingers had been inside Angelina. Angelina wanted to be on her knees, take them in her mouth. The rough pad of Jagvi's thumb against her teeth. "I'll call if anything happens. First her, then you."

"Good kid," Patrick said. Angelina flipped him off and he grinned at her. "Okay. I'll pick you up at six, and we'll figure out a plan with the others." He leaned over her to pop open her door, and stayed leaning over to call, "Hey, Marcella, take care of my sister, okay? She's still feeling delicate!"

Marcella, who worked in the cubicle next to Angelina, walked past nodding and blushing.

"She has such a crush on you," Angelina observed. "You want to get in there?"

"Stay unpossessed for a whole week and then you can fix me up," Patrick said.

Whoever had worked in Angelina's cubicle before her had scratched a long list of curse words into the desk. Angelina had never been able to discern whether the neat column of profanity was an expression of their own frustration or a record of everything they'd been called by irate callers: cunt, motherfucker, whore, bastard (which appeared twice), stupid bastard (only once), and a whole variation of bitches—ugly bitch, fat bitch, stupid bitch, cuntbitch. For a while Angelina had notched a check next to each curse as it landed in her own ears, but she'd grown bored of this several years ago and would probably have carved her desk to matchsticks if she'd kept it up any longer.

Today she made the calls on autopilot, reading from the script and often missing the moment when her subject hung up. Her attention flickered between the memory of the stone hand crushing her to the memory of Jagvi's hands, on her, inside her. Halfway through every mind-numbing survey, she wanted to say, Hey, do you know what happened to me last night? She wanted to tell them about that stone clamp closing around her waist with Jagvi desperate and afraid by her side; wanted to add to that Jagvi's tongue stroking into her mouth.

She twitched through a morning of calls and hated every person she spoke to for not being Jagvi. After lunch, when she hit dial on the next number and was greeted with Jagvi's brisk "Yeah, hello?" it took a moment to sink in.

"Good afternoon, my name is Angelina, and I'm calling on behalf of your elected representatives to ask you—" She stopped, startled, and said, "Jag?"

"Angel?" Jagvi said.

"Jagvi," Angelina repeated, and turned to shoot her supervisor such a winning, radiant smile that he walked into a wall.

Angelina had worked here for two years, and the closest she'd come to dialing someone she knew was the owner of a head shop in Myrna who called her a fascist instrument of government surveillance. Mostly she got people living in distant provinces beyond the mountains. There were no odds that allowed for this. And yet here was Jagvi's voice.

"I thought you were working?"

"I am."

Jagvi sounded panicked. "Has something happened? Are you okay?"

"I'm A-OK, daddy-o," Angelina said. "You're the next number on my list. It's a random dialer."

"That's ridiculous," Jagvi said, and started laughing, like she understood the wildness of the coincidence as instinctively and happily as Angelina.

"Dumb luck," Angelina said. "My favorite kind."

"So this must mean you have questions for me."

"Yeah," Angelina said, and spun in her chair, the headset cord twisting around her elbows and chest. "Are you at my place right now or your dad's?"

"Yours."

"Hmm," Angelina said, and pictured Jagvi leaning against that familiar wall in her T-shirt and basketball shorts. Pinching the cord of the landline between her finger and thumb, pulling it tight and letting it bounce back. "How can I be sure of that? What if you're in a high-tech lab and you've hacked my call?"

"Hacked it," Jagvi echoed.

"Sure."

"Well, I'm looking at one of your bras."

"Maybe that's just the decor in your underground hacker lair."

"It's fallen off the washing line," Jagvi said, "and My Dog has been chewing it—"

"Your Dog," Angelina corrected.

"Hang on," Jagvi said, "I thought My Dog was *your* dog—"

"I know you're just doing this to annoy me," Angelina said, and Jagvi laughed again. Heat crawled down Angelina's spine.

"What would you prefer I do?" Jagvi said lazily. "I'm very open to your suggestions."

Angelina squeezed her thighs together. "This call may be recorded for quality and training purposes." She cast a quick glance around, but her neighbors were all reading their scripts with glazed eyes. "We have a deal, Jag. Remember?"

"Only vaguely," Jagvi said. "Will you tell me one thing? I bet you will, you love telling me things."

"I don't know," Angelina said, "you're being extremely inappropriate, harassing me in my place of work—"

"I think you seem like a lap girl," Jagvi said. "Am I right?"

Angelina's breath came out in a rush. "What?"

"I think you'd fit nicely," Jagvi said. "I'd put you in my lap and get you settled right where I want you and then turn your head off."

"Shut up," Angelina said. She wanted to put her tongue out and pant. "We agreed we can't do it again—"

"Are you saying you don't want that? Don't you enjoy it when I take Control?"

"Jag, it's not fair—"

"Well, you shouldn't have Left Me behind."

There was an edge of annoyance to Jagvi's voice, like she was genuinely piqued, enough to make Angelina protest, "I have to work."

"Your work Bores Me," Jagvi said.

The fear started like a prickle in her feet, so soft and easy that Angelina could pretend her leg had fallen asleep and she just needed to stomp it back to life. "Not funny."

"No? I thought It was a little Funny." There was quiet on the other end of the line. Angelina noticed for the first time that she could not hear Jagvi breathing. "You're Not Jealous, Are You? You're Still My Favorite."

Angelina's voice hunched in her throat, waiting for safety.

"Others Are Appealing In Their Own Way. This Body Is Fun. But You Always Do Exactly What I Want."

Angelina cleared her throat. She managed to say, "Are you hurting her?"

"I Don't Know." The voice was both curious and unconcerned.

"What do you want?"

"Lots Of Things," the thing said. She could still hear the smile in Jagvi's voice.

"Don't hurt her," Angelina said.

"It's A Nice Body. I See Why You Like It So Much."

"Please. Let her go."

"No," Jagvi's voice said, so close to the real thing except for that thin whine hovering underneath every word, the drone of a wasp, or a falling missile. "I Think I'll Keep It. Besides, I've Thought Of A Good Joke. See Ya Soon, Angel."

Angelina yanked her headset off and tossed it aside before she could hear the line going dead or any other awful noise that might be waiting for her. She shoulder slammed a flabbergasted Marcella on her way out, and when she tried to shout an explanation, only gurgling sounds came from her throat, garbled syllables in a high-strung note of tension. She'd been wrong about the kiss, wrong about the fairy tale. None of them were safe.

She couldn't stand to think of Jagvi's easy walk hijacked by the thing from the pit. She felt sick at the idea of something living behind Jagvi's high, handsome features; something else picking up her hands and jerking them about like a marionette; something taking Jagvi's big, generous mouth and speaking with it; something trying out her shoulders and forearms and hips. Angelina would sail straight into its stinking maw and wrap her arms around Jagvi's neck and drag Jagvi back to herself and back to Angelina. She ran alone toward the mountain.

On an evening when she dawdled and stopped to talk to people and smoke a joint while the sun went down over Big Joe, it took Angelina fifty minutes to get home. On a bitter winter afternoon when she slipped over snow and ice and every step was, by necessity, full of trepidation, maybe thirty. Today she made it in fifteen, her breath rattling at her chest, her heart pounding until she skidded through the front door howling Jagvi's name.

The house was quiet and still. Just the low hum of the fridge, a cricket trapped behind a mesh window, and the wild sounds Angelina made as she gulped for air. She yelled Jagvi's name again, and again. Then Jagvi called, "Here! I'm Here!"

Angelina tore up the stairs and pushed into each empty room. Their stained bathroom, Patrick's unmade bed, Angelina's cluttered cupboards. Angelina checked in closets and under piles of clothes and in the bathroom cabinet, as though Jagvi would come tumbling out of each improbable place. She heard Jagvi's voice calling mournfully back to her.

"Jag," she panted, eyes prickling, "come on—"

"Out Here! I'm Outside!"

Angelina tumbled downstairs and into the backyard, which was empty except for My Dog, who had escaped her tether and wandered over cheerfully to say hello. Angelina sank to her knees. She was so frightened she was nearly crying, breath hitching, sweat gathering in the hollows of her neck and her elbows.

My Dog, oblivious, snuffled closer to lick it up. Angelina hugged an arm around My Dog's neck. Every breath she took wobbled all over the place. She leaned in closer to her dog, nuzzling into her fur, and wondered if Jagvi was dead. My Dog caught one of Angelina's nostrils with her big flat tongue.

"Hey, baby," she mumbled, scratching My Dog's ears, "hi."

"Hi," My Dog said in Jagvi's voice. "Told You I Had A Good Joke."

XXIV

My Dog sat panting in front of Angelina. Angelina kept trying to catch the ventriloquist's trick, the moment when Jagvi or even the thing revealed itself to be waiting on the sidelines and not here, inside her dog.

"Take Your Time," My Dog said. Her mouth didn't know how to shape the human words; it flapped and pouted, gray lips and pointy canines gleaming through. Yet each sentence drifted free, neat and easy into the clear air, as though it came from somewhere much deeper than her muzzle. Her throat. The depths of her belly and bowels. Jagvi's voice seeped out of the animal while the chill of oncoming evening shrank tight around Angelina, boxing her into her body.

"Are you hurting My Dog?" she managed. "Hurting me isn't enough?"

"I Didn't Hurt You," My Dog said, and her tongue lolled out in that hopeless doggy grin. Were her eyes darker than normal? Or was it just that Angelina could see the rooms opening up behind them, something cavernous settling into her dog's skull, and a shadow flitting from doorway to doorway, out of sight. "Not Much."

It was hideous, and also hilarious: My Dog talking in Jagvi's slow, easy voice, especially after Angelina had been so frightened. Instead My Dog was like a chatty companion from a children's show, and Angelina started laughing, flattening her palms against her thighs and cracking up at the sheer, ridiculous absurdity, howling so that she didn't cry, wiping tears of mirth from her cheeks so she didn't vomit from the wrongness of it all.

My Dog laughed along. Jagvi's laugh. My Dog lifted her long face and didn't howl or bark excitedly or leap in circles around Angelina as usual; instead she stayed neatly upright and laughed. She sounded somehow polite. The shock got worse and worse as the thing kept her company, My Dog's eyes trained on her with something awake behind them.

"Stop," Angelina said, still hitching over her own hysterical laughter, "stop—"

"Okay, Angel," My Dog said, and the laughter switched off like a radio. Birds cried close by.

"You said," Angelina said, "you said you got tired after, how are you back already?"

"You Fed Me So Well."

Angelina shuddered. "What do you *want*?"

My Dog leaned forward and licked her, a broad swipe of tongue that left a sticky trail up Angelina's cheek. Revulsion ran down her spine, but she couldn't bring herself to shove My Dog away. She felt like she was pulling a daisy apart petal by petal: My Dog, not My Dog.

"What Do *You* Want, Angel?" My Dog said, in the same low, flirtatious voice the thing had used to speak as Jagvi on the phone, only now that Angelina had noticed the whining undertone of the thing, she couldn't stop. She staggered to her feet.

"I want to call Jagvi," she said, "and make sure that she's okay."

"Let's Call Jagvi!" My Dog agreed, bounding in circles around Angelina's feet, her tail wagging.

Angelina had a sinking feeling that she'd run straight into a trap, the thing from the pit baiting her with the exact fear that would ensure she didn't approach with caution, didn't call Patrick, didn't stop to think. It was dangerous and humiliating, how much she'd lost her head over Jagvi. But it also wasn't a good idea to sit here and talk with this thing alone.

The phone rang just long enough that Angelina thought Jagvi might not be there before the line clicked. "Hello?"

"Hi," she said in one gulped syllable of relief.

"Angel," Jagvi said, and she didn't sound like she was smiling, she didn't

sound flirty, she sounded as though every molecule in her body were straining toward Angelina, and she was angry about it. The Jagvi feeling. Angelina
didn't know how the thing had tricked her. "What's wrong?"

"I'm okay, it's not in me, I'm—I'm home now." Part of Angelina was frightened to warn Jagvi explicitly, with My Dog leaning against her legs, panting
attentively up at her. She hated how good the thing was at being My Dog,
how naturally My Dog lolled at Angelina's feet. Her hand flexed around the
receiver.

"Are you alone?" Jagvi asked.

"No," Angelina said.

"I'm coming," Jagvi said, and hung up.

"I'm Excited To See Jagvi," My Dog said.

Fear and nausea churned in Angelina's stomach. "She'll get rid of you."

My Dog ignored her. "Things Happen Around Her." Its voice was shifting
and changing, like a radio dial screwed fast one way and then another, setting Angelina's teeth on edge; now Jagvi's voice, now something more like
Angelina's, now a rough undercurrent of a growl. "She Makes Things Happen. She's A Very Interesting Person."

What had Angelina done? The dog's tail thumped happily on the floorboards. To what fate had she lured Jagvi? She dialed again, fingers clumsy
on the phone, but this time the line just rang and rang and Angelina could
imagine it too clearly, the empty house and Jagvi already barreling down
the mountain. My Dog's shadow grew denser, her furry head etched more
sharply against the surrounding air, like menace made her more vivid, too
real for the world. Angelina couldn't look away. My Dog stared back at her,
mouth open in a goofy doggy grin.

But when the door banged open, Jagvi didn't even glance at the dog. She
stormed across the floor and grabbed Angelina by the back of her neck with a
big square palm, hauling her into Jagvi's body. Angelina made fists in Jagvi's
T-shirt, dark green today and slightly damp with sweat. She dropped her
cheek against Jagvi's hair and let out the frightened moan she'd held back on
the phone. Jagvi's hands were inside her T-shirt, squeezing her belly, making
her squeak. Shaking Angelina back into herself and sending her wild and

out of her head at the same time, so it took her a second to work out what Jagvi was doing and another to stutter—

"No, Jag, it's not in me—" And Jagvi didn't stop touching her, but she did go still, hands cupping Angelina's hips.

"It's Me," My Dog said in Angelina's voice. "But I'll Moan Like Angel If That Gets Your Attention." Angelina felt Jagvi's grip flex and tighten around her. She lifted her head in time to see Jagvi's face knocked blank with shock for a moment before her lip curled, revulsion spreading like ripples on a pond.

It was only a moment, and then she took control of the situation with vexing practicality. She grabbed My Dog by the scruff of her neck and, when My Dog yelped and squirmed, she wrestled the dog down, arms around My Dog's chest, between her front legs, huddled in close like she was play fighting except for the grim expression on her face. Her hands carded through fur, trying to reach My Dog's skin underneath and set her free.

"Careful," Angelina said, voice cracking, kneeling beside them. She wondered if she had the strength to haul Jagvi—or the dog—away if she needed. "It tricked me, I think it wants us here."

My Dog jerked and wriggled, voice ratcheting all over the spectrum now, a small child giggling, the high-pitched grunting squeals of a pig, howling curses in Angelina's voice and then Patrick's. For all the cacophony, the thing seemed to be having a good time. My Dog turned that lolling grin up at Angelina each time she wriggled out of Jagvi's grip, and no amount of Jagvi scratching at the furry back or clamping her hands around the long snout did anything to force the thing out.

"We Can Keep Cuddling If You Want, But You Don't Want Me Out Of The Dog. You Don't Care."

Jagvi pulled back, giving Angelina an incredulous look. Angelina said, "Wanna bet?"

"She Doesn't," My Dog said. "She Cares When It's You. She Doesn't Want To Fuck The Dog."

"Jesus," Jagvi said. Both of them stared at My Dog, Jagvi's hands half raised like she still wanted to grab for it.

"It's An Annoying Trick," My Dog told Angelina. "It's Hard To Get Under Your Skin When She's Fighting Me For Space."

Jagvi's shoulder moved against Angelina's, like maybe she had flinched, but her face was smooth and unconcerned, glittering condescension in her dark eyes. Angelina looked from Jagvi to the dog, baffled. "That's how she gets rid of you? And that's why you had to go in the fountain instead?"

"I Always Find A Way Around Things," the thing from the pit said, and it laughed. That horrible wheezing sound of rocks scraping over dead earth, rodents squealing as they fled. "Any Other Questions? We Have A Little Time."

"Time before what?" Angelina said.

The thing didn't answer.

Angelina narrowed her eyes. "Let's go, Jag. It can spew its mysterious bullshit to the door..."

"And Leave Poor Doggy Alone? When She's So Scared Already?"

Angelina recoiled, but Jagvi put her hand on Angelina's knee, squeezed once. "Don't listen to it. It's not reliable. It's pathetic."

My Dog howled with laughter. "I Can't Decide Which Of You I Like Best," it said in Angelina's voice. "Nini's More Useful, Obviously. But Look How Much Fun You Are."

"If she's so useful, why did you try to kill her?" Jagvi said.

"Did I Try To Kill Her?"

Jagvi's teeth were gritted. "From my perspective."

"I Guess I Don't Know My Own Strength," My Dog simpered, eyes drawing wide before they narrowed as she jerked her head up and snapped her teeth in one motion. Lips peeling back, frothing saliva against dark gums, rushing close so that Angelina had to scramble backward on her knees. My Dog's front paws were on her thighs, and her snarling fangs were inches from Angelina's neck as the thing growled, "I'm Just HUNGRY."

Angelina yelped and tried to push it away, but My Dog jumped again, knocking her off balance, falling hard on her elbow.

"I'm STAAAAARVING," My Dog howled, and her teeth snapped at Angelina's throat, a hot breath of air before Jagvi's arm was around its body, pulling it back, dragging it away from Angelina. Her arms strained around the frothing, snarling My Dog. "You Think I Want To Kill Her? I Want To *Eat*! I Want That Good, Full Life! And Then All The Memories Will Be Mine, And You Won't Be Able To Keep Them From Me Anymore, You Stupid Little Girl, And There'll Be No Future Left For You To Steal, All Of It Will Belong To Me—"

Jagvi grunted and hurled her weight against My Dog hard enough to send the possessed creature skidding and yelping out into the hallway. Angelina lunged forward and caught Jagvi's hand, and the two of them stumbled backward into the kitchen, slamming the door behind them. Jagvi grabbed a chair, and Angelina helped her jam it under the handle.

"We need backup," Jagvi said. "I'm calling Patrick."

Angelina nodded. It took five seconds to dial, and another five before he picked up. He asked no questions, hung up fast, saying he'd be home in fifteen minutes or less.

"Then what?" Angelina asked. My Dog was silent out in the hall. "You think the three of us can fight it off?"

"Yeah," Jagvi said. Angelina kept waiting for Jagvi to look afraid, but she was at her most untouchable. Her expression was so flat she almost looked bored, those concrete walls raised seamless around her, with no way that Angelina or anything in Cadenze could have hammered their way through. It should have been reassuring that Jagvi didn't look frightened, but that detachment made a fistful of warning tighten in Angelina's chest. "It's stronger than My Dog, but not unbeatable if Pat's here, too. And then we leave."

"I'm pretty sure it'll be able to chase us up to your house."

"I mean leave Cadenze. Run away."

Angelina's stomach flipped. "Would that even work?"

Jagvi shrugged. "Always worked for me before."

"Did It Really?" My Dog called through the door in Riccardo's grizzly voice. "Did It Really Feel Like You Were Gone?"

"I fucking hate that thing," Jagvi said.

"I'm Misunderstood," it said. A bitter old man's lament, all the violence from before drained away. "Jagvi Doesn't Understand Me Like Angel Does."

"We could try and—talk to it," Angelina whispered to Jagvi, cautious. "It sounds calmer. We could try to work out what it's planning. It never mentioned the memory thing before."

Jagvi shook her head. "It's a Cadenze monster. It's not going to say anything worth listening to."

"We learn things, sometimes," Angelina argued. "It just told us why you can get it out of me." Jagvi sucked in a rough breath, emotion passing over her face too fast for Angelina to track.

"It doesn't know me," Jagvi said.

"Guess Again."

There was a thud, and the door shook, almost knocking the chair away with the force of it. They heard My Dog whimpering—it sounded like her for real, although there was no way to tell. Angelina made for the door, but Jagvi pulled her back, hands firmly around her waist. A high, sharp yelp and the door shook again, like My Dog was throwing herself at it. The third time they heard a crack like wood on bone, and the chair skidded aside. My Dog howled with pain. Jagvi had to let go of Angelina to hold the door shut, her back up against it and her hand white-knuckled on the doorknob. But nothing tried to get through.

The two of them stood frozen. The silence was awful. Angelina pictured My Dog broken and bleeding in the hallway. She would be so confused. The thing said she was frightened, and it probably wasn't lying. Angelina went to the door and touched Jagvi's hand.

"Please," she said.

Jagvi nodded.

Angelina wasn't sure what she was expecting: My Dog dead, or unconscious, or entirely gone. A leg twisted the wrong way, fur matted with blood. But when Jagvi opened the door, My Dog sat on her haunches, entirely unhurt and watching attentively, tongue hanging out of her mouth and that alien intelligence smiling at them.

"Do You Think You Can Put Me In Time-Out?"

"I don't like this," Angelina said. "Jag, I really don't like it, why would it possess my fucking dog? What's the *plan*?" she demanded, crouching to stare at My Dog. "What do you *want*? If you want to eat me, why not fucking eat me already? You could've killed me last night!"

"If You'd Died, That Wouldn't Have Been A Very Interesting Future."

"So you do want that," Jagvi said, reluctant. "Her future."

"You Don't Mind Some Friendly Competition, Do You?"

Jagvi took hold of the back of Angelina's collar.

"Little Town Runaway," My Dog continued, in Angelina's softest and most beguiling voice. "It's Nice To Finally Speak To You, You Know. One-On-One."

"You're not one-on-one," Angelina said.

"You Don't Count," My Dog said happily, peering up into Jagvi's eyes.

"What, then?" Jagvi said. "What do you want to say to me?"

"Patience. Everything In Its Time."

"How do you take Angel's future, if you don't kill her?"

A knot in Angelina's throat put pressure on the bruises on her neck and conjured the fountain's hand around her again, the unbearable pain, the tight squeeze like she was going to burst and be smeared all over the stone palm. A thin and gory residue that the thing could lick up in its own time, at its own pleasure. "And why are you back now, if you're still not gonna—just fucking *do* it?"

My Dog didn't answer. Her ears were pricked and her head tilted, attentive.

"Tell us," Jagvi said.

Now Angelina could hear it, too. Patrick's tires on the gravel outside and the sound of his truck shutting off. His key was in the lock when My Dog smiled at Jagvi and said, "Because I Want You To Be Happy."

XXV

"Hello?" Patrick called. Light filtered through the front door, and he faltered when he saw them, two women and a dog in conversation. He'd come with his sleeves rolled up, fists raised, and Angelina loved him for it. Jagvi ought to let go of her shirt, they were clutching each other too obviously, but the fear could account for most of that.

"It's still in My Dog, Pat," Angelina said. "Come in slowly. It's talking to us."

"Are either of you hurt?"

He didn't come slowly, marching down the hall toward them with his eyes darting from My Dog to Angelina to Jagvi and back again, something of his onstage presence in the puff of his chest and jut of his chin, like he wanted to make himself a more imposing contender to the monster. He reached My Dog sitting in the doorway. Her tail thumped against the ground, and then she winked at Angelina and went for Patrick's throat.

Patrick landed hard, a sickening thud against the laminate floor. He slammed his fist into the dog's side and yelled aloud, voice tearing and breaking. Seconds flitted by like freeze-frames, and blood spattered everywhere.

The dog snarled over him, a deep, wet sound more human than animal. Patrick shouted again, and Angelina and Jagvi scrambled together to throw their arms around the heaving mass of dog and man and whatever else was in there. Her earlier snap at Angelina had been nothing compared to this violent

181

storm of claws and teeth. Jagvi didn't hesitate, threw ruthless blows with her fists and her elbows, but My Dog barely flinched, undistracted from her prey.

Angelina went for My Dog's snout. Straining and digging her nails in, she got the dog's jaws unlocked, but it revealed a big red gash at Patrick's throat, leaking fast, flash of something yellow like cartilage that had Angelina letting out a panicked yelp as her grip slipped. The dog snapped again, Patrick's shoulder this time, Patrick's face white and his eyes dark, spasming on the floor. He shoved at My Dog's face, curled fingers bouncing off her cheek, the power of the punch already faltering. Angelina grabbed My Dog's tail and pulled, throwing her weight away from the tangled mass. Jagvi lifted her fist and crashed it hard onto My Dog's head, and the dog made a murmuring affectionate noise and nuzzled up against Patrick's collarbone like a lover. Patrick gasped and jerked.

Jagvi switched positions, pressing her knees into the dog's rib cage and trying to push it wriggling down to Patrick's other side, forcing it to break its hold. It happened in slow, awful motion, the dog snapping and howling, Patrick bellowing mangled curses, and Angelina could already see that Jagvi would get toppled over in another minute and then the dog would be back at Patrick's throat, even as its teeth unlocked and it separated from Patrick in a froth of saliva and blood, laughter that still sounded like Angelina's ringing in the air. Angelina could run for a hammer or a knife, hurt or kill My Dog into stopping, but would it even work? She could picture her poor dog's corpse still snapping with the monster's teeth.

"Drop it," Angelina begged helplessly. "My Dog, please. Drop it!"

The command rarely worked even when My Dog wasn't possessed. This time she saw My Dog's eyes roll back, a brief flash of anguish.

"Drop it!" Angelina tried again. "Come on, girl. Be good. Drop it!"

Jagvi joined in, following Angelina's lead. Angelina put her hand on My Dog's head, the downy fur between her ears, and they both chanted, "Drop it, My Dog, drop it!" Patrick's lips moved, soundless and white.

The dog's mouth opened. Her pink tongue flashed. Blood stained her teeth. Angelina staggered backward, a feeling like a cloud of starlings diving at her, but Jagvi grabbed her elbow, fingers tacky against Angelina's skin, and hauled her back into the group. The feeling, that empty hungry mass that towered over her and pressed her into the ground, collapsed over her head like a wave, slid thick and greasy down her back—and ran onward, and away.

My Dog skittered off Patrick's chest and into Angelina's arms. Angelina held her tight, yanking My Dog's head up so she could check her face for any sign of a monster hiding within. Jagvi bent over Patrick, saying his name over and over with an awful, determined calm. Pat's blood dripped like drool from My Dog's jaws, but her eyes were huge and brown and dumb, and the only thing Angelina saw reflected in them was her own sorry face.

XXVI

Patrick staggered alongside Jagvi as she half carried him to the kitchen sink, bending him to the faucet and washing the deep wounds with warm water and dish soap. Angelina stood babbling beside them, begging Jagvi to hurry up. Blood pooled at Patrick's throat and shoulder, and he was paler than Angelina had ever seen him. He didn't speak; when he tried, his teeth chattered too hard for them to understand the words.

"Go start the car, Angel," Jagvi said. As Angelina ran from the kitchen, Jagvi began to murmur to Patrick in a low voice Angelina couldn't catch. She was still talking to him long minutes later when they came stumbling out of the house together, Patrick draped over Jagvi's shoulders with a towel pressed to his neck, and into the waiting back seat of Angelina and Caro's battered Skoda. A steady stream of words that Patrick followed as closely as always, his eyes fixed on Jagvi's face.

"Pat?" Angelina said, pulling out with a screech of tires onto the road and sending them barreling down the mountainside. The sun sank before her, deep red shadows across her town. "Are you okay? Is he—Jag, he's gonna be okay?"

"All good, Nini," Patrick said, voice strangled tight in his throat.

"None of your major arteries have been hit, which is great," Jagvi said. Like she was going to hand him and his arteries a shiny school medal. "But you've lost a lot of blood, and it might be infected, so we need to get you to the hospital right away—Angel, you don't have to be polite right now!"

184

Angelina jumped, slamming on the gas again after she'd slowed to wave the turning car in ahead of her. "Sorry! Sorry, it was automatic—"

But she couldn't help stealing glances at Patrick in the back seat, white and wounded, and slowing so the potholes didn't hurt him.

"Angel," Jagvi said. "Speed up."

"Right, sorry."

"Hurts," Patrick admitted through gritted teeth as he tried to shift his weight farther onto his side.

"Just lie still. It won't kill you to do what I tell you for once. *Fucking* Siccos."

Angelina flicked another glance in the rearview mirror. Jagvi's face was tight with worry, but Patrick smiled up at her, eyebrows raised as though invoking a familiar joke. *Please do not be jealous of your brother bleeding out in the back seat*, Angelina told herself, with a lurch of self-loathing.

"You're doing really well," Jagvi said, and ran her free hand over Patrick's hair. Angelina gave up and was jealous.

"Nini?" Patrick rasped.

Angelina jerked guiltily, but Patrick only sounded confused. "What?" she said, then realized she had taken the wrong turn, swinging east. They were driving fast along Cadenze's border, the road that limned the town and curved in under Little Joe toward Franco's farm. "Fuck! Sorry, I'm on auto-pilot." She made an illegal U-turn, hurtling back toward the intersection that connected the highway. "Sorry, shit—"

"All good," Jagvi said, "just...Angel, there's the exit."

"Yeah." Angelina looked at the turn as they sailed past it again, her sweaty palms steady on the wheel.

The silence in the car changed. Angelina pulled over to the side of the road, poised and waiting for a break in the traffic.

"Easy," Jagvi said. And then, as Angelina waited and waited: "Maybe faster than that, though. Come on—Angel, you could have made that!"

"Not all of us are used to gunning in and out of traffic," Angelina said, which made Patrick and Jagvi relax a little. Angelina did not have to relax: the fear lapped around her ankles, climbed higher, the ocean roar of terror not so far off now, but she stayed loose all through her spine. She knew now that tension made no difference, except that maybe it hurt a little more when it climbed in.

The turn was on Angelina's left now. She watched another car ahead of her take it, foreign plates, probably only passing through Cadenze on its way to a better destination. No one ever came here unless they had to. Angelina stayed focused, and the car was quiet and expectant and everyone saw the turn, and everyone saw Angelina keep the wheel straight.

Jagvi spoke first. Her voice was deliberately light. "Why don't I drive?"

"Good idea," Angelina said, and pulled over again.

She came around to the back seat, and Jagvi grabbed her, leaving sticky traces of blood on her arms, shoving her face against Angelina's neck. Brief graze of teeth. Angelina shook her head miserably.

"It's not in me," she said. "I don't know what's happening. Don't waste time, we gotta get Pat to the hospital. Get in the front, Jag, I've got him."

Patrick slumped against the window with his arm around Angelina's shoulders as she pressed the towel tight against his neck. It had been white when they got in the car, and now it was drenched with shadowy blotches. The blood looked murky, like something dredged up from the bottom of a lake and not sprung from Patrick's living veins.

Jagvi drove fast, cars honking in outrage as she swerved neatly into the gap she made for herself. Her shoulders climbed up around her ears, eyes on the rearview mirror more than they were on the road, pupils flashing back at Angelina and her brother. Angelina kept waiting for the thing's voice, for the hook at the back of her neck, for the feeling of it sliding into her brain. But she didn't feel anything, and so she was still frowning to herself and wondering what was happening and where it was and why she hadn't been able to drive out of Cadenze when she leaned forward over the seats, laid a gentle hand on the wheel and swerved the car away from the turn.

They barreled across the road, an oncoming car blaring its horn. Jagvi dove for control of the wheel and jerked them into a frantic U-turn, and then they were cruising back into Cadenze.

"Nini!" Patrick choked out, clutching his own shoulder where Angelina had dropped it. Jagvi was breathing hard. Angelina didn't say sorry. She didn't say anything.

"We have to go to Myrna," Jagvi told her, "we have to take Pat to the hospital." Her matter-of-fact tone sliced through Angelina, its blind hope, as though Angelina were just a confused kid who needed reminding. Angelina swallowed around the hurt in her throat and nodded. No sign of the thing, except for what it had left behind in her. Like it had occupied her enough now that its residue rested in her bones, her tendons. She couldn't trust her body anymore. She stared at her own hands, clumsy traitors still streaked in Patrick's blood. The sight gave her motion sickness, and she had to swallow repeatedly to keep the bile from rising.

This time Jagvi drove well over the speed limit, like she could trick the thing into missing the point where they swung out and left Cadenze city limits. But Angelina knew these roads better than Jagvi. She caught the wheel at the exact right moment, and Jagvi had to slam on the brakes to keep them from skidding.

"You could hold her down," Jagvi said. Patrick tried to nod, but the movement made him flinch. His eyes were wet from the pain.

"You're too hurt," Angelina said. "I'm going to make it so you can't get to a hospital, and then…"

She gripped Patrick tighter, as though that would do any good.

"We could," Jagvi said, and stopped, shaking her head. "We could…"

"Tie me up? Knock me out?" Angelina's chest hurt. Pat's bandage was wet under her fingers, her fingers were sticky, there was liquid sliding down her wrist. "Do you want to see it cornered? Do you want me even more out of control? I nearly got us all killed just now as it is." The car wouldn't leave Cadenze as long as Angelina was in it, and they didn't have time to figure out a loophole. "You'll have to leave me here. I can walk home."

"Can't do that," Jagvi said. "What if it comes back? It probably *wants* us to do that."

"I'll go to Old Timers, then, or Franco's."

"Jag," Patrick said. His voice was quiet, and getting quieter. "Stay with her. You can get it out, if it…" He trailed off, voice a scraping burble from the mess of his throat.

"Pat," Angelina said, "then who will—"

"Caro," Patrick said, closing his eyes like he was drifting off to sleep. He sounded dreamy and faraway. "Get Ma."

"I'm not leaving you," Jagvi said. "Pat. I'm not. I'm not leaving you."

"Please," Patrick murmured. Each word was punctuated with a gasp of desperate breath. "She's—my sister."

Jagvi stared out at the slick of the road and the rising mist. It had started to rain. She switched the wipers on and set her jaw, and turned the car toward Little Joe. Angelina's chest was a hive of panic, but the rest of her body greeted the change in direction. Hands that had been poised to tilt the wheel were free to pet Patrick's hair. Eyes that had been sharply focused on the road were permitted to drift to Jagvi's knitted brow in the rearview mirror. The monster was a creature of Cadenze, and she saw now that it had no intention of chasing her beyond its borders. Instead it hauled her back like an errant kitten. She had been stupid to try to run away.

Caro was standing outside her shack. Not many cars came up this way, and the noise must have stirred her. Her face went bright with surprise when she spotted Jagvi behind the wheel, and then Angelina got her door open and called, "*Mama*," and Caro came running.

Caro spent fifteen seconds gibbering over her son while Jagvi and Angelina explained in a garbled rush that she needed to take him to the hospital, here were the keys, Jagvi already listing things Caro should tell the emergency room doctors, dog bites to the neck and shoulder, no sign of rabies, moderate blood loss. Angelina hustled Caro into the driver's seat. She twisted to look at Patrick spread out across the back, and he raised one hand in a weak greeting.

"He's bleeding," Caro said. "Girls. He's bleeding everywhere."

"That's why you need to go now." Angelina reached over to buckle Caro into her seat.

"But what happened?"

"Call me when you're there. I'll tell you everything." Angelina slammed the door, but Caro wound down the window to stare aghast at her daughter.

"You're not coming with us?"

"No, Mama, that's why you have to drive. I can't go."

"But he's your brother!"

Jagvi leaned down to the window. "Caro, he's lost a lot of blood."

Caro nodded. Her hands shook as she reached for the ignition, but she took a few steady breaths, drawing on some inner well of strength. Angelina hoped that it would last long enough to get Patrick to the hospital.

"A dog bit him?"

"My Dog." Caro's eyes widened in shock. "I promise everything will be okay. Just get him to Myrna."

"Right." Caro started the car, with one more brief glance at her mangled son behind her. "I'll call you when I can."

"We'll be waiting," Angelina said. Patrick waved one shaky hand from the back seat.

They watched the car careen back down the mountain, moving fast this time like, at last, it understood that it was part of an emergency. It rounded a bend and the taillights disappeared.

All along, complacency had been Angelina's curse—and perhaps too much faith in the power of Jagvi's hands. She had assumed the thing would step in and out of her body and leave Angelina entirely herself when it was gone. As though Angelina didn't know that the more you touched something, the more you left an impression; whether it was Jagvi's mouth on hers or the thing leaving traces of itself in Angelina's body. It had touched her just enough that she would never exit the cage into which she had walked. Angelina felt as though she could see the borders of Cadenze in her mind's eye and the curtain slowly lowering before them, closing her off from the world beyond. She would never leave this place.

Cadenze was a network of fluorescent and yellow lights, the hum of cars and factories and the ripe smell of rocks and dirt all around her. Angelina's knees thumped against one another; she was shaking, she realized, and sank to sit on a tree stump, her trembling, bloodstained hands jerking like trapped birds in her lap.

189

XXVII

They didn't speak on the long walk home. Angelina was occupied with visions of Patrick's face, pale and shivering and small. With every step, Jagvi's knuckles brushed hers, a charm to ward off the thing from the pit and keep her, but each time their skin caught, it reminded Angelina that both of their hands were tacky with blood.

My Dog greeted them mournfully at the door. Angelina knelt to pet her fur and told Jagvi where to find the travel carrier. Normally Angelina had to lure My Dog with treats, but this time she trooped into the crate with solemn understanding. Her paws were pinkish, like she'd been trying to clean them.

There were bloody pawprints all through the hallway and kitchen and a sloppy pool of red where Patrick had fallen. They used kitchen towels and toilet paper to soak it up, and scrubbed what was left with cheap disinfectant. It was the same process that Angelina followed after fights at Old Timers. It just took longer and felt worse.

It was late by the time they were done. They washed their hands together at the sink, elbows overlapping. Angelina could remember watching Patrick and Jagvi jostling for space here as teenagers, cleaning themselves up after a long day building the porch or fixing up the truck. She didn't realize she was crying until she felt Jagvi's arms around her. Angelina hooked her chin over Jagvi's shoulder and screwed her eyes shut. Her tears were hot and heavy and seemingly endless, her whole body shuddering with their force. Jagvi held her so tight that it hurt.

The knock on the door startled both of them. Angelina wiped her damp cheeks with a dish towel while Jagvi swung to face the empty hallway.

"Is it back?"

Another series of knocks, heavy enough to make the doorframe rattle. Her uncle Franco called, "Angelina? Are you there?"

"It can change its voice," Jagvi said under her breath.

"But it doesn't usually knock," Angelina said.

"We know about Patrick," Franco called. "Your mother called us from the hospital. Angelina?"

"I'm here," Angelina called back. Jagvi's hand was tight around her wrist. "Is Pat okay?"

"Come outside and talk to me properly," Franco said. Angelina loved the way he spoke: stoic, commanding, always soothing in the undertone. She waited for Jagvi's nod. They went to the door together.

Franco stood illuminated by the porch light in his hunting jacket, the dark brown collar framing his thickset jaw, and his brother Sam fidgeting by his side. They'd parked out on the road, but the car's headlights were still on, and Angelina could see Jethro and Ricky leaning on the bumper and watching the house.

Sam tucked the plug of tobacco he'd been chewing against his gum and said, "What the fuck took you so long?"

Angelina repeated her question. "Is Pat okay? Why didn't Ma call me?"

"He's sedated. They're checking for infections."

"But he's gonna be okay?"

"We think so," Franco said, and Angelina grabbed Jagvi's arm and squeezed. She wanted to cry again; she laughed wildly instead. The sick weight in her belly lifted, just a fraction. Franco watched her, nodding a little, more to himself than to her. "Caro is with him."

"Is he on a ventilator?" Jagvi asked.

Franco considered them both, their damp hands and disheveled hair,

Angelina's eyes still puffy from crying, Jagvi's face grave and cast in shadow. "What the fuck happened?"

"It got into My Dog," Angelina said. "It used her to attack him."

"Where is it now?"

"We don't know. We chased it out of My Dog, but I don't know where it went."

Part of her hoped that it had retreated again, but she could never trust that it had gone away again. She'd made that mistake too many times. Her hands trembled as she remembered jerking the steering wheel over and over, her body refusing to leave Cadenze. She reached for Jagvi again and touched her bare arm. Franco's eyes were roving searchlights, catching everything.

"Chased it out," he repeated. "What does that mean?"

"I told My Dog to drop it. It's what we say when she's eating trash or a shoe or something. She must have been able to let it go."

Sam said, "That dog doesn't follow commands." Franco kept looking at Jagvi. Her T-shirt was covered in blood.

"She does sometimes, when she wants to." Angelina glanced behind her at My Dog, curled up in her cage. "She didn't want it in her either."

"You didn't want it in you, the last time," Franco argued. "Could you 'chase it out'?"

"No," Angelina said. "I don't know. Look, it wasn't immediate, okay, I had to yell it over and over, Jagvi did, too—"

"Jagvi told her to stop?"

"Jagvi said *drop it*, she heard me doing it and she joined in—"

"And that's when it stopped?"

Angelina nodded. "Yeah, Jagvi helped."

"It stopped on her command."

"What?" Angelina frowned. "No, that's not what I said."

But Franco was not finished. "What happened to your neck?"

"Pat already told you, I was in the fountain and it crushed me. I don't know why, it felt like it was angry but then it stopped—"

"It just stopped on its own?"

Angelina shifted her weight and exhaled harshly. "I don't *know*. We think that—I thought maybe we'd beaten it."

"We?"

"Me and Jagvi."

"She was there?"

"What? Yes, Uncle, she was trying to save me." They'd explained all this to the family already, but maybe they hadn't understood. "We asked Jagvi to stay close. Me and Patrick."

Franco nodded slowly, which meant that he was making a decision. He'd nodded in the same way when he found Patrick and Angelina living alone, all those years ago. He'd probably been wearing the same coat. The only difference was the gray in his hair.

He beckoned Angelina forward. She stepped out of the house, shooting a reassuring smile over her shoulder at Jagvi and receiving only a tilt of Jagvi's chin in return.

"Angelina," Franco said, "you need to come with us. The family will keep you safe. Matthew has found some records of the ruins on Big Joe, and your nonna wants to do another ritual. Your mother is going to meet us there."

"Okay, good," Angelina said, relieved. "Just let us get changed. Jagvi, do you have a clean shirt down here?"

"No," Franco said harshly, but the hand he put on Angelina's shoulder felt gentle, coaxing. "Just you."

Angelina paused. She willed herself to keep calm. She was barefoot but they were still almost equal height, their eyes the same murky green-gray. "You don't understand the situation, Uncle. You haven't been here."

"Here's what I understand," Franco said. "Every time you're hurt, she's there. Every time it ends, it's by her command."

"Because she's *saving* me."

Sam interrupted with vicious exasperation. "Don't be so blind. Your brother's in a hospital bed right now!"

Angelina closed her eyes and tried to put herself in her uncles' position. They loved Patrick, had essentially raised him together, and she could only imagine what the phone call from Caro had been like, the picture of disaster she had painted. Her baby boy mauled half to death, the girls refusing to explain. Such news required an action plan, some practical defense against the encroaching darkness. The Siccos believed in spirits and curses but they believed more deeply in the power of family, the importance of those ties, and now one of them was wounded and another was haunted and they were looking for the weak spot in their ranks.

"She's always been bad luck," Sam said, glowering at Jagvi.

The relish in his voice made Angelina's blood boil. Bad luck was an insult reserved for the worst offenders in her family's moral universe. It meant you drew bad things toward you with purpose. Meant you were a magnet for the devil. But all Jagvi ever did was try to keep bad things away. Monsters, Cadenze, Angelina herself: all things that had to be fought or defied. Look at the way she'd tried to resist Angelina. Jagvi made mistakes, she was cold and then impulsive, but *bad*? Angelina thought of Jagvi in the house today, squaring up to the monster, in the back seat holding Patrick together, or poised over Angelina in the fountain and kissing her with senseless desperation until the stone hand opened wide.

"Jagvi's the only luck I've had so far," Angelina said. "I know you want to help, but none of us know what this thing is, or how to stop it. Jagvi's the only one who's actually done anything to protect me."

"How?" Sam demanded.

"What?"

"How did she protect you? How does it work?"

Angelina swallowed. *It's Hard To Get Under Your Skin When She's Fighting Me For Space.* "I don't know how it works. I just know it's not her fault."

"What do you have to say then?" Sam said, addressing Jagvi. "How are you protecting her?"

"Angel already said we don't know," Jagvi said.

"That's it?" Sam put on a dumb, mocking voice. "*I don't know, I don't know, I don't know.* You seemed to know a lot last week when you were telling us all it's not real."

"Yeah, I don't pretend to understand things when I don't," Jagvi said. Same smooth-toned condescension that she'd turned on the thing earlier today. "You could try it sometime."

"Fuck you," Sam said. "Fucking bitch, what the fuck are you doing to my family—"

Angelina clapped her hands, hard enough that the moths clouding around the porch light flittered back. "This is crazy. I'm telling you that Jagvi's not the problem. We have a real honest-to-god monster here, okay, it tried to kill me and then it tried to kill Patrick, and it's not going anywhere. I know you're all scared, but you can't just overreact like this. We have to think it through."

"Why don't *you* think it through," Sam said. "Carl's been asking around, and the other families all have the same story. There's always a companion, and it always makes you turn on your own. It makes you *want* to take its side."

"We can't make decisions based on fairy tales," Angelina said. She turned to Franco. He had a jaw that sloped left, just like Patrick's. My Dog's possessed fangs thrashed behind her eyes. She needed her family onside, but she felt drained of all her usual charm, and there were no clever jokes left in her. "Uncle, please."

But Franco wasn't looking at her anymore. His eyes were on Jagvi, and he looked almost regretful, his pity directed either at Jagvi or his own niece, in the outsider's thrall.

"There's a bus leaving for San Michele tonight, girl," he said. "You'd better be on it."

Angelina could feel a headache building. She put one hand on her forehead, wishing her own palms were as cool and wide as Jagvi's. The night felt fragile, everything threatening to splinter, and Angelina held herself taller to block Jagvi from view.

"Or what?" she asked. "What are you gonna do, Franco? Shoot her? Put a bounty on her head? Has Sam got the tar and feathers ready?"

"Your mother agrees with me," he said. "She doesn't want the Marino girl in her house."

"This is my house. Mine and Pat's."

"It's Caro's name on the lease."

Angelina took a step forward. Over by the car, Jethro and Ricky straightened, poised for a fight, even as Sam leaned back. She remembered Patrick's old prediction or accusation, that Angelina had been picked as successor for Franco, the leader of her Sicco generation. But she didn't hold that power yet. "It hasn't been her house for a long time, Franco. You know that."

"She's your mother, Angelina. She wants you safe."

"Jagvi isn't some demon from a story," Angelina said. "She isn't the 'dark companion' or whatever they're saying. She's one of us. And, listen, the only person this thing's ever been inside of is me. If anything you should be protecting *her* from *me*."

"Angel," Jagvi said. Angelina turned back to see Jagvi leaning against the doorjamb with her arms crossed. "Maybe you should go with them."

"No."

"If you think it would be better for me to leave—"

"It wouldn't be," Angelina said. "It won't be better. Everything will be worse." She tried to smile. "I already knew that, but now there's a monster, too."

Jagvi's expression stayed cool and unimpressed, that old barricade, and from the side of her mouth, she said, "Huh." Last week Angelina would've interpreted it as amusement, like Jagvi was laughing at her plea. Tonight it sounded more like wonder.

Sam waved at Ricky and Jethro for backup, and Angelina's favorite cousins shuffled over together. Jethro was still in his work uniform, shabby warehouse coveralls with his sleeves rolled up to his elbows, his eyes fixed on his father. Ricky flicked the smoking butt of his cigarette into the gravel. "What's going on?"

Angelina feigned a laugh. "Oh, you know. They're just trying to kick me out of my own house." She wanted them to see how ridiculous the whole thing was. The older Siccos might be reactionary, superstitious, but the younger ones always had her back. It had been Ricky who told the others to cut out the dyke jokes, Jethro who helped Patrick beat up that kid who drew a swastika on her school locker.

But Ricky shook his head. "Not you." He squinted at Jagvi. "Just her."

Angelina's smile faded. She swallowed hard; the bruise on her throat felt like a clamp. "You're all agreed, then?" She directed the question at Jethro, who only shrugged and looked away.

Sam waved his hand impatiently in Angelina's face. "Listen. She's not fucking staying here, and that's the end of it."

"We can go up to my dad's place," Jagvi said. "My place, I mean."

"Absolutely not," Franco said, but Angelina spoke over him.

"Perfect!" She took a step back so that she and Jagvi were side by side. "There, you can tell Ma we're not staying in *her* house. We'll leave right now."

"What about Your Dog?" Jethro asked.

"Bring her up," Jagvi said.

"You'd fucking like that, wouldn't you?" Sam spat at her, but Franco held his hand up, and Sam went silent.

"It's too dangerous," Franco said. "I won't leave you alone with her and that dog."

My Dog sat awake in her cage, stirred by the men's voices and watching with her nose pressed up against the wire. She looked placid enough, but Angelina couldn't trust appearances any longer. The thing might already be in her again, crouching and observing. My Dog, not My Dog.

"She'll be okay on her own for one night," Angelina said finally. "I'll come down and feed her in the morning." She dug into her pocket and found the paper scrawled with Jagvi's home number. "Jethro." He took the paper reluctantly, like he was waiting for his father to knock it out of his hands. But Franco's eyes were fixed on Jagvi. "Can you call this number if anything changes with Pat? Even if it just stays the same, call so I know he's okay?"

"Sure, Nini. We're going to the hospital tonight. You could come with us."

Angelina's stomach clenched in on itself, grief cramping like blood. Patrick was only a handful of miles from her, his hospital window looking out onto the same mountains; he might as well have been on the moon. "I can't. It won't let me leave Cadenze." Angelina touched the corner of Franco's jacket. "Uncle, it really doesn't have to be like this. We can deal with it together. I'll come to the farm with you if Jagvi can come, too."

"No fucking way," Sam said. Ricky spat on the ground. Franco said nothing at all. Part of him probably wanted to hit her, beat her until she complied; if she were some other girl, he might have tried. The look he gave Angelina was hard and heavy with fatherly disapproval, but he wasn't her father.

"All right," Angelina said. She clapped her hands again. She needed to leave now or risk crying in front of all of them. Every time the Siccos might have turned from her, Angelina had always counted on blood winning out. When she came out, or that train wreck fight she'd had with Franco when he voted for the nationalists, or when Caro had decided her children needed a "break" from the wider family influence. With every schism, she'd braced herself to lose them, without ever really believing it could happen. They loved her too much. They would do anything for her. It had never occurred to her that there was something she would not do for them.

"Jethro, you call me. And tell Ma to call me, too, as soon as she can. I'm— If you see Pat tonight, will you tell him I love him?"

"We'll tell him you chose that girl over your own family," Sam said.

Angelina shrugged. "Pat would've done the same. Ready to go, Jag?"

"Yes," Jagvi said. She pulled her leather jacket from its hook in the hallway and handed Angelina her raincoat, and led the way up the tarmac road with the headlights still burning behind them, the men of Angelina's family watching them leave and My Dog whining from her cage. Angelina had never denied her family anything, never turned her back on them. Good Siccos never struck out on their own, even during the worst fights; they stuck together to feud in company. She should feel lonely. But she wasn't alone.

XXVIII

"It's nice," Angelina said tentatively. The front door of Jagvi's family home fed them into its kitchen. The linoleum was stained yellow, the counters old and faded, as though no one had lived here for decades. Depressing, considering that Riccardo had died only six months ago.

The living room was mostly taken up by a pulled-out sofa bed where Jagvi had evidently been sleeping. There was a heap of discarded shirts and underwear by the corner of the mattress. Angelina had the urge to kneel down and bury her face in it, crawl straight into fabric and the smell of Jagvi's body. Like prey trying to hide her scent in the undergrowth, making herself small and invisible to everything—monsters, brothers, blood, guilt. Jagvi pulled her bloody T-shirt off and added it to the pile. Angelina licked her lips.

"I left my backpack at your place," Jagvi realized, taking a clean shirt from a stack on the armchair. "I'm going to end up in my dad's old shirts by the end of the week. You should try to sleep."

"It's going to come back," Angelina told her. "It doesn't need to rest anymore."

"I know." Jagvi clicked on a lamp by the side of the couch. "But you do."

Angelina wanted to protest, but she didn't have a better suggestion tonight. They couldn't leave. Her family was at a loss. Patrick was in a Myrna hospital bed, My Dog alone in her cage. Angelina watched Jagvi smooth down the blankets and figured this house was as safe as any other.

Angelina went back into the kitchen and dragged one of the chairs out to the front door. She jammed it under the doorknob to keep it shut. When she returned to the living room, Jagvi gave her a questioning look.

"In case it sends My Dog up here to kill us, I guess." Angelina smiled, though she wasn't really joking.

Jagvi handed her a bottle of water. "I'm more afraid that your uncles are gonna come blast down the door with a shotgun."

"They're just spooked about Patrick." Angelina took a long swig, swilling the water in her mouth to wash out the bitter aftertaste of adrenaline. "I'm sorry for how they treat you."

Jagvi shrugged. "Nothing new."

"I know," Angelina said. "I'm sorry."

Jagvi opened her mouth, breath catching in her throat. For one terrible second Angelina thought Jagvi was going to cry, but instead she yawned, her jaw cracking with the force of it. When she was done, she rubbed her chin sheepishly.

"Didn't get much sleep last night."

"Me either." They stood on opposite sides of the mattress. Pulse skittering, Angelina said, "I promise not to jump you if you promise not to jump me."

Jagvi watched her for another long moment before she nodded.

Angelina stripped down to her T-shirt and underwear before she crawled under the blankets. Jagvi lay down in her jeans without getting under the covers. They stared at the ceiling together. Mold fringed the corners of the plaster.

"I really hope Pat's okay," Angelina said. "Thank God you were there."

"You're the one who stopped it," Jagvi said.

"I would've been screwed on my own," Angelina said. "You were so tough."

Jagvi turned on her side to face Angelina, resting her cheek on her folded hands. "I was really, really scared."

"Oh," Angelina said. "I couldn't tell."

"No?" But Jagvi didn't sound surprised.

Riccardo's house was quiet on its high perch on the mountain. Not even a gurgling pipe disturbed them. Angelina imagined the years Jagvi had lived in this silent house, sitting opposite Riccardo at every meal, following his orders, letting him pick and pull at her, gritting her teeth and squeezing any sign of weakness down into nothing. While Jagvi spoke with Angelina's uncles this evening, her face had been so calm that they might have been discussing some town gossip about the Calvanese twins.

"You're pretty brave, Jag."

Jagvi wrinkled her nose. "I don't know about that."

"You could've left, tonight," Angelina pointed out. "You could leave now."

"I would if you wanted me to."

"I don't," Angelina said.

Jagvi's jaw worked. Angelina watched, fascinated, as Jagvi scrunched her mouth up and still took a moment before she could speak. Finally she said, "Your family isn't going to like that you came with me."

Angelina shrugged.

"Really, Angel," Jagvi said. "You said Pat would do the same but—they're used to him and me. And he's always been a bit outside them. Not like you."

"So?"

"I don't know," Jagvi said. She stared straight up at the ceiling. "I know it's because I'm the only one who can get it out of you."

Angelina's voice came out in a low, embarrassed scrape. "But you know that's not the only reason."

"Uh." Jagvi let out a long, shivering breath, almost the most affected Angelina had ever seen her. "Yes. I guess I do know that. Thank you."

Angelina flushed. "I nearly got Patrick killed, and I've fucked your life up—"

"Ah, but that's nothing new," Jagvi said. "Turn over."

She moved in closer, draping herself along Angelina's back and wrapping one arm firmly around Angelina's waist, catching Angelina's hand in her own. Her nose brushed the back of Angelina's neck. They were touching in too many places for the thing from the pit to intrude.

The trill of the phone jolted them awake. Angelina sat bolt upright, and Jagvi grabbed her wrist and said, "Fuck!" and for a moment the noise racketing through the dark house felt like an alien sound, unfamiliar and frightening. Then Angelina recognized it and dragged Jagvi out of bed with her, stumbling into the kitchen. The digital clock on the microwave read 3:43 a.m. Angelina picked up and said, "Mama?"

"It's me," Patrick said.

"Pat!" Angelina yelped. Jagvi squeezed her wrist and crowded close to the receiver. "Are you okay?"

"Fucking groggy. They gave me the heavy shit. I'm just waiting for my next dose." His voice was torn, like he'd spent the night screaming into a microphone.

"Is Ma with you?"

"She's asleep on a chair. The boys were here while I was passed out."

"Does it hurt a lot?"

"Not too bad," Patrick said. "I'm all ripped up, though. They've got me in this giant neck brace. Thanks, sweetheart."

"Who's that?"

"Suze, she's the nurse on duty. She's letting me use the phone at reception."

Angelina started giggling helplessly. "Oh yeah? Think you're in with a shot?"

"Jethro told her I went hand-to-hand with a wolf, so I'm not sure how she could resist." Jagvi dropped her forehead against Angelina's shoulder, either in exasperation or relief.

"Good to hear you're already milking this for all it's worth."

"Are you guys okay? Why are you up at Jagvi's place? I tried the home phone but nobody picked up."

Angelina sighed. "Franco's got everyone thinking it's Jagvi's fault. They're looking for a scapegoat."

Patrick swore under his breath. "Caro, too?"

"She wanted Jag out of *her* house. It's been a shit show."

"I'll handle her," Patrick said. "You stick with Jagvi, all right? Don't listen to them."

"I haven't," Angelina said. "I wouldn't."

"And the thing? Have you seen it?"

"No. I'm with Jagvi."

"Good kid. Look, just stick together, okay? I'll talk to Ma and I'll call back in the morning. We're gonna kill this thing together."

"Yeah we will. Don't worry about us."

"Can I speak to Jag?"

Angelina didn't want to admit her irritation. "Sure."

She moved away to give them privacy, but her treacherous ears strained to overhear what Jagvi was saying. Apologies, assurances. Questions about his wounds and a sly comment about the nurse. Angelina found her jeans crumpled on the living room floor and pulled them back on. The lamp flickered. Angelina looked up, and it stilled again. She went to the kitchen.

After they'd hung up, Jagvi asked, "Are you sure it was really him?"

"I think so." Angelina couldn't really see any benefit for the thing in imitating her brother. It already had them trapped. And besides, if Patrick really *wasn't* okay, then the rest of the Siccos would be up here for blood before long.

Jagvi switched on the overhead light and offered Angelina a box of crackers. The phone call had energized her, her foot bouncing beneath the table, bare toes brushing Angelina's ankle. Angelina examined the picture frames lining the wall, a dozen different versions of Meera and Jagvi peering out from dusty glass. She tapped a photo of teenage Jagvi looking sullen and distrustful of the camera, playing with her braid like it was too heavy for her. She did not look as intimidating or grown-up as she had seemed to Angelina at the time. She was wearing an outfit Angelina had never seen, draped in sunshine yellow silk that wrapped around her waist and scooped over her shoulder. "What's this?"

"Just a sari. My aunt sent it for my birthday." Jagvi surveyed the photos on the wall, her eyebrows drawn together, mouth sloping down. "I don't know why he left all these up. It's like a fucking museum of women who left him."

"Maybe he missed you," Angelina said.

"Maybe he preferred the versions of us who couldn't speak. What are you doing?"

Angelina paused, halfway through unclipping the frame and claiming the sari photo for herself. "Someone's gotta keep the museum going."

"Angel," Jagvi said, and laughed, but Angelina shrugged, folding the photo in half and tucking it in her pocket, deadly serious. She'd keep it, the Jagvi Archives, possess all the shreds of Jagvi she could claim, even the ones she hadn't understood at the time, even the ones that had been Patrick's first.

They sat side by side on the floor surrounded by papers in a room so full of boxes that Angelina couldn't tell what its original function was. They were still a long way from morning, but neither of them could sleep, visions of Patrick's mangled cartilage swimming behind Angelina's eyes whenever she tried. Jagvi sorted papers while Angelina attempted to untangle a giant string of Christmas lights. Angelina stretched one leg out and Jagvi tucked her bare ankle neatly over Angelina's.

"What makes me so mad," Angelina said, "is that Franco and Sam are basing this 'companion' shit off of folktales and myths like that's a science. Everyone in these hills has some story about fucking a witch or punching the devil."

"Those stories would get warped pretty fast. Every time someone retells it, they get to add their own spin." Jagvi shook an ultrasound scan out of an envelope, examined it, and set it aside. "That's what I was trying to say the last time we were at Franco's place."

"You were right," Angelina said. "And half the stuff they said about the thing from the pit was useless. If they know enough to decide it's all your fault, why didn't they know enough to predict this shit with Patrick? Where in any story does someone get mauled half to death?"

"I would have liked a warning about that."

"You wouldn't have believed it," Angelina said and then added, "Sorry. I understand why."

"Doesn't matter now." Jagvi picked up the next stack. As far as Angelina could tell, Riccardo had kept every scrap that crossed his path: bills, letters, advertisements, as if he couldn't bear to let a single record out of his sight. "What did it mean when it talked about your memories?"

"It's just been going through my head a lot," Angelina said. She pointed

at the papers Jagvi was rifling through. "It kind of feels like that. Only...
wetter."

Jagvi grimaced. "But it said it's hungry, right? It was mad at you about it."

Angelina nodded. She plugged in the string of Christmas lights and raised
a thread of five shining bulbs. "Maybe this is how it feeds. It starts with my
past." She unscrewed the first two lights, and they popped out into darkness.
"Like, stealing my memories, forcing me to show it things. Then it shows
up in my present. It starts destroying things, it hurts me, it tries to kill Pat."
Two more lights came unscrewed and went out. "Then it moves on to my
future, somehow." She touched the last few lights on the chain. "That's why I
can't leave. 'Cause it's not done."

As she finished speaking, the whole bundle of lights fizzed and blinked
out. Angelina frowned, unplugged and plugged them in again, but they
wouldn't come back on.

"They're thirty years old," Jagvi said.

"Yeah," Angelina said. She glanced behind her, anyway. Nothing but the
wall splattered with stains. "Stay close to me, okay?"

Jagvi shifted across the floor until their bare elbows overlapped. "I'm not
going anywhere."

"That makes two of us," Angelina said, and laughed mirthlessly. She worried one of the lightbulbs between her finger and thumb. "It's not like I never
thought about moving away. But I hated that trip to San Michele so much,
and then there's Ma, and I don't have any money and I always worried that
I'd miss Cadenze more than I'd enjoy being somewhere else. I know this
thing has me in a trap, but it's not like I was very free before."

"You're lucky to have a place where you feel like you belong. Most people
don't have that."

"Don't you? In San Michele?"

"Nobody's ever threatened to run me out of the city," Jagvi said, "but yeah,
I don't know. I always felt like the odd one out, growing up here. That feeling
didn't go away just because I left. Maybe it's just me." Her teeth flashed, that
wolfish grin.

"But you have friends there," Angelina said.

"Oh, sure. I still see the college group sometimes, and my cousins. And there's three other butches in my station," she added. "We get pizza sometimes. Complain about girls."

"If I come to the city, will you introduce me to them?"

"No," Jagvi said. Heat sank through Angelina like a feather, swinging lazily down her abdomen to find its seat in her lower belly. Jagvi put her hand on Angelina's knee, her big palm cupping the kneecap. "Yeah, there's a nice crowd. And I hang out with my ex a lot."

The lights went out.

"Shit!" Angelina said, jumping to her feet, and she heard Jagvi swear, too, grabbing for Angelina in the dark, her warm hand wrapped around Angelina's forearm.

"That lightbulb's been on the fritz for ages," Jagvi said. "Hold my hand." She led Angelina to the other side of the room, where she slapped her palm hard against the crumbling plaster by the light switch. The lights came back on. They eyed each other.

"I can't believe it's fucking toying with us now." Fear prickled in Angelina's chest, but now the thing had come for her brother, and she was mad at it, too, full of biting disdain as if it were another asshole picking a fight with Patrick in Old Timers on a messy night.

"Should we run?" Jagvi asked.

Angelina raised her hands helplessly. "Run where?"

"Right."

For a moment neither of them moved. Then Jagvi shrugged and led Angelina back to their spot on the floor. Angelina tried not to feel like the thing from the pit had looked after her. Dropped the lights at the exact moment Angelina needed, so Jagvi couldn't see Angelina's expression when she mentioned her ex.

"So," she said, when she could trust her voice to stay light. "Who were you talking about?"

Jagvi seemed reluctant to start the story, glancing up at the lightbulb again. "Rosa. We met when I was twenty-three and she was thirty-two. She had so much more of her shit together than me."

"Why'd you break up?"

"Um, a few things. We didn't really have conversations. I always felt like she was coaching me to be a better person."

"Do you have conversations with her now?"

Jagvi laughed. "No, but it bothers me less. And it's kind of nice to have someone encouraging you to try harder. I should be a better person."

"I don't want you to be a better person," Angelina said. "Actually, I'm finding the fact that you're a good person pretty frustrating."

"Thanks, Angel," Jagvi said. "Likewise."

"One day I'm gonna tell Pat about the torment that he's caused us," Angelina said. It was nice to imagine there'd be a day when she could actually talk to him about it, and it would be lighthearted.

"Please don't," Jagvi said.

"Well, he has a lot to answer for." Jagvi didn't say anything. "I'm teasing."

"I know."

"You shouldn't listen to me," Angelina said. She flopped backward onto the floor, resting her head on a garbage bag filled with old curtains and rags and draping her legs over Jagvi's. "I'm still in shock."

She watched a spot of mold on the ceiling. She couldn't be entirely sure, but she thought it might be growing, spreading out sly, faded tendrils. But the only sense of presence in the room was Jagvi, who always seemed to take up more air than other people. Jagvi, who left Angelina desperate and shameless and able to say things like, "And from last night."

"It's pretty shocking to get attacked by a fountain," Jagvi said mildly. "Or did you mean something else?"

"Yeah," Angelina said, "at this point getting choked by a disembodied hand is kind of par for the course. What happened with you was much crazier."

"I'm gonna take that as a compliment," Jagvi said.

Angelina leered without taking her eyes away from the mold. "At least the thing can't take that away from me, huh? I got a night with Jagvi Pussyhound Marino."

"You should put that on a T-shirt," Jagvi said, and finally looked back at her, her face carefully untroubled.

207

"You liked it, too," Angelina said.

You're perfect, Jagvi had said. She'd looked like she meant it. She still looked like she meant it. "I liked it, Angel."

On the ceiling, the mold shifted into a design half-decipherable: G O.

"Go where?" Angelina said, and pointed.

Jagvi's voice dropped low. "Get out? Is that what it—"

But the mold wasn't done. Curling, languorous letters. G O O D G

"I'm feeling targeted," Angelina said.

G O O D   G I R L, said the mold on the ceiling.

"Let's try another room," Jagvi said.

XXIX

Aged fifteen, when Jagvi was a fascinating mystery, Angelina used to fantasize about Jagvi's bedroom. At the time she did not consider the fantasies to
be sexual. She used to lie in her own bed, close her eyes, and imagine that
when she opened them she would be in Jagvi's room. She tried to add detail,
populate books on shelves and posters on walls, the heavy denim jacket that
Angelina secretly coveted thrown over a chair, homework spilling over the
desk.

Tonight Angelina hesitated at the threshold to Jagvi's old room. It was full
of broken furniture. A burnt-out toaster lay next to a stack of phone books,
a box inexplicably crammed with dented saucepans alongside three planter
pots filled with dirt, an old bed frame with no mattress.

"I haven't really looked in here yet." Jagvi swept some of the crap off the
desk, perching on the cleared space with her back against the wall.

To the untrained eye maybe it was only a collection of junk, but Angelina could pick out the traces of Jagvi's teenage presence—peeling biology
and math textbooks on a scratched-up desk, a crappy stereo in the corner with a stack of metal albums, and, intriguingly, several CDs featuring
dreamy-looking girls with acoustic guitars. Peeling flyers for Myrna rock
concerts covered one wall. She studied them one by one, aware of Jagvi's
eyes on her. Seeing where Jagvi had slept for all those years somehow felt
more intimate than sharing a bed. Angelina touched the purple hair of an
old G!rlzone doll on a shelf.

"Angel?" Jagvi leaned forward, and Angelina put her hand out and let Jagvi touch it, their palms splayed against each other. Angelina knew what those fingers felt like inside her.

"Still me," she said. As if in response, the lights dimmed a little. It felt inviting.

Jagvi grabbed Angelina's hand and squeezed hard. "Come on, I'll let you go through my clothes. You can have that old jacket if you're good." The moment *good* came out of her mouth, they both cringed, and the light flickered back to full brightness.

"Which jacket?" Angelina asked, trying to sound casual.

"The denim one. You liked it, right? Help me move this out the way."

They hefted more boxes up onto Jagvi's bed frame. Jagvi pulled her wardrobe open with a creak.

"So many linen shirts," she marveled. "I can't believe I thought I was straight—"

"What's that?" Angelina interrupted. She pulled at a sparkling corner of fabric in the back. "Is this what you're wearing in the picture?"

"Yeah." Jagvi pulled the sari out. Its yellow had faded to mustard, but the embroidery shimmered. She shook out fold after fold of silk.

"I thought it was a dress?"

"You wrap it around you and tuck it in."

"But this is ten times longer than you."

Jagvi shrugged. "You want me to show you?"

Angelina knew her grin was too wide. "Yes! Absolutely."

"Okay," Jagvi said. "Only because you're being haunted, and because I can't find my jacket."

It took her a few false starts. Eventually she stripped off her T-shirt and loosened her belt enough to tuck folds into the waistline of her jeans. Angelina sat on the floor with her hand on Jagvi's bare foot.

"Ma always did this for me," Jagvi said, twisting her shoulders around. "I'm going to fuck it up. I'll need to pin it—there should be a couple pins hooked on that corner." Angelina crawled down the length of cloth to find them, and her knee hit a shoebox under the bed. She dragged it out and flipped it open, hoping to find an old pair of Jagvi's boots to steal. Instead there was the briefest stroke down her neck—an indulgent, conciliatory touch—and a sex toy.

Angelina hollered with joy. "Titty mags! Titty mags and a vibrator!"

"They're not titty mags," Jagvi said, looking amused, but they were *extremely* well-worn paperbacks with half-dressed heroines on the front, which counted, in Angelina's opinion. The vibrator was small, and very pink. Angelina wondered if she should feel weird about picking it up.

"Pins," Jagvi said.

Angelina found two safety pins hooked on a corner of golden netting. She handed them up to Jagvi, who held one in her mouth and used the other to pin the sari to the shoulder of her sports bra. Angelina clicked the vibrator, but its battery had died. "This is so cute."

"I didn't use it much," Jagvi said. "I can never be bothered with vibrators."

"Really?" Angelina was intrigued. She and Gemma had a biannual date where they visited a sex shop in Myrna and bought a new vibrator each, then went to a divey bar and split several bottles of red wine.

Jagvi shrugged. "Better with my fingers."

"Ha," Angelina said, face going hot, and blurted out, "but you like— You use other stuff, too. Like the packer."

"I told you that wasn't for sex," Jagvi said. "It's cute that you like it so much. Yeah, I use other stuff."

"So if I keep digging," Angelina said, "if I go through the rest of the stuff under your bed, am I gonna, what, will there be a strap there?"

"No."

Angelina let out a breath. She put the lid back on the shoebox. "Guess you never had much need for one in Cadenze—"

"It's in my backpack." Jagvi paused. "Back at your place."

Angelina stared at her. "You travel with one?"

Jagvi shrugged, silk ruffling around her. "Gotta be prepared."

"Ah." Angelina's mouth was wet. "You know, I've actually never."

"Yeah," Jagvi said, like she'd already guessed as much. The room was hot and still. Jagvi took in Angelina's wide, upturned eyes, and grinned. She turned her attention back to her sari. "I'm done."

The gold made Jagvi's skin glow even under the dingy light, and under the shimmering fabric, the line of her arm and her gesturing hand looked elegant, her stomach a decadent curve.

Angelina cleared her throat and managed to say, "It's more femme than you usually go, huh?"

"Yeah," Jagvi said, amused but not embarrassed. It added another layer to the way Jagvi looked, something campy, like a wink drenched in gold. Angelina wanted to snap another picture to match the one in her pocket. Being in this house with Jagvi was doing things to her that she hadn't expected. She could feel something tragic rising in her, a bittersweet nostalgia for what hadn't been, could not be. And then the thought of Patrick in the hospital came swinging through like an ax falling lower and lower, his ragged breathing, the thing playing with the lights, flicking out a shadow that looked like nothing so much as a long hand, outstretched, reaching.

XXX

In Riccardo's room there were still the remnants of life, grimy shirts, a drawer of faded bed linen. Jagvi hesitated over touching anything. She was getting tired again, Angelina had caught her hiding yawns, and she had to hold a fistful of sari at her hip to keep it on. Angelina made a pretense of sorting through Riccardo's old shirts on the floor so that Jagvi could sit on the bed in her silks and finery. The easiest way for them to touch was for Jagvi to rest her palm on the back of Angelina's neck. Her thumb skated over the skin below Angelina's left ear. It took physical effort to keep from tilting into her hand.

"Is it weird to be packing up all your dad's stuff?" Angelina asked.

"Not really weird," Jagvi said. "Just awful, you know."

"I'm sorry I didn't... I didn't think you'd have wanted me at the funeral."

"Huh?" Jagvi shook her head. "It's okay. Pat was there. It would probably have just, uh—confused me, if you showed up."

"Because you're so used to me being an asshole?"

"Because you confuse me," Jagvi said.

Angelina turned and looked up, her head resting against Jagvi's knee. There was something huge in her chest that she didn't have words for, and when she looked across the space between them, she found Jagvi just as overwhelmed.

They had made a big mistake yesterday. They had spent a decade spitting at each other from either side of a boundary, and now they had crossed it and there was no going back, no forgetting how it felt to wrap her legs around Jagvi's hips, taste Jagvi's tongue in her mouth. Every conversation was like a whirlpool, a drain they were circling, dragging them both back into the center.

Jagvi's voice was rough. "We should keep talking."

"What?"

"I don't think it likes it when we go quiet," Jagvi said. Behind her the faded wallpaper's ugly paisley print was resolving into words that Angelina tried to avoid reading.

Angelina swallowed. "What if it was just—your dad. Just a regular kind of haunting."

Jagvi laughed, short and unimpressed. "No. He's worm meat for sure."

"Even now that we know there are..." Angelina gesticulated wildly, conjuring up hauntings and monsters.

Jagvi nodded. "There's nothing mysterious about him. His life feels like a pathetic map to me. This thing—I don't know where it's taking us."

A breeze caught in the curtains, making them dance and twitch. The windows in the room were sealed shut. Outside only the black of night.

"Like, if it was your dad, it would be easier to deal with."

"Maybe in some ways, yeah," Jagvi said. "He was more transparent. But the thing from the pit feels both...more dangerous and less damaging. It feels like something you can be free to hate, without the obligation to forgive. Unlike parents." She kicked at the bedside table. "Even if you know they treat you like shit."

"Are you talking about Meera as well?"

"Oh, Meera!" Jagvi cackled, brightening. "No, we get on pretty well. She loves me."

"She always sort of scared me. Even when we were kids, she was so...cold."

"She was like that on purpose."

"You do it, too. Close yourself off."

"Maybe." Jagvi spoke gently. "Cadenze was hell on earth for her. She'd been trying to convince me to leave for a while, even before I came out. It was amazing, when we finally did. Seeing everything I'd missed."

"I'm still not enough proof there are queer girls here, too?"

"Baby," Jagvi said, and Angelina whipped around to stare at her, but Jagvi was exhausted and trying to outtalk a monster, and she didn't seem to notice the word as it left her mouth, continued smoothly, "I'm talking about brown people."

"Oh." Technically, Angelina wanted to say, her original response was still accurate. But it was something she didn't talk about.

"You know, when we first left Cadenze, we stayed with my aunt—my ma still lives with her. She's a really strict Hindu, and the first night I was there, I ordered noodles with beef and she gave me this forty-minute lecture. And the whole time my cousins were like, winking over the sofa at me. It was like familial disapproval and familial approval at the same time."

"How many cousins do you have?"

"Eleven. Ma has four sisters and they all have kids. I was always shy around them."

Angelina barked a laugh. "You?"

"It's weird with them," Jagvi said, and paused, trying to work it out. "I don't know. When I realized I was gay and especially when I found that group in San Michele, it was like, *Ah fuck, here's who I am, thank god I found you.* But it was the opposite with my cousins. They're all so—I'm the only one with a white parent, and I grew up *here*, and Ma did her best, but I don't speak any Bengali and I never went to temple and we didn't celebrate any holidays. That's what I mean. In Cadenze, Ma and I were always—we were the odd ones out, but when we're with the rest of her family, it's just me sticking out on my own."

"So why does it— Why did you say it was amazing," Angelina said, stumbling over the words, "if it—that sounds like it's shit."

Jagvi shook her head. "It's hard sometimes. But I like being around them, we have fun together. It's nice to be able to see where you come from and then choose another direction."

She gave Angelina a look like a dare, but Angelina didn't want to disagree with her. She suspected that Jagvi was talking about Cadenze as well, but her knee-jerk instinct to defend Cadenze had lost its usual power. "Caro would agree with you. Even me and Pat were too much direction for her. She had to run off to the other side of town to make sure we didn't point her anywhere."

Jagvi's face hardened. "Well, Caro."

"I know, I know." Angelina blew out an annoyed breath. "She's being stupid tonight, but Pat will talk her around."

"We shouldn't need her permission to stay in your house."

"We don't really," Angelina said. "She just let the others get to her. She would never do something like that on her own."

"Maybe," Jagvi said.

"You don't think so?"

Jagvi shrugged. "I mean, she's never been strong for you guys, has she?"

"She drove Pat to the hospital all on her own," Angelina said defensively. "I know she can be unreliable, but she cares about us. You saw her after I got hurt up on the mountain. She wouldn't leave my bedroom."

"She got in the way," Jagvi said. "Pat had to spend all his time comforting her instead of taking care of you. And as soon as she'd had her fill of attention, she ran away again, just like she did when you were kids."

"She didn't run away from us," Angelina argued, then realized she'd just said exactly that. Jagvi was kind enough not to point it out, but her raised eyebrows said enough. "She...doesn't do well with responsibility."

"But whenever she needs you or Pat, you have to drop everything to be there for her. Being a mother was too much for her, but you're both supposed to baby her, and you can't ever depend on her for anything because she's *so* fragile." This last was delivered with thick, cloying sarcasm, and Angelina turned around fully to study Jagvi's face.

"You really hate her," she said, surprised.

"No," Jagvi said. "Sorry. I know she's your mother. She just makes me angry."

"But you don't even interact."

Jagvi blinked. "Not because of how she treats me. I just hate how she is with—with you and Pat."

"Oh," Angelina said. Jagvi looked sympathetic, but not quite apologetic. "You mean leaving when we were young."

"Well. Yeah. To start."

The room was colder than before. Angelina felt abruptly childlike, staring up at Jagvi and arguing her mother's case. If Pat were here, he'd take Angelina's side, but he was broken and bleeding, miles away. She stood up. "She didn't abandon us. She was around all the time."

"Sure," Jagvi said.

"What do you mean, to start?"

"I don't want to have a go at your ma—"

"But?"

"I just don't like the way she talks to you both," Jagvi said. "She treats you like... it's high school and she wants to win the popularity contest. Or like you're these terrible burdens she has to bear."

"Have you told Pat you think this?"

"Yeah, we talk about it a lot," Jagvi said, and Angelina jerked backward, blinking rapidly. "Angel—"

"No, it's fine. I know Pat has a—a hard time with her."

"And you don't?" Jagvi said, her voice careful, like she thought Angelina was about to snap. Was Angelina about to snap?

"She's harder on Pat. He's not the Sicco girl."

"When you were seventeen, you told me the Sicco girl thing was a myth," Jagvi said. "And every time I've heard Caro talk about it, it just seems like another burden she's putting on you."

"It's complicated," Angelina said. She felt frozen under Jagvi's observation, which had been keen and trained on her for longer than she'd realized.

"Maybe," Jagvi said. "But it's not great. And I think it's messed up that she didn't tell you anything about your dad."

The lights shuddered above them, a momentary respite from Jagvi's attention. Angelina walked out of the room to slap her hand against the hallway wall and see if that helped. Remembering they were supposed to stay together, she came back to stand in the doorway, but she couldn't make herself return to Jagvi's side. She stood just beyond the threshold and said, "I'm not sure it would have been better if she told me about my dad. Pat knew a lot about his dad, and it made him feel worse."

Jagvi nodded; she already knew.

"Yeah, I mean that was its own shitty thing," Jagvi said. "But I think… everyone was always speculating about you, and she just let it happen."

"Uh." Angelina swallowed. She walked backward until she could lean against the hallway wall, watching Jagvi on the bed in her golden silks. Angelina had never thought of her father as something her mother should or could handle. It was just something that had happened to Caro, the same way her family's disappointment had happened to her, or her children's demands. The loss of Angelina's father had always been Caro's burden, Caro's life, Caro's luck, nothing to do with Angelina. But he was Angelina's dad. "Yeah. Maybe."

"Do you want me to stop talking about this?"

Angelina shook her head. Her fingertips tingled, guilt and fascination shoving at each other. "I want you to tell me more."

Jagvi pushed her hand back through her hair. "It's not like you *needed* a father, but I think it would have been helpful if you had any idea who he was, especially given that you were a little brown kid growing up in a mostly white town. She must know something, and she's just choosing not to tell you. I feel like you were robbed of your dad."

The door between them slammed shut. Angelina swung around, searching for the thing from the pit, and found nothing, no voice or presence. She ran for Riccardo's bedroom door.

Jagvi slammed against it at the same time. "Angel, hey, Angel—"

"I'm here," Angelina said, and rattled the handle: it was fixed shut. "Do you have a key?"

"There's no lock. Move back, I'm gonna try and break through."

Angelina pressed herself flat against the wall. There were several hard thuds. The door was scratched and cheap. It should have splintered easily. But it stood firm and unmoving as Jagvi threw herself against it.

"This fucking house," Jagvi snapped, and her voice had shifted down into that brutal, practical tone that meant they were in real trouble. "You okay, Angel? Angel?"

Angelina stayed where she was, palms flat against plaster. Rabbit in the headlights, or idiot teetering on the edge of the cliff; all night, something like this had been coming for her, and now she stood frozen to watch it arrive. Mold rolled across the opposite wall. A clean green sheet, a base layer, before the words started to stream out.

NOT ROBBED

"Angel! Angel, are you—"

"It's talking again," Angelina said. Her voice stayed so steady.

The letters weren't languorous anymore. Streaky capitals, dashed out in rage and resentment. *HE WAS NOT STOLEN HE WAS SAVORED*

"Angel," Jag said, "you gotta stand really back, okay—"

Angelina peeled herself away from the wall. She could still move, but everything was slow, and it took a gigantic effort to take a few steps. The door splintered, and Jagvi said her name, agonized. Angelina drifted away. The thing had her in its current, the whole house oozing with its power, and Angelina suspended like a wasp in a jar of honey. Another second and an ax slammed through. Jagvi followed, shouldering her way past the wreckage of the door, her sari billowing around her and catching on the jagged wood.

"Where did you get the ax from," Angelina said dreamily.

Jagvi grabbed her by the back of her neck and hauled her in close. "Under Dad's bed. Stay with me."

A callus thumbed over Angelina's nape and sent her shuddering back into herself. She grabbed Jagvi's hand, squeezed it tight, and said, teeth chattering, "I think it's talking about my dad—"

HE WAS NOT FOR YOU, screamed across the wall. *HE WAS TOO GOOD FOR YOU TOO DELICIOUS.*

"Come on!" Jagvi dragged Angelina along the hallway. Doors slammed behind them, the sound of chairs scraping across linoleum, as though a hundred ravenous guests were storming through. "See, this is what happens when we give Caro too much fucking attention—"

The lights blared brighter and brighter as they stumbled down the stairs, and the banisters turned in on themselves, wood cracking back to form letters that read *S L U T.*

"Are you seeing this, too—"

"Yeah," Jagvi said, voice ragged, and Angelina squeezed her eyes shut, trying to escape. In the dark she saw dots swarming together: *S T U P I D SLUT LIKE MOTHER LIKE*

Her eyes flew open. They'd made it to the front door. Jagvi dragged the chair out of the way, but the door wouldn't open. The ax bounced off and away, wresting itself from Jagvi's grip, and when the blade hit the opposite wall, it shattered. Dodging shards, they threw themselves to the ground, hands over each other's heads. Jagvi's thumb against her forehead dripped sticky liquid.

"Hold on to me," Jagvi said, and they scrambled to their feet. Angelina wound her arms around Jagvi's waist, smoothing her hands under where the sari was coming loose and baggy at the sides so she could get her fingers on bare skin. She pressed her palms flat against Jagvi's stomach and tucked her face against Jagvi's neck.

"Should have stuck to possessing stone," Jagvi yelled, furious and gleeful. "This house is cheap bullshit, and I've wanted to knock it down for years."

She picked up one of the discarded chairs and slammed it against the closest wall. Plaster splintered; something screamed. Jagvi tried it again and left a hole in the drywall. The chair broke, which didn't seem to faze her. She reached for anything heavy enough to work, and the paper-thin house was full of solid junk, a broken stool, a rusted cast-iron pot. Angelina curled close against Jagvi's back and they shuffled through the house like some slow and formidable animal, bashing their way through the walls and doors that tried to press back at them, plaster rising and crashing like waves.

"Down!" Jagvi snapped, and Angelina threw their clutched-close bodies to the floor in time for every kitchen window to shatter, so the house opened up and seemed to lean toward Little Joe's grim slope limned by the coming dawn. Everywhere Angelina looked was jagged glass. Jagvi shook glittering shards out of Angelina's hair, cradling her scalp. Walls swung toward them;

the roof bowed and bucked, like its rafters wanted to break free and embrace them.

"Pat's gonna be so mad if we die here," Angelina said.

Jagvi grinned, all of her heightened and gleaming with adrenaline. "He hates to be left out."

"He needs to get used to it."

"Angel—"

"Better save my life first," Angelina said, and they lunged to their feet, picking up the dining table like a shield. Shoulder to shoulder, steel legs digging into their palms, they hurtled forward in a desperate charge through the mangled panes of the kitchen window. Plaster rained from the ceiling, glass sliced up through their sneakers, and they spilled outside onto the long grass. They lay curled around each other on the undersurface of the table, Angelina's face pressed blindly into the curve of Jagvi's throat. The house sagged in on itself behind them, the ground rippling with aftershocks, an indignant earthquake meant just for them.

Her knees throbbed where she'd landed on them, and she could taste hot salt, liquid on her lip that she realized was Jagvi's blood. She startled, but it was only a small cut beneath Jagvi's ear from an errant shard of glass. Before she could think better of it, Angelina fit her mouth to the jagged red line and sucked, lathing the cut with her tongue.

"Angel," Jagvi said, and put her hand on Angelina's arm, which was how Angelina discovered she was shaking. She wriggled closer into Jagvi's space, swung one leg over Jagvi's hip, her mouth still pressed to Jagvi's skin. She could feel Jagvi's pulse now, quick beneath her tongue, and Jagvi said her name again, and then caught her by the chin and pulled her down to the kiss.

She dragged Angelina in, mouth deep as a cavern and her breaths coming hard, a heavy, frantic kiss, both of them shocked to be alive. They were chest to chest now, open-mouthed, and Angelina knew distantly that there was pain waiting for her, but her body was singing, and Jagvi's hands were all over her.

The house roared behind them. They stopped at the same time, Angelina's face hovering an inch above Jagvi's. There was an awful groan of metal from inside, like the belly of a ship tearing open as it sank. Before Angelina could catch her breath, Jagvi hauled her up, and they limped away. Angelina didn't know where the thing was. She wished she could believe that it had died on their way out, crushed under the wreckage, but she knew better by now. Things happened when it wanted them to. It drip fed them clues when it wanted them to know more. It used violence to force their hands and retreated when it wanted them to catch their breath. Farther up the path, the roof of the ugly house seemed to spasm and then caved in on itself, a dark, ugly mass collapsing against the gray-blue pall of early dawn. A white sun rose from the other side of town, climbing through the clouds like some other beast called up from some other pit.

"It was talking about your dad," Jagvi said, dazed. "We need to speak to Caro. Maybe we'll find out why she doesn't talk about him."

"Yeah," Angelina said, and stopped walking. Jagvi looked at her, her sari undone, trailing behind her in a golden path back to the debris. They stood alone on the empty mountain road. "Jag. You said you weren't gonna do it again."

She watched Jagvi's face change into an expression that Angelina had first seen when she was sixteen and never, ever forgotten. Shame and desire intertwined. Something helpless. The kind of hunger that had to be fed.

"I didn't mean to kiss you," Jagvi said.

Angelina wiped something wet on her forehead, blood or sweat. "That makes it worse. That means you can't help it."

Jagvi yanked the sari the rest of the way off, bundling it under her arm and standing in her sports bra and heavy jeans. "I know."

"Well, join the club," Angelina said. They leaned close, foreheads touching. Angelina's heart was pounding. "It's enough now. I'm done. Aren't you?"

"I'm done," Jagvi agreed. "I give."

They turned down toward Angelina's house, slow and sore, leaning close together. Like they were members of the same sports team, walking exhausted off the pitch after a game they'd given their all to and lost. Part of Angelina wanted to cry, something deep and sad. Then Jagvi's fingers brushed against her hand, and the sorrow slipped its chains and found a comfortable place at the back of her head. She let Jagvi tangle their fingers together.

"Let's go home," Jagvi said.

Angelina looked at her. The dim dawn was a relief after the burning bulbs in Riccardo's home, and Jagvi looked back, not quite serious. Something joyful and expectant grew in her face. Angelina drew in a quick breath. "You wanna hurry?"

"No," Jagvi said. "I've waited long enough. Ten minutes isn't going to kill me."

"Speak for yourself," Angelina said, and they ran hand in hand down the mountain.

XXXI

Jagvi liked to carry her: something Angelina had already suspected and now knew for sure. Jagvi liked the heavy weight of Angelina slung over her shoulder, she liked to nudge Angelina away from agency. Angelina couldn't have escaped from Jagvi's arms if she'd wanted, and the thing couldn't take her from Jagvi either. Jagvi's grip was hard and possessive with no space for anything else.

When they crossed the Sicco threshold, Jagvi scooped Angelina into her arms and pressed her back into the dark turn of the stairwell, the silk tip of Jagvi's tongue on her palate, the crush of her teeth on Angelina's lower lip. Angelina's breath came in rough pants, and Jagvi carried her higher through the house, pausing only to scoop up her backpack from the hallway. Downstairs, locked in her cage, My Dog howled for company. *I feel you, babe*, Angelina thought. *But it's my turn to fuck something up.*

On Angelina's small bed they jerked each other out of their clothing, practical and desperate, no more time left for them to waste. Angelina's loose hair trailed over her chest until Jagvi pulled it aside in an easy fist, Angelina already down to her underwear and grinding messily against Jagvi's denim-clad thigh. They yanked Jagvi's bra up over her head, and Angelina groaned in despair at her pointy tits, the hair in her pits, her knuckles grazing Angelina's hips as she drew Angelina's underwear down.

Easing away, panting and lovely, Jagvi reached for the strap. Angelina pushed up on her elbows and watched as Jagvi drew the harness tight. The clear gray light of morning flooded her bedroom, and Angelina had been up most of the night, her body shuddering between anguish and alarm and desire, and Jagvi looked unreal, like Angelina had dreamed her up. Angelina nursed at her own fingers, making anxious, urgent noises.

"I'm gonna fuck it up if you keep doing that." The sound of Jagvi's voice in the still house startled Angelina, and she rolled up to knee walk over the mattress until she was before Jagvi, laying a flat hand over her stomach, tilting her mouth up for the kiss, still frantic and restless until Jagvi's tongue stroked hard and soothing against hers. The reminder that Jagvi was here, to take care of it—break them out of the house, save her from the thing, take Angelina to bed. Everything Angelina needed, along with the full-breath relief of tipping responsibility into Jagvi's competent grip.

Jagvi nipped Angelina's bottom lip, and Angelina smiled against her mouth, mumbled, "Is it as tricky as the sari?"

"Almost as complicated," Jagvi agreed, but she didn't falter, fingers sure on the buckles. Her dick was the same color as her inner thigh, a paler brown than her biceps, her stomach, her dark nipples. Angelina reached for it, but Jagvi batted her hand away. She shoved Angelina, tipping her back against the bed.

"I don't want you to feel it until it's inside you."

"Jag," Angelina ground out. Waves of electricity swept over her as Jagvi lifted Angelina's knee and hooked it over Jag's shoulder, first touch of her fingers sliding down. Like Jagvi had found a switch inside her and was casually flipping it on and on and on. Angelina could feel sweat pooling everywhere, in the crooks of her knees, in the small of her back, a sheen on her forehead and her neck: if she were to disappear right now, she'd leave a perfect damp imprint of her body on the sheet behind her. But she hadn't disappeared, she hadn't been taken, she'd escaped the crumbling house; she tipped her head back, baring her throat, whining, and Jagvi used her slick fingers to get the dick wet, a sure, confident circle with her fist.

Angelina had thought it might hurt. She'd thought she might need time to adjust, or that she would have to ask Jagvi to slow down. But it didn't hurt at all. From the first blunt breach, she was moaning, clutching Jagvi's shoulders, hips tilting up into it, Jagvi's hot face pressed against her neck. Jagvi panted hard against her, sharp breaths like a whine, and when Angelina hooked her legs up around Jagvi's waist, Jagvi actually shouted, hips jerking forward, pressing in deep and hard.

"It's honestly a disgrace no other girl has done this for you," Jagvi said, and fucked her hard enough that Angelina saw stars. "Not when you look so pretty taking it." Her voice was breathless, devoted and mean. Somehow Angelina knew that she could feel every part of this, every spasm, every inch of the strap as Angelina clenched around it. "But I'm glad."

"I can't talk," Angelina stuttered out. "When you're— I can't—"

"I know, baby," Jagvi said, mouth at Angelina's cheek, her jaw, the sensitive tip of her ear. Angelina was coming apart fast. Her body felt like hot liquid, a pool that Jagvi was swimming in, and as Jagvi licked a possessive line along Angelina's throat, Angelina sent out a frenzied prayer to her monster, *Thank you for allowing us this, thank you for letting me have her*, and felt the satisfaction of the monster far away, somewhere out in the hills or the splinters of Jagvi's old house. The silence that meant, You're Welcome. The gift of a moment that it would come back for later, and take to sate its own hunger.

She didn't want to think of her monster when she came, but she did. She thought of both of them. Trembling, full of internal gratitude like a prayer, clutching Jagvi close until Jagvi kissed her again and pushed her back flat against the mattress. But Angelina couldn't let her go, wouldn't let her go; she twined her legs around Jagvi's waist, arms around her, heels knocking in the small of Jagvi's back. Jagvi gasped, one elbow on the mattress for balance and her other hand gripping Angelina's hip, keeping her close, and she fucked Angelina hard and fast, took her pleasure, jerking her clit against the strap's ridged base and pushing it deep enough that Angelina yowled. When Jagvi came, her face was vicious and triumphant, the conquering hero come home at last.

XXXII

Outside rain fell on the mountain. Torn wallpaper swelled to new breadths with the first steady patter of water as misty droplets sank into frayed paper and found they liked it there. Mud set up camp through the ruin of Riccardo's house. The floor was submerged. The mountain observed the roof cracked open, the shattered walls, and hurried to reclaim the corpse for itself.

It was still raining late in the morning, but Angelina didn't notice. She'd woken to find Jagvi watching her. By the time Angelina managed to blink her eyes open completely, Jagvi already looked rueful. Angelina reached out to catch her before she turned, thumb sliding over her bottom lip. Jagvi caught the tip between her teeth. Angelina blinked, and they both began to crow at the same time.

"Don't fucking *watch me sleep*," Angelina started, already breathless with laughter, and Jagvi countered, "Who wakes up and sticks their hand in someone's mouth, what kind of evolutionary response is that?" She was laughing, too, that low, rough laugh that interrupted speech, but her hands were matter-of-fact and sure of themselves on Angelina's body.

"Because I'm so hungry," Angelina protested, trying to claw back some authority and losing it immediately as she nosed along Jagvi's rib cage, up into her armpit, feathery hair against her nose. "I'm starving, when are you going to give me some food, haven't you taken enough liberties without starving me to death as well—"

"This is your house," Jagvi said, grabbing Angelina's chin, wrestling her into a kiss.

"And I'm just meant to cook?" Angelina demanded. "For myself? You're just gonna fuck my brains out and then order me into the kitchen—"

Jagvi cackled, tipping Angelina onto her back. Hot mouth against Angelina's neck, drag of her teeth against Angelina's collarbone. "Order you? Is that a request?"

Angelina wriggled, one of Jagvi's legs slotting between her thighs, making her breath escape in a whine. "I bet this was your plan all along," she said. "Turn me into your messed-up little housewife—"

"Again," Jagvi said, grinning, "this is your house. Mine just got torn down."

"Convenient excuse," Angelina said, and pushed up, shoving Jagvi off her and immediately losing all haughty power by collapsing on top of her, ear against Jagvi's chest. "You won't get me that easily."

"Bet I will," Jagvi said. Her heartbeat was so steady. Her thumb slid along the line of Angelina's jaw. "Where do you think it is?"

"I don't know."

"Do you still think it was toying with us?"

"I think we made it angry eventually, but yeah, it was playing games before that." The shape of that twining mold kept coming back to her, words reaching like hands across the ceiling. GOOD GIRL. Like it was praising its pet. Was that what she was?

My Dog was still cowering in her cage downstairs. They would need to let her out to pee soon, poor sweetheart, and she must be hungry. She was just a pet as well, confused and anxious as they were, bearing punishment for crimes that were not her own.

"I want to call Pat," Angelina said. "Tell him we're here."

Unless she had slept through it, no Siccos had come back up Big Joe to check on them. Perhaps Pat had already gotten through to them. Perhaps they were too afraid to return. When they came here last night, they'd not yet seen the state of Patrick and what that thing had done to him.

"We can do that," Jagvi said. Her hand was in Angelina's hair, but she didn't stroke: she wove her fingers through the roots, keeping a gentle grip.

"We have a plan now, Angel. It gave something away, and we're gonna chase it."

"Right," Angelina agreed, but she didn't move. Jagvi's rib cage rose and fell beneath her cheek, and what Angelina really wanted was to sink into the cavern of Jagvi's chest, hide within the deepest part of her, and never come out. "I have to work tonight. We could drive to Caro's and talk to her before my shift."

Angelina called the number Pat had given them last night, but Suze had clocked out, and it was a new nurse on shift who told them that Patrick was doing more tests and she didn't know when he'd be back. She refused to take a message but did grudgingly confirm that Pat had gotten some sleep. Jagvi made Angelina breakfast while Angelina showered. She came downstairs to find Jagvi frying pancakes shirtless in a pair of black underwear, the bulge of her packer visible.

She looked impossible. She looked holy, like San Rocco himself had shown up to make Angelina breakfast. If Angelina spoke, she was going to say something terrible, so instead she tiptoed up behind her to fit close against Jagvi's back and grab her tits.

Jagvi, unbothered, handed her a cup of coffee.

"Hey," Angelina said, grinding against Jag's ass, "shall *I* fuck you?"

"If you like," Jagvi said politely.

"I totally could!"

"I know," Jagvi said, voice thick with amusement.

"You'd love it, Jag. I'd be the greatest top in the world."

"I can't wait," Jagvi said, and pinched her ass.

"You should be nicer to me," Angelina complained. "I think you broke me." Jagvi turned, backing Angelina up, taking back the coffee mug to put Angelina up on the counter and stand between her knees, hands in Angelina's hair, licking into Angelina's mouth. Angelina folded against her. "Fuckin' big-city dyke with your big-city dick taking advantage of little old me—"

"I can get a smaller one," Jagvi said, smiling against her mouth, "if you want. But I don't think you do."

"You can't just always call my bluff and assume you'll win! Maybe I want a bunch in all different sizes!" Angelina pulled back from Jagvi, curious. "Hey, what do straight girls do? Like, do you just accept whatever you get? That sucks."

"I think about that *all the time*," Jagvi said fervidly.

All through the dregs of morning the phone rang, like a summons away from Jagvi's mouth, like a reminder that they had more important things to be doing, like an alarm shrieking at Angelina's betrayal. There were monsters to fight and brothers to heal. Three separate people called Angelina to ask if it was true her dog had attacked Patrick. Gemma rang convinced that San Rocco was wreaking punishment, and needed talking down from hysteria; Angelina's boss at the call center checked in to ensure the latest Sicco mystery wouldn't interfere with Angelina's next shift on Wednesday. At each new jangle of the phone, Angelina leapt out of her place in Jagvi's lap like she'd been electrified, grinding her teeth at every caller who had the gall to not be Patrick.

He finally phoned in the early afternoon, his voice already steadier. Joy and guilt in equal measure churned in Angelina's stomach.

"Why are you so hard to track down?" Patrick complained. "What's going on, did Ma let you back in the house?"

"She hasn't left a guard or anything," Angelina said. "And we had to feed My Dog. We managed to get her out back, Jag tied her up but she seems calm now. Oh, uh, and we kind of destroyed Jagvi's dad's house." She rushed through an explanation.

"But it's gone now? It's not speaking to you?"

"No," she said, which wasn't technically a lie. The *You're Welcome* she'd heard could have been imagined, or implied in its silence, and Angelina kept straining her ears for conversation that never came.

"Just stay close to Jagvi," Patrick said. "Give her a high five or a handshake every so often, yeah? Don't stop touching."

Angelina's mouth tasted of ash. "We won't. Did you speak to Caro?"

"I tried. She left this morning. She kept saying I need to rest my voice, and to let the uncles handle it. You know what she's like."

"Yeah. We'll go and see her soon. How are you feeling?"

"Fine. Bored. They want me to stay another few days to finish the drugs. I'm not allowed any beer."

"We'll buy you a gallon when you're back," Angelina said. "Barrels of beer."

"Toast the end of that house. Was Jag pleased?"

A tentative note in his voice, like he already knew it was more complicated than that. Angelina held out the receiver and said, "Ask her yourself."

Jagvi came forward from where she'd been lingering in the doorway. "Hey, Pat. How's the bite?" A faint, dismissive murmur from the phone. Jag's shoulders relaxed. "Yeah, pretty satisfying."

She beckoned and Angelina slunk closer to eavesdrop. Arm around Jagvi's shoulders for balance, Jagvi's hand on her hip. Quick regretful dip of Jagvi's eyes at her, though neither of them let go as Patrick continued: "...destroy the thing that haunts you."

"Childhood home done," Angelina chimed in. "Just the monster to go."

"Exactly," Jagvi and Patrick said at the same time.

When he hung up, Jagvi didn't move. She held the receiver lax in one hand, her other still resting on Angelina's hip, their bodies like brackets curving toward one another with Patrick cupped in the space between. Jagvi's expression was far and remote, which meant Angelina could look down into it without fear of being caught.

"You wanna talk about it?" Angelina said eventually.

"I don't think there's much to talk about." Jagvi rubbed her eyes. "Are you used to lying to him?"

"Yeah, sure. Most of it's dumb shit, you know, stealing his weed or saying I took the trash out last time, whatever, but I mean...I didn't tell him I was gay for ages. I barely told him anything about Dani. You know that. What else." She searched for more secrets to offer up. "I hooked up with this woman last summer and we had a fight and she kicked me out of her car and I was too drunk to get home, slept in a ditch. He would've freaked if he knew, so I said I slept at Gemma's. When I was seventeen I stole a twenty from his wallet and we had no money and I felt *really* bad about it and couldn't sleep for weeks and I still never told him." Jagvi smiled a little but didn't say anything. "Does that help?"

"Not really. We have a different relationship."

"He loves you as much as he loves me."

"No."

"Maybe more. He actually chose you. He just got stuck with me."

Jagvi snorted. "That's not true."

"If he finds out, you can blame it on me," Angelina tried. "You can tell him it was all me. You tried to stay away and I wouldn't let you. The *thing* wouldn't let you. You did everything you could, Jag, and I'm the one who can't get enough—"

She'd gone too far. She couldn't stop talking, and she had Jag's attention back, Jagvi's eyes hot and dark, her mouth twisted unhappily, so Angelina should shut up but she couldn't.

"I'm the one who's been obsessed, I'm the embarrassing teenager in this scenario, you were just throwing me a bone—"

"Angel." Jagvi kissed her, slow and careful, thumb stroking the line of Angelina's jaw. Angelina was shivering. She felt humiliated and small, and some part of her liked feeling that in front of Jag, comfortable in her old habits. Jagvi murmured against her mouth, "You know none of that's true, right?"

"Isn't it?"

Jagvi drew back, cocked her head to the side. "Not even close," she said, rapping Angelina over the head with her knuckles. "C'mon. Let's go talk to Caro."

XXXIII

They took Patrick's truck. Jagvi drove. Angelina could have driven herself; the thing only stepped in when Angelina tried to leave Cadenze. But she wanted to sit in the passenger seat beside Jagvi, prop her feet up on the dashboard and watch Jagvi's forearms draped over the wheel. Patrick lay quiet and unspoken between them—but laid aside, for now. They had to interrogate Caro first. One Sicco at a time.

"Will it just be your ma?" Jagvi asked. "Or are your uncles gonna be there, too?"

"I don't know," Angelina said. Caro was unpredictable in times of crisis, as likely to announce breezily that it was nothing to do with her as she was to seek comfort and security in her brothers' arms. "Either way, nothing changes, okay? We're just there to ask for some information."

Jagvi glanced at her.

"What?"

"And if your uncles want to take you away from the big bad dyke?"

"First off, Jag, I'm taller than you, and second, they don't like you because they think you're an associate of the devil, not because you're a lesbian. This time, anyway. And third, they can want whatever they like. It didn't work last night, remember?" After she finished speaking, Jagvi kept looking at her. Angelina's face went hot. "What?"

"Nothing." Jagvi took the turn up onto the Pepper Grinder. "It feels good to be on the road."

"Yeah? Even driving to see Caro?"

Jagvi nodded. "It's a good time, riding around with Angelina Sicco."

The rain had slowed to a fine dew, and mist rose up all around them, green and gray trails swathing the car, fogging up the windows. The valley was unwilling to give up its warmth, even as they barreled through September. Angelina felt like she was caught in a hothouse, as though her life were blooming around her, too fast to control. If she didn't keep smiling, she was going to cry.

"Do you ever think about what it would have been like if it had been—you and me?" she said. "In high school?"

She half expected Jagvi to flinch, but instead Jagvi laughed. "A lesbian romance in Cadenze? With two teenage brown girls? Yeah, that would have been a very sweet hour before I got run out of town."

"They're not *that* bad," Angelina protested. "They've seen me with plenty of girls."

"Oh, plenty?" Jagvi said, and laughed again when Angelina sulked back into her seat. "You learned how to manage them. It's impressive, but I think ten years ago we would have been eaten alive." She paused, then added, with that gentle note, "You pass better than me, too."

"Yeah." Angelina's features and her missing father gave her away, but her skin was lighter than some of the more tanned farmers, and she slipped easily into crowds. Jagvi stood out everywhere she went. Angelina tried, "We could have kept it secret."

"That's true," Jagvi said, flashing a grin at her. "Tortured dyke Romeo and Juliet. Very romantic."

Angelina ran her hand along Jagvi's leg, squeezed her thigh. "C'mon, Jag, play with me. I could have climbed out my window at night to meet you. Secret looks across the school bus—"

"We're riding the bus in this fantasy? I seem to remember teenage Angelina thought the bus was for losers only."

"You're so annoying," Angelina said. "I never get indulged."

A lazy dip of Jagvi's eyes reminded her that wasn't true. Angelina's face went hot, and then she had a new idea and started tracing her fingers up the inseam of Jagvi's jeans.

"Okay, fine, keep it safe and heterosexual," she said. "What if you'd been my *boy*friend, huh?"

Jagvi laughed again, but not in the same way. Rough catch of her throat.

Angelina lowered her eyelashes modestly, because it was that or start howling with joy and greed. "Come pick me up on Friday nights? Have to shake Patrick's hand and promise to have me back by midnight? 'Cause you were older, Jag," she added, pressing her thighs together restlessly as she sank further into it, "you'd have to promise to be so, so respectful, and then you could—we could drive out to the hookup spot at night, instead—"

"Angel," Jagvi said breathlessly.

"Everyone would wanna know what a sweet girl like me was doing with a guy like you." Angelina's hand slid up, knuckling over Jagvi's crotch, turning her hand around and cupping the dick that wasn't there right then. Jag's hips jerked up into her palm. "Sitting on your lap while you had beers with the boys? Wearing a long pretty skirt so no one could see where your hands were?"

Jagvi pulled the car over and dragged Angelina into her lap. "No one who knew you," she said, "would ever call you sweet."

They made out with the steering wheel digging into Angelina's back for ten minutes before they realized, with a jolt, that they were parked beside Caro's little house.

"Fuck!" Angelina scrambled back, craning her head over her shoulder to peer at the hut, which looked empty, even though the Skoda was outside. Angelina stuck her fingers into her mouth automatically, licking them clean. Jagvi lifted her hips to button up her fly. The exact moment they put themselves back to semi-rights, Caro came around the corner in her walking boots and raincoat.

Caro saw the truck and frowned, and then she put her hand to her eyes and considered the women sitting behind the windshield. She stood there, unmoving, until Angelina got out of the car.

"You said you'd call from the hospital," Angelina said.

"Nini," Caro said, and her face crumpled into tears.

Angelina got her mother into one of the white plastic chairs set up outside the hut, and cradled her while she cried. The rain picked up again, and Caro sobbed in Angelina's arms until she was soaked through. Her poor, lovely mother, desperate for comfort and unable to focus on much other than her own pain. Angelina couldn't help her own crumbling sympathy, the way she instinctively moved to smooth back Caro's hair and coo to her, "I know, Mama, it's all right, it's all okay." Maybe she shouldn't coddle Caro like this, but Caro had still had to drive her son to an emergency room yesterday, she was still embroiled in a supernatural disaster, she was still Angelina's mama. She wept into Angelina's chest, and Angelina held her close and did not rush her. Jagvi waited beside them, standing with her hands in her pockets and examining the flowerbeds. She looked patient enough to wait for days.

Finally, when Caro's ragged inhalations had smoothed out, Angelina said, "Ma, do you want to go in and we'll get dry?"

"I can't let her in," Caro said through a gulping sob, gesturing toward Jagvi. "It's not up to me. It isn't my fault."

"I don't care," Jagvi said. "We can stay out here."

"I need a drink," Caro said. "Can you believe it's been hours and nobody has come and offered me a drink?"

"All right, Ma," Angelina said. She looked up at Jagvi apologetically. "There's a bottle of whisky in the glovebox." Jagvi fetched it without a word. Caro took a neat nip and winced before taking another.

"Thank you. I've had the worst night of my life."

Angelina wondered how long it would be polite to wait before she snagged the bottle for herself. "I know, Mama."

"I've never been so afraid."

"Patrick's okay. He called and told us himself."

"He's putting a brave face on it. He's always been brave. You should've seen him in the hospital, he looked like a little boy again. I had to watch them do all these horrible things to his body. Blood transfusions and rabies shots and all kinds of atrocities," Caro said, biting the words out between her teeth. "It felt like they were doing it to me. And they asked me all sorts of questions about Your Dog. As though it was my fault, like I'm some idiot woman who let my son get hurt!"

"Pat's an adult, Ma. I'm sure no one blamed you."

"They looked at me. You know how they look at you in Myrna." Caro glanced up at Angelina and then sharply away. Another hard sip of the whisky. "And now you're looking at me like that, too. The family's in crisis, girls. We had to make a decision."

"It was the wrong one," Angelina said, but gently, like she understood Caro's reasoning. It was strange to coax Caro along under Jagvi's nonjudgmental gaze, knowing that Jagvi was in fact judging Caro extremely. It made Angelina feel both on show and protected. "Jagvi's not the problem here. You know that."

"I don't know anything," Caro said dismally.

"I'm telling you, Ma. You gotta listen to me." She put her arm around Caro's shoulders. "Us Sicco girls have to stick together, huh?"

"What about the dog?" Caro said.

"Jag chained her up in the backyard. She's okay. We'll work out what to do about her." They'd left My Dog whining and confused, Angelina hovering back out of reach while My Dog howled for her. Angelina knew it was the thing's fault, but it felt like something she had done to My Dog personally. Another creature Angelina had let stand in front of her and take her fall.

Caro sniffed and rubbed her nose. "Patrick told me off, too. And my mother thinks all of this is my fault, somehow, just like everything is." She finally looked up at Jagvi, who met her gaze without blinking. "Do you have anything to say for yourself?"

"Ma—"

"What would you like me to say, Caro?" Jagvi was gentler than she'd been with Angelina's uncles. "I'm not lying to you. I don't want to get between you and your kids. I'm trying to help them."

"I have to protect my children," Caro said. "I won't be criticized for protecting my children."

"Of course not," Jagvi said.

Caro's hands were shaking. Angelina took the bottle of whisky from her and set it in the grass. "We need the house, Ma. We don't have anywhere else to go."

"Your uncles won't like it," Caro said.

Part of Angelina felt desperately sorry for her. Caro hated to be cornered like this, caught in a situation in which she had no interest or control. She liked her children to take care of themselves and her brothers to step in and fill any gaps; she did not like demands coming at her from both directions. Pressure Caro like this, Angelina knew, and she would withdraw further into her own unhappiness.

"How has this happened to me?" Caro lamented. "First my daughter is attacked, then my son. I feel so helpless."

She hunched over with her head in her hands and started to cry again, her shoulders shuddering. Angelina rubbed her mother's back. She hesitated, but Jagvi nodded encouragingly.

"Actually, Ma, there is a way you can help us."

Caro shook her head without taking her hands from her eyes. "I can't do any of the spells. Your nonna never bothered to teach me."

"No, it's something else," Angelina said. "I wanted to ask about my dad."

The heaving pile of Caro went still. "Why on earth do you want to talk about him?"

"We're just covering all of our bases. Family history, you know, trying to find any clues." They had already agreed not to tell Caro what the thing had said last night. Angelina didn't think Caro would react well if she knew the monster had mentioned her specifically. "Why did he leave?"

"I'd had enough of him," Caro said into her hands.

"Sure, okay, but like... logistically. Did you fight? Did he just drive away one day? Did he know you were pregnant?"

"Don't remember."

"You don't remember if you told him he had a kid?" Jagvi said.

"No." She curled further down into herself.

"Okay, well, what was he like when he was around? Did he look like Angel?"

"Don't remember," Caro repeated.

"What was his name?" Angelina tried.

"Don't remember!" Caro sat up and stared at Angelina. Her face looked wrong. Her cheeks were an ugly red from crying, and her pupils had dilated so wide that her eyes looked entirely black. "Why are you doing this? What are you trying to prove?"

"I'm not," Angelina protested. "I just want to know what he was like!" She didn't want to defend herself for asking what suddenly seemed to be an entirely justified question. Why did no one remember the circumstances of her conception, or an extra man hanging about Cadenze? Why was Angelina's dad shrouded in mystery?

"Nothing," Caro said. Angelina watched something open in her mother's face. A kind of hungry emptiness, a yawn. It snapped shut around nothing. The black pools of her eyes shone straight through Angelina, and there was no space for anything else within them. "He was like nothing."

"Is he dead?"

"Probably. Maybe. I don't know." Caro clutched at her temple like she was in pain, and Angelina exchanged a swift look with Jagvi. This wasn't the vague fuzziness of memory that twenty-six years would achieve, not even the drunken blackout of a one-night stand; this was something else, Caro squirming before them like a trapped insect.

"I remember his scream," she said finally. "Long. Very loud. There isn't anything else. If there was, it's gone now. If you don't mind, girls, I need to go to bed."

Angelina and Jagvi sat side by side in Patrick's truck.

"If you've eaten someone's future," Jagvi said, in her calm, capable paramedic voice, the one Angelina had learned meant she was throbbing with terror, "then any flash of them later is yours, too. That's what the story says. Someone saying their name. Someone remembering their face. So maybe you just keep eating, every day."

"Until they're all gone and you get hungry again," Angelina said. She almost wanted to laugh. There was a strange ringing in her head. The moment after the explosion before anyone had a chance to survey the damage.

"Maybe for something similar," Jagvi said.

XXXIV

Absurdly, Angelina had to work. Jagvi helped her take down the stools, refill the ice bin, pull up the shutters, and then they sat in helpless silence on either side of the bar. Four thirty, before the patron influx began, the window streaked with rain so the square beyond blurred into gray.

Angelina cleared her throat. "Caro must have been really close to it, if it ate my dad and she got away. So that's good."

"How's that," Jagvi said, voice flat. Angelina smiled at her, chin on her hand.

"Because it means it might not hurt you and Pat."

"Well, that's not true," Jagvi said. "Because it already hurt Pat. So why don't you tell me what you're really thinking?"

Angelina looked away. "I'm thinking that...maybe it's a curse. A Sicco curse."

"Angel."

"My uncles say the other families talk about it, but it's our pit, on our land. And what about my great-great-whatever who threw her baby in the pit? And what about my uncle Lou?"

"You remember those people and Caro doesn't remember your dad—"

"We don't remember the baby. Just that its mother was a baby killer."

"And your uncle Lou didn't disappear!"

"Yeah, I've been thinking about him. But what if it tried to eat him and fucked it up somehow, and it just got...half of him? Half his future, half his life, half his mind, whatever, and that's why it was hungry again so soon after? I was born three years after Uncle Lou had his accident. It must have eaten my dad around then."

She could feel it reaching for her across centuries of Sicco spawn, the long, cold shadow of a curse falling over her. Angelina had always been marked out, her birth a once-in-a-generation anomaly, but it turned out that everyone had been focusing on the wrong thing. It wasn't her girlhood that set her apart; she belonged to a separate lineage altogether. This was her true inheritance.

"It's still not a Sicco curse," Jagvi said stubbornly. "Because your dad wasn't a Sicco."

Angelina swallowed. "But...Jag, I think it wanted Caro."

Jagvi flinched. "You think she'd do that?"

"Push someone else in?" Angelina could almost imagine it, her mother hovering by the edge of the pit, whimpering as she offered someone else up in her stead. "Yeah, I do. Especially if she never had to remember it. You said it, Jag. It's not exactly out of character for her to shirk responsibility."

Jagvi's hand shot across the bar top, and she grabbed Angelina by her wrist, squeezing tight. "That's not the same thing. Angel, listen to me, it's not the same thing. She owed you and Patrick a parent. She didn't owe the thing her *life*. That's not a responsibility people take on."

"Right," Angelina said, and smiled so that Jagvi would believe her. "Sure. I know."

"Good," Jagvi said, and her thumb traced the rapid pulse in Angelina's wrist until the bell above the door jangled and she had to let Angelina go.

A normal night in Old Timers, cheerful greetings and people exchanging gossip and accusations, and Angelina did her best to serve drinks and smile back and keep the bar humming, no matter how wrong it felt, like a radio station playing gibberish. It helped to have Jagvi there, back straight and eyes alert, nursing a glass of whisky, and untroubled by the regulars who stared at her. Angelina snuck covert looks at her and stole a moment with her when she could.

"It talked to me in here, the first time," Angelina said, leaning across the sticky bar. "No, the second time." A flash of writhing on the bathroom floor, the nightmare she'd been so confident in her ability to banish. "It snuck up on me in the cellar. And now I don't want to restock the vodka."

"I'll go with you." Jagvi tried to smile. "I'll hold your hand."

Angelina shook her head. "We gotta be careful, everyone here knows Patrick." Jagvi paled like Angelina had slapped her, and Angelina hurried on. "Anyway, that's not the point. It's everywhere, it's like it's taken over my town. I think about it when I see my bar or the fountain or even my fucking house…" Her town, all of it infiltrated and possessed, violence erupting through buildings and fountains, leaving a trail of wreckage in Angelina's wake.

"That's a paramedic thing, too," Jagvi said absently. "All of San Michele is like that for me. Parks where kids have broken their necks or intersections with motorcycle accidents. There's this one block my shift buddy calls Suicide Corner. Everywhere I look is a disaster scene."

"Jag," Angelina said, startled, and Jagvi shook her head like she was clearing a fog.

"Anyway, Cadenze was meant to be shitty in a different way," she said, and shot Angelina a quick smile. "I spent years sitting in your kitchen and what, all I'm going to remember is Pat…"

"You did hang out there way too much, it's true," Angelina said, trying to be funny, and stood up to serve a customer. When she turned back, Jagvi was emerging from the cellar, arms full of vodka and cobwebs in her hair. Knight-errant, Angelina thought again, poor twentieth-century hero. Someone should give Jagvi a sword. Someone should find Jagvi a worthier damsel than Angelina. Someone should take Jagvi back to the city and all the monsters she could actually fight: the car crashes and stabbings, the overdoses and falls. She was wasted here. Angelina knew now, she felt it in her Sicco veins, that it was over; they were beaten.

The bar filled and emptied, demographics washing in and out with the hours. It was a weeknight, so Angelina worked alone, but plenty of people in Cadenze were still thirsty. Angelina couldn't stop looking at Jagvi, handsome and frowning, her hands loose around the whisky glass she wasn't drinking. Angelina couldn't see how Jagvi didn't attract more attention. To her it felt like Jagvi was lit up, like Jagvi was obscene, her presence making Angelina pulse.

No one talked to Jagvi the way they might another familiar face, no one bought her a drink, no one even really smiled at her, but they didn't harass her either. No muttered slurs, no aggressive approaches. Angelina wondered, bitter laughter caught in her throat, if maybe Angelina herself had really done a good job. If all the gibes she'd endured about turning Old Timers into a gay bar had run their course, and the locals found a new dyke in their space too familiar to be agitating. If in Angelina's determination to set Cadenze up as some kind of hidden queer heartland, she had at least made it a place where they would go ignored. A few summers ago she'd heard a regular describe a gay tourist as "one of Angelina Sicco's lot," and maybe that taunt was also a gift, handing Angelina possession of the queer population in all the queer places she'd worked to carve here, in her home.

And now that Jagvi sat waiting for Angelina right in the pocket Angelina had built for her, Angelina realized this was what she'd been waiting for. Never mind the scene she'd told herself she was creating, the tourist hookups she'd pretended to be enticing. No wonder she'd never called any of her one-night stands for a second date, no surprise that she'd ignored every invitation to visit a fling in their own town. Every film, every pamphlet, every girl whose eye she'd ever caught: they'd been for Jagvi. Angelina had thought she was trying to put a flag out for everyone, but instead she was a beacon transmitting a desperate signal for the only woman she'd ever really wanted. The woman who came back every few years to cast a dismissive eye around and leave again. *Is it good enough for you yet? Am I good enough for you yet?*

"What," Jagvi said.

"What what?"

"You're looking at me funny." She tilted her head, her tired and lovely face trained on Angelina, her hand open and palm up on the bar top in case

Angelina needed it. Angelina wanted to crawl into her lap. Instead she looked away.

"Did you think it was weird when Caro showed up today?" Angelina asked. "Like, right on time? If she'd come a minute earlier, she would have caught us."

Jagvi nodded.

"It could come back anytime," Angelina said. "But it hasn't."

"It told you it gets tired. Maybe that's why?"

"Maybe." But Angelina wasn't convinced. The way it had howled after them in Jagvi's house felt like a natural disaster, an avalanche cresting, something at the height of its power. And there was something very deliberate about the new bubble of quiet around them. "I feel like we're being left alone. Like it's not letting anyone intrude on me. Like it's waiting."

"Let it wait," Jagvi said. "Patrick'll come back, and the three of us will work out what to do, and then it'll be sorry it was so patient."

Angelina nodded uneasily.

"Angel. I'm not going to let it touch you." Jagvi set her mouth, tilted her chin up. The lazy arrogance that meant she was frightened. "Who's the only one who gets to touch you?"

"Ah," Angelina said, breath sliding neatly out of her, pulse in her cunt.

"Well?"

"You are," Angelina said, and Jagvi smiled at her. She didn't look so frightened now.

"I am," she agreed.

Old Timers was too busy to risk anything, but when Angelina made a desperate, jerky gesture, Jagvi followed her into the crappy little bathroom.

"Such a bad idea," Angelina panted, voice hitching over a squeak as Jagvi's fingers crooked, *Gimme*. Angelina moaned, head falling back against plywood with a thunk. Jagvi kissed her hard, her free hand almost tender tilting Angelina's jaw down, and despite the drunk men outside, despite the one cubicle and the paper-thin walls, despite the lack of another bartender and the dry throats waiting at the bar, no one banged on the door, no one yelled for Angelina, no one realized where she was or with whom.

In the space left around her, in the way Jagvi was kissing her, Angelina could feel her future growing in great jagged pulses, a nature documentary on fast-forward, hope like greenery cracking up through concrete. Maybe they could beat it. Maybe Jagvi would stay. Maybe Jagvi would leave and Angelina would leave with her, break her brother's heart for good. Maybe Patrick would get over it, shout and stomp and then give Angelina away at an impossible wedding. Jagvi wanted kids. She wanted Angelina. Maybe Angelina could be the doctor's girl, maybe she could follow Jagvi to all the places she'd told Patrick he was dumb for wanting to go. Maybe she'd leave her town to her monster, or maybe she'd stay in Cadenze to rule the roost and drive out to the city once a year to fuck Jagvi senseless.

All that potential should have felt good, a wide vista stretching before her, a thousand interesting mountain trails to amble down. But Angelina knew what it was. It was a banquet, spread out on the shining tablecloth and waiting.

XXXV

Five long and tense days later, Jethro's car pulled up outside the house, and Angelina and Jagvi opened the door, braced for disaster, expecting an invalid. Instead Patrick climbed out reeking of chewing tobacco with gnarly black stitches crawling up his neck. He looked like he'd been on a bender: deep circles under his eyes, stubble creeping into a beard, greasy hair pulled back, somehow an air of dangerous charm, as though he'd spent the past week charging about and breaking hearts.

He rapped on the hood of the car. "Come back when all of you stop being such dipshits, huh?"

"You're welcome for the ride!" Jethro hollered after him.

Patrick flipped him off without turning back, long legs eating up the ground to Angelina. He hugged his arm around her shoulders, gave Jagvi a fist bump, and said, "C'mon. I want a fucking drink."

Angelina hovered in the doorway. Jethro looked out the car window at her, and the good humor on his face died, something confused and forlorn taking its place, like a child punished for a crime he didn't understand. Like My Dog, chained up in the backyard for a week now, making her weary circle in the dirt and wondering why Angelina didn't love her anymore. As though My Dog had been transported back to the forsaken side of the highway where Angelina had found her. Angelina's heart throbbed. She wanted to run to all the family she'd distanced herself from; she wanted to be back at that party when she'd been surrounded and safe. Jethro shook his head and swung the car out onto the road.

"You want to talk to him?" Patrick said. "He's spewing the same family bullshit as the rest of them."

"I wanted to make sure he actually left," Angelina said. "They've been driving by the house all week."

"Seriously?" Patrick led the way to the kitchen, throwing a bag of pills on the table and retrieving a beer from the fridge. He handed it to Jagvi, who knocked the cap off against the counter and handed it back. "Just in case Jagvi gets snacky and takes a bite of you?"

The fridge hummed. No one laughed. Patrick peered over his shoulder, frowning, and Jagvi took a step forward.

Angelina jumped in before she could speak. "Guess so!"

Jagvi's jaw clenched, but all she said was, "How are you feeling, Pat?"

"Fine, you know. Annoyed. What a waste of time. But at least the thing didn't get to you two, huh? Why's it so quiet?"

"We don't know," Jagvi said. "It doesn't feel like a good sign."

"You don't think you took it down with your old house?"

Angelina and Jagvi shook their heads.

"Angel still can't leave town," Jagvi said. They'd tried over and over, driving in the middle of the night when the roads were empty, and it didn't matter when Angelina swerved them across the road. They'd tried it with her hands tied, in the back seat, even shut up in the trunk. Angelina's body had kicked the lock so hard that the hatch burst open while they were still moving, and Jagvi had to use the emergency break before Angelina could kill herself leaping out, out of her head, her body willing to risk anything just to stay within Cadenze's borders.

The thing had not spoken or made any other move, but there was nothing soothing about the silence they stood in. If they'd fought their way through the storm, that night in Riccardo's house, it was only to stand in its eye.

In the uneasy quiet, Angelina had crouched like an expectant animal. She'd called in sick to the call center three days in a row, then stopped bothering to call. She'd likely lost that job, but doomed girls didn't need to worry about how they were going to afford groceries. Instead, she satisfied other appetites. She'd taken calls from her brother, sick of hospital food and lonely and trying to hide it, and fed him fluent, soothing lies. She'd watched her family cruise past the house, frozen on her knees with Jagvi's fingers curled through her hair, and then breathed out when the headlights passed on and left them undetected. She could feel her life rotting before her, a fruit ready to drop off the bough.

"Pat," Jagvi said. "I need to talk to you about something."

"Fucking now?" Angelina demanded, but she'd known, she'd known for days, watching Jagvi's tension grow, her misery every time Patrick called, the way she gripped Angelina like she was expecting Angelina to be hauled out of reach. She'd seen the stubborn bitterness about Jagvi's face, the only time she ever looked like Riccardo.

Jagvi had told Angelina last night, when they were half-asleep, crammed close in Angelina's tiny bed. Jagvi's leg draped over her hip, arm around her waist, nose brushing the apex of Angelina's spine.

"I'm going to tell him," Jagvi had said.

Angelina thought about pretending she was asleep, but she was trying to be brave enough to deserve the way Jagvi looked at her. "You don't have to do that."

"Yeah, I do."

Angelina rolled around to face her. "Jag. He's gonna be really upset and we made a deal not to upset him—"

"We made a deal not to do this," Jagvi had said, stroking Angelina's cheek. "But we did, and I can't lie to him again."

"Can it wait?" Angelina pleaded. "Everything's all fucked up and there's a monster and you gotta do this, too?"

"I'm sorry," Jagvi said, and kissed her. "I'm really sorry. I'll tell him it's my fault, but I have to tell him."

"And he's sick and hurt and—"

"Baby," Jagvi said, and she looked implacable. The girl who had sat across from Riccardo every night and been determined not to become him. The girl who had actually made it out of Cadenze and fashioned herself anew.

Jagvi, who was always on alert, every situation an emergency that she had to resolve. Angelina had known there was nothing she could say to change Jagvi's mind.

Still, when Jagvi said, "Yeah, now," Angelina turned, throwing her hands up in the air. She felt like a little sister, left out of Patrick and Jagvi's long and complicated relationship. Her best and most practiced way to fight this frustration was to treat Patrick and Jagvi as the children, forever stuck in their adolescent tangle while Angelina rose above the squabble to adulthood. But Angelina hadn't risen anywhere this time; she'd sunk deep and obsessive into Jagvi. And beneath her habitual sneer, she could feel her heart pounding, panic seething. Her family had all turned away from her. What would Patrick do?

Patrick looked between them, eyebrows raised. "What?"

"I broke a promise," Jagvi said.

"Did you pick a fight with Caro?" Patrick said, amused, and then set down his beer and frowned. "What's going on?"

Angelina slipped away, heading for the door with the vague pretense of checking on My Dog, but Patrick said, "Where are you going, Nini?" She looked back over her shoulder and watched his face change: eyes sharpening, mouth curling into something resigned and bitter.

"Ah," he said. "That promise."

Was there a part of Angelina that wanted him to know? Wanted to win, to beat Patrick, to come out on top? Chosen and in possession? A part of her that wanted to punish Patrick for his unending devotion to Jagvi, for every puppy dog look and helpless crawl back to her, a portion of her brain still controlled by the sixteen-year-old girl who had never stopped howling, *Didn't I fucking tell you?*

If it was something she wanted, it was a poisoned wish. Patrick's gaze traveled slowly between the two of them. She wasn't even standing next to Jagvi, couldn't take her hand or lean against her shoulder. And the realization dawning on Patrick's face wasn't betrayal or despair, wasn't even real anger. He just looked annoyed.

Patrick said, "Are you *fucking kidding me*?"

"Pat," Jagvi said. "Pat, listen—"

"You said it was just a crush," Patrick said. "You told me not to worry about it!"

"What?" Angelina said.

"I tried," Jagvi said, her eyes fixed on Patrick's face. She stepped forward, but Patrick reeled back. "I tried to stay away! I told you, I knew it was all going to go wrong if I came back, I didn't want to come back, but—"

"For the last three fucking years?" Pat said, and now he sounded angry, but not the way Angelina had expected. He was cold and irritated, watching a disaster unfurl just as he'd predicted. He looked like her uncles, red-blooded male disapproval rising to the surface, the jaw jut of generations of disappointed Sicco men.

"No, fuck," Jagvi said, running her hands through her hair.

"She's my little sister!"

"I didn't mean to—"

"Pat," Angelina interrupted, because she didn't want to hear the end of that sentence. "Pat, listen—"

He ignored her, focused on Jagvi. "And what happens when you leave again?"

"Can't we fix the monster first?" Jagvi said, voice cracking.

Patrick shook his head, the stitches on his throat creasing with the movement. "You've got it in for both of us. You want to fuck us both up? Is that the plan?"

"Pat—"

"It's so depressing, Jag, it's so shit and stupid—"

"You're my best friend," Jagvi tried, and Patrick snorted in disdain. Angelina felt something give in her chest at the misery on Jagvi's face, the way her mouth crumpled. She wanted to go to Jagvi's side. She wanted to throw herself in the midst and be useful. But she was already in the middle; she was the splinter in Jagvi and Patrick's life, the reason Patrick was attacked, the reason Jagvi was afraid, the reason they were standing angry and alienated from one another.

"I told you," he said. "I told you in the first place it was a bad idea, and you agreed, and I asked you not to, and you promised! Jag. You promised."

Jagvi looked like he'd hit her. "Yeah."

"Can you two not talk about me like I'm not here?" Angelina managed.

"But you're always here, Nini," Patrick said, without looking away from Jagvi. "That's the whole problem."

All the air rushed out of Angelina's lungs, as though he'd caught her in an iron grip and squeezed. When she could speak, she said, "Christ," and left.

XXXVI

Angelina followed the time-honored traditions of her town and sought out Cadenze's greatest refuge: she went to Old Timers.

"Nini!" Gemma said, hailing her with pleasure, and sat her at the bar with a spritz and a bowl of potato chips. Angelina picked at the peeling polish on her fingernails. When Gemma finished serving and collecting the empties, she mimed a cigarette, and Angelina followed her outside. Gemma's ex-husband had broken up with his new girl and fed Gemma's parents sob stories about wanting to give his marriage another try. "I told them if they want to live with a guy who doesn't know how to flush a toilet, then they can be my fucking guest."

Angelina managed a weak smile. "Good for you. Sorry I haven't been around as much."

Gemma shook her head. "I wanted to come see you, but your cousins told me not to go up Big Joe anymore. Are you okay?"

"Uh," Angelina said. She leaned back against the brick and shook her head when Gemma offered her a drag. "Not really." Gemma reached out and took her hand, eyes full of sympathy, and Angelina said, "I kind of started sleeping with Jagvi."

"Oh. Fuck."

Angelina laughed weakly. "C'mon, I thought you'd be a little pleased. It's good gossip at least, right?"

Gemma squeezed her hand. "Sure, yeah," she said, but her heart clearly wasn't in it. "Does Patrick know?"

Angelina jerked out a nod.

"How'd that go down?"

"I'm here, aren't I?"

"Well. That sucks. I thought you agreed it was a really bad idea?"

Angelina hunched her shoulders. This wasn't the comfort she'd come looking for. "Sometimes you don't do something 'cause it's a good idea."

"I guess," Gemma said. She sighed, tapping ash against the wall. "Still. Poor Jagvi."

"What?" Angelina blinked at her. "Why poor Jag? I'm good in bed, Gemma," she added, trying to turn the situation into something familiar, to get Gemma to laugh or coo over her. But Gemma's mouth only twitched, like she couldn't muster the full energy for a smile.

"Sure, but it's a lot more complicated for Jagvi than it is for you, isn't it? Or is it just a fling?"

"I don't...I'm not...I dunno—"

"Well, if it's not, that's an awful position for Jagvi to be in," Gemma continued. "She hates this town, everyone knows that. And she only just escaped it, her dad just died and she finally got rid of her last tie or, like, responsibility, whatever. And you love Cadenze, you'll stay here forever. *And* she has all that history with Patrick—everyone thought they were gonna get married! It's an impossible choice. There's nowhere good this can lead for her."

Angelina stared at her friend. "When you said it was a bad idea," she said slowly. "You weren't talking about me?"

"Nini, you know I love you, but your worst-case scenario here is a little heartbreak." Gemma patted her hand. "Heartbreak won't kill you. What about Jagvi? She loses her best friend and her freedom and her cool job in the city if she stays. And if she goes, it's still weird with Patrick and she doesn't get you either. She's in a shitty spot." She dropped her cigarette and ground the butt beneath her heel. "Man. Cadenze is hard to escape once it gets its hooks in you. I thought Jagvi had made it. I kind of admired her for it."

She laughed humorlessly, and Angelina stared at her.

Francesca-Martine put her head out the door. "Nini? Your brother called. He said it would be great if you could come home before a monster eats you?"

Gemma laughed again, realer now. "Siccos," she said, shaking her head.

At home, Patrick waited at the rickety kitchen table, halfway through a beer with another empty beside him. He looked at her and raised his eyebrows. "Anything follow you up here? Jagvi's out back if you need a dose of anti-possession."

"I'm fine." She was discomforted by how easily he referenced Jagvi. "What's on your sandwich?"

"Roast beef. Nonna brought some around. She called you a scallywag." He got up and took another wax paper–wrapped sandwich from a towering pile, putting it on a plate and setting it on the table. Angelina eyed him warily.

"Are you meant to drink when you're on antibiotics?"

"Shut up, Nini."

"Hey, fuck you, man." Angelina dropped into the seat opposite him and stole a swig of his beer, waiting, but Patrick didn't react. "Well, this is a fucked-up little family dinner."

Patrick snorted.

Guilt and annoyance curdled in her stomach, an unpleasantly familiar, teenage feeling. "You're not even gonna acknowledge it?"

"What do you want me to say?"

"If you're mad, you might as well start yelling," Angelina said.

"I'm not mad at you."

"Well, don't lie."

"I'm not," Patrick repeated. He took a tight swallow of beer, bob of his Adam's apple. "It's between me and Jag. It's not even really a surprise. You've always been obsessed with her and you always just grab for what you want—"

"Hey, fuck *you*," Angelina repeated, now with venom.

Patrick shrugged. "You do, Nini. I'm sure you felt kinda bad about it, but did you even hesitate? Tell me the truth, were you the one who talked her into it?"

"What did you want me to do?" Angelina demanded. "I didn't want to hurt you, but fuck, Pat, I can't help it if I—if I—"

"If you what? You don't even know!" He smacked his palm onto the table. "Christ, Nini, I want you to *think*! For once in your fucking life to stop and think before you do something! Think about me, or about the fact that there's a monster that wants to eat you, or that Jag is never, ever going to stay here, and then be an adult and realize that you don't always get everything you want. What part of growing up here didn't teach you that?"

"Maybe it was you!"

"Maybe it was," Patrick agreed. "Yeah. I actually worry about that a lot."

"Oh, fuck off—"

"I'd like to," Patrick said, "but none of us can do that. Eat your fucking sandwich."

She found Jagvi outside, motionless in the grass with My Dog pressed up against her side, the day dying around them and shadows crawling out to claim their territory. Angelina tripped down the steps with a cry caught in her throat; for a moment all she saw was Jagvi's stillness and My Dog nuzzling in at her throat, but then Jagvi propped herself up on her elbow and looked over at Angelina guiltily.

"I felt bad for her," Jagvi said. "Tied up all alone."

Angelina's heart was still pounding. She crossed the yard toward Jagvi. "She might be dangerous."

"Yeah." Jagvi scratched My Dog's chin. My Dog gazed up at her, big wet eyes, tail thumping in the dirt. "Poor old thing."

"Should I be worried? One fight with Patrick and you're baring your throat?"

"I don't think she's going to hurt me. But maybe don't come any closer, Angel," Jagvi added, and Angelina stopped, just out of reach of the chain. Jagvi caught My Dog's head between her hands and rubbed her silky cheeks, her ears, as though to distract them, as though Angelina and her dog weren't both quivering at the end of their chains, wishing they could close that last small gap. My Dog stood up, waving her tail with her old foolish optimism, determined to be happy no matter how often the world proved her wrong.

Jagvi glanced between them and stood up, guiding Angelina back to the porch with a hand on the small of her back. They sat on the steps together. My Dog whined and lay back down in the dirt.

"You think it's only 'cause I was there?" Angelina asked, chest tight. "That Patrick was hurt?"

"Well, we already knew that. It's after you. But we'll beat it, Angel, I promise," Jagvi said, and she touched Angelina's thigh and then flinched away. "I talked to Pat. I'm not going anywhere until we get rid of it. I won't let you get hurt."

Jagvi avoided her eyes, talking fast and low with her gaze trained on the dog still watching them from the shade. Angelina wanted to ask if she and Patrick had any sense yet of the hopelessness of their situation. They had won no victories, had no real information except the fact that Jagvi wanted Angelina so badly Angelina couldn't be taken on her own. Instead, Angelina's town and her family and her dog would turn on her, or each other, until they were ripped to shreds and Angelina sat waiting for the thing in the wreckage.

And in the meantime, Angelina was still pathetic enough that the real issue she wanted to address was, "And after we get rid of it?"

Jagvi looked at her properly then. Her handsome, beloved face was quiet with unhappiness. "I don't know, Angel."

"Is he really angry at you?"

Jagvi shrugged. "He's right to be."

"I guess." Angelina drew in a breath. "Did you promise Patrick not to date me?"

"That would have been presumptuous. You didn't like me very much."

"So what did you promise?" Angelina felt like she was sifting her way through a mess of confusion, the triangulation around her only slowly coming into focus, but Jagvi looked perfectly calm. She looked as though she had never expected anything but this, her relationships with the Sicco siblings crumbling at her feet.

"I promised not to go after you."

"Three years ago?"

Jagvi nodded.

"When you and Patrick had that really bad fight?"

Jagvi hesitated, then said, "Yeah. He was furious. And I got angry, too, I felt like he thought I was doing it on purpose or that I'd been lying to him for fun or something..."

"Doing *what*?" Angelina said. "I don't understand. I thought you didn't like me."

Jagvi laughed, and looked away. "Remember when you came to the city with Pat and told me you were going to run your town?"

"That was like seven years ago," Angelina said, embarrassed. "I was a brat."

"I've loved you my whole adult life," Jagvi said.

Angelina laughed, cracked and disbelieving. "What?"

Jagvi shrugged. "I don't know. It took me ages to realize. I could never stop thinking about you after that. And then every time after, every time I saw you, I wanted you more. I couldn't—I've never been able to get enough."

Angelina's breath caught in her throat.

"But that's all I've got, Angel. I've spent years trying to work out how to get myself out of Cadenze, and it was for nothing. I know how to keep people alive, and I know how to fuck you, but I don't know how to resolve this, and everything I want is going to fuck something else up."

"But, Jag," Angelina whispered, and couldn't think of anything else. She plucked at Jagvi's sleeve, restless, almost too frightened to put her hands on Jagvi properly. "Jag."

Jagvi rested her forehead against Angelina's shoulder and closed her eyes. She looked very tired but she kept speaking in that low, sensible voice. "I want you and also I want to be best friends with Patrick. I want you to come live with me in San Michele and also you were obsessed with this town and never going to leave it way before the monster showed up and made sure that you couldn't, and I want to leave this town forever and also I want to stay here with you. It's *my* hometown, too, I want to make it mine, and also everyone in this place hates me. There's not a single decision I can make that will fix anything, and so far every decision I've made has made everything worse."

Angelina's hand trembled on Jagvi's knee. She bumped her face forward, and they kissed slow and clumsy in the growing dark, the sting of Jagvi's teeth on her bottom lip. Then Jagvi stood up, touching Angelina restlessly as she went out of reach, gripping her shoulder, stroking her hair.

"Sorry I've made things so weird with you and Pat," Jagvi said. "I'll sleep on the couch tonight, okay? I'm there if you need me."

The mountain sank into night. Angelina went to bed early, unable to face the occupants of her house. Somehow, she managed to sleep a little. When she woke it was still dark, but the morning birds were singing, and she was thinking about that deep knot of contradictions in Jagvi's head, the bundle of impossible desires that strained and shoved at one another. Typical Jag, Angelina thought, to sit there for hours trying to unpick everything so that she could be fair to everyone. She needed someone selfish, like Angelina, to take a knife and slice right through.

Angelina had spent so much of her life furious with Jagvi for turning her back on Cadenze. But for the first time, Angelina could feel not just the rejection and abandonment of Jagvi leaving Cadenze, but the joy of it, too. The pleasure of imagining Jagvi strolling out of town, her backpack slung over one shoulder, her thumb hooked in her belt loop. Jagvi serene and safe behind her sunglasses. Jagvi climbing onto the bus and the wheezing doors shutting behind her and all the horror of Cadenze receding from her view.

The Sicco girl of her generation could not beat a curse, but she would not be a monster, and she would not be her mother. All her life Angelina had wanted to keep people together, to hold on to what she loved, to stay; maybe the best thing to do now was shake off those ties and let them have a fresh, clean morning free of Angelina and the wreckage that trailed her. No more complications, no more monster, no more splinter in Patrick's and Jagvi's lives. She could bring peace to her family and her town. She could get Jagvi on that bus.

She went downstairs quietly. Patrick snored behind his door, Jagvi a silent mound on the couch. She couldn't risk taking the car and waking them with the engine, but she didn't mind walking. Angelina slipped out the back door and tiptoed across the dewy grass.

"Hi, baby," she said, kneeling and unlocking the chain. My Dog bounded into her arms, licked her face, shivered and whimpered with happiness. Angelina cried a little into her fur and then drew back, dashing the tears off her face. Angelina's poor, sweet companion, conscripted into something else's service. If the stories were right, then the monster would need an accomplice to finish her off. My Dog seemed as good a choice as any. She'd rather fall under a loving pair of fangs.

"C'mon. It's time to go."

XXXVII

Angelina and her dog walked down the paved road. Dizzy with freedom, My Dog jumped against every fence post to check the fields beyond. She stopped at a pothole filled with water and dunked her entire head in, came up with her fur plastered back against her face, shaking her head in the blue predawn light. It was colder today, and the sharp air felt like a taste of the coming winter. A season that Angelina would never see.

Toward the base of Big Joe, a car pulled up beside her. She froze, thinking it was Franco or one of the other boys come to get her, but the man who rolled down the window was no Sicco. It was Francesca-Martine's husband, David, the burly football fan who brought them baked ziti before their shifts. His eyes were bloodshot and puffy, and he was wearing an undershirt and sweatpants. He'd been at a poker game all night, he said. He asked if Angelina needed a ride somewhere.

On the road to Franco's place, David nodded at My Dog in the back seat, her head jammed out the window, and asked if Angelina was taking her to the farm to be put down.

"I heard she took a chunk out of your brother," he said.

"It wasn't her fault," Angelina said. "She's a good girl, really."

David studied her in the rearview mirror. Half-dressed, faded bruises on her throat, dead eyes. "People keep asking us at Old Timers, what's going on up on Big Joe. All that fuss when you were sick, and then this dog attack and

Riccardo's place collapsing overnight. Me and Francesca keep telling them that it's Sicco business."

"That's right," Angelina said. "It's nobody else's problem."

"But people are worried about you," David added. "If we can help at all..."

Angelina shook her head. "It's like you said. Sicco business." Handed down the line from one to the next. However many other victims back down the line, wiped from the memories of her ancestors before they could mourn. And Caro, who had offered up a proxy in her place. But Angelina Sicco did not shirk responsibilities.

David dropped her off at the border of Franco's farm. He didn't ask why she didn't want to drive up to the house—more Sicco business, not for others to pry. He wished her luck.

Franco's farm faced east, and beyond the far hills Angelina could see the first traces of sunlight. But the path to the caves led downward, and a fog had settled in the gorge, obscuring the trail that Angelina stumbled along. She almost missed the turn at the ravine, realizing only when she was a few feet away that she'd nearly tripped over the cliff. My Dog appeared at her side, head on Angelina's thigh, nudging her back onto the path.

"Thanks, baby," Angelina said.

"You're Welcome," My Dog said. "Going To My Cave?"

It was almost a relief. Angelina's monster had come for her, and it was nearly over.

"Yes," she said, "that's where I'm going."

"How'd You Escape Your Keepers?" My Dog asked. Its voice was a close approximation of Gemma's, although maybe it was just the tone that was reminiscent; knowing, intimate.

"They're asleep."

"How Nice!" My Dog said. "I Love Asleep."

She stuck close now, plastered to Angelina's left leg like she wanted to form a moving barrier between her and the ravine. Her tongue lolled from her mouth, and every few strides Angelina felt the pink caress on the back of her calf, wet nose nudging her onward. She had that early morning sickness, her stomach curdling in protest. Once that light crept far enough over the hill, Jagvi would wake and realize Angelina was gone, and she would guess. Angelina knew she would guess.

"Was Patrick Very Upset?" My Dog asked. "I'm Sorry I Missed It. I Wanted To See Him Finding Out."

"Shut up."

"I'm Sorry I Missed Your Consummation With Her, Too. Although You Did Beg Me To Leave You Alone. And," the dog added, satisfied, "I'll Get It Soon, Huh?"

Angelina said nothing. She could see the cave mouth yawning up ahead. A great black mouth in the wall of rock. The party cave. The cave where she came to tell stories and share laughter. The cave where her monster had slept patiently, waiting for Angelina to call. Angelina's hands dangled by her sides. My Dog stood beside her and peered into the mist. Her wet nose twitched.

"Can't Stand Out Here Forever. In You Go. Or Shall I Force You?"

"Fuck off," Angelina said. She walked inside on her own.

Thin dawn cut through the fog and painted the cave floor gray. Angelina squinted in the gloom, walked right into a pile of blackened sticks from the last fire, and cursed, jumping back. She could hear My Dog's claws clattering on stone as she clambered up to one of the higher ledges. The ancient paintings looked down on the scene, silent eyes long obscured, the weapons disfigured by time. Remnants, maybe, of whoever had thrown the thing down into this pit in the first place, but they had not subdued it. Only contained it. Made it the problem of the people who dared to live up above, the Sicco monster that watched them and hunted them and then erased them altogether.

"I'm ready," Angelina said.

"That's Good," My Dog said, and yawned wide, turning in a circle once before settling down with her chin on her front paws. From her rocky perch, she looked down at Angelina expectantly.

Angelina swallowed sour fury. "Please. I don't have long."

"Not Very Long," My Dog agreed.

Sunlight lapped at her bare ankles. Jagvi and Patrick would be up soon. The ride from David had helped, but she was still running out of time.

"I don't want anyone else getting hurt," Angelina pleaded.

Uninterested, My Dog licked her own paws, badly. Great slobbering swipes of her tongue, drooling over her claws until they were spit slick.

"You won't even block them off? Can't you trigger an avalanche or something?"

"No."

"But I'm here, I'm ready for it! I want to make it easier for you!"

My Dog looked up, and Angelina saw something of the animal in there, the eyes gone wide and pleading like the thing had given her a little more space. Then she heard the thing inside her own head. That voice that sounded like it was coming from behind her, clear as her own thoughts.

I Appreciate That. But She's Not Here Yet.

"What? Who?" Angelina had an awful thought. "Caro?"

Laughter reverberated through her skull, and each *Ha* was a punch to her brain, flattening the cells, a hot hammer swinging through pink matter to make room for itself. She Already Fed Me! the thing crowed. I Told You. He Was Delicious. Now It's Your Turn.

Angelina was breathing fast. "Okay. Okay! Then do it."

She's Not Here Yet.

"Who!" Angelina demanded, but she was in no position to make demands. Power swarmed down her back and out toward her limbs, and the thing had her. It forced her to the ground, her knees buckling and landing hard on the stone, and already the pain didn't feel real because it wasn't hers. It seized her body in its grip, pincer on the back of her neck until she couldn't move at all.

That's Better. Nice And Still. Don't You Worry, You're Going To Be Fine.

But she wasn't going to be fine. That was the point. It was supposed to swallow her up. Split her open and suck everything out, everything she'd ever been and everything she was going to be, drag out each moment of memory and then devour everything that came next, every Angelina that she might become, and in doing so it would leave her town and her family alone, for a generation at least, and Jagvi and Patrick would wake cleansed and unafraid. A Patrick and Jagvi who had never known Angelina, a Patrick who could do what he liked without the burden of his little sister hanging from his neck, a Jagvi who didn't have that miserable, complicated knot inside her, the love that couldn't do anything or go anywhere. And the two of them would love one another, and stay in step with one another, and they would be safe.

But still nothing happened. Patrick and Jagvi would be awake by now, find Angelina's empty bed and My Dog's empty chain, climb into the truck and come racing toward the only possible place that Angelina could have gone. They would be speeding down the road and they would park the truck with a screech and Jagvi would hurtle down the path toward the cave.

Yes. She Won't Be Much Longer.

And finally, Angelina understood.

XXXVIII

The thing laughed while Angelina tried to thrash it off. Heaving and writhing, slamming herself against the contours of her skull, her body as still and tranquil as though she were in prayer. Adrenaline rocketed through her with nowhere to go, hands that couldn't shake, teeth that couldn't rattle, and when Angelina screamed her fury and her fear, her lips didn't even attempt to part.

I Told You Before. I Want That Good, Full Life. I Don't Want Sicco Scraps.

My Dog drew her head back and said in Angelina's own voice: "I Want Something With Some Meat To It."

When My Dog spoke, Angelina flailed anew, jerking and squirming in the strong grip of its alien presence. But the thing was untroubled, strong enough now to hold them both at the same time. Its voice flittered between My Dog's jaws and the steady presence behind her. It let My Dog move, whining and slinking over the ground, rolling over like she wanted to shake off the presence riding within her, too, and occasionally coming over to lick Angelina's face, unable to understand why Angelina wasn't helping her. Now and then the thing flexed its control over My Dog, and she cringed, whites of her eyes rolling. It was hurting her.

It forced My Dog's face to the side in an involuntary gesture of sympathy. Sweetly, it asked Angelina, "Why Would I Want You?"

Inside her head: I've Seen Your Life.

"We Both Know What's Up Ahead For You."

Boring, Boring, Boring. Your Life Isn't What You're Good For. Now You Understand What You're Good For, Don't You? Little Fisher?

Angelina's breath heaved and caught in her lungs. The thing from the pit and Angelina Sicco kneeling together on the rock, two Cadenze beasts, born of this earth and unable or unwilling to leave it, destined to repeat the same patterns over and over. But they had more in common than that. They cast out nets. They did their best to lure people in, offering whatever they could to attract beauty and adventure to a place that had never fostered either.

And You Know How It Feels To Look At Her. All That Potential, All That Energy, All That Power.

Its creeping interest delved through Angelina's mind. Jagvi smashing through the door in her sari. Jagvi poised over her on the mattress, hot fingers beckoning. Jagvi appearing at Franco's birthday party, fresh off the bus from the city with her chin held high. The bravest and strongest person Angelina had ever met. Gritted teeth and stoic face. A teenager so determined that she slept with her fists clenched. Angelina considered each piece of evidence with numb understanding. Jagvi was everything Angelina wasn't. She had real courage and real guts, and a real future ahead of her.

"I Know, I Know," My Dog soothed. "You Wanted To Be The One To Ruin Her Plans. I Didn't Even Have To Help You That Much."

A kiss in the fountain to break the possessed stone—which was a temper tantrum, Angelina realized dumbly, the hand closing around her in fury when Angelina and Jagvi made their deal to part ways, and releasing her when it could trust Jagvi to stay close. And this past week, the welcome silence around them, a protection that descended between them and the Siccos, so that Angelina had the time she'd needed to bind Jagvi to her.

Now You're Getting It.

What else? *You've Been Feeding Me So Well*: every memory of Jagvi it had devoured. Every time Angelina had tried to steer away from Jagvi, the thing had pointed her straight back into Jagvi's path. It had put Angelina in enough danger that Jagvi had no choice but to stay to protect her; it had woken not at Angelina toeing a stone into its pit, but at the introduction she had offered.

Yes. She Smelled Delicious. It's A Good Future. I'm Not Surprised You Want It, Too.

Outside the cave, morning had broken. A sound cut through the silence: two boots, running toward them.

But I Called Dibs.

"Angel!"

Jagvi arrived alone. Angelina couldn't look up, but she saw Jagvi's shadow cast by the sunlight streaming in through the cave mouth, her beloved outline coming closer, exactly as she was supposed to. And she came for Angelina just like she always did, deliberate and hard and fast, slamming against her, on her knees with her arms around Angelina and her hands delving up under Angelina's shirt for skin.

It hit Angelina like a spike of energy, a great gulping gasp of oxygen, her ears ringing and her mouth already open and yowling warnings. "You gotta go, you have to leave right now, Jag, you have to run—"

"Come on, then!" Jagvi grasped her hand, but Angelina didn't feel her touch. She stared down at her hand, at Jagvi's fingers tangled and squeezing with hers. No sensation at all. The thing peeled back but now that the shock of Jagvi's touch had faded, she could feel it, still hanging grimly about her neck.

"Told You I Got Stronger," My Dog remarked, and panic flashed across Jagvi's face.

"Angel," Jagvi said, and thrust her hands up Angelina's sleeves, fingernails catching on her skin, every part of Angelina that she could touch—elbows, shoulders, belly, knees—and with every point of contact, Angelina could feel the thing digging in deeper, her body slipping further out of her control as Jagvi and the thing tussled for ownership.

Sorry, the voice in her head said. But I Don't Mind You Talking.

"It's too strong," Angelina said, her voice barely scraping out of her. "It doesn't matter, Jag, we were wrong—it's me, I'm the companion, I delivered you right to it. It wants you!"

Jagvi raised her head. For a moment she seemed to look right through

Angelina, that sharp, penetrating gaze, as though she could catch out the thing hunkered like a spider in Angelina's brain or leaning casually against her back, keeping her still. Then she blinked and shook her head. Her shoulders relaxed.

"Okay," Jagvi said, and caught Angelina's cheek in her palm, stroked her thumb over Angelina's mouth. "Listen, Patrick is getting your uncle and your cousins, they'll be here soon. Focus on me. Keep trying to move your arms."

"*Jag*," Angelina said, "you're not listening to me—"

"I'm listening," Jagvi said, and kissed her, a sure and warm kiss except that Jagvi's hands dug at her, begging for Angelina's body back.

"That Won't Work This Time," My Dog said, bored.

"Shut up," Angelina snarled, and started to cry, sobbing and terrified and wishing she could move even her head, smash Jagvi away from her with her forehead, topple forward and roll Jagvi out of the cave. "Jagvi, you have to go. Please go, please, just run—"

"Not without you," Jagvi said.

"Your Mother Was Easier," My Dog said. "She Understood Right Away. She Was So Polite And Sweet And Then I Helped Her Forget. She Never Felt Guilty. None Of You Remembered Him, Wasn't That Nice?"

Angelina shook her head fervently, but yes, yes, it was nice. She hadn't even cared about her father, for most of her life, fleeting nightmares and idle daydreams before she dropped his image again. She'd thought she was brave and realistic, when actually this thing in her head the whole time had been blocking her from even really wanting to know who he was, accepting it every time Caro palmed her off with *I don't know* because she'd understood exactly what the not-knowing felt like. And now it wanted to take Jagvi the same way.

"You have to leave now," Angelina begged. "You have to go."

Beg All You Want. She Isn't Going To Run.

"Baby," Jagvi said. She was so calm, so still, as straight-backed and confident as ever. "It's going to be okay. Pat's coming, it can't fight all of them—"

"It fucking *can*, it's got My Dog, too, it can control stone—"

"And it doesn't matter anyway, okay? It can't have you."

"It wants *you*. I'm the bait." Sniffling and gasping, her face wet, Jagvi's careful hands on her cheeks, rough thumbs stroking the tears away.

"It's a good trap," Jagvi said. "I get it now. It's a really good trap."

"Jag, *please*—"

"I'm not me if you don't exist," Jagvi told her. "So it doesn't matter. We get you away or it gets me. That's okay, baby. You're gonna be okay."

Angelina would not be okay. She felt like a wildcat tearing in her own mind, flinging herself toward Jagvi's warm palms, and she couldn't tell if it was the thing slipping or gravity finally giving in to the inevitable that sent her tripping forward, landing hard against Jagvi, sending them tumbling against the ground.

Jagvi grunted and then shoved up to her elbows, hope flaring across her face. Angelina clutched her, staggered and thrilled.

The thing loomed up close behind her.

That's Enough.

It sank through Angelina so fast she felt dizzy, shoved aside in her own body. A moment later she realized the hands moving before her eyes were her own; it took even more time to recognize what they were doing, one idly resting on Jagvi's shoulder, the other catching her arm. Angelina's hands flexed—stronger now, filled with a power that was not their own—and then yanked Jagvi's shoulder out of its socket. The two hands that no longer belonged to Angelina caught Jagvi's strong forearm and snapped it in two. Bone punctured its way up to the surface, froth of blood, Jagvi screaming and screaming, the quiet calm wiped away from her face at last.

Angelina smiled down at her.

"Here Come The Men," she said.

XXXIX

They came quietly, without bluster or bravado. The line of Sicco men: her uncles Franco and Sam leading the way with their guns, and her cousins Jethro and Ricky and even Matthew clutching a pitchfork, and in the center of the mass Angelina's brother.

"Brave Heroes One And All!" the thing said, and its amusement rolled through Angelina and stretched her mouth into a grin. Patrick recoiled when he saw her. Angelina could almost see her reflection in his wide, startled eyes, his little sister leering over Jagvi crumpled on the ground, her arm smashed between them. A frozen tableau, with the snarling dog at the threshold to stop anyone from disturbing it.

Settle Down, the thing said irritably, and its voice was like a thumb to Angelina's head, forcing her into the tiny corner of her mind she had left.

"Pat," Jagvi said, voice strangled, "it's strong and it's in the dog, too—"

"What happened?" Patrick demanded. He took a few quick steps forward, and then My Dog leapt at him, snarling, and he faltered back, out of the range of snapping teeth.

Matthew raised his pitchfork, and Sam cocked his gun but Franco said, "Wait!"

"That One Understands," My Dog said. The thing was using Angelina's nonna's voice at her most malicious. "You Can Kill The Dog If You Like. I Don't Mind. It Would Be Less Crowded Inside."

"If you hurt my sister, I'll kill you and everything you ever touch," Patrick said.

The thing used Angelina and the dog to laugh at the same time, an ungodly chorus of hilarity. They spoke as one. "Your Sister Will Come Through This Just Fine."

"It's hurt the Marino girl," Franco said. His voice was measured.

"Jag," Patrick said, voice cracking, "can you touch Nini, can you get it out?"

"It hurts pretty bad, Pat," Jagvi said thinly. She breathed fast and shallow, little hiccuping gasps between words. "I can't concentrate. I think it's too strong now. Pat," she said, and in the corner of Angelina's mind that Angelina was allowed, she was screaming at the way Jagvi sounded, the sweet exhaustion. "It's okay. Angel's gonna be okay."

"What?" Patrick said, and then he understood and he dove forward, trying to reach them, but My Dog leapt to stop him. The two of them wrestled on the ground, Patrick trying to keep the snapping jaws away from his throat.

The men swarmed around him, but the dog was so strong, stronger than My Dog had ever been. Jagvi raised her strained, hurt voice and called, "Drop it! My Dog! Drop it, girl!"

"If You Like," the thing said with Angelina's mouth, and sat a little heavier in Angelina. "The Dog Doesn't Really Matter Now. Siccos Know What To Do With Me."

Across the cave, My Dog whined and crumbled under the weight of the men around her. For a moment everyone's harsh breath was the only sound in the cave, and then My Dog leaned up and licked Patrick's cheek, tentative and confused.

"Jag," Patrick said, and sprang to his feet. The men and Angelina's dog ran with him.

The dog got there first, faithful friend, and the thing inside Angelina picked up her hand and used it to smack the dog away. My Dog's body made an arc through the air. The thing turned Angelina's head to watch with curiosity as the dog sailed across the cave until it slapped hard against the cave wall. A silly noise, a splat, and the snap of bones. Vibration in Angelina's throat: the thing was using her to laugh. The heap of My Dog lay silent and broken on the cave floor, her body pointing in several directions.

"Getting Stronger," the thing said, and flexed Angelina's fingers.

Patrick flung himself forward, but he didn't get far. The Sicco men he had brought to assist caught him, their arms around his shoulders, Franco gripping his wrist, Jethro's hand fisted in his shirt, Patrick struggling in the midst of them.

"What?" Patrick demanded. "It's gonna—it's got Jagvi, you have to let me—"

"Pat!" Jethro said. "It's stronger than any of us, and it's going to eat. It's over. It's done."

"Let me go," Patrick said, writhing, trying to shake off his family. He landed a punch to Sam's stomach and twisted Ricky's wrist until Ricky cried out, but for every hand he escaped another grabbed at him, hauling him back until Patrick was almost off his feet, panting and red in the face, hair falling over his eyes, flabbergasted desperation rising off him. The thing watched, interested. Jagvi tried to say something, and Angelina reached out caressingly and put her hand over Jagvi's mouth.

"It's over," Franco echoed, and gave Patrick a shake. "Don't you see, kid? It's her or your sister."

"It can't be either of them!"

Franco's face was grim and regretful. "You won't have to remember for long."

"*Jag*," Patrick cried.

"I Like Siccos," the thing said. "They're So Reliable."

Franco spat on the ground, and the thing laughed in Angelina's head. So reliable and so predictable. The strong ones were sensible, and the weak ones, like little Angelina, could wriggle in its grip as much as they wanted. She was still such a good pair of hands, sharpened to the point and ready to feed.

Jagvi lay slack and sweating on the ground, filthy with blood, those dark eyes certain and clear as ever. Brave, Angelina wanted to say; the thing took the word and considered it and then agreed. Yes. She didn't know if she was speaking aloud, or if it was speaking to her, or if it had filled her to the brim and they didn't even need to speak now, its consciousness blanketing her, the last twisting figments of Angelina floating in the oil slick of the thing from the pit. Yes, Jagvi Was Brave: they were in agreement. She didn't even cry, but that didn't matter. The thing would have her tears soon enough. Angelina didn't understand?

Look, I'll Show You. And it bent their face to Jagvi and ate.

It came in a flood. Hunting for tears, maybe, so that was what they got first: a tiny, eight-year-old Jagvi crying bitterly at the foot of her bed, Riccardo striding out of the room, and then a present-day Jagvi hanging up a phone in an apartment Angelina didn't know. A stranger looked up from where he was drinking a glass of wine and said, *Everything okay?* and Jagvi said, *Uh, my father just died*, and excused herself for the bathroom. She sat on the closed lid of the toilet and stared out the window at the busy San Michele street below, and she laughed once, shortly, and then her face fell.

They came in seconds, dripping images like the way the thing hunted through Angelina's own mind, and yet there was time to savor everything. Angelina hung on to her own senses by the tips of her fingers, and so she tasted them all, meaty and satisfying, filling her deep. Tiny Jagvi all alone in her private school uniform, waiting for her ma at the bus stop when a stranger approached to tell her to go back where she came from. Finding her in tears, Meera kissed her cheek and told her she'd need to grow a thicker skin. Teenage Jagvi alone in bed running her hand along the border on a map, Patrick's denim vest thrown over the back of a chair. Then the Christmas adult Jagvi came back to Cadenze, standing outside the Sicco house, rugged up against the cold, wishing she could go inside and stay. Jagvi listening to Patrick tell another bratty Angelina story with her heart pounding, her hand curled in her pocket, trying to keep her face smooth. Jagvi in Old Timers with Angelina, knowing that Angelina wanted Jagvi to kiss her, Angelina within reach and willing to be grabbed, at last.

The thing laughed: It knew the feeling. It would eat it all. Jagvi's capable hands, the big palms that Angelina loved and the deft fingers. Jagvi's dick, all the variations of it over the years, from the first lurid pink strap her ex had coaxed her into buying to the soft packer, the thing ate out of existence, like it had never been there at all. Jagvi's left eye, the pop of vitreous between Angelina's teeth.

Now Jagvi screamed without cease. Her voice rang through the cave—they would eat that soon, all in good time—and her eye was streaming and her nose running. Patrick made broken, anguished noises in the grip of the men, and Angelina could feel the thing getting stronger, like a weight leaning on her back, forcing her closer and closer against Jagvi, squashing her down against the body that would soon be gone. Right now she could still feel the panicked thud of Jagvi's heart and the twist and arch of her body in pain, but the thing turned Angelina's tongue into sandpaper, and she licked up mouthfuls that the thing swallowed greedily down. Soon it would have no need for Angelina; Angelina could feel the claws forming at her hips, the teeth grazing her neck, as with every bite of Jagvi the thing became more itself.

Here's The Good Stuff.

Jagvi's hands flat over the stranger's chest as she pumped and counted and put her mouth down to breathe for them until they came coughing and spluttering back to life. Jagvi with a backpack on her shoulders, setting out down a crowded street in an unknown country, rickshaws jangling past and bright paint and streamers hanging from windows. Jagvi leaning over a hospital bed to speak to the patient within it; Jagvi carrying a small child with his arms wound around her neck; Jagvi with a streak of gray in her hair rattling down a set of stairs to catch a much older Angelina by the hips and back her up against a wall.

Yes, You're In Some Of It, the thing said, uninterested. But See How Much More There Is? How Did You Think You Could Ever Offer Anything Like This?

Degree certificates hanging in frames on a wall. Family crowded around her. Parties seething with girls who wanted to catch her eye. Dozens of lives caught and saved in her hands. Jagvi coughed up her future in painful gags while her skin went dull. It reeled around her like smoke, obscuring her from view, and the thing grunted over its meal, shoveling it down.

With every bite the thing grew stronger, until it shoved Angelina to the side and left her discarded by the pit. This was how Caro had lain, decades before, until it was over and the thing allowed Caro to pick herself up and limp home, already forgetting why she was sore.

Angelina hadn't forgotten anything; that would come last, as it slurped the final traces of Jagvi out of this world. But her mind felt unfamiliar. She hunkered in the periphery she had been pressed into. When she reached out for emotion or thought, she did so flinching, expecting to be beaten back. The easiest—though not easy—thing to reach for was her body, which belonged mostly to her again. Laboriously, Angelina stood.

The thing crouched over what was left of Jagvi. Jagvi's body was half gore and half shadow, as though with every bite it was tearing away less of her physical shell and more of something greater, spirit or soul, the psychic space Jagvi took up in the universe. And the thing grew as it ate; it was almost visible now. Something vast and vicious, a strong smell like burning tires, sticky dripping limbs.

Angelina stood looking at it for a while. Every thought seemed a long way off. By the time she noticed something—like Patrick's broken begging, or the heat rippling off the thing—she had already stopped caring. The only emotions to rise were easy ones, things so natural that they required little effort. Affection. Fatigue. And the strong desire to have Jagvi all to herself.

Mine, mine, mine. She wasn't horrified by the thing's attack: she was *jealous.* The feeling reverberated back and forth inside her head, shattering more space for itself, swelling like a wave that dragged her upward. Jagvi's future was not for this thing. Jagvi's body did not belong in the pit. Angelina wouldn't let her be stolen this way. Her thoughts fled out of reach, a jumble of words and distress, but once that jealousy took hold, it could not be beaten back. *Mine. Mine.*

The thing's power thrummed through her still, a little doll held loosely in her owner's other hand. She couldn't think properly. Logic was gone, and reason, and fear. When she stooped and picked up one of the rocks that bordered the edge of the pit, the strength with which she wielded it was not her own. Still, it was her shoulder that swung and her hand that aimed and smashed the thing from the pit off Jagvi and deep down into the hole from where it came.

A shriek of rage bounced from wall to wall of the cave and Angelina's skull.

"Nini!" Patrick howled. "Fix her! Put it back in her!"

Angelina looked down. At her feet, Jagvi lay mangled and dying, all that future draining out of her. From this angle it looked like smoke. Looked like life. Looked like a promise. Angelina already knew it was delicious.

"Give it back to her!"

Angelina looked at Jagvi, then at Patrick. Her brain moved in fits and starts, its synapses unused to belonging to themselves.

Stupid Little Girl. From deep within the earth, Angelina could hear the thing scuttling back up the steep walls of its pit. Stupid Empty Little Girl.

The thing was right about some things, Angelina thought. She was hollow. She was starving.

"Angel," Jagvi said as Angelina bent to her, and what was left of her hand fell in Angelina's hair, a gentle caress. Angelina smiled. She put her face back to that future and began to eat. It was hers, not the thing's. It belonged to her and it filled her so good. It was hers and it was meant for her, and Angelina would eat every morsel, even as Patrick sobbed and begged her to stop and the outrage and penetrating hatred of the thing behind her rang through the broken earth.

Faintest return of her smile. Jagvi's fading face, last eye brightening as it disappeared. Like maybe it didn't hurt anymore.

Patrick cried out. The men were clustered around him, but their voices blurred together, their vocal cords vibrating at a frequency that Angelina no longer responded to. At least one of them was shrieking in high terror. Steps lurched toward Angelina. Angelina was annoyed, distracted from her meal, although the distraction reminded her that she liked Jagvi's smile, and wouldn't mind seeing it again. With the thing knocked back, she could find her own way through her mind again. Her hunger for Jagvi was not the same as the thing's. She didn't want to lock Jagvi inside her gut and own her in silence. She didn't want to gorge on Jagvi's future until there was nothing left. She wanted to watch it unspool, let Jagvi keep her black eyes and wide palms, her chivalry and humor and tough, thorny mind. She wanted Jagvi to live out those days that tasted so good.

She put her hand through the drifting particles of Jagvi and bent to where Jagvi's mouth had once been. She fed it back, all the future she had taken and all the future the thing had taken through her, which was hers, after all, her body, her meal, hers to return. She pushed the future out until she felt Jagvi's tongue stroke against hers, solid enough to meet Angelina's mouth again, more and more until Jagvi's ragged breathing was audible and Angelina could smell Jagvi's sweat and fear and hope. Angelina made her as whole as she could, gave her back her eye and her memories and the blood-streaked shirt and the broken arm, and then she peeled herself reluctantly away and turned to the thing behind her.

She could see it now. She had something of its capacity in her, and it could not hide from her anymore. It was bright with hate and power, but starved, too; it had been starving for years. The thing had managed a few measly bites of Jagvi, but it had also taught her how to pick up the cutlery and feed herself, and it had left too much of itself within her. It had entwined its hands with hers; it had shown her how to dig through Jagvi's mind, how to crouch over something and consume it. She knew how to eat now. She smoothed her sleeve over her mouth and found that she was still smiling.

Angelina caught it by the neck. The first bite was a bitter mouthful, and the monster screamed in fury, trying to take her over. Angelina only tightened her grip. Jagvi's future had looked like smoke and teemed with images of memory and possibility, but the thing's future was a void, an empty space demanding to be filled, and Angelina clamped her mouth down on it and tasted years of darkness and hunger and didn't know how to stop. She chewed faster than she could swallow. Textures on her tongue reminded her of a body, rocky chunks of teeth and hot strings of sinew. Maybe the thing had been a person once, maybe a fallen angel sent from heaven to challenge San Rocco, or a demon from hell come to prey on the living.

It was nothing like Jagvi, nothing like the gleaming life Angelina had licked all over before she returned it. But Angelina had grown up in Cadenze with Caro. She had looked after herself since she was thirteen. She had choked down worse meals.

"I'm still hungry," she said regretfully, and helped herself to the feast.

The Future

The people of Cadenze called Jagvi doctor, even though Jagvi would never get her MD now. Sometimes ironically, as though it were a title Jagvi had bestowed upon herself; sometimes with uncomfortable sincerity. Jagvi tried not to pay it any attention. She diagnosed flus, she treated allergic reactions, she set broken bones, she pretended that even half of the patients she referred to a doctor in Myrna would actually go. She worked out of a small shop front on the town square, a few doors down from Old Timers, and charged on a sliding scale that Patrick said was charitable to the point of lunacy. Angelina's uncle Franco had found her the space, lent the money for the rental deposit, and dismissed any concerns that Jagvi's new business might not be entirely legal with a laconic wave of his hand.

One cold evening in spring, Jagvi locked up the shop front and climbed into Angelina's car and drove to Patrick's garage. Not far from Cadenze, but far enough. He stood out front in his coveralls talking to a customer. His hair was newly short, cropped close around his temples and leaving his face strangely bare. His breath hung in a cloud.

Jagvi parked and watched him until he could join her, an old and beloved pastime. When she was a teenager, Jagvi had wanted to crawl inside Patrick's skin. She loved the way he moved, slinging himself into chairs, shrugging on a jacket, clocking her down a stretch of school hallway and switching to an easy jog so he could catch up faster. Her stomach had squirmed at a hundred

279

of Patrick's everyday gestures. She still thought it had been fair to interpret that as desire. It *was* desire, in a way.

Patrick finished up with his customer and crossed the road to slide into Jagvi's passenger seat. "How you doing?"

"Starving, I didn't break for lunch. You want pizza?"

"Sure. We could check out that new place in Myrna."

"Let's just go down the road," Jagvi said, and touched his arm. Soothing, conciliatory. "They have cheap wine."

Patrick's mouth tightened. He didn't argue, and only halfway through the third slice did he look up at her. The guarded expression had also become familiar, though part of Jagvi always wanted to go down onto her knees, seize him by his wrists, beg him not to look at her like that.

These days Patrick spent more and more time out of Cadenze, long hours at the garage, nights in Myrna, the occasional trip to San Michele. For a while in the winter, Jagvi made regular visits to the big building supplies outlet off the highway, and it was the happiest Patrick had been in months, riding along with her. When they did hang out at home, his shoulders stayed tight, his eyes alert. Jagvi recognized an old version of herself in his expression, in the way he held his body.

Patrick felt it, too, Jagvi knew. The presence in Cadenze. It was hard to shake off, and it made him anxious. He talked often about leaving town for a while, or forever. He told the family that he might find a job in San Michele or open his own garage somewhere down the coast, but to Jagvi he admitted that what he really wanted was to pack up his truck and drive.

"You could come," Patrick said casually over the last slice of pizza. "We could road-trip those routes we planned out. Or you could go somewhere on your own, or with your ma. Give yourself some space."

"I don't want to do that," Jagvi said.

Patrick studied her face. "Don't want to, or can't?"

"Is there a difference?"

"Yes. There is."

Jagvi rested her chin in her palm. "Okay, Pat. You want to split dessert?"

If she hadn't convinced him before, she wouldn't now. Their fights had died down, not like the weeks right after the cave, when Jagvi's arm was still in a cast and Angelina was a seething delight and Patrick waited until they were out of his sister's earshot to say, "I watched her try to *eat* you."

"Yeah, you and I watched a lot," Jagvi had snapped. "How else was she gonna beat it?"

Patrick said, "I guess we'll never know."

They found other things to talk about; they always had. They kept track of each other's injuries, swapping the painkillers that Ricky provided. Months later, Patrick looked well. He had two jaw-shaped scars on his shoulder and collarbone, and he'd bulked up a little. He was dating a friend of Ricky's wife's. She joined him for his Sunday morning Caro visits and at rock shows in Myrna. She was young and clever, and the most normal girl that he'd dated in a long time. No anger issues, no mysterious past, and she looked at Pat with uncomplicated adoration. She would probably run away with him if he asked.

"Try to see it as a good thing," Jagvi said gently. "No matter what happens, you know I'll be here. I'm holding down the home front."

"It's still weird to hear you call it that."

"Good?"

"Home," Patrick said.

Driving back into Cadenze always made Jagvi aware of how much being away hurt. Something switched the second she crossed the town border, an attention that snapped to her, and the weary strain in her chest eased, the prickle of discomfort along her limbs dissipated. Sometimes it felt like being licked all over by a happy, rough tongue; sometimes it felt like being dunked into icy water and coming out laughing and shivering. Jagvi couldn't help grinning under the force of the feeling. She knew what it meant: *Angel has been unhappy while you were away, and now she knows you are back and is reaching for you.*

The daylight lingered even this far into the evening, a sure sign of spring, but the sky above rolled with lilac clouds. Strange weather ahead. Jagvi cruised around the main square, raising a hand to Gemma, sitting by the fountain with a couple of guys. She nodded at a few locals. Most people still avoided Jagvi if they could, but it didn't trouble her as much as it once had.

It wasn't just that Cadenze was less lonely than it had been when she was a teenager, though of course it was. But there was something lonely and solitary in Jagvi herself that she had learned to recognize. All those years in the city chasing girls and danger and companionship, as though she didn't know that each one of those things was waiting in its purest form for her back home. She'd imprinted on a pair of siblings too young to look back and change her mind. She didn't need Cadenze to like her.

The worst she'd dealt with were the groups of men who liked to stare; on occasion, they would also shout or spit. Jagvi knew the best reaction was to leave, but once or twice a different instinct took over and she responded with hocked spit of her own or a slow, deliberate "What did you say to me?"

Just when fights began to brew, Angelina had a habit of appearing. Lounging against walls, smiling at anyone who looked at Jagvi too closely. Angelina's preferred method of confrontation still involved laughing it off, and she found plenty to laugh about, but she had finally lost interest in playing nice with her town. People strutted about as though they weren't trailing these pathetic little lives, Angelina said lightly, with empty futures promising only more of the same. Barely worth a bite, Angelina said, and snapped her teeth, a gesture that should have been ridiculous. Instead it made grown men pale.

Jagvi always stepped in before it went too far: bundling Angelina under her arm, steering her away, keeping her content and hidden up on the mountain. The beady-eyed people of Cadenze recognized Jagvi as Angelina's keeper, and occasionally they asked her to mention it to Nini if they had some sheep who'd strayed too far, or extended an invitation to a party or baptism. "Bring your little lady, of course," they said, eyes darting about in fear, unsure whether it would be better if Angelina came or not. But they wanted her blessing, this new Cadenze creature, Angelina Sicco, who was still beloved but no longer familiar.

The story around town was that Angelina had fought a demon and won but lost a part of herself in the process. No one could quite agree on which part. Her soul was the most popular suggestion, her sanity a close second. Gemma and Francesca-Martine didn't allow that kind of talk in Old Timers but still, it was in the air. Even Gemma once whispered to Jagvi, "It's not so much that she's lost something, is it?"

Jagvi nodded. If anything, Angelina had gained a lot. There was a newness to her. She had expanded beyond her previous borders. She was stronger and healthier, her colors more vivid, like all her life she'd been undernourished and now she was finally getting what she needed.

"Not that it matters," Gemma said. "She's the same in every way that counts. This town can't handle strong women, that's all."

"Correct," Jagvi said, and thought of Caro, who practically cowered at the sight of her only daughter, made excuses not to be left alone with her, asked them to always call ahead before visiting. Maybe she could see something of what Angelina had swallowed on her face. It must be frightening to recognize a monster and have no idea where you knew it from.

But it was hard to feel only sorry for Caro. The last time Jagvi saw her, Caro had asked how Meera felt about her moving back to Cadenze.

"She's happy for me," Jagvi said, and wondered if that was true. Jagvi sent postcards to San Michele and called Meera a few times a week, but she'd never found her mother the easiest to read. "She might visit us in the summer."

Caro blew on her tea. "That'll be the day."

It upset Jagvi more than it should have. After Caro left, she'd gone out to sit on the thin grass, not even noticing the evening's chill until Angelina came to find her. She fetched Jagvi's jacket and draped it over her shoulders before collapsing next to her.

"Caro's not a trustworthy source," Angelina said. She shrugged, matter-of-fact, the way the Sicco siblings always talked about their mother. "She doesn't know Meera. You can't take her word for anything." Angelina managed a smile. "Even when there's not a monster involved."

Last month Jagvi had sat with Angelina while she studied a list of census records from the year before she was born, for Cadenze and all the surrounding villages. Jagvi had brought them home from the public library in

Myrna; they'd wondered if maybe the remnants of the thing inside Angelina would react at the sight of a name. Angelina pored over each one, but nothing hinted at a connection. She became obsessed with hard evidence, even spent a weekend excited about the idea of DNA testing, until Patrick said, "Aren't you worried about what else they might find in you?" and she reluctantly gave it up.

Jagvi didn't know if the fact-finding mission was futile. She suspected the thing did not leave tracks, let alone newspaper articles. But she thought about Angelina's dad a lot, the man whose fate she had almost shared. She wondered at what point he'd realized what was going to happen, if Caro had taken him to the cave or if he'd run to find her there. She wondered if he had loved Caro right until the thing slurped up the last traces of him with Caro's tongue.

Out in their backyard, Angelina had offered Jagvi her wineglass and Jagvi accepted it. Strong and sour, from Franco's vineyard. She allowed herself to get drunk now, from time to time. The old sense of panic still reared up, but she ignored it long enough to get giggly with Angelina, making out sloppily in a corner of Old Timers after they'd closed. Jagvi rediscovered the pleasure of a beer with Patrick on one of Cadenze's dozy afternoons; she accepted the shots Angelina's cousins bought her as the tentative peace offerings they were.

Sometimes Jagvi looked around her home and imagined showing it all off through Meera's eyes, the flowers on the table and the wine in the kitchen and Angelina in her armchair, halfway through a magazine and a smart comment. She wanted to put Meera in a chair at the dining table Jagvi had built herself, sanding down the wood with Patrick on a freezing weekend early in the year. She imagined pointing each detail out to her mother in turn, all her luck cataloged and possessed.

Up Big Joe and around the bend, past Patrick's house and closer to the misty peak, her windshield fogged up until she turned the heater on. In the dying light, she could see the first spots of snow, tiny enough that they could have been dust in her eyes. Driving this way used to give Jagvi a sick feeling in her gut, knowing that around the next corner she would see the dark scribble of her childhood home against the slope. Riccardo smoking in the kitchen, his mouth preemptively curled into a sneer. Her cramped and hateful bedroom. Even Meera's silhouette flickering from room to room, like she had never actually escaped.

Still, it was her land. When she came back to clear out the house after her dad's death, she'd been resentful of the burden, and the night that she and Angelina had fought their way out felt like giving in to all of her worst impulses. By the time they escaped, there was nothing left to preserve. And here was Jagvi's reward, at the end of the gravel road: an entirely different house coming into view.

The Siccos helped build it. They spent the first month just clearing the site of the old house. Broken furniture, old appliances, splintered remains of walls. Jagvi was bunking at the Sicco house downhill, and she'd been out of her head most of the time with the combination of pain medication for her arm and the dumb satisfaction of getting what she wanted. She was so unused to rest that it was a shock to her system, to wake up in the morning and not immediately have something she ought to be doing. Plus, she and Angelina were still working out their limits. Sometimes they went too far, and Jagvi spent a few days feeling like a sleepwalker, only half there, Angelina clinging to her arm with that big, frightened look on her face.

In early November Jagvi got her cast off, and the property had been razed clean to its foundations. Angelina's uncle Robert drew up some blueprints, and Franco put a construction team together, mostly composed of Sicco cousins and their offshoots. The family had never formally apologized for their treatment of her, but Jagvi was glad not to have to discuss it. She didn't want to feel pressured to forgive them. If they wanted to work their guilt out by building her a house, she was inclined to let them. What they'd had to witness in the cave felt like punishment already.

Jagvi's own memories of that morning blurred and splintered halfway through. She could hold on to everything up to the point that the thing in Angelina snapped her arm in two. Then Angelina had crouched over her, and she did not look like Angelina at all, her smile so wide it split across her lips. Abruptly Jagvi had not been able to remember where she was, or who was with her, or even her own name. Her arm hammered with pain, and thunder blared in her head like a drill. She'd heard patients talk about their lives flashing before their eyes, but all Jagvi saw was a life she didn't recognize, people she hadn't met and streets she'd never walked down, a panic of memory and fantasy and all of it sliding out of sight before she had time to parse it, like each image was a streetlight and one by one they were extinguishing. And all along, beside her own screams, the chomping and lip smacking of the feast.

By the time Angelina fed it all back, Jagvi's brain was a hot stew. She barely caught the final meal, but she remembered the faces of the men as they watched their beloved Sicco girl tear that monster apart with her teeth. The gun hanging limp from Sam's hand. Matthew's guttural sobs. Jethro and Ricky running out to vomit. It took all of Franco's strength to hold Patrick back, both arms wrapped around Patrick's chest and his mouth to Patrick's ear muttering words of comfort or warning.

Now they struggled to look Angelina in the eye. When they had questions about the construction, they preferred to consult with Jagvi alone. They dropped off food, rather than staying to eat. Jagvi thought it troubled Angelina a little, but Angel wasn't one to dwell on things she couldn't change.

The house sprang up from the ruins in a matter of months. All of them were aware that the job was going too well; the roof was in place strangely early, just after Christmas, as though determined to block out January blizzards that never arrived. When the snow fell that year, it was mild and not enough to halt construction. Every shipment arrived on time or early. Workers who came to help with the pipes or the wiring commented on the rapid progress, fewer roadblocks than they'd ever seen, especially on a property this high up the mountainside. The Siccos exchanged looks. They knew that something in Cadenze wanted a home of its own very badly. And Angelina had always loved the mountain. She would not settle for a pit.

Several times that winter, Angelina and Jagvi drove to the edge of town and walked over the crunchy snow until they found some boundary that

Angelina could not or would not cross. She stood pink-cheeked and smiling across the divide, while Jagvi walked farther into whatever it was—the next county, the next town, a patch of trees that simply did not belong to Angelina. Jagvi ducked in and out of sight, behind scrubby patches of rock or farther down the slope until trees blocked her from view, and Angel waited more or less patiently. If it was cold, she stalked back and forth along the boundary line, whining until Jagvi snuck back up behind her and seized Angelina kicking into her arms.

Jagvi had expected Angelina to be panicked at the revelation that she still couldn't leave Cadenze. But with the thing gone—or under control—Angelina no longer seemed concerned, and particularly not about staying in Cadenze. Instead she was luxuriously pleased, as though a burden had been stripped from her. No more doubts, excuses, guilt for staying in her hometown. She was exactly where she wanted to be.

In February, when the bulk of the exterior work was complete, Jagvi went to tour the insides with Franco. He asked her opinion on the layout and the fixtures and committed each of her requests to his notebook with somber dedication.

"It's a lot of work," Jagvi said. "I can help, now the cast's off."

But Franco shook his head. He put his hand on her good arm. It might have been the first time he'd ever touched her. "You're doing enough, girl."

After he'd driven away, Jagvi stood outside the half-finished structure, trying to see it through the Siccos' eyes. It was certainly more stable than Riccardo's old house had been. Thicker walls, a solid foundation. Somewhere secure to put the girl and her keeper.

Until the building work was done, they lived in Angelina's old house. Without announcing it, Patrick stayed at the Sicco farm, only visiting to check on Jagvi and pick up his mail. He could sometimes be coaxed to stay for a movie, but he always left as soon as the credits rolled. Angelina herself was patient, gentle and friendly with her brother like he'd been ill and she was pretending not to notice. Jagvi didn't know whether that was the right approach; she'd never been any good at mediating the relationship between the Sicco siblings, something she thought both of them actually appreciated.

She was closer than anyone, and had been for years, and yet there was a space into which she was not invited and could not understand.

And still it was a surprise when Patrick forgave Jagvi: grudgingly, and with enough barbs that Jagvi knew carrying on with his sister would always be a sore point. But he didn't seem to have forgiven Angelina. He loved her helplessly and avoided her as much as he could.

The only thing that kept their new distance from breaking Jagvi's heart was how unconcerned Angelina seemed to be. She could not quite be hurt in those early months, and especially not by Patrick. She seemed sure everything would work out, and she told Jagvi one night that she knew Patrick would come back to her sooner or later. "He's just a man. He needs to sulk and then he'll get over it. Wait and see."

Angelina had always had a possessive streak, Jagvi knew, and now it had been given complete rein, pushed full throttle and roaring to the surface. Still, she was not a tyrant or a bully, lurking deep in a pit until it climbed out to stalk some ill-fated stranger. Angelina wanted the people she already loved, and she was content to wait for them to come to her. The way Jagvi did every night.

Sometimes, Jagvi had nightmares that the thing was still tricking her, smiling with Angel's pretty mouth, leading her back to the pit. She woke up struggling, convinced that the Angelina sleeping beside her was an imposter, leaping out of bed to the other side of the room. She pressed her back up against the wall and panted, ready for Angelina to attack, Angelina's tongue and teeth ripping strips off her. Angelina waited, the sheets pooling around her hips, until Jagvi was calm enough to approach. She took Jagvi's hand and placed it on her bare chest. Jagvi felt her heartbeat, slipped down to cup her tit, felt Angelina shiver at her touch.

"It's me," Angelina said. "It's gone."

Angelina said she never heard it anymore. She thought she'd digested its mouth, or the part of it that could speak. Jagvi shuddered at the image, but maybe Angelina was right and the thing had broken down in Angelina's stomach, her enzymes latching on to its ancient, ephemeral corpse and seizing up the dissolute parts, distributing them throughout her body. Perhaps her stomach had integrated a part of the thing into its chemistry, or perhaps the thing sat whole, alive and waiting, in the depths of her gut.

Whatever had happened to the thing from the pit, it had left Angelina with an appetite, and so Jagvi had learned how to feed her girl. Curled up in their bed or out on the dewy grass. Braced over her or lying with Angelina sitting on her lap, Jagvi fit her mouth to Angelina's and gave a part of herself over.

An hour. An evening. The sun glowing red beyond the mountains, the apricots budding in the tree, the hair in Jagvi's pits getting thicker, the silver river of the night drifting by. All that she might see or do or feel in the coming minutes or hours, lapped out of her by Angelina's sandpaper tongue. For that stretch she was gone. Angelina watched over her, fearsome as any guard dog, her hands restless in Jagvi's hair until enough time had passed that Jagvi's life was her own again.

"Are you sure it's safe?" Patrick said. He had asked Jagvi to explain it to him and promised not to react, but still he paced back and forth in the backyard with his hands in his hair, comical image of despair. My Dog's chain lay loose on the ground. "You make her sound like a vampire."

"She isn't," Jagvi said. For one thing, as far as they knew, vampires weren't real. For another, they hungered for blood. Crucially, they gave nothing back.

On the evenings Angelina was full and content—which were most of them—Jagvi could brace above her, straps digging into her hips, fuck so hard that Angelina's back arched off the bed and her mouth went ragged with wanting. Pin her wrists to the floor and fill her so entirely that she couldn't speak anymore, her mouth open and gasping, eyes fixed wide and astonished on Jagvi's face. Then Jagvi would lean down and murmur, "I gave you two hours tonight, Angel. What do I get?"

"Everything," Angelina managed, panting in her ear, Jagvi's good girl finding words even when Jagvi fucked them out of her.

And afterward, Angelina limp and curled against Jagvi's side, Jagvi said, "What about next year?"

"That's yours."

"And your kids, when you have them?"

"Jesus," Angelina said, and laughed, weak and overwhelmed. "Yes. Yours."

"And if you ever feel like breaking the law and getting married?"

Angelina's fingers dug into Jagvi's arm, clinging tight. "Yes."

Jagvi shifted, propping herself up on an elbow, grinning down at Angelina. "And when the new millennium shows up?"

"That's yours, too," Angelina said. "Jag. Jag—"

Jagvi gave her the kiss she was looking for, hand cradling Angelina's jaw. She didn't need Angelina's guilt or Patrick's fear. She understood the feeling. She'd been hungry for Angelina's future for years.

"I guess it doesn't really feel one-sided," Jagvi told Patrick.

He shook his head. "Didn't you see enough fucked-up relationships growing up in this town? In that house?"

"But it doesn't feel like any of those." Jagvi considered. "Maybe it's a dyke thing."

"Oh, fuck off," Patrick said, making her laugh.

Early spring: they'd been living in the house for a month now, the final coats of paint and fittings springing up around their new domesticity. Just yesterday Franco and Jagvi had installed the last window seals, so that when she opened the front door this evening it still felt warm, despite the plummeting temperature. Jagvi took a beer to sit on the porch. It should have been dark by then, but the sky wavered and shifted into a heavy purple hue, patches of orange, clouds thick and heavy with snow. The cold seemed to be inching down from Big Joe's peak and racing up from the valley at once, a circle of frost closing in on Jagvi. She wore her university hoodie under her jacket and waited.

Jagvi could tell when Angelina was coming, these days. It felt like fear, or some panicky instinct of danger, the way animals raise their noses to the wind and scatter, or when a phone rings and the pulsing in your gut tells you it's bad news. Except along with the prickle of sweat breaking out on Jagvi's lower back and the way her heartbeat amped up, it also made her mouth go wet. Made her palm herself, curl her knuckles over her crotch, ready and hungry for her monster.

Jagvi's girl, Cadenze kept, came storming up the mountain. She rarely felt the cold now and even tonight wore only her loose blue jeans and one of Jagvi's T-shirts, plus a forgotten dish towel from Old Timers slung over her shoulder. Hair wrestled up into a knot, big eyes and the generous mouth that Jagvi loved. Angel moved a little differently now, swarming across the ground like she had more legs than she should, though when Jagvi looked down it was just the same two long ones with the neat curve of ankle that fit perfectly into Jagvi's palm. But her grin was the same, cocksure and bratty as she crossed the distance between them and dropped herself into Jagvi's lap.

"Gone for ages today," she complained. Jagvi dragged her in with her hands on Angelina's hips, kissed her hello, friendly touch of her tongue before she leaned back, and Angel chased after her, still talking. "I thought you were gonna come over to Old Timers for lunch?"

Thick flakes of snow began to drift into Angelina's hair, but Angelina didn't seem to notice. Jagvi brushed them away. "Mrs. Ruiz showed up with her migraine again."

"Jag! It's not a migraine, I told you, she wants you to fuck her. You should write her a prescription, *Find another dyke*, and then she'll stop coming around and asking you to test her temperature and look deeply into her eyes in search of broken blood vessels, or hope that you treat her for hysteria with some kind of Victorian-era vibrator—"

"Oh, should I not have done that?" Angelina pressed her laughing face closer, mouthed against Jagvi's hairline. Scrape of her teeth. But there was something hesitant in her, a snag about her smile, and Jagvi said, "What?"

"I was thinking about My Dog today," Angelina said.

Jagvi's fingers spanned her hips, squeezed. She waited.

"It's dumb. It's not like I remember the exact date I found her. But it was this time of year."

"Yeah," Jagvi said. Angelina had found My Dog one day in the spring four years ago. Five months after Jagvi had made a fool of them both outside Old Timers that New Year's. Patrick had told Jagvi on a call. She was skin and bones, he said, and would probably be dead by the end of the week. But the next time he called, the dog was still alive and following Angelina everywhere she went, and Angelina was full of triumph.

"Fucking brat," Patrick had said on the phone. "So I guess we've got a dog now."

"Sucks to be you," Jagvi said lightly, and carried the story around with her for weeks. She couldn't stop thinking about it, obsessive and painful, picking at it like a scab. She wanted to call back and ask questions: Where did Angel find her, how had she nursed the dog back to health, had she ever doubted her own capacity? Had the dog been afraid of her at first, or had it loved her instantly or was it both, a knot of anxiety and devotion that Jagvi knew all too well? Jagvi told four separate people the story as a funny anecdote about "this girl I know," until she accidentally told it twice in front of Rosa, who asked her who this girl was, anyway, and then Jagvi knew she'd given herself away.

"My dog," Angelina said now, not a name but a claim. She blew out a breath. "My poor pup. Maybe we eat dinner out back tonight, hey?"

In the backyard of their little house stood a small circle of stones, away from the shadow of the mountain with bellflowers and Silene di Elisabetta springing up all around. Jagvi didn't know who had carried My Dog's corpse back, but she hoped—perhaps irrationally, given that he'd been busy trying to pull his sister back from the edge and put Jagvi's body back together—that it had been Patrick. She wanted someone who loved My Dog to have held her; she didn't like to think of My Dog's poor broken body heaped into a blanket or truck bed. She liked to imagine the impossible, that awful morning in the cave. Patrick taking My Dog into his arms. The long, slow walk across the valley and back up their mountain.

However she'd made it, she was here now. Angelina's friend in her last spot in the sun.

But there was no sun left tonight.

"Baby," Jagvi said, "I think we're about to be snowed in."

"Wait, really?" Angelina said. She tilted her head up to the sky, bright-eyed and expectant, and noticed for the first time the flakes drifting around them.

They kept catching in her hair, white on dark curls, and then melting away into nothing on her warm skin. "Shit! Lucky you and Franco finished the windows. Good timing, huh?"

"Uh-huh," Jagvi said.

They made dinner together, thick, dark stew with the venison an Old Timers regular had shyly offered Angelina a few days earlier, asking her to keep his wife and her new pregnancy in her thoughts. Their kitchen was a cube of golden light in the dark, the snow falling thick and heavy enough now that Jagvi couldn't see beyond to the glimmer of Cadenze's lights in the valley or even Patrick's house farther down the hill. Of course, they were still there. She crowded Angelina against the kitchen counter, tasted salt and copper in the kiss. The feeling of fury and gratitude she couldn't shake, hating everything that had happened to them and loving the trap they were caught in. Good timing.

The phone clattered against the wall, and Angelina extracted herself, breathless, to answer it while Jagvi attended to the stew.

"We're fine, yeah, we're well stocked," she said. "You could make a run for it up here if you—well, okay, good."

"Okay?" Jagvi asked when she hung up.

"That was Pat," Angelina said. She thumbed her bottom lip, dark-eyed and careful as she considered Jagvi. "He heard it's going to snow all tonight and tomorrow, at least. Might take a week before the roads clear."

Jagvi grinned at her.

"Shut up," Angel said, flushing. "It's not anything to do with me."

"If you want me all to yourself," Jagvi said, "all you have to do is ask."

"I'm not doing it deliberately," Angelina said. Some part of her looked panicked, like she didn't trust her own power. Those eyes were like deep chasms into the earth, something hungry and mad living there, something that wanted to eat Jagvi up. Frightening, sure, but nothing new; Angelina had looked at her like that for years. "Can you spare a week?"

Jagvi beckoned. The saint and scourge of Cadenze slunk over to her. Jagvi caught her close.

"I can spare a week," she said. "I've got time."

Acknowledgments

Thank you to Andrianna deLone, who steered us expertly through some choppy seas. Thank you to Seema Mahanian, a champion who saw the potential in a very messy few chapters and knew how to coax it forth, and to Jacqueline Young for instinctively getting this novel and bringing it as high as we could climb. We're also so grateful to Angelina Krahn, Mari Okuda, Caitlin Sacks, Albert Tang, Leena Oropez, Kamrun Nesa, Theresa DeLucci, and everyone at Grand Central Publishing. Thank you to Charlotte Trumble for swooping in like an actual superhero to give this book such a wonderful home in the UK and Commonwealth. Thank you to Sarah Jeffcoate, Laurie McShea, Karin Seifried, Steve Turner, Matt Johnson and everyone at Simon & Schuster UK, as well as Rachel Aitken at Simon & Schuster Australia — we're so glad to be bringing this book about weird hometowns to our weird hometowns with you. Thank you also to our beloved Lucy Morris, Rosie Pierce, Peppa Mignone, and all the lovely people at CAA and Curtis Brown. Thank you to John Darnielle for the song "Steal Smoked Fish" and his gracious permission, and thank you also to Nicola Taddonio for teaching us about Matera and driving us to the Crypt of Original Sin.

We're so grateful to and for: Sophie Evans, Jack Roberts, Flora Bell, Marina Manoukian, Charlie Wührer, Marc Yates, Monica McInerney, Martha Perotto-Wills, Avery Curran, Rosalie Bower, Julia Armfield, Yael van der Wouden, Emery Kennedy, Wulf, and the staff of Other Nature.

Acknowledgments

Thank you to our families for all their love and support, especially Marie McInerney, Daniel Clements, Ulli Clements, Ruby Clements, Rafael Clements, Pranesh Datta, Liz Datta, Shirmilla Minaya Datta, Victor Minaya Datta, Lea McInerney, Maura McInerney, Mary McInerney, and Monica Clements. Ruby and Ulli are always our first readers and deserve extra support and gratitude in these trying times; RIP to Ruby's tattoo. A special shout-out to our combined thirty-nine cousins, the conceit of whom we plundered extensively in the course of writing.

Finally, over the time that we wrote this novel, two men bravely taught Mik how to drive. Thank you to Daniel, who shepherded four children to their licenses in one increasingly battered Holden, and to Matthias, with our apologies for the state of his neck and our thanks for an excellent winter spent cruising Berlin's streets. Four wheels, baby!!!! Beep beep!!!!!!!!!!

About the Authors

Photo © Camila Berrio

Mikaella Clements and Onjuli Datta are also the authors of *The View Was Exhausting*. They are married and live in Berlin.